'Peter James is one of the best crime writers in the business'

**Karin Slaughter**

## Praise for the Roy Grace series

'James just gets better and better and deserves the success
he has achieved with this first-class series'
*Independent on Sunday*

'The tense plot is laced with fine humour . . . never before has
Brighton Pavilion appeared so sinister. James is on top form'
*The Times*

'One of the most consistently readable crime writers, James
seems to have shifted a gear with this latest meaty offering
featuring his excellent Brighton detective Roy Grace'
*Daily Mail*

'Peter James is on a roll with his Roy Grace novels . . . an
authentic, well-researched and compelling read'
*Daily Express*

'An incredibly strong book in a strong series. Peter knows
how to spin a yarn!'
*Sunday Express*

'What sets James apart is his extraordinary attention to detail
and sheer authenticity of his police procedurals'
*Daily Mirror*

'Peter James has established a series that is taking over from Ian Rankin in sales'
*Front Row*, **Radio 4**

'Another of James' sophisticated, complicated and well-informed snap-shots of the Brighton police at work . . . His research is obviously careful. It's well worth the effort, as the result is a superior thriller'
*Literary Review*

'An incredibly gripping tale . . . Peter James has managed once again to keep his latest book fresh and bang up-to-date in its themes and style'
*WeLoveThisBook*

'*Dead Man's Grip* brings a whole new dimension to this series, and in my view lifts it way above its peers . . . I really couldn't wait to finish, to see how it would be resolved . . . Excellent'
*Shots Mag*

'The latest crime thriller from Peter James is just as gripping and detailed as ever – you'll be hooked!'
*OK!*

# NOT DEAD YET

**Peter James** was educated at Charterhouse, then at film school. He lived in North America for a number of years, working as a screenwriter and film producer before returning to England. His novels, including the *Sunday Times* Number One bestselling Roy Grace series, have been translated into thirty-four languages, with world sales of 11 million copies. Three books have been filmed. All his novels reflect his deep interest in the world of the police, with whom he does in-depth research, as well as science, medicine and the paranormal. He has also produced numerous films, including *The Merchant of Venice*, starring Al Pacino, Jeremy Irons and Joseph Fiennes. He divides his time between his homes in Notting Hill, London and near Brighton in Sussex.

Visit his website at *www.peterjames.com*
Or follow him on Twitter @peterjamesuk
Or Facebook: *http://www.facebook.com/peterjames.roygrace*

*Also by Peter James*

DEAD LETTER DROP
ATOM BOMB ANGEL
BILLIONAIRE
POSSESSION
DREAMER
SWEET HEART
TWILIGHT
PROPHECY
ALCHEMIST
HOST
THE TRUTH
DENIAL
FAITH
PERFECT PEOPLE

*Children's Novel*
GETTING WIRED!

*The Roy Grace Series*
DEAD SIMPLE
LOOKING GOOD DEAD
NOT DEAD ENOUGH
DEAD MAN'S FOOTSTEPS
DEAD TOMORROW
DEAD LIKE YOU
DEAD MAN'S GRIP

# NOT DEAD YET

# PETER JAMES

PAN BOOKS

First published 2012 by Pan Books
an imprint of Pan Macmillan, a division of Macmillan Publishers Limited
Pan Macmillan, 20 New Wharf Road, London N1 9RR
Basingstoke and Oxford
Associated companies throughout the world
www.panmacmillan.com

ISBN 978-0-330-51557-3

Copyright © Really Scary Books / Peter James 2012

The right of Peter James to be identified as the
author of this work has been asserted by him in accordance
with the Copyright, Designs and Patents Act 1988.

All rights reserved. No part of this publication may be
reproduced, stored in or introduced into a retrieval system, or
transmitted, in any form, or by any means (electronic, mechanical,
photocopying, recording or otherwise) without the prior written
permission of the publisher. Any person who does any unauthorized
act in relation to this publication may be liable to criminal
prosecution and civil claims for damages.

The Macmillan Group has no responsibility for the information provided by
any author websites whose address you obtain from this book ('author websites').
The inclusion of author website addresses in this book does not constitute
an endorsement by or association with us of such sites or the content,
products, advertising or other materials presented on such sites.

1 3 5 7 9 8 6 4 2

A CIP catalogue record for this book is available from
the British Library.

Typeset by SetSystems Ltd, Saffron Walden, Essex
Printed and bound in Great Britain by CPI Group (UK) Ltd, Croydon, CR0 4YY

This book is sold subject to the condition that it shall not,
by way of trade or otherwise, be lent, re-sold, hired out,
or otherwise circulated without the publisher's prior consent
in any form of binding or cover other than that in which
it is published and without a similar condition including this
condition being imposed on the subsequent purchaser.

Visit **www.panmacmillan.com** to read more about all our books
and to buy them. You will also find features, author interviews and
news of any author events, and you can sign up for e-newsletters
so that you're always first to hear about our new releases.

**For GEOFF DUFFIELD**

**You believed in me and you made it happen**

# 1

I am warning you, and I won't repeat this warning. Don't take the part. You'd better believe me. Take the part and you are dead. Bitch.

# 2

Gaia Lafayette was unaware of the man out in the dark, in the station wagon, who had come to kill her. And she was unaware of the email he had sent. She got hate mail all the time, mostly from religious nutters or folk upset by her swearing or her provocative costumes in some of her stage acts and music videos. Those emails were screened and kept from bothering her by her trusted head of security, Detroit-born Andrew Gulli, a tough ex-cop who'd spent most of his career on close protection work for vulnerable political figures.

He knew when to be worried enough to tell his boss, and this piece of trash that had come in, on an anonymous Hotmail account, was not something he figured had any substance. His employer got a dozen like this every week.

It was 10 p.m. and Gaia was trying to focus on the script she was reading, but she couldn't concentrate. She was focused even more on the fact that she had run out of cigarettes. The sweet, but oh so dim-witted Pratap, who did all her shopping, and who she hadn't the heart to fire because his wife had a brain tumour, had bought the wrong brand. She had her limit of four cigarettes a day, and didn't actually *need* any more, but old habits die hard. She used to mainline the damned things, claiming they were essential for her famed gravelly voice. Not so many years back she'd have one before she got out of bed, followed by one burning in the ashtray while she showered. Every action accompanied by a cigarette. Now she was kicking free, but she

2

*had* to know they were in the house. Just in case she needed them.

Like so much else she needed in life. Starting with her adoring public. Checking the count of Twitter followers and Facebook *likes*. Both were substantially up again today, each nearly a million up in the past month alone, still keeping her well ahead of both the performers she viewed as her rivals, Madonna and Lady Gaga. And she now had nearly ten million subscribers to her monthly e-newsletter. And then there were her seven homes, of which this copy of a Tuscan palazzo, built five years ago to her specification on a three-acre lot, was the largest.

The walls, mirrored full length floor-to-ceiling to create the illusion of infinite space, were decorated with Aztec art interspersed with larger-than-life posters of herself. The house, like all her others, was a catalogue of her different incarnations. Gaia had reinvented herself constantly throughout her career as a rock star, and more recently, two years ago at thirty-five, had started reinventing herself again, this time as a movie actor.

Above her head was a huge, framed monochrome signed photo of herself in a black negligee, titled WORLD TOUR GAIA SAVING THE PLANET. Another, with her wearing a tank top and leather jeans, was captioned, GAIA REVELATIONS TOUR. Above the fireplace, in dramatic green was a close-up of her lips, nose and eyes – GAIA UP CLOSE AND PERSONAL.

Her agent and her manager phoned her daily, both men reassuring her just how much the world needed her. Just the way that her growing social networking base – all outsourced by her management company – reassured her, too. And at this moment, the one person in the world she cared about most – Roan, her six-year-old son – needed her just as much. He padded barefoot across the marble floor, in his Armani Junior pyjamas, his brown hair all mussed up, his face scrunched in a frown, and tapped her on the arm as she lay on the white sofa, propped against the purple velvet cushions. 'Mama, you didn't come and read me a story.'

She stretched out a hand and mussed up his hair some more. Then she put down the script and took him in her arms, hugging him. 'I'm sorry, sweetie. It's late, way past your bedtime, and Mama's really busy tonight, learning her lines. She has a really big part – see? Mama's playing Maria Fitzherbert, the mistress of an English king! King George the Fourth.'

Maria Fitzherbert was the diva of her day, in Regency England. Just like she herself was the diva of her day now, and they had something profound in common. Maria Fitzherbert spent most of her life in Brighton, in England. And she, Gaia, had been born in Brighton! She felt a connection to this woman, across time. She was born to play this role!

Her agent said this was the new *King's Speech*. An Oscar role, no question. And she wanted an Oscar oh so badly. The first two movies she had made were okay, but had not set the world on fire. In hindsight, she realized, it was because she hadn't chosen well and the scripts were – frankly – weak. This movie now could give her the critical acclaim she craved. She'd fought hard for this role. And she'd succeeded.

Hell, you had to fight in life. Fortune favoured the brave. Some people were born with silver spoons so far up their assholes they stuck in their gullets, and some, like herself, were born on the wrong side of the tracks. It had been a long journey to here, through her early days of waiting tables, and two husbands, to the place she was now at, and

**NOT DEAD YET**

where she felt comfortable. Just herself, Roan and Todd, the fitness instructor who gave her great sex when she needed it and kept out of her face when she didn't, and her trusted entourage, Team Gaia.

She picked up the script and showed him the white and the blue pages. 'Mama has to learn all this before she flies to England.'

'You promised.'

'Didn't Steffie read to you tonight?' Steffie was the nanny.

He looked forlorn. 'You read better. I like it when you read.'

She looked at her watch. 'It's after ten o'clock. Way past your bedtime!'

'I can't sleep. I can't sleep unless you read to me, Mama.'

She tossed the script on to the glass coffee table, lifted him down and stood up. 'Okay, one quick story. Okay?'

His face brightened. He nodded vigorously.

'Marla!' she shouted. 'Marla!'

Her assistant came into the room, cellphone pressed to her ear, arguing furiously with someone about what sounded like the seating arrangements on a plane. The one extravagance Gaia refused to have was a private jet, because of her concerns over her carbon footprint.

Marla was shouting. Didn't the fuckwit airline know who Gaia was? That she could fucking make or break them? She was wearing glittery Versace jeans tucked into black alligator boots, a thin black roll-neck and a gold neck chain carrying the flat gold globe engraved *Planet Gaia*. It was exactly the same way her boss was dressed tonight. Her hair mirrored her boss's, too: blonde, shoulder length, layered in a sharp razor cut with a carefully spaced and waxed fringe.

5

Gaia Lafayette insisted that all her staff had to dress the same way – following the daily emailed instructions of what she would be wearing, how her hair would be. They had, at all times, to be an inferior copy of herself.

Marla ended the call. 'Sorted!' she said. 'They've agreed to bump some people off the flight.' She gave Gaia an angelic smile. 'Because it's *you*!'

'I need cigarettes,' Gaia said. 'Wanna be an angel and go get me some?'

Marla shot a surreptitious glance at her watch. She had a date tonight and was already two hours late for him, thanks to Gaia's demands – nothing unusual. No previous personal assistant had lasted more than eighteen months before being fired, yet, amazingly, she was entering her third year. It was hard work and long hours, and the pay wasn't great, but the work experience was to die for, and although her boss was tough, she was kind. One day she'd be free of the chains, but not yet. 'Sure, no problem,' she said.

'Take the Merc.'

It was a balmy hot night. Gaia was smart enough to understand the small perks that went a long way.

'Cool! I'll be right back. Anything else?'

Gaia shook her head. 'You can keep the car for the night.'

'I can?'

'Sure, I'm not going anywhere.'

Marla coveted the silver SL55 AMG. She looked forward to driving the fast bends along Sunset to the convenience store. Then to picking up Jay in it afterwards. Who knew how the night might turn out? Every day working for Gaia was an adventure. Just as every night recently, since she had met Jay, was too! He was a budding actor, and she was

6

determined to find a way, through her connection with Gaia, to help him get a break.

She did not know it, but as she walked out to the Mercedes, she was making a grave mistake.

# 3

Thirty minutes earlier, the valium had started kicking in as he set off from Santa Monica, calming him. The coke he had snorted in a brief pit stop in the grounds of UCLA in Brentwood, fifteen minutes ago, was giving him energy, and the swig of tequila he took now, from the bottle on the passenger seat beside him, gave him an extra boost of courage.

The '97 Chevy was a rust bucket, and he drove slowly because the muffler, which he couldn't afford to fix, was shot, and he didn't want to draw attention to himself with its rumbling blatter. In the darkness, with its freshly sprayed coat of paint, which he had applied last night in the lot of the deserted auto wash where he worked, no one would see quite how much of a wreck the car was, he figured.

The tyres were totally bald in parts, and he could barely afford the gas to get across town. Not that the rich folk around here, in Bel Air, would have any concept of what it meant or felt like to be poor. Behind the high hedges and electric gates were huge mansions, sitting way back, surrounded by manicured lawns and all the garden toys of the rich and successful. The *haves* of LA. Some contrast with the *have-nots*, like the decrepit rented bungalow in the skanky part of Santa Monica he shared with Dana. But that was about to change. Soon she was going to get the recognition she had long deserved. Then they might be rich enough to buy a place like the ones around here.

The occupants of half the homes he passed by were

named on the copy of the *Star Maps*, so it was easy to figure out who was who. It sat, crumpled and well-thumbed, beside him, beneath the half-empty tequila bottle. And there was one sure way to cruise the streets of Bel Air without drawing attention to yourself from the infestation of police and private security patrols. Hey, he was an actor, and actors were chameleons, blending into their roles. Which was why he was dressed in a security guard uniform, driving right along the outside perimeter of Gaia Lafayette's estate, passing the dark, fortress-like gates in a gleaming Chevy station-wagon emblazoned with large blue and red letters: BEL-AIR-BEVERLY PRIVATE SECURITY SERV-ICES – ARMED RESPONSE. He had applied the wording, from decals, himself.

The arrogant bitch had totally ignored his email. It had been announced in all the Hollywood trade papers last week that she had boarded the project. She was going to be playing Maria Fitzherbert – or *Mrs* Fitzherbert as the woman had been known to the world – mistress of the Prince of Wales of England and secretly married to him. The marriage was never formally approved because she was a Catholic, and had the marriage been ratified, then her husband could never have become King George IV.

It was one of the greatest love stories in the British monarchy. And in the opinion of the showbiz gossip web-sites, one of the greatest screen roles ever to have been offered.

Every actress in the world, of the right age, was after it. It had *Oscar potential* written all over it. And Gaia was so not suitable, she would make a total screw-up. She was just a rock star, for God's sake! She wasn't an actress. She hadn't been to drama school. She hadn't struggled for years to get an agent, to get noticed by the players in this city who mattered. All she had done was sing second-rate songs, peel off her clothes, flaunt her body, and sleep with the right people. Suddenly she decides she's an actress!

In taking this part, she had screwed a lot of genuinely talented actresses out of one of the best roles of the past decade.

Like Dana Lonsdale.

And she just did not have any right to do that. Gaia didn't need the money. She didn't need to be any more famous than she already was. All she was doing now was feeding her greed and vanity. Taking bread out of everyone else's mouth to do that. Someone had to stop her.

He patted the pistol jammed in his pocket, uneasily. He'd never fired a gun in his life. The goddamn things made him nervous. But sometimes you had to do what you believed was right.

It was his pop's gun. He'd found it beneath the bed in the old man's trailer, after he had died. A Glock. He didn't even know the calibre, but had managed to identify it, from comparisons on the internet, as a .38. It had a loaded magazine of eight bullets, and on the floor beside the gun he had found a small carton containing more.

At first, he had planned to try to sell the thing, or even just throw it away. And right now he wished he had binned it. But he couldn't. It was there, in his home, like an ever-present reminder from his father. That the only way to stop injustices was to do something about them.

And tonight the time had come. He was intending to stop a big injustice.

Oh yes.

# 4

Like many farmers, early morning was Keith Winter's favourite time of the day. He liked to be up before the rest of the world, and he particularly loved this time of year, early June, when the sun rose before 5 a.m.

Although, on this particular day, he walked out of his house with a heavy heart, and crossed the short distance to the chicken shed with leaden steps.

He considered Lohmann Browns to be the best layers, which was the reason he had 32,000 of this particular breed of hens. By looking after them and nurturing them carefully, free range, during their short lives, the way he did here at Stonery Farm, he could get their eggs to taste consistently better than any of his rivals.

He kept the birds in humane, healthy surroundings, gave them all the space they needed, and fed them on his secret diet of wheat, oil, soya, calcium, sodium and a programme of vitamins. Despite the fact that his hens were aggressive in nature, and cannibals if given the chance, he was fond of them in the way that all good farmers cared for the animals that gave them their livelihood.

He housed them in a dry, clean, modern single-storey building, with a large outdoor run, that stretched out for over one hundred yards across the remote East Sussex hilltop property. Alongside were shiny steel silos containing the grain feed. At the far end were two lorries that had arrived a short while ago, at this early hour. A tractor was parked near by and sundry agricultural equipment, a rusting shipping container, pallets and sections of railing lay haphazardly around. His Jack Russell bounded around in search of an early rabbit.

Despite the strong breeze coming in off the English Channel, five miles to the south, Keith could feel the approach of summer in the air. He could smell it in the dry grass and dusty soil and the pollen that gave him hay fever. But although he loved the summer months, the advent of June was always a time of mixed emotions for him, because all his cherished hens would be gone, to end up in markets, with their final destinations being as nuggets, or soup, or ready-to-eat chicken dishes.

Most farmer acquaintances he talked to considered their hens to be nothing more than egg-laying machines, and in truth his wife Linda thought he was a little nuts the way he became so fond of these dumb creatures. But he couldn't help it; he was a perfectionist, obsessive about the quality of his eggs and his birds, constantly experimenting with their diet and supplements, and forever working on their accommodation to make it as conducive as possible for laying. Some eggs were trundling out of the conveyor belt into the grading machine, as he entered. He picked one large sample up, checked it for blemishes and colour consistency, tapped the shell for thickness and set it down again, satisfied. It trundled on past a stack of empty egg-cartons and out of sight.

A tall, solidly built sixty-three-year-old, with the youthful face of a man who has retained all his enthusiasm for life, Keith Winter was dressed in an old white T-shirt, blue shorts, and stout shoes with grey socks. The airy interior of the shed was partitioned into two sections. He entered the right-hand section now, into an echoing cacophony of noise, like the incoherent babble of a thousand simultaneous cocktail parties. He had long got used to, and barely even noticed, the almost overpowering reek of ammonia from the hen droppings, which fell through slats in the gridded metal floor into the deep sump below.

As one particularly aggressive hen pecked, painfully, at the hairs on his leg, he stared along the length of the shed, at the sea of brown and white creatures with their red crests, all strutting around in a busy manner, as if they had important engagements awaiting them. The shed was already starting to thin out, and large areas of the gridding were visible. The catchers had started early this morning, nine workers from Eastern Europe, mostly Latvian and Lithuanian, in their protective clothing and face masks, grabbing the hens, carrying them out through the doors at the far end and placing them in specially designed cages in the lorries.

The process would take all day, at the end of which the shed would be empty, leaving just the bare grid. A team from a specialist company would then come in to lift up the grid slats and remove the year's four-foot-deep collection of droppings with a mechanical bobcat.

Suddenly, he heard a shout from the far end, and saw one of the workers running towards him, dodging through the hens, his face mask removed. 'Mr Boss!' he shouted urgently at Keith, in broken English, with a look of panic on his face. 'Mr Boss, sir! Something not right. Not good. Please you come have look!'

# 5

The electric gates were opening!

Shit!

He was so not expecting this. He was jumpy, his thoughts all over the place. And he remembered he had forgotten to take his medication today; the one that kept the insides of his head all cohesive. Who was coming out? Probably a change of security guards, he thought, but this was too good an opportunity to miss. Just in case it was the bitch herself! She was known to like going out on her own. Although most of the time when she went jogging, according to the press, she had more security guards around her than the President of the USA.

He braked hard, switched off the Chevy's engine and pulled the gun out of the front pocket of his pants. He stared at the gates. At the blazing headlights of a car at the bottom of a winding drive, waiting for the gap to be big enough to drive through and out into the street.

He sprinted across the road and in through the gates. He saw the Mercedes halted, waiting. Smelled its exhaust mingled with the scent of freshly mown grass. Music pounded from its stereo, a Gaia song!

How sweet was that! Listening to her own music in her last few moments of life! She would die listening to it! How poetic was that?

The roof was down. Gaia was driving! She was alone!

*I warned you, bitch.*

The big Mercedes engine rumbled away, a steady, musical

boom-boom-boom. A gleaming metal beast waiting for the driver to press the pedal and thunder forward into the night. The gates continued opening, jerkily, the right-hand one faster than the left.

In a clumsy, fumbling movement, despite all his rehearsals, he flipped off the safety catch of the Glock. Then he stepped forward. 'I warned you, bitch!' he said. He said it loud, so she could hear. He saw her stare at him out of the shadows of the cockpit, like she was full of questions.

He had the answer in his shaking hand.

He saw the expression of fear on her face as he came closer.

But this was not right, he knew. He should turn away, forget it, run. Run home? Run home a failure?

He pulled the trigger and there was a much louder explosion than he had imagined. The gun jerked as if trying to break free of his hand, and he heard a thud, as if the bullet had hit something in the distance. She was staring at him wide-eyed in terror. Not a scratch on her. He had missed.

He aimed again, pointing the gun closer at her. She raised her hands in front of her face as he fired again. This time a piece of something flew off the back of her head and some of her hair stood up, in a row of spikes. He fired again, straight into her forehead and a small, dark hole appeared in the centre. She slumped back, quivering like a landed fish that had been hit several times with a hammer, her eyes still staring at him. Dark liquid leaked from the hole and ran down and along the bridge of her nose. 'You should have listened,' he said. 'You should have obeyed me.'

Then he turned and ran away, back to his car, in a daze.

# 6

Gaia was coming to Brighton! The icon coming back to the city where she was born. Brighton's most famous living star was returning home to play Brighton's most famous historical female. It was a match made in heaven. A dream for Gaia.

And an even bigger dream for Anna Galicia. Her biggest fan.

Her number one fan!

Only Anna knew the real reason why Gaia was coming here. It was to be with her! The signals had all been very clear.

Unequivocal.

'She's arriving next week, Diva, what do you think of that?'

The cat stared at her without any expression she could read.

The star of stars was arriving next week. Anna would be there at the hotel to greet her in person. Finally, after years of adoring her, and of communicating with each other from afar, she would have the chance to meet her. Perhaps touch her hand. Even, if things went really well, she might be invited into her suite, to drink cocktails with her – and then?

Of course you could never tell whether Gaia was into men or women at any given time. She flaunted each new relationship openly. Going through lover after lover, in search of – *the one*! She had been married twice, to men, but that was a long time ago. Anna followed her life online, on television, in newspapers and magazines. And she and Gaia had been flirting secretly with each other for years in code. Their own secret code that Gaia used as her emblem on all her merchandise. A tiny, furtive fox.

*Secret fox!*

Gaia had been sending more and more signals to her in recent weeks. Anna had the evidence stacked in neat piles of newspapers and magazines neatly laid out, each individually protected in a cellophane folder, on the table in front of her.

She had rehearsed that moment when they would finally meet a million times over, in her mind. Struggled with her doubts. Maybe start with asking for her autograph to break the ice? This wouldn't be too much to ask for her number one fan, would it?

Of course not.

*Secret fox!*

Gaia was famed for adoring her fans. And none was as devoted as herself. She had spent her entire inheritance of her late mother's house, and on top of that, almost every penny she had ever earned collecting her memorabilia.

Anna had always bought the best seats at Gaia's concerts when she had performed in England. She had made sure she was first in line, either in person, or on the internet. She had secured a front row ticket for every single night Gaia had performed in her smash hit West End musical, *Sainted!* – the life of Mother Teresa.

And of course she always sent Gaia an apologetic email if she was going to be unable to attend because she had not been able to secure tickets. Wishing her well. Hoping the evening would be fine without her. And of course, the sign.

*Secret fox!*

Anna sat, dreamily, in the upstairs room of her little

house in Peacehaven, close to Brighton. In her *shrine*. The *Gaia Museum*! If she breathed deeply – really deeply – ignoring the smells of dried-out cardboard and paper and plastic and polish, she believed she could still detect Gaia's perspiration and perfume from the costumes her idol had worn at concerts, which she had bought at charity auctions.

Every inch of wall space was covered in images and souvenirs of Gaia. Autographed posters, glass cabinets, shelving stacked with her CDs, a silver balloon which she kept continually inflated, printed with the words GAIA INNER SECRETS TOUR which she had bought two months ago when the singer had last been in the UK. Framed tickets of every Gaia concert around the world she had ever attended, concert tour schedules, bottles of her health-giving mineral water, and a treasured collection of her personalized monogrammed coat hangers.

Several headless mannequins stood around the room, each wearing a Gaia dress she had bought at online auctions, and encased in transparent covers to protect them – and above all, to preserve the scent and bodily smells of the icon, who had once worn them on stage. More items of Gaia's clothing lay, in labelled boxes, wrapped in acid-free tissue paper.

There was also a treasured fly-fishing rod that Gaia had been photographed using for one of her GREAT OUTDOORS GAL posters, that Anna had lovingly framed, with the rod beside it. The rod reminded Anna of her father, who used to take her fishing when she was very young. Before he'd abandoned her and her mother.

She sat, sipping from a Martini glass the Gaia special cocktail she had lovingly mixed from the recipe Gaia had published – a mojito, with loganberries added for health-giving properties and guarana for energy – while listening to her idol's greatest hit playing at full blast, 'Here To Save The Planet Together!'

She raised the glass in a toast to one of her favourite images of all, the close-up of the icon's lips, nose and eyes, titled GAIA UP CLOSE AND PERSONAL.

Diva, her small Burmese cat, walked away from her, back arched as if in anger. Sometimes Anna wondered if she was jealous of Gaia. Then she turned back to the cuttings on the table and stared at one, the Spotted section of *Heat* magazine. It was a photo of Gaia, in black jeans and top, shopping in Beverly Hills, in Rodeo Drive. Beneath was the caption:

Gaia shopping for new movie role?

She smiled excitedly. Black! Gaia had put that colour on just for her!

I love you, Gaia, she thought. I love you so much. I know you already know that! And of course, soon I will tell you in person, face to face here in Brighton. Next week. Just five days' time.

Please be wearing black then, too.

Secret fox!

# 7

The partially complete skeleton lay on the steel table, bathed in the glare of the overhead lights of the post-mortem room. Detective Superintendent Roy Grace stared down at the skull, its creepy rictus grin like a final Parthian shot of mockery. *Goodbye cruel world, you can't hurt me any more! I'm gone! I'm out of here!*

Grace was eight weeks shy of his fortieth birthday, and in his twenty-first year with Sussex Police. Just under five feet eleven inches tall, he kept his figure in shape by relentless exercise. His fair hair was cut short and gelled, thanks to his styling guru, Glenn Branson, and his nose, squashed and kinked after being broken in a scrap when he'd been a beat copper, gave him the air, on first acquaintance, of a retired prize fighter. His wife, Sandy, now missing for almost a decade, once told him he had eyes like Paul Newman. He'd liked that a lot, but had never quite believed it. He just considered himself a regular guy, unexceptional, doing a job he loved. Although, despite his years working on homicides, human skulls always spooked him.

Most police officers claimed they got used to dead bodies, in any form, and that nothing bothered them, except for children. But every body he encountered still bothered Grace, even after all his years in this job. Because every corpse was once a person loved by their family, their friends, their lover, however fleetingly for some tragic people that might have been.

At the start of his career he had promised himself that

he would never turn cynical. Yet for some of his colleagues, becoming a cynic, alongside gallows humour, was their emotional carapace. Their way of staying sane in this job.

All the dead man's component parts that they'd recovered so far had been neatly and precisely laid out by the forensic archaeologist, Joan Major. It was like a flat-packed piece of furniture that had arrived from a DIY store with some key bits missing, he thought, suddenly and irreverently.

*Operation Violin*, on which he was the Senior Investigating Officer, was winding down. It was the investigation into two revenge murders and an abduction. Their prime suspect, who had been identified by New York detectives as a known Mafia contract killer, had disappeared. It was possible he had drowned attempting to avoid arrest, but equally likely, in Grace's view, he had left the country and could now be anywhere in the world, under one of the host of aliases he was known to use – or, more probably, a new one.

Nearly four weeks on from the suspect's disappearance, *Operation Violin* had moved into *slow time*. Back on the roster as Duty SIO for this week, Roy Grace had stood down most of his team, retaining just a small workforce to liaise with the US. But there was one more element to the operation that remained – and lay in front of him now. And time didn't get much slower than for fully decomposed, and picked clean, skeletal remains. It had taken the best part of a week for the Specialist Search Unit's team to cover every inch of the massive tunnel and surrounding inspection shafts, and to recover the remains, some of which had been scattered over a wide area by rodents.

The Home Office pathologist, Dr Frazer Theobald, had done much of his painstaking post-mortem in situ, before the remains were brought here last night, without being able to come to any conclusions as to the cause of death. He had departed a few minutes ago. Without any flesh or body fluids, with the absence of any signs of damage to either the skull or the bones, such as from a heavy instrument or a knife or a bullet, the chances of finding the cause of death were slim.

Several members of the investigating team remained in the room, gowned up like himself in green pyjamas. Cleo Morey, Grace's fiancée, thirty-two weeks pregnant, was the Senior Anatomical Pathology Technician, as the Chief Mortician was officially termed. Her green PVC apron lay draped over the bulge of their baby, as she slid a body wrapped in white plastic sheeting out of a door in the floor-to-ceiling bank of refrigerators, eased it on to a trolley and wheeled it through into another section of the room, to prepare it for a post-mortem.

Philip Keay, the Coroner's Officer, a tall, lean man, with swarthy good looks beneath short dark hair and bushy eyebrows, remained dutifully present, although engrossed at this moment with his BlackBerry.

This stage of the investigation, which was focused on trying to establish the identity of the dead man, was being led by Joan Major, a pleasant-looking woman, with long brown hair and fashionably modern glasses, who had a quietly efficient manner. Grace had worked with her several times in the past, and he was always impressed by her skills. Even to his experienced eye, all skeletons looked much the same. But to Joan Major, each was as individual as a fingerprint.

She dictated into her machine, quietly but clearly enough so that anyone who wanted to listen, could. She began with the skull.

'Prominent brow ridges. Sloping forehead. Rounded superior orbit. Large mastoid process. Extended posterior zygomatic arch. Prominent nuchal crest.'

Then she moved on to the pelvis. 'Narrow sciatic notch. Oval obturator foramen. Pubic bone shorter. Narrow sub-pubic angle. Subpubic concavity absent. Sacrum curved.'

Roy Grace listened intently, although much of what she said was too technical for him to grasp. He was tired and stifled a yawn, glancing at his watch. It was 11.45 a.m., and he could do with another coffee. He'd been up late last night, playing in his weekly boys' poker game – where he'd ended forty pounds up. It had been an exhausting few weeks, and he was looking forward to having a curry with Cleo tonight, and kicking back, watching some Friday night junk television, ending, as they usually did, falling asleep watching their favourite talk show host, Graham Norton. And, glorious thought, they had no plans for the weekend. He was particularly looking forward to some time alone with Cleo, enjoying those precious last few weeks before, as he had been warned by his colleague Nick Nicholl who had recently become a father, their lives changed for ever. Originally, they had hoped to have their wedding before the baby was born, but the process for having Sandy declared legally dead, and work, had got in the way of that. Now they had to make new plans.

He also needed the breathing space, after the past hectic weeks, to focus on the vast bundle of trial documents of a snuff movie murder case involving a particularly nasty specimen of humanity he'd arrested, Carl Venner, whose trial was listed to come up at the Old Bailey in the next couple of weeks.

He turned his focus back to the forensic archaeologist. But within a few minutes, although he tried not to be, inevitably he was distracted by Cleo. A few weeks ago she'd been in hospital with internal bleeding. She had been warned not to do any heavy lifting, and it worried him to see her now, removing the body and rolling it on the trolley. Working in a mortuary, it was inevitable you would have to lift things. He was scared for her, because he loved her so much. Scared, because as the consultant had warned, with a second bleed her life could be in jeopardy as much as their baby's.

He watched her stop the trolley alongside the naked cadaver of an elderly woman she had just finished preparing. The skull cap had been removed, and her brain lay on a Formica tray above her chest. On the white wall chart above there were blank spaces for the dimensions and weight of the dead woman's internal organs. At the top, the name Claire Elford was handwritten in black marker pen.

It was a grim place to work and the job was tough. He could never fully understand its appeal to Cleo. She was a statuesque beauty, her long blonde hair clipped up, hygienically; she would have looked more at home in a smart London advertising agency or art gallery or magazine publisher – but she truly loved her job. He still could not believe his luck, that after almost ten years of hell, following Sandy's disappearance, he had found love again. And with someone so gorgeous and such fun to be with.

He used to consider that Sandy was his soulmate, despite their constant arguments. But since beginning his relationship with Cleo, the word *soulmate* had taken on a whole new meaning. He would die for Cleo, he truly would.

Then turning his focus back to the forensic archaeologist, he asked, 'Joan, can you give us any indication of his age?'

'I can't be too precise yet, Roy,' she said, moving back to the skull and pointing. 'The presence of a third molar suggests adult. The medial clavicle fused suggests he is older than thirty.' Then she pointed at the pelvis. 'The auricual surface is phase six, which would put him between forty-five and forty-nine. The pubic symphysis is phase five – less precise, I'm afraid – which could put him anywhere from twenty-seven to sixty-six. The wear in his teeth indicates towards the upper end of this age spectrum.'

She pointed at parts of the spine. 'There are some osteophytic growths which again are suggestive of an older individual. In terms of race, the skull measurements suggest Caucasian, European – or European region – origin, but it's difficult to be more precise. As a general observation, pronounced muscle attachments, particularly noticeable in the humerus, suggest a strong, active individual.'

Grace nodded. The skeletal remains, along with a pair of partially gnawed sea boots, UK size nine, had been discovered by chance in a disused tunnel deep beneath the city's principal harbour, Shoreham. He already had a pretty good idea who this man was, and all that Joan Major had said was helping confirm this.

Six years earlier, an Estonian Merchant Navy sea captain called Andrus Kangur had disappeared after berthing his container ship loaded with timber. Kangur had been under observation by Europol for some years on suspicion of drugs trafficking. The man wasn't necessarily a great loss to the world, but that wasn't for Roy Grace to judge. He did know there was a probable motive. According to information from the Divisional Intelligence Unit, which, following a tip-off, had had the ship under surveillance from the time it entered the port, Kangur had tried to double-cross whoever was behind this cargo, and had not been too smart in his choice of whom he had screwed: a high-profile New York crime family.

From the evidence so far gathered, and from what Grace knew about the likely assailant, the unfortunate captain had been chained up in what amounted to an underground dungeon, and left to starve to death or be eaten by rats. When they had found him, all of his flesh and almost all of the sinews and his hair had gone. Most of his bones had fallen in on each other, or on to the floor, except for one set of arm bones and an intact skeletal hand, which hung from a metal pipe above him, held in place by a padlocked chain.

Suddenly, Roy's phone rang.

It was a cheery and very efficient Detective Sergeant from Eastbourne CID, Simon Bates. 'Roy, you're the Duty SIO?'

Immediately Grace's heart sank. Calls like this were never good news.

There were four Senior Investigating Officers in the Sussex CID Major Crime Branch, taking it in turns to be the Duty SIO, one week on, three weeks off. His shift was due to end at 6 a.m. on Monday. *Shit.*

'Yes I am, Simon,' he said, about as enthusiastically as a dental patient agreeing to root canal work. He suddenly heard a strange clicking sound, which lasted for a few seconds; interference from somewhere.

'We have a suspicious death at a farm in East Sussex.'

'What information can you give me?'

The clicking stopped. He listened to Bates, his heart sinking, his weekend down the khazi hours before it had even begun. He exchanged a glance with Cleo, and could see, instantly, that she understood what was going on. She gave him a wan smile.

'I'm on my way,' he said.

He hung up and immediately dialled the Chief Constable's Staff Officer, Trevor Bowles, informing him that it sounded like there was another murder in the county, and that he would report back with more details later. It was important to keep the CC informed of a potential major incident, as well as the Deputy Chief Constable and the Assistant Chief Constables, to avoid the risk of their being in the embarrassing position of hearing the news third hand from the media.

Next he dialled his colleague and friend, Detective Sergeant Glenn Branson.

'Yo, old timer, what's popping?' Branson answered.

Grace grinned at his use of rap language, a recent affectation that he had picked up from a movie. 'I'll tell you what's about to be popping – your ears. We're going up a hill.'

# 8

I made a mistake, bitch. You were lucky. But that
changes nothing. Next time I'll be the lucky one.
I will get you anywhere in the world that you go.

# 9

In the stop-go rush hour traffic heading down into the Valley, Larry Brooker sat in his black Porsche cabriolet. It was a 911 Carrera 4-S, he told anyone who would listen. He needed to make sure people knew he'd bought the 4-S, and not the less expensive 2-S, and that it had the $25k ceramic brake upgrade. Details. He was a detail guy. It wasn't just the Devil that was in the detail. The gods of success were, too. People needed to know you were one of life's winners; players in this business had no time for losers.

He was on his cellphone, his veneered teeth flashing brightly in the strong morning sunlight. His eyes, raw from a sleepless night, were shielded by his Ray-Bans, and his shaved dome gleamed with a healthy California tan. He was fifty, short and lean and spoke in a rapid, staccato manner; he was like a video on permanent fast-forward.

To the occupants of other vehicles crawling alongside him, he looked every inch an archetypal successful LA entertainment industry mover and shaker. But inside the plush leather cocoon of the Porsche's cockpit it was very different. He was squirming in his ripped jeans. The sun might be shining on Ventura Boulevard, and on his exposed dome, but it sure as hell was shady in his heart right now, and sweat was trickling down his neck, sticking his black John Varvatos shirt to the seat-back. Not yet 9 a.m. and he was already perspiring. It was going to be a clammy day – in more ways than one.

Folks called this city Tinseltown because so much here

was a glittery illusion where, like the facelifts of fading stars, nothing was permanent. And sure as hell there wasn't anything permanent in Larry Brooker's life right now.

He remained in deep conversation on the phone all the way along Universal Boulevard, and continued talking as he reached the security gate at the studios. Even though the guard had seen him a thousand times before, the surly old stalwart still stared at him like he was some dog turd that had floated downstream on the morning tide – which was about how he felt today. The guard went through the ritual of asking his name then checking down his list, before giving him a more respectful nod, and opening the barrier.

Larry pulled up into one of the allotted spaces marked *Reserved for Brooker Brody Productions.*

As any producer who had free offices on a studio lot knew, you were as good as your last few productions, and unless you had the stature of Spielberg, you had zero assurance of permanent tenure.

He hung up and mouthed the words, *Oh fuck!* The call had been from a Californian internet billionaire, Aaron Zvotnik – who had funded his last three productions – giving him the reasons why he was not going to continue beyond the current one. That was some start to a day, to have lost a revolving fund of $100 million.

But he could hardly blame Zvotnik. They'd delivered three movies in a row that had tanked. *Blood Kiss* at a time when vampire movies had peaked. *Genesis Factor* when the world had become bored with *Da Vinci Code* follow-ups. And more recently their massively over-budget sci-fi flop, *Omega-3-2-1*.

Three previous expensive divorces had taken their toll on his finances. The bank owned most of his house. His vehicle finance company was closing in on his Porsche. His fourth wife's divorce lawyer was closing in on the kids.

Twenty years back, after his first mega hit, *Beach Baby*, every door in this city swung open before he'd even reached it. Now, in Hollywood parlance, he'd struggle to get arrested. This was an unforgiving place. There was the old adage, *be nice to people when you're on your way up . . . because you never know who you're going to need on the way down.*

But there was no need to bother with that here. When you were on your way down in Tinseltown it didn't matter how nice you once were. You became Dick Shit. You became an unreturned phone call. A scrawled name on a Post-it note that got flicked into the trash can. You became *air*.

Movie producers like himself were gamblers. And every gambler believed their luck was going to change on the next throw of the dice or spin of the wheel. Larry Brooker didn't just believe it right now – he *knew. The King's Speech* had been a global phenomenon. *The King's Lover* would be, too. The very title sent shivers of excitement down him. Let alone the script, which was awesome!

The damned thing had to work.

King George IV. Gorgeous Brighton, England, locations. Sex, intrigue, scandal. This was a no-brainer. They'd negotiated with Bill Nicholson, who wrote *Gladiators*, to do a polish on the screenplay. Nicholson's dialogue was smart. Everything about this project was smart. George IV lived life high on the hog, was a friend of dandy socialite Beau Brummell. He was a king who was vain but also very human. He enjoyed going to prize fights and cock fights, and was comfortable mingling with low-lifes – he was a true man of the people – at least in the script, he was.

Suckered into an arranged marriage, George IV's first words to his best friend, when he saw his betrothed, were, 'For God's sake, man, give me a glass of brandy!'

They were already in pre-production, but the entire project was in danger of falling over for the same reason so many productions never got the crucial green light. Cast.

Brooker entered the suite of offices on the first floor of the tired-looking low-rise block. His secretary, Courtney, was bent over the coffee machine like an Anglepoise lamp, with her skirt riding high up her slender legs, revealing her panties. It gave him an instant prick of lust despite his woes. He'd hired her because he fancied her like hell, but so far had got nowhere with her, thanks to the fact she had a hunk of a boyfriend who, like almost everyone in this town, was an actor in search of a break.

He greeted her with a cheery, 'Hi, babe, could murder a coffee,' and walked through into his office, which was a large square box with a fusty smell, decorated with a full-size BP petrol pump, a pinball machine, several wilting pot plants, and framed posters of his movies. The window looked out on the parking lot.

He slung his black Armani jacket on a chair and stood at his desk for some minutes, checking his emails and the stack of messages on Post-it notes simultaneously. He was in the Last-Chance Saloon, but what a big chance they had right now! They had their female star but lacked the male lead to complement her. That was all that mattered right now, finding that man, and it was a big problem. They'd had A-lister Matt Duke all lined up and ready to sign, but two nights ago, high on coke, he'd trashed his car on Mulholland Drive and would be spending months in hospital with multiple fractures and internal injuries. Goddamn dickhead!

Now they were in a panic to replace him. Their female lead, Gaia, had a reputation for being difficult and demanding, and a lot of people did not want to work with her. If they didn't start shooting in three weeks they would lose Gaia's window and have to wait another ten months for her. That was not an option; they didn't have the cash to survive ten months.

He sat down just as his partner, Maxim Brody, slouched into the room, reeking as ever of cigar smoke. He looked hung over and was clutching a Starbucks coffee in a container the size of a fire bucket. While Larry Brooker could pass for a decade younger than his fifty years, Brody, who was sixty-two, looked all of ten years older than that. A former lawyer, with thinning hair, watery eyes and a jowly face like a big, droopy bloodhound, he had the air of a man who perpetually carried the troubles of the world on his shoulders.

Dressed in a pink polo shirt, baggy jeans and worn trainers, Maxim peered around suspiciously, in his usual manner, as if he didn't trust anything or anyone, sat down on the sofa in the middle of the room, and yawned.

'Tally tiring you out?' Brooker said, unable to resist the barb.

Brody was on his fifth wife, a twenty-two-year-old with gargantuan breasts and a brain smaller than her nipples, a wannabe actress he'd met waiting tables in a café on Sunset.

'Do you think she could play George's real wife?'

'George's real wife was a dog.'

'So?'

'Get real, Max.'

'Just a thought.'

'Right now we need our male lead. We need goddamn King George.'

'Yuh.'

'Yuh. Are you with us? On planet earth?'

Brody nodded. 'I've been giving it thought.'

'And?'

Brody fell into one of his habitual silences. They infuriated Brooker because he could never tell whether his partner was thinking, or had momentarily, in his drug-addled brain, lost the plot. Without their male lead the whole shooting match was in danger of crashing and burning around their ears. At the period of their movie, George IV was in his late twenties, with Maria Fitzherbert six years older. So Gaia was perfect, if a little thin. To get a major male star in the right age range who either was English or who could pass as English, was proving even harder than they had anticipated, and they were running out of options. In desperation, they'd cast their net wide. They weren't making a biopic, for God's sake, this was a movie, fiction, George IV could be any damned age or nationality they chose. Besides, weren't all those Brit royals foreign?

Tom Cruise wasn't available. Colin Firth had passed, so had Johnny Depp, Bruce Willis and George Clooney. They'd even tried a different tack and put an offer out to Anthony Hopkins, which had come back with a curt no from his agent. That completed the most bankable names on their sales agent's list. Now, focusing on Brits, they were looking at a wider roster of stars. Ewan McGregor did not want to work outside LA while his kids were growing up. Clive Owen was unavailable. So was Guy Pearce.

'Gaia Lafayette is screwing some hunk. What about him?' Brody said, suddenly.

'Can he act?'

Brody shrugged. 'How about Judd Halpern?'

'He's a drunk.'

'So? Listen, we got all the presales we need on Gaia's name – does it matter who plays fucking George?'

'Actually, Maxim, it does. We need someone who can act.'

'Halpern's a great actor – we just have to keep him off the juice.'

Larry's phone rang. He picked up the receiver. 'I have Drayton Wheeler on the line for you,' Courtney said. 'It's the fifth time he's called.'

'I'm in a meeting. Who is he?'

'Says it's very urgent, to do with *The King's Lover*.'

He covered the mouthpiece and turned to his partner. 'You know a Drayton Wheeler?'

Brody shook his head, preoccupied with removing the lid of his coffee bucket.

'Put him through.'

Moments later a voice at the other end of the phone, the tone aggressive and nasty, said, 'Mr Brooker, do you have a problem reading emails?'

'Who am I talking to?'

'The writer who sent you the idea for *The King's Lover*.'

Larry Brooker frowned. 'You did?'

'Three years ago. I sent you a treatment. Told you it was one of the greatest untold love stories of the world. According to *Variety* and the *Hollywood Reporter* you're going into production. With a script based on my treatment that you stole from me.'

'I don't think so, Mr Wheeler.'

'This is my story.'

'Look, have your agent call me.'

'I don't have a fucking agent. That's why *I'm* calling you.'

This was all Larry needed today. Some jerk trying to

cash in on the production. 'In that case, have your lawyer call me.'

'I'm calling you. I don't need to pay a lawyer. Just listen to me good. You've stolen my story. I want paying.'

'Sue me,' Brooker said, and hung up.

# 10

Eric Whiteley was remembering every second, as clearly as if it were yesterday. It all came back every time he saw a news story about bullying, and his face felt flushed and hot now. Those ten boys sitting on the wall chanting, 'Ubu! Ubu! Ubu!' at him as he walked by. The same ten boys who had been on that low brick wall every evening since the start of his second term at the school he hated so much, some thirty-seven years ago. Most of them had been fourteen – a year older than him – but a couple, the smuggest of them all, were his age and in his class.

He remembered the paper pellet striking him on the back of his head, which he had ignored, and just carried on walking towards his boarding house, clutching his set of maths and chemistry books which he'd needed for his afternoon classes. Then a pebble hitting him really hard, stinging his ear, and one of them, Spedding Junior it had sounded like, shouting out, 'Great shot!' It was followed by laughter.

He had walked on, the pain agonizing, but determined to get out of their sight before he rubbed his ear. It felt like it was cut open.

'Ubu's stoned!' one of them shouted and there had been more laughter.

'Hey Ubu, you shouldn't walk around stoned, you could get into all kinds of trouble!' another of them had shouted and there were even more guffaws and jeers.

He could still remember biting his lip against the pain,

fighting off tears as he carried on along the tree-lined avenue, warm blood trickling down the side of his neck. The main school grounds, with the classrooms and playing fields, were behind him. Along this road were ugly boarding houses, big Victorian mansion blocks, accommodating sixty to ninety pupils, some in dormitories, some in single or shared rooms. His own house, called Hartwellian, was just ahead.

He could remember turning into it, walking past the grand front entrance, which was the housemaster's, and around the side. Fortunately there had been no boys hanging around to see him crying. Not that he really cared. He knew he was no good, useless, and that people didn't like him.

Ubu.

Ugly. Boring. Useless.

The other kids had spent all of the previous term – his first in this school – telling him that. John Monroe, who had the desk right behind him in Geography, had kept prodding him with a ruler. 'You know your problem, Whiteley?' he said, each word emphasized with a prod.

Whenever he'd turned around he got the same answer. 'You're so fucking ugly and you've no personality. No girl's ever going to fancy you. None, ever, you realize?' He remembered how Monroe's horsey face would then break out into a snide grin.

After a while, he had stopped turning round. But Monroe used to keep on prodding, until Mr Leask, the teacher, spotted him and told him to stop. Five minutes later, when the teacher began drawing a diagram of soil substrates on the blackboard, Monroe's prodding started again.

# 11

Detective Sergeant Glenn Branson was struggling to insert his thirty-three-year-old, six-foot-two, nightclub bouncer's frame into a white protective paper suit. 'What is it with you and weekends, boss?' he said. 'How come you always manage to screw them up for both of us?'

Roy Grace, perched alongside him on the rear tailgate of the unmarked silver Ford Focus estate car, was struggling equally hard to get his protective suit up over his clothes. He turned to his protégé who was dressed in a shiny brown jacket, even shinier white shirt, a dazzling tie and tassled brown loafers. 'Lucky you never chose farming as a career option, Glenn,' he said. 'Wouldn't have been your style.'

'Yeah, well, my ancestors were cotton pickers,' Branson retorted with a broad grin.

Glenn was right about the weekend, Roy thought ruefully. It seemed that every damned murder he had to deal with came in just when he had his weekend all sorted out.

Like now.

'What did you have planned, matey?'

'The kids. One of the few weekends Ari is letting me have them. I was going to take them to Legoland. Now she'll have something else to use against me.'

Glenn was going through a bitter divorce. His wife, Ari, who had once encouraged him so hard to join the police, was now using the unpredictability of his hours as part of her argument for not agreeing contact arrangements for the children to see him. Grace felt a sharp twinge of guilt.

Perhaps he shouldn't have requested Glenn join him. But he knew his marriage was doomed, whatever happened. The best favour he could do his friend was to ensure his career came out of it intact. 'You think taking the weekend off would help save your marriage?'

'Nope.'

Grace grinned. 'So?'

'You ever see that movie, *Chicken Run*?'

He shook his head.

'You've lived a sheltered life.'

'Lot of sex in it, was there?' Grace retorted.

'Yeah, right.'

They put on face masks, raised their hoods and snapped on protective gloves. Then the pair of them signed in on the scene guard's pad, and ducked under the blue and white police crime scene tape. It was a fine, blustery day. They were high up on the ridge of a hill, with open farmland stretching for miles in all directions, and the glinting blue water of the English Channel visible on the horizon to the south, beyond the Downs.

They walked towards a long, single-storey shed with clapboard walls and a row of roof vents that stretched away into the distance, two tall steel silos standing beside it. Grace pushed the door open. They went inside to the glare of artificial lighting, to the sour stench of confined animals, and the din of thousands of protesting hens.

'Had eggs for breakfast, old timer?' Branson asked.

'Actually, I had porridge.'

'Guess at your age, cholesterol matters. Low fat milk?'

'Cleo's put me on soya.'

'You're under her thumb.'

'She has pretty thumbs.'

'That's how every relationship starts. Pretty face, pretty

thumbs, pretty damned everything. You love every inch of her body and she loves every inch of yours. Ten years on, you're struggling to remember one damned thing about each other that you once liked.' Branson patted him on the shoulder. 'But hey, enjoy the ride.'

Roy Grace stopped and Branson stopped beside him. 'Matey, don't become a cynic. You're too good for that.'

'I'm just a realist.'

Grace shook his head.

'Your wife vanished on your thirtieth birthday – after you'd been together several years, right?' said Branson.

'Uh huh. Getting on for ten years.'

'You still loved her?'

'As much as the day I met her. More.'

'Maybe you're an exception.'

Grace looked at him. 'I hope not.'

Branson stared at him, his face full of pain. 'Yeah, I hope not too. But it hurts. I think of Ari and the kids constantly, and it hurts so much.'

Grace stared down the length of the shed, with its gridded steel floor, a section of which, towards the far end, had been lifted. He could see, suited up, the stocky Crime Scene Manager David Green; three SOCOs including the burly, intensely serious Crime Scene Photographer James Gartrell; DS Simon Bates; the Duty Inspector Roy Apps, and the Coroner's Officer Philip Keay.

'Let's rock and roll.' Grace stepped on to the grid.

'Not sure I feel much like dancing,' Glenn Branson said.

'So, you and the dead body have something in common.'

# 12

The dead body was very definitely not dancing. Partly on account of the fact that it was embedded in several feet of chicken excrement, partly because its legs were missing, and partly because it had no hands or head, either. Which would have made co-ordination difficult. A cluster of blow-flies buzzed around, and the stench of ammonia was almost overpowering.

Glenn, close to retching, turned away. Grace stared down. Whoever had done this had little forensic awareness, and even less finesse. The headless, limbless torso, with desiccated flesh missing in patches, covered in excrement and crawling with flies and maggots, was barely recognizable as human. The skin, which appeared acid-scorched in the patches where it was visible, was a dark, leathery brown, giving it the air of a shop-window dummy that had been salvaged from a bonfire. The rank stench of a decaying body, all too familiar to Grace, rose all around him, making the air feel heavy and cloying. It was a smell that always accompanied you home, in your hair, on your clothes, in every pore of your skin. You could scrub yourself raw, but you'd still smell it again the next morning.

The only person he never noticed it on was Cleo. But maybe Glenn was right, and in ten years' time he would. He hoped not.

'Coq au vin for dinner, Roy?' the Crime Scene Manager greeted him, dressed in a white protective suit, with breathing apparatus, his mask temporarily raised.

'Not if it does that to you, thanks!'

Both men stared down into the space, four foot below the grid, at the torso. The first thought in Roy Grace's mind was whether this was some kind of gangland killing. 'So, what do we have so far?'

In answer to his SIO, David Green picked up a sealed polythene evidence bag from the floor, with an air of pride, and held it up with a gloved hand.

Grace peered inside. It contained two jagged pieces of badly soiled fabric, with an ochre checked pattern just visible. What looked like parts of a man's suit.

'Where did you find these?' Grace asked.

'Close to the body. Looks like it might have been something he was wearing – for some reason the only parts that didn't decompose or get taken by rats for a nest. Maybe we'll find more when we start our fingertip search.'

'*He?*'

'One of the few bits that weren't cut off, chief, if you get my drift.'

Grace nodded, uncomfortably getting his drift.

'Must have been a made-to-measure suit,' Glenn Branson said.

Grace and Green looked at him. 'Can you tell that from the cut of the cloth?' Grace asked.

'No, chief.' Branson nodded down at the remains and said, drily, 'I'm imagining they would have had a bit of a problem finding something off-the-peg to fit him.'

# 13

Inside the house, just like all Gaia's homes, the floors looked like Italian marble. Just like the stone that had been imported slab by slab from the Fantiscritti quarry in Carrara that, historically, had supplied the Medicis with the marble for their palaces, and in more recent years, one of the Los Angeles landmarks, Hernando Courtright's Beverly Wilshire Hotel.

The walls were hung with Aztec artefacts and stage shots of Gaia. In pride of place, on the wall facing the sofa, was the signed monochrome photo of her with wild, just-out-of-bed hair, wearing a black negligee to promote her world tour. To the left, above one of the armchairs of the white leather three-piece suite, which was a clone of her one in LA, was another tour poster, also signed. In it she wore a green tank top and leather jeans. Gaia would have felt totally at home here! Okay, so maybe the rear aspect wasn't as fine as in some of her residences. Gaia probably had a better view from her kitchen window than this one, an old woman's smalls hanging on a washing line, and a disused breeze-block garage.

Above the fireplace, with fake electric coals burning, was a blow-up of her idol's lips, nose and eyes in green monochrome, captioned GAIA UP CLOSE AND PERSONAL. Again, personally signed.

One of her favourite items!

She had fought a fierce bidding war on eBay for it.

Securing it with just five seconds to spare for £1,750. Money she could not afford. But she had to have it.

*Had* to.

Like everything else in this small semi, with the irritating street light outside that shone an amber glow every damned night into her bedroom.

Anna had bought the house in daytime, six years ago. It had never occurred to her that street lights might be a problem. Gaia would not have to put up with street lights keeping her awake, that was for sure.

Anna had written to the council, written to the *Argus*, the *West Sussex Gazette*, the *Sussex Express*, the *Mid Sussex Times*, but no one had replied, no one had done a single damned thing about that street light. So she bought an air rifle, and shot the bulb out in the middle of the night. Two bloody workmen from the bloody council replaced it two bloody days later.

But none of that mattered right now. All forgotten for the moment, because Gaia was coming to Brighton! And Anna had now found out where she was going to be staying. In the Presidential Suite of The Grand Hotel. Where else? They should have had an Empress Suite for her. She was the greatest, the queen of rock, the queen of the silver screen, the greatest star of all time. She was an empress! A truly Grand Empress! Returning to the city where she was born. Coming home to her roots. Coming to meet her number one fan!

And Anna really was her number one fan. Everyone conceded that. Gaia herself had! One of her assistants had replied to one of her emails saying, *Dear No 1 fan!* And of course, all of the other Gaia fans like herself, who shared snippets of information on chatlines, by email, by Facebook and sometimes Twitter, yet who became deadly enemies in bidding wars on eBay, all of them conceded that, as of this moment in time, Anna had them beat. She had the biggest collection, by far.

Number one.

And the secret signals from Gaia confirming their special relationship.

*Secret fox!*

Gaia had millions of adoring fans. But how many owned one of just six *Call Me Your Baby* vinyls in the world? How many fans had paid £1,000 for the signed single, 'Shady Babe'? How many fans had paid £2,500 for a single roll of her acid-free toilet paper? How many had gone to £16,000 against every other damned Gaia fan for a signed jacket Gaia had worn and thrown into the audience during the last night of her world tour?

She had already been offered, and rejected, £25,000 for it.

The world was full of Gaia fans. But just twenty-three of them, like herself, were hardcore, bidding on all and everything that came up. How many were willing to pay everything they had for the smallest trophy? Like the limited edition Corgi Mini car labelled *Gaia World Tour Courtesy Car*, which she had secured for a mere £500! Or the Gaia health tonic miniature Martini, a bargain at £375. And how many others did Gaia communicate with via coded signals? None, that was how many!

She had spent over £275,000. That might be the equivalent of the earnings from one appearance by Gaia, but it was every penny she had in the world, and every penny she earned went towards this collection.

She was Gaia's number one fan, no question.

That was why Gaia communicated with her. Their secret!

Anna could barely contain her excitement. She was not only ticking off the days, she was ticking off the hours, minutes, and sometimes, when she got really excited, the seconds!

'I love you, Gaia,' she said. 'I love you to death.'

# 14

Roy Grace, followed by Glenn Branson, stepped out of the stench and din of the birds in the chicken shed, into the blustery sunshine, and breathed in the fresh air with relief.

'Shit,' Glenn said.

'Good observation!'

Glenn lowered his mask. 'Foul play, I'd say.'

Grace groaned. 'That's truly terrible, even by your standards.'

'Sorry.'

'I'd like you to be my deputy SIO on this. I'm going to get you sanctioned as a temporary Detective Inspector. Does that appeal?'

'What's the catch?'

Grace grinned. 'I have my reasons.'

'Yeah, well, they'd better be good.'

Grace patted him on the shoulder. 'I know I can rely on you – you've done a good job on *Operation Violin*. ACC Rigg has noticed that.'

Glenn's face lit up. 'He has?'

'Yes – and I bigged you up on it. I have a feeling this case now could be a runner. Handle this well and it could count a lot in your promotion boards.'

Branson had all the qualities for promotion to the rank of Inspector, and Grace was determined to help his friend up the ladder. With his ongoing marriage problems that had been dragging him down for months, promotion, he was certain, would be the fillip that could really lift Glenn out of his increasingly frequent bouts of depression.

Grace remembered, a few years back, when he'd got that crucial promotion to Detective Inspector, how everything had changed for him. Starting with the surly uniform stores manager, whose whole demeanour had altered the day he had gone in requesting an Inspector's tunic with the two pips instead of stripes, and that coveted cap with its band of black braid. When you became an Inspector you truly felt you had become officer class, and everyone's attitude in the police – and public, too – towards you changed.

'I want you to handle the media on this one,' Grace said.

'Media – I don't – don't have much experience. You mean I'll have to deal with that toerag Spinella?'

Kevin Spinella was the senior crime reporter on the local newspaper, the *Argus*, who always managed to find out about any crime long before anyone else. He had an informant inside the police somewhere, and it had long been one of Grace's ambitions to find and nail that person, and he · was working on it. 'Spinella and everyone else. You can do your first press conference later today.'

'Thanks,' Glenn said doubtfully.

'I'll help you,' Grace said. 'I'll hold your hand.'

Branson nodded, staring around. 'So where do I start here?'

'By clearing the ground beneath your feet. Okay? First thing, get a POLSA up here and a team from the Specialist Search Unit to do a fingertip search beneath the gridding and above. Second, we need to know all the access roads in the surrounding area, and we need to start a house-to-house in all the villages. You have to inform the Divisional Commander for East Sussex Division, and tell him you'll need some help from uniform and local PCSOs, and maybe the Specials. Contact the local MP and the Police Authority member. Tell them it looks neat and tidy to you, at the moment, and that you feel there is minimal community impact.'

'Anything else, boss?'

'Think of a holding statement for the media. Start planning about your communications strategy for public reassurance. Get the names of everyone who has access to this place – who delivers the mail, the milk, the newspapers, the animal feed, the heating oil or Calor gas – everyone who could have been here in recent months – every visitor. I'd suggest setting a parameter of one year back. Find out if there is any CCTV.'

As with every major crime investigation that he ran, Grace needed to establish a range of parameters for all aspects, and to plan out the immediate steps in his Policy Book. One of the first problems he needed to address was the business of this farm. The owner, Keith Winter, would want the minimum disruption to his livelihood.

His immediate impression was that, unlike some farms he had visited, everything here looked clean and modern. The long, single-storey shed. The shiny silos. The handsome farmhouse that looked newly built. The gleaming Range Rover, its registration plate indicating it was less than a year old. The Subaru Impreza, two years old according to its index, signalling someone who liked fast cars. The good things in life.

Someone who would kill for such things?

There was a smart electric gate at the start of the mile-long driveway up here. Okay, people were security conscious these days, but how many farmers had security gates? Hiding something? Or a precaution against travellers?

Going through his mind right now were potential sus-
pects, or those he needed to know more about. The first
notes he made on his pad were to get intelligence on the
owner of this place. Who was Keith Winter? What was his
background? How long had he owned Stonery Farm? What
was his financial situation? Did he have partners? When
had that grid last been cleared? Who did he employ here?
Each of his employees, current and past, would need to
be identified and questioned. Would Winter really have put
a murder victim in his chicken shed? Perhaps he thought
it would be completely dissolved. Certainly it was a known
fact that the Italian Mafia used pig farms as an effective
means of disposing of bodies, and there had been a case in
the UK a few years back. But pigs were omnivores.

He shared his thoughts with Glenn Branson.

'Ever see that Pasolini film, *Porcile*?' the DS replied.

'No, never heard of it.'

'It's a classic. A bloke gets eaten by a pig in that.'

'Think I'll give it a miss,' Grace said.

'You already have missed it, it came out in 1969.' Then
Branson frowned. 'I know someone who might be able to
tell us a bit about the cloth, if we're right about it being suit
fabric.'

'Oh?'

'A tailor in Brighton, works at Gresham Blake.'

Gresham Blake was Brighton's society tailor. 'That
where you get your clothes made these days?' Grace looked
at him quizzically.

'I wish. I met him a few years ago when his flat was
burgled. Gresham Blake's where you should go though, on
your Big Cheese salary.'

There was no certainty, Grace thought, that the clothing
fabric was even connected to the victim, but it was an

important line of enquiry. Most murder investigations began with a missing person and until that person was identified, it was hard to make real progress. One of the key things he needed to establish at this moment was the age of the body, and how long it had been here. He pulled out his phone and called forensic archaeologist Joan Major, asking her if she could come here as soon as she was finished at the mortuary. She told him her work on the skeletal remains was almost completed.

It was possible they could get DNA from the victim, which might help identification. Failing that, if the age, or at least the age range, of the victim could be established, they could make a start by looking at the county and region's missing persons list.

He stared around again. There were some farm buildings beyond the shed, and another, smaller dwelling. One immediate decision he needed to make was whether to treat just the chicken shed as the crime scene, or the entire farm including the farmhouse. He did not feel he had enough to justify that draconian measure, which would have meant Winter and his family having to move out into temporary accommodation. His view was to treat the farmer as a person of interest to his enquiry for now, but not a suspect.

Despite his wariness of the danger in making assumptions, Roy Grace always made hypotheses at every crime scene. And the first one he made here was that money might be involved. A dead man in expensive clothes. A business partner? A blackmailer? Winter's wife's lover? Winter's own lover? A creditor? A business rival? Or was it someone totally unconnected with Winter, who had merely used this place as a dump site?

'Glenn,' he said. 'Early in my career I had a very wise

Super in Major Crime. He said to me, *there is no case colder than one in which the victim is unidentified.* Remember that. Identifying the victim is always the first priority.'

Sending Branson back inside with his head spinning, Grace walked over to the car, sat in the driver's seat and closed the door for some privacy. He started to jot down the names of the enquiry team he wanted to put together, hoping that some of his regulars, recently stood down from *Operation Violin*, would be available. After a quiet start to this year, everything had kicked off in May. Sussex had an average of eighteen murders a year. So far in these first five months, there had been sixteen already. A statistical blip, or a sign of the times?

He stared through the windscreen at the expensive Range Rover and the Impreza – a rich man's toys – and the architect-designed farmhouse. Maybe there was money to be made in farming chickens?

But, as experience had long taught him, wherever there was money to be made, there was killing to be done, too.

# 15

'We're fucked!' Maxim Brody's gloomy voice said.

Larry Brooker, in his First Class seat, held the cellphone to his ear. 'Why? What do you mean, Max?'

'I just came off the phone with Gaia's agent. She's walking.'

'Whaddya mean she's walking?'

'The insurance company won't let her go to England,' said Brody, sounding even more defeatist than ever.

'So, okay, worst case scenario, we shoot everything here in LA!'

'Sir,' the stewardess insisted, 'you have to turn that off.'

'Yeah, right, Larry,' Brody replied. 'We're gonna build a replica of the Brighton Royal Pavilion here on the Universal lot? On our budget? Rebuild the whole goddamn city of Brighton, England, here?'

'I'm flying to New York right now to meet with our broker, Peter Marshall, at DeWitt Stern – he's gonna—'

The grumpy stewardess reached out her hand, imperiously.

'Sir, I'm sorry, I'm going to have to take your cellphone for the duration of the flight if you don't switch it off.'

'Do you know who I am?' he shouted at her.

She frowned. 'Having memory problems are you, sir?' She glanced down at the list she was holding in her free hand. 'Seat 2B? You're Mr Larry Brooker! Does that help you, sir?'

He balled his fists in frustration. 'Jesus!'

'God delusions. I'm sure we can find a chaplain to assist you.'

Larry Brooker drained the remains of his glass of champagne before the bitch seized that, too.

Then he sat, in silent fury, as the plane jerked and bumped along its taxi path, his thoughts veering between ritually disembowelling the harridan, and the prospects of salvaging his rapidly collapsing film production. They had Gaia, one of the world's most bankable stars. They now had their leading man, Judd Halpern, a senior B-lister to replace that coked-up shithead A-lister, Matt Duke, who'd trashed himself in a car wreck. They had their director, ageing Jack Jordan, a two-times Academy Award nominee, a prima donna who had a reputation for being impossible, but who was hungry for this project because he saw it as possibly his last chance to bag an Oscar.

They were not going to get shafted by a goddamn insurance company wimping out. No way.

No fucking way, baby.

He ordered a Bloody Mary as soon as the drinks started after take-off. Then another. Followed by another. Then some wine with his meal, until he finally reclined his seat and fell into a stupor.

At eight o'clock the next morning he staggered off the plane, clutching his overnight bag in one hand and a bottle of water, understanding, as he did each time he made this domestic journey, why they called it the Red Eye Special. His mouth was parched and his head felt like it had a heavyweight title fight going on inside it.

An hour later he climbed out of the limousine, clutching another complimentary bottle of mineral water, and entered the front door of 420 Lexington Avenue, the headquarters of the insurance company DeWitt Stern. He'd worked with one of its principals, Peter Marshall, on several previous productions. Marshall was a good guy, who had never let him down. His mission today was to persuade the insurance broker not to be put off by a little thing like an attempt on Gaia Lafayette's life. They were going to be in England. The UK, for fuck's sake. The safest goddamn place on earth. If someone was seriously out to kill Gaia, then where better for her to be? A country that had no guns.

Marshall would agree. He was smart, he would get it.

Larry popped a sugar-free mint gum into his mouth to mask the alcohol on his breath. Then he stepped out of the elevator and walked up towards the reception desk with a big, warm smile on his face.

His winning smile.

# 16

Roy Grace was smiling.

'You look so happy, my love,' Cleo said in greeting as he let himself in at the front door of her home. It was twenty to midnight. Her hair was pinned up and she was wearing a slinky, powder-blue nightdress beneath her bathrobe. Humphrey, their young rescue dog – a Labrador–Border Collie cross – barked enthusiastically, jumping up at his suit trousers, wanting attention too, his high-pitched yip-yap-yips echoing around the cobbles of the gated townhouse development.

'You make me happy,' he said and kissed her, then tugged Humphrey's ears. The dog immediately rolled on his back. Grace knelt and rubbed his belly. 'How was your evening?'

'Apart from crawling around in chicken shit, it was fine!' she replied. 'Yours?'

'You went there? Yourself?'

'With Darren.' She shrugged. 'We're short staffed. And hey, I like free-range cadavers.'

He shook his head. Then as he stood up, Cleo thrust an ice-cold vodka Martini, with four olives on a cocktail stick, into his hand. 'Thought you might be in need of sustenance!' She gently fended off Humphrey, who was jumping up again.

'You're amazing!' Grace sipped the drink gratefully, put the glass down on a shelf and kissed her again, putting his arms around her white towelling bathrobe, holding her firmly but gently, feeling the bulge of their baby against his stomach, smelling her freshly shampooed hair, then took the glass and drank another slug of it. The dog lay on his back, paws in the air again. 'Okay, jealous one!' He knelt and rubbed his belly once more.

'I know!' she said. 'I am amazing! Totally amazing. Never forget that, will you, Detective Superintendent Grace?'

He grinned, standing up again. 'Why would I want to?'

He looked into her clear blue eyes, feeling so incredibly happy. Happier than he had any right to be. He loved her. He loved being here in her home, especially this living room, with the lights dimmed, candles burning all around.

A City Books carrier bag lay on the floor – their favourite bookshop in Brighton. On the table lay a copy of *The World According To Joan*, held open by a solid glass paperweight.

He'd long been a Joan Collins admirer, and he loved that Cleo had actually made the effort to get the book in order to try to understand why.

For all these past years now since Sandy had gone, he had never believed it would be possible to feel happy – or even at peace – ever again. Cleo had changed that, and he felt almost guilty to be so happy again. Guilty because in all these years he had never stopped looking for Sandy. Her disappearance had been so sudden, so completely unexpected, without the remotest hint of any foreshadowing. One moment they had been totally happy together, and the next she was gone. On the morning of his thirtieth birthday they'd made love, as they always had done on each other's birthdays. He'd gone to work, and when he had arrived home, looking forward to a celebratory dinner with Sandy and another couple, their closest friends, she had vanished. There was no note. All her belongings were still in the house, except for her handbag.

Twenty-four hours later, her elderly black VW Golf was found in the short-stay car park at Gatwick Airport. There were two small transactions on her credit card on the morning of her disappearance, one from Boots, and one from Tesco. She had taken no clothes, and no other belongings of any kind. Her credit card was never used again.

In all the years since there had not been a single night, even when lying in Cleo's arms, when he hadn't fallen asleep wondering what had happened to her. Had she run off with a lover? That was possible, of course – how much did anyone really know about their partner? Had she decided, for whatever reason, to disappear and totally re-invent herself in a new life? People did that. But, when she had never given any hint that she was unhappy, why would she have? Another possibility was that she'd had an accident. But that didn't fit with her car being at Gatwick.

More likely, he thought, she had been abducted, and whoever had taken her had left her car at the airport to throw pursuers off the scent. The grim reality was that in most abductions the person taken was killed within hours. Then again, there had been cases of abductees being held against their will for years.

For a long time now his friends and his sister had been urging him to move on, to accept that Sandy was gone and that he had to live his life in the present, not the past. He was trying so hard to do that, and Cleo made it easier than he could ever have imagined. He loved her, totally, utterly, madly. Yet there was still something that he could not quite let go of.

The nightmare that would wake him, screaming, every few months. Sandy down the bottom of a well shaft, like the abducted senator's daughter in *Silence Of The Lambs*.

And the guilt that followed in those sleepless hours

listening to the dawn chorus – that he had not done enough to find her – that there was one key, something blindingly obvious, staring him in the face, that he had overlooked.

His eyes fell on the copy of *Autocar* that was lying on the coffee table. He had bought it because it had a road test of the Alfa Giulietta. Ever since his own beloved, ageing Alfa had been written off following a chase last summer, he had hankered after another. They were cars that, in his view, had *soul*. At least, the only ones within his price range that did. There had been months of wrangling with the insurance company who had been trying to wriggle out of responsibility because, they argued, he should not have been using it on a police pursuit. But they had finally caved in.

He'd fallen in love with one of their models, a two-seater, but with the baby on the way, that was completely impractical. A couple of friends, including Glenn Branson, had advised him that a people carrier would be the sensible option, with all the paraphernalia he would have to carry around once the baby was born. He'd looked at a few but they did not appeal. Now he had seen on a Tates garage forecourt a two-year-old Giulietta, and was totally smitten. It was a hatchback, big enough to take a pushchair.

'What's troubling you, my love?' Cleo asked as she sat beside him on the huge red sofa. On the television on the wall opposite, with the sound muted, chef Hugh Fearnley-Whittingstall was demonstrating how to fillet a mackerel.

'Cars!' he said.

'Go with your heart.'

'I need to be practical.'

She shrugged. 'You know what? I have so many friends whose lives have been totally changed by their children. They don't have time for each other any more. They hardly ever make love any more. Their lives are consumed by their kids. I don't want that to happen to us. Surely we can be good parents, but still find the time for each other? Get the car you want, not the one that you think will be most practical. We can adapt. Bump will have to learn to fit in with us!'

He smiled again and drank some more of the Martini. On an empty, caffeine fuelled stomach it was hitting the spot, making him more relaxed by the second. It suddenly occurred to him how incredibly understanding Cleo was. If he'd arrived home to Sandy at midnight on a Friday, with the knowledge that he was going to have to work over the weekend, she would have been sound asleep, and extremely bolshie when he'd disturbed her, leaving for work at dawn the next morning. But there was total understanding from Cleo, who was herself liable to be called out in the middle of any night, weekday or weekend.

'You know, the other thing that's troubling me is . . .' he paused as Humphrey jumped up on the sofa beside them and then rolled on his back in his favourite position, belly up, expecting his tummy to be rubbed yet again. Grace obliged.

'What's troubling me is – ' he kissed Cleo's soft cheek – 'I love you so much,' he said.

'Oh, is *that* what's troubling you?'

'Uh huh, maybe.' He kissed her again. Then again, feeling increasingly pleasantly woozy as he drank some more of the massive Martini. 'I love you and I can't get enough of you.'

'You never read what it said on the tin,' she said, smiling. '*Use Cleo sparingly with caution.*'

'I'm a bloke, I don't read instructions.'

He stared into her eyes for some moments, then at the

rest of her face. It was true, what he had read, that women could blossom in pregnancy. She looked even lovelier than ever.

'Yep, well, I'm a female, so I read instructions and warning labels. But luckily for you I missed the one that said, *Engaging with Detective Superintendent Roy Grace could make you dangerously horny.*'

'I think I must have missed a similar one about you.'

'So?' she leaned across, kissed him on the lips, then lowered her hands between his legs, and pressed, provocatively. 'What are you going to do about it?'

'I thought – you know – that we weren't meant to—?'

'We're not, Detective Superintendent,' she said. Then she grinned. 'Well, not really. Are you hungry?'

'No, just horny.'

She kissed him again. Then after a moment, she said, 'Tell me something.'

'What?' he murmured.

'When you made love to Sandy, what did you think of? I mean – *who* did you think of?'

'Who?'

'Was it always her – her naked body that aroused you? Or did you think of other women?'

'It was a long time ago,' he said.

She kissed each of his eyes. 'Don't be evasive, I'm interested.'

He shrugged. 'I guess in the early days it was her. But later on, probably other women, too.'

'Who?'

'I don't recall.'

'Movie stars? Models?'

'Some.'

'And when we make love? It can't be attractive to make

love to a plump woman with blue veins all over her breasts. Who do you fantasize about now?'

'You,' he said. 'You are a complete and utter turn-on for me.'

'You're lying, Grace.'

'I'm not!'

'Yeah? Prove it?'

He gently lowered her right hand down his body. Her eyes widened in surprise and she smiled seductively.

'I rest my case,' he said.

She kissed him again. 'Not sure I want you having any rest, not for a little while, my love!'

# 17

He was angry.

Not many people knew more about anger than he did. That world-class superbitch, formerly known as his wife, and once upon a time – incredibly – his blushing bride, had made him go on an anger management course.

There were all kinds of anger. Like the frustration you got at a damned parking machine that took your coin and didn't give you a ticket back. Like the silent fury you felt when you saw a lout toss litter from a car window. Like the neighbour below you throwing a party that went on playing loud music into the night.

But nothing he had learned on that course taught him how to deal with the rage that burned inside him now. The anger of being screwed, right royally, totally and utterly. Of having the one big break in your life taken away from you.

People couldn't do that and get away with it.

But the thing was, they did, all the time.

When that happened some people shrugged their shoulders in defeat. Some went to lawyers, and all that happened then was they got more broke and the lawyers got more rich. He didn't have that kind of money. Maybe it was the kind of case that a lawyer might take pro bono.

But he didn't have the time.

He wasn't going to sit back and accept it and let them get away with it. He wasn't going to bend over and hold out a pot of Vaseline to them. He was going to do something about it. He didn't know what yet. Nor how.

*Don't get angry, get even.*

He had made a start. He'd bought a plane ticket.

He was going to make the bastards regret this.

They taught him an old Chinese proverb at the anger management course. *Before you seek revenge, first dig two graves.*

He'd dig as many graves as he needed. If one was for himself, that was fine by him. Shovels were easy to buy. And he was going to need it anyway, he didn't have long to live.

# 18

At 8 a.m. Roy Grace sat in his office, with his Policy Book open in front of him. Every Senior Investigating Officer kept one, and if at any point they were required to account for their actions on a major crime investigation, by any subsequent review of their case, they could refer back to it.

An important part of the entries into Grace's Policy Book was his hypothesis for the motives of any murder and how the victim came to meet his or her death.

His first note today was:

1. *No arms, no legs/head. Organized crime? Killed by unknown person.*
2. *Drugs deal reprisal?*
3. *Person known to police – get rid of identity?*

There was a whole raft of other motives, but in his view, none that led to this kind of mutilation of a corpse.

When he had finished, he just had time to make himself a coffee, then hurry through to the morning briefing.

*

'The time is 8.30 a.m., Saturday, June the fourth,' Roy Grace read out from his typed notes. 'This is the second briefing of *Operation Icon*, the enquiry into the death of an unknown man whose headless, armless and legless torso was discovered at Stonery Farm, Berwick, East Sussex, yesterday.'

'Legless, chief?' interrupted Norman Potting. 'Was he pissed?'

There was a titter of laughter, which Grace silenced with a glare. His good mood from last night remained with him this morning, and Potting wasn't going to spoil that. He'd got up early, done a five-mile run along Brighton seafront in glorious early morning sunshine, with Humphrey loping happily alongside him, and had arrived in his office in the CID HQ, on the edge of the city, an hour ago.

From his early days as a Senior Investigating Officer, Roy Grace had learned the value of cultivating the friendship of the Senior Support Officer Tony Case, who allocated the Major Incident Suites – of which, since the budget cuts, there were now only two in this county and two in neighbouring Surrey – to the enquiry teams. Case knew that Grace favoured this one in Brighton, MIR-1, in the same building as his office, and had managed, yet again, to secure it for him.

The two Major Incident Rooms at Sussex House, MIR-1 and MIR-2 were the nerve centres for major crime enquiries. Despite opaque windows too high to see out of, MIR-1 had an airy feel, good light, good vibes. Grace always felt energized here.

Already some wit – Glenn Branson he suspected – had stuck a cartoon on the inside of the door. It was an image from the film *Chicken Run*.

Seated attentively at the curved desks around him were the twenty members of his team he had assembled since leaving the farm shortly after midday yesterday. The regulars he had present were Detective Sergeant Bella Moy, in her mid-thirties and still living with her mother; even at this early hour she was busily attacking the inevitable red box of Maltesers in front of her; Detective Constable Nick Nicholl, beanpole tall, yawning as usual after yet another sleepless night with his baby son; Glenn Branson, in a cream suit and a pistachio coloured tie; and Norman Potting, who had joined the police relatively late in life, a curmudgeonly but very effective Detective Sergeant, who had a string of failed marriages behind him.

Normally shabbily dressed, with a greasy comb-over and reeking of pipe tobacco, Potting looked different today, both younger and smarter. His grey hair had turned dark brown. He was wearing a smart blue suit with a cream shirt and a tie that, for once, had not been decorated with his breakfast. And he exuded a reek of not unpleasant cologne. Someone had given the man a very thorough and effective makeover. Yet another new woman?

The only one of his regulars absent today was attractive, young DC Emma-Jane Boutwood, who was away on honeymoon. Among the rest of the team were several more detectives, including two DCs he had worked with previously, Emma Reeves and Jon Exton, a detective Grace was keeping his eye on because he thought him exceptionally bright; David Green, the Crime Scene Manager; a crime analyst; an indexer and Sue Fleet, the press officer.

On the work surface in front of Grace lay his agenda and his Policy Book. 'DS Branson has been appointed, temporarily, Acting Detective Inspector,' he announced. 'He will be my deputy SIO and will be doing much of the running of this case, as I'm still very involved with *Operation Violin*.' He turned to his colleague, seated next to him, and could see he looked nervous. 'What do you have to report?'

Glenn Branson studied his notes for a moment, then, choosing his words carefully, and being uncharacteristically pedantic, said, 'Home Office pathologist Nadiuska De Sancha attended at 4.20 p.m. yesterday. I had no news from her to report at our evening briefing yesterday. She completed her in situ investigations at 7 p.m., after which the body was recovered to the mortuary. The pathologist is due to return at midday today to continue with the post-mortem. As yet we are unable to put an age on the victim, although the pathologist estimates him to have been between thirty and fifty years old. Forensic archaeologist Joan Major will also be continuing her work and I'm hoping she may be able to give us a more specific age range.'

He checked his notes carefully then added. 'One fact of possible significance from the pathologist's findings pertains to the dismemberment of the body. It would appear to be an amateur job, clumsily done – not by someone with surgical skills.'

Grace made a note, then looked at his protégé proudly. So far, Glenn was doing fine. He had a presence and natural air of calm authority that inspired confidence and made people take him seriously – despite, at times, his garish clothes.

'A search of the void beneath the gridding was carried out until midnight, and has started again this morning, under the supervision of a POLSA, Sergeant Lorna Dennison-Wilkins from the Specialist Search Unit. As yet no more body parts have been found, nor any further items of clothing. The fabric will be sent for DNA testing, but I'm first going to try to find out about its provenance.' He pointed at four colour blow-up photographs of the fabric segments that had been tacked to a board, two showing the entirety of the samples, two showing details of the loud yellow ochre colour and check pattern.

'Like it, do you, Glenn?' Norman Potting asked. 'Want to get yourself a new whistle?'

Glaring at Potting, with whom she had long sparred, Bella Moy asked, 'What's a *whistle*?'

'You've led a sheltered life, haven't you, doll?' Potting said patronizingly. 'It's Cockney rhyming slang. Whistle and flute – suit. Get it?'

As a response, she huffily scooped another Malteser out of the box and crunched it noisily in her mouth.

'I like that noise you make,' Potting said. 'Nothing sexier than a bolshie young lady.'

'Thank you, Norman,' Grace cautioned, then raised a hand to stop Bella from commenting.

Looking back at his notes, Glenn soldiered on. 'Local East Division officers are conducting a house-to-house on all roads in the vicinity, within an initial parameter of two miles, that I have set. All farm workers, regular and itinerant, are being interviewed.' He paused, then added, 'This is an unusual location, situated one mile up a private driveway, because the property is not visible from any public road, so no ordinary passing member of the public would be aware of it. In my opinion, whoever used this as their dump site had prior knowledge of the location. We're working on a list of everyone who has visited or had access to the property in the past twelve months.'

'Have you considered someone over-flying in a light aircraft or helicopter, boss?' asked DC Jon Exton. 'And seeing it as a possible deposition site because of its remoteness?'

'That is another possibility,' conceded Branson. 'According to what I've been able to ascertain so far, in a very limited time frame, the farmer is a popular man, no one local has a bad word to say about him. One hypothesis I'm working on is that this could be an enemy of Keith Winter – a business rival trying to set him up – but I don't at this point know enough about the world of chicken farming to make that fly – no pun intended. My other hypothesis is that someone familiar with the farm felt this would be a good place to dispose of a body.'

'What about mispers?' Bella Moy asked. 'Shouldn't that be an immediate line of enquiry for us?'

Branson shook his head. 'That will be an important one. We have carried out an immediate local check, but it didn't produce anything. First I need an estimate on how long this person has been dead, before we can proceed too far down that route. I'm hoping to get this either from the pathologist or from the forensic archaeologist tomorrow. Until I get that information, I don't know what parameters to set for looking at missing person reports.'

Roy Grace smiled, watching the indexer making notes. It was the answer he would have given. He made a note himself, for either Glenn or himself to write in the Policy Book.

'In terms of media strategy, I have some welcome news to give out!' Branson went on. 'Our friend Kevin Spinella from the *Argus* is on holiday.'

There was a muted cheer. Glenn grinned. 'I'm calling a second press conference for five-thirty this afternoon, by which time I hope to be able to give out information that may generate some response from the public. I will of course keep enough back to enable us to weed out crank calls.'

It was normal in any major crime enquiry to withhold key information that would be known only to the perpetrator. That way time wasters could be quickly eliminated.

At that moment, Grace's new phone, which he had switched to silent, vibrated. He glanced at the display, fully expecting it to be Spinella. But the display said BLOCKED

NUMBER. He answered it, as quietly as he could, and heard the voice of the Chief Constable's Staff Officer, DCI Trevor Bowles.

'Roy,' he said. 'The Chief needs to see you as soon as possible. Are you free this morning?'

Grace frowned. The Chief Constable, and the other brass, tended to keep to office hours and their weekends free. For Tom Martinson to want to see him on a Saturday, there had to be an important reason.

'I could be with him in half an hour.'

'Perfect.'

Grace ended the call, worried. As soon as the briefing finished, he agreed to meet Glenn Branson at the tailor at 11 a.m., then hurried out to his car, in his precious reserved space at the front of the CID HQ building.

# 19

It was love at first sight. The first time Eric Whiteley saw Brighton's Royal Pavilion, he was smitten. He was fifteen, on a day trip to Brighton with his parents, and he had never seen anything like it before in his life. It was a place that belonged in someone's imagination, someone who tried to escape from the nastiness of the world into the labyrinth of beauty inside his head. It was not a place that belonged in the middle of an English seaside resort.

Yet there it was.

He was mesmerized by the mad splendour of its sprawling design, by its part-Indian, part-Chinese influences and its curious domes. And even more by its totally extravagant interior. From then on during his school holidays he spent all his pocket money on the train fare from Guildford, where he lived, to Brighton, and on the entrance fee, going there when it first opened every morning, and staying until it closed. It was a world away from his boarding school which was full of bullies who told him constantly he was ugly, boring, useless, Ubu.

He felt safe inside its ornately decorated walls, surrounded by the richness of its art treasures. This royal palace, built by King George IV, and used by him for secret – and not too secret – seaside love trysts with his mistress. He doubted that George, nicknamed Prinny, vain and increasingly rich, had ever been bullied by anyone, nor been told he was no good or ugly. No one would have ever called him Ugly Boring Useless. Even though he actually was.

One of the things he liked most to imagine was himself wearing the costumes of the time. He particularly fantasized about dressing up as the king, in those fine robes. He could picture himself sweeping into class, sword hanging to his side, king. No one would call him Ubu then.

One summer, when he was eighteen, he applied for a holiday job as a guide and to his joy he was accepted. He would escort parties of tourists around, telling them of the love the king had for his mistress and how frustrated he was by the protocols of his age. But what he loved most of all about this job was the access it gave him. The freedom to wander around the Pavilion's interior when there were no tours for him to guide, without the security guards taking any notice of him.

He liked best of all its hidden parts. The secret corridors that ran behind the kitchens to the grand rooms, where servants could move around with drinks and food, slipping in and out of secret doorways. There was a hidden spiral staircase, that the public never saw, because the banisters were dangerously rickety, up which he could climb to an area, beneath one of the domes, to which the king invited his guests to see the spectacular views, and later where occasional senior household staff were rumoured to have lived.

It was now derelict, the floorboards were in poor condition, and there was a very large trapdoor secured with just two bolts, and carrying a warning sign, below which was a forty-foot drop down into a store room above the kitchens. There was a rope-and-pulley system from the 1800s, which Eric imagined to have been a very primitive kind of dumb waiter. And from this rooftop eyrie he had the finest view of Brighton he had ever seen.

He'd sneaked a sleeping bag up here and made it his

private place. Sometimes, if he could avoid the security guards when they closed up the building in the evening, he would bring a picnic here and hole up for the night. Safe. No bullies up here. He would close his eyes and imagine himself living here, a king, worshipped and adored.

Then one night he got caught by a bully security guard.

They fired him as a guide. He was told he could never come back here again.

# 20

Cleo loved her little town house in the trendy North Laine district of Brighton; she felt secure here and she liked the convenience and the buzz of living in the centre of the city. It was great to walk across the courtyard and out of the gates, and be able to stroll through the maze of cafés and small independent shops, and down to the beach on a fine day. But there were some drawbacks. One was that Humphrey needed a garden to be out in when she was at work – and she planned to return to the mortuary as soon as practicable after the baby was born. A bigger problem still was that she only had one tiny spare room and needed that for her studies – she was doing an Open University degree course in Philosophy – and for Roy to have a workplace at home. The baby would be born in a matter of weeks, perhaps even sooner, and they would be short of space. As soon as Roy sold his house they could start looking for a bigger place together. Another less serious, but constant, irritant was having to park on the street, and it was getting harder and harder to find spaces when she came back from work in the evenings.

Throughout her life, Cleo's favourite time of the week had always been Saturday mornings – even though in this job she frequently had to work part of her weekends. People who died suddenly were rarely obliging enough to do so only during office hours, which meant that when she was on call, which was most of the time as they were short-handed in the mortuary, she frequently had to go out on weekends and holidays to help recover a body.

The one last night had been particularly unsavoury, and today she had to attend and assist at the post-mortem, which had now moved from the deposition site to the mortuary. But she wasn't daunted. The torso lying in a tank of chicken droppings was grim work, but mangled and sometimes disembowelled bodies in car crashes were far worse and more harrowing. So were charred corpses in fires. And it always made her sad to see lonely, elderly people who had died in their homes and not been discovered for months. But by far the worst of all were children. A couple of weeks previously she'd had to recover a six-month-old baby who'd died of suspected sudden infant death syndrome.

Removing that tiny girl from the little cot in the house had been traumatic for her, thinking all the time of how she might feel if that had happened to her and Roy. And the frightening prospect that it could.

But she wasn't thinking of any of that now as she stepped out of her front door into the early June sunshine. Above her was a cloudless sky, and she smelled the tang of salt in the air from the English Channel, a short distance to the south. The forecast was good, and although she was destined to spend much of the day in the mortuary, she hoped to get away by late afternoon, and meet her sister for a coffee and catch-up in a café on the seafront. Afterwards she planned to get prawns and avocado and some nice Dover sole and cook Roy one of his favourite meals this evening – after which they could watch a DVD, if she could stay awake that long!

She strode across the courtyard, dressed in a long lycra T-shirt, with her bump out loud and proud, her Crocs – which Roy didn't care for – slapping on the cobbles. She ignored her almost constant backache from the weight of the baby, feeling so blissfully happy she was almost high. She was carrying the child of the man she truly, deeply loved. A wonderfully kind, caring and strong person. And she genuinely believed he loved her just as much.

Two seagulls swirled overhead, shrieking, and she glanced up at them for a moment, then carried on towards the wrought iron gates. She clicked the lock and stepped out into the narrow street. This part of the city was always teeming with people on a Saturday morning, spilling out of the rammed Gardner Street bric-a-brac market a couple of streets away. It was 9.30 and the antique dealer across the road, who specialized in fireplaces, already had some of his goods out on display, propped against the shop front.

She walked up the hill, taking the first right turn, and strode along the even narrower street, lined on both sides with small terraced Victorian houses, past the nose-to-tail parked cars. She saw her black Audi TT halfway along, where she had parked it last night – relieved as ever that it had not been stolen.

As she neared it, she witnessed the standard hazard of parking out in the open in this city – thanks to all the gulls, half of the vehicles looked like Jackson Pollock paintings. Even from a hundred feet away, she saw the streaky, swirly white and mustard-yellow splodges all over her beloved convertible.

But then as she got closer, her mood suddenly changed. With a tightening in her gullet, she broke into an anxious run, ignoring the fact she wasn't supposed to run. Then she stopped beside the car.

'Shit,' she said. 'Shit.'

The fabric roof had been ripped open, both lengthways and sideways.

Feeling a flash of fury, her sunny mood totally gone,

she peered inside, looking for the damage. But to her surprise the CD and radio player were intact. 'Bastards,' she mouthed. 'Scumbags.'

Then she saw the marks on the bonnet. At first she thought it had been someone tracing in the dust with their fingers, until she looked closer. And froze.

Someone had used a sharp instrument, a screwdriver or a chisel, and had engraved the words in the paintwork, gouging right down to the bare metal.

*COPPERS TART. UR BABY IS NEXT.*

# 21

Malling House, the headquarters of Sussex Police, was on the outskirts of Lewes, the historic county town of East Sussex, eight miles north-east of Brighton.

The sprawling, ragged complex of Police HQ buildings, from where the administration and key management for the force's 5,000 officers and civilian employees was handled, was fronted by a handsome red-brick Queen Anne house, once a private stately home, and faithfully restored after it had been gutted by fire over a decade ago. It housed the offices of the Chief Constable, the Deputy Chief Constable, the Assistant Chief Constables and other chief officers together with their support staff.

When Roy Grace halted at the security barrier, he felt the same kind of butterflies he always had when he came here, as if he were still a schoolboy and had been summoned to the headmaster's study. He had only met the recently appointed Chief Constable, Tom Martinson, very fleetingly at a social event, and had not had the opportunity to talk at any length with him. He would need Martinson's confidence and backing if he were to rise any further from his current rank of Detective Superintendent.

The rank of Chief Superintendent was the next goal on his career ladder, but he had no ambition to rise beyond that into the Assistant Chief Constable realm, partly because he didn't think he could play the required politics, but more importantly because it would make it almost impossible to do any frontline police work, which was what he loved. In those elevated roles you were predominantly desk-bound managers. True, in his current role he was desk-bound to a large extent, but he always had the option to get out into the field – and took every opportunity to do so.

In any event he was very content with his current position, as Head of Major Crime. It was a position he could only have dreamed of when he had first joined the police, and it was a job that gave him so much satisfaction he would happily stay in this position for the rest of his career.

If he had one regret in life, it was that his father, also a police officer, and his mother, had not lived to see his success.

But at the moment he was preoccupied by a big concern, which was that nothing stayed still in life. As a result of recent government budget cuts, police forces were required to amalgamate divisions and share resources, and some had to implement compulsory retirement after thirty years' service. Sussex Police was now having to share its Major Crime Branch with Surrey. Which meant he could no longer be sure of remaining in this job. And his fear at this moment was that this summons to see the Chief meant bad news. Police officers could not be made redundant before retirement age, but many were currently being shunted sideways.

The security guard gave him a cheery wave and he drove through the open barrier, then turned right, passing the police driving school and parked in front of the modern glass and brick Comms building. As he switched off the engine his phone rang.

The display showed BLOCKED NUMBER.

He answered, and to his dismay he heard an all too familiar voice down a crackly line, accompanied by what sounded suspiciously like the roar of waves.

'Detective Superintendent?'

'That you, Spinella? Thought you were on holiday?'

'I am – in the Maldives on honeymoon,' the Chief Crime Reporter of the Brighton *Argus* said. 'Flying back tomorrow.'

Bloody hell, you actually found someone to *marry* you, Grace thought, and nearly said. Instead he replied flatly, 'Congratulations. I'm afraid your wedding invite must have got lost in the post.'

'Haha,' Spinella said.

'What's so important that it takes you away from your bride?' Grace asked.

'I hear you've got another murder.'

'Finding married life boring already, are you?'

There was a brief silence followed by another 'Haha'.

'I'd return to your bride, if I were you, Kevin. Leave us to sort out whatever we have to deal with. I'm sure the city can cope in your absence.'

'But you and I have a responsibility to the citizens of Brighton and Hove, don't we, Detective Superintendent – especially when it involves a headless human torso?'

How the hell, Grace wondered, as he did every time Spinella called him, did the reporter have this information already? 'I think our responsibilities are a bit different, actually,' he replied.

'Is there anything you can tell me about the body at Stonery Farm?'

Grace did not answer him immediately. It had been decided that the information that the torso was missing its head and limbs would be withheld from the press for the time being. 'Why do you suppose it is headless?' he asked.

'Well, it's got no arms or legs, so it probably hasn't got a head either. Not much point leaving the head on if you're going to that much trouble, is there?' Spinella said. 'Not like he's going to be much use as a football player.'

Every time during this past year that there had been a murder in the city, Spinella had the information way before anyone else. Any Sussex police computer would instantly have access to the log of the incident – which meant the leak could be coming from anyone inside Sussex Police.

The moment he had time, he was determined to investigate and find out who that mole was. But right now, with the case of Carl Venner coming up to trial, the unidentified dead body in the tunnel beneath Shoreham Port, their prime suspect in *Operation Violin* missing and now the torso on the chicken farm, he had more important issues on his plate. 'What would you like to tell me, Kevin?' he asked. 'Sounds like you know more about it than I do.'

'Haha!' Spinella said again. That damned laugh, which was almost the reporter's catchphrase, irritated him every time. 'Thought you might have a bit of inside track for me, Detective Superintendent.'

As always, Grace was forced to hold back his anger. Sussex Police needed the co-operation of the local media and there was nothing to be gained – the reverse in fact – from being too confrontational.

'Acting Detective Inspector Branson is the deputy SIO on this case and he's handling the media,' Grace said. 'You'd best speak to him.'

'I just did,' Spinella said. 'He told me to speak to you.'

'I thought the point of going on holiday was to switch off,' Grace said, silently fuming at Glenn Branson. The bastard, passing the buck! But he needed, as ever, to keep Spinella onside. 'I really don't know anything at this stage. DI Branson is holding a press conference at five thirty this afternoon. If you'd like to call me just before, I'll tell you what I know then.'

Grace tried to work out the time zone in the Maldives. He had in his mind that they were four hours ahead. That would make the press conference at 9.30 p.m. – hopefully messing up a romantic honeymoon dinner for the toerag.

'Umm, well, okay, I'll try.'

'Tell your beloved it's something she'll have to get used to.'

'Haha!'

'Haha!' Grace replied.

Then, as he ended the call, Cleo rang.

# 22

Grace had noticed throughout his career that the more senior the rank of his fellow officers, the tidier their offices seemed to be. Perhaps there was a clue here: to rise successfully to the elevated status of Chief Constable, you must be adept at managing your paperwork, or was it just that you had more people, like a Staff Officer as well as an assistant, to manage it for you?

His own office was a perpetual tip, his desk, floor and shelves stacked with bundles of files. Earlier in his career, when all he'd had was a desk in the Detectives' Room, its surface was permanently invisible beneath the sprawling paperwork. His untidiness had been one of the things that frequently annoyed Sandy, who had been almost obsessively neat and had a taste for minimalism in her home. Curiously, since Glenn Branson had left his wife Ari and moved into Roy's now empty house as his permanent lodger – and caretaker of Marlon, his goldfish – he had gone through something of a role reversal, constantly irritated at the mess Glenn left the place in – especially his CD collection. Although recently, since he had put the house on the market, Glenn had started being a lot tidier.

One of the things he loved about Cleo was that she was almost as naturally untidy as he was. And having a boisterous pet added to the sense of permanent chaos in her home.

But there was nothing out of place in the Chief Constable's spacious office as he entered now. The huge, polished wood L-shaped desk was uncluttered, apart from a leather blotter, some silver-framed photographs, including one of the Chief Constable flanked by sports presenter Des Lynam and another local celebrity, a pen set in a leather holder, and a solitary sheet of paper, that looked like an email printout. Two black sofas were arranged in a corner with a coffee table, and there was an eight-seater conference table. On the walls hung photographs of sports stars, a map of the county and several cartoons. The huge sash windows gave magnificent views out across Sussex. The whole room gave off an air of importance, but at the same time felt comfortable and warm.

Tom Martinson shook his hand firmly and asked him to come in, speaking in a cheery Midlands accent. The Chief, who was forty-nine, was slightly shorter than himself, a strong, fit-looking man, with thinning, short dark hair, and a pleasant, no-nonsense air about him. He was dressed in a short-sleeved white shirt with epaulettes, a black tie and black trousers.

'Take a seat, Roy,' he said, indicating one of the chairs at the coffee table. 'Can I get you something to drink?'

'I'd love a coffee, sir.' Roy Grace was trying very hard to put, temporarily, what Cleo had just told him out of his mind and focus entirely on this meeting, and trying to impress Martinson.

'How do you take it?'

'Muddy, please, sir, no sugar.'

The Chief smiled, raised the phone on his desk and ordered it, then sat down beside Roy and folded his arms – distancing body language, Grace thought warily, despite Martinson's cheery demeanour.

'I'm sorry to drag you over here on a Saturday.'

'It's no problem, sir. I'm working today anyway.'

'The Stonery Farm enquiry?'

'Yes.'

'Anything I need to know?'

Grace quickly brought him up to speed.

'I have to say,' Martinson replied, 'that when I heard you were the SIO on this I felt very confident the investigation was in good hands.'

'Thank you, sir,' Grace said, pleasantly surprised and somewhat relieved.

Then Martinson looked more serious. 'The reason I asked you to come and see me is a rather delicate situation.'

*Shit*, Grace thought. This *is* going to be about the Sussex–Surrey Major Crime branches merger.

He then had to wait for some moments while the Chief's assistant, Jean, who was, unusually, working this weekend, came in with his coffee and a plate of biscuits. As she left, he continued.

'Gaia,' Martinson said, then fell silent for a moment.

'Gaia?'

'You know who I mean? The rock singer and actress? Gaia Lafayette.'

'Absolutely, sir.'

You'd have to have been living under a rock in this city to have missed all the media coverage during the past couple of weeks, Grace thought.

'I personally think she's a better singer than she is actress, but who am I to judge?'

Grace nodded. 'I'd probably agree with you. I've never been a great fan, but I know someone who is.'

'Oh?'

'Detective Sergeant Branson.'

'You're aware she's coming to Brighton next week, to star in a film about the love affair between King George the Fourth and his mistress Maria Fitzherbert?'

'I knew her visit was imminent. DS Branson's very excited, hoping to get a chance to meet her! Presumably the producers know that Mrs Fitzherbert was English, not American?' Grace said.

Martinson smiled and raised a finger. 'Ah, but did you know that Gaia was born in Brighton?'

'Indeed, in Whitehawk.'

Martinson nodded. 'The girl done good, as they say.'

Whitehawk had for many years been one of the city's poorest areas. 'She has.'

'But we have a big problem, Roy. Over the past two days I've had conversations with a senior homicide detective from the Threat Management Unit of the Los Angeles Police Department, as well as her personal head of security, the head of Tourism and Leisure, Adam Bates, and the Chief Executive of Brighton Corporation, John Barradell. A few days ago, apparently, one of Gaia's assistants was shot dead leaving Gaia's house in Bel Air. The police view it as a case of mistaken identity, and that the true target was Gaia herself.'

'I didn't hear about that.'

'I don't think it's made much impact in the UK press. She received an email warning her not to take the Maria Fitzherbert part. Apparently her security advisers weren't too concerned about it at the time – it was just one of a number of crank emails she gets constantly. But their concerns are that, if they are right in their assumption, she could be targeted again. This email was sent to Gaia the next day.' He then handed Grace the sheet of paper from his desk. The Detective Superintendent read the words with a chill.

I made a mistake, bitch. You were lucky. But that
changes nothing. Next time I'll be the lucky one.
I will get you anywhere in the world that you go.

'Roy, I don't think I need tell you the enormous PR value of
having this film shot here, in terms of tourism and world
exposure, obviously.'

'I understand that, sir.'

The Chief gave him a worried smile.

Brighton had a criminal history dating back to the mid-
1800s. After a series of particularly violent murders in the
early 1930s, including two separate dismembered torsos
being discovered in trunks in station left-luggage lockers,
Brighton acquired the unwelcome sobriquet of 'Crime Capital of the UK' and 'Murder Capital of Europe'. For years,
the Tourist Board had been trying to shake off that reputation, and the police had been making good progress in
reducing the crime rate.

'If anything were to happen to Gaia while she was here,
the damage to this city would be incalculable. You understand my drift, don't you, Roy?'

'Yes, sir. I get that completely.'

'I thought you would. But there's a problem. I've had a
discussion with Scotland Yard's Close Protection Unit.
Under their mandate, only royals, diplomats and government ministers qualify for high-level protection. Rock stars
– and movie stars – are not on the approved list – they're
expected to provide their own security.'

Grace shrugged. 'That makes sense – they have the
money to do that.'

Tom Martinson nodded. 'Under normal circumstances,
yes – to keep fanatical fans at bay. But they're not permitted to carry firearms in this country. So that gives us the

problem of how to protect them against someone with a gun.'

Grace took a sip of his coffee, thinking hard. Despite Brighton's dark side, one blessing was that it had never had the kind of gun problem that afflicted some inner cities in the UK. Of all the murders in the county of Sussex in recent years, only a handful had involved guns. But that did not mean that guns were not readily available to anyone with intent, who knew where to ask. 'We could make an exception with our own Sussex Close Protection Team, I would have thought, sir.'

Martinson nodded. 'I want you to do a risk assessment and write a security strategy for Gaia while she's in Brighton – knowing that there's a possibility someone may try to kill her with a firearm. I'd like to meet again on Monday morning to go through it, and later on Monday with the team leaders we'll need to implement it, including the ACCs and the Divisional Commander of Brighton and Hove. I'm sorry to throw this at you at the start of the weekend.'

'It's not a problem, sir.' The Detective Superintendent tried not to show his excitement at the challenge. This was really going to give him the chance to shine in front of the Chief Constable. But equally, he knew, a massive burden of responsibility had just been dumped on his shoulders. Keeping Gaia alive while she was in Brighton was now interlinked with keeping his chosen career path alive. And the most recent case he had worked on, *Operation Violin*, showed that Brighton was easily within the reaches of a professional US hitman.

Martinson unfolded his arms, took a biscuit from the plate, then held it without taking a bite. He frowned, as if searching for the right way to say what was on his mind next. 'Changing the subject totally, I also wanted to tip you off about something, Roy.'

'Oh?'

'I believe you had a bit of an unpleasant experience some time back, with a certain Brighton villain, name of Amis Smallbone?'

The creep's name made Grace squirm. 'I put him away on a life sentence, and he didn't like it. Not that many of them do.'

Tom Martinson grinned, fleetingly. 'That was twelve years ago?'

Grace did a quick calculation. 'It would be, yes, sir.'

Amis Smallbone was, in Grace's opinion, the nastiest and most malevolent piece of vermin he had ever dealt with. Five foot one inch tall, with his hair greasily coiffed, dressed summer and winter in natty suits too tight for him, Smallbone exuded arrogance. Whether he had modelled himself on some screen mobster, or had some kind of Marlon Brando *Godfather* fixation, Grace neither knew nor cared. Smallbone, who must now be in his early sixties, was the last living relic of one of Brighton's historic crime families. At one time, three generations of Smallbones controlled protection rackets across Kemp Town, several amusement arcades, the drugs going into half the night-clubs, as well as much of the city's prostitution. It had long been rumoured – a rumour circulated with much enthusiasm throughout the police – that Smallbone's obsession with prostitution came out of his own sexual inadequacy.

When Grace had personally arrested Smallbone on a charge of murdering a rival drug dealer in the city, by dropping an electric heater into his bathtub, the villain had threatened retribution against him personally, and against his wife Sandy. Three weeks later, with Smallbone banged up in the remand wing of Lewes prison, someone had sprayed every plant in the garden of Grace's home – Sandy's biggest passion – with weedkiller, turning all the borders into an arid wasteland.

In the centre of the lawn had been burned two words.

*UR DEAD.*

Grace had been present in court when the jury had returned their guilty verdict. Amis Smallbone, in the dock, had curled his fingers around an imaginary gun, pointed it at Grace and mouthed the word *bang!*

'I've got possibly worrying news for you, Roy,' Tom Martinson said. He looked at his biscuit, but still did not touch it. 'I thought I should warn you, as I doubt anyone from the prison service will bother. I'm an old university friend of the Governor of Belmarsh Prison, who kindly tipped me off. Amis Smallbone was freed from there, on licence, three days ago.'

A chill rippled through Grace, thinking of the phone conversation he'd just had with a very distressed Cleo. 'Does he have a release address, sir?'

Grace knew that a prisoner serving a life sentence would have his release address set by his probation officer, with numerous reporting conditions attached.

'He does, Roy, a hostel on Brighton seafront. But he's in breach. I'm afraid he hasn't been seen for two days.'

# 23

You needed to know the right time and wrong time to buy in the icon's cycle. Like all the fervent Gaia memorabilia collectors, Anna Galicia knew this only too well.

She sat in the gilded, white velour upholstered armchair that was an exact copy of one she had seen Gaia lounging back in, in a *Hello!* magazine feature on her Central Park West apartment. Anna had had the replica made by a firm in Brighton, so that she could lounge back exactly the same way Gaia did, unlit cigarette gripped louchely between her forefinger and middle finger. Sometimes, sitting in this chair, she could imagine she was in the Dakota building, and that her view was over Central Park. The same building where John Lennon had been shot dead.

Something had always excited her about stars who met violent deaths.

She took an imaginary drag on her cigarette then tapped the end in the ashtray enamelled with Gaia's face. Saturday morning was her favourite time of the week, with the whole weekend stretched out in front of her. A whole two days to spend indulgently immersed in her idol! And next week, oh God, she could barely contain her excitement. Next week, Gaia would be here, in Brighton!

In the local paper, the *Argus*, open in front of her, was a photograph of the tiny house in Whitehawk where Gaia was born. Of course she wasn't called Gaia Lafayette then. She was Anna Mumby. But hey, Anna thought with a wry smile, who didn't change their name?

She carefully lifted her computer from her lap and set it on the floor, took a sip of her *Gaia Save Exploited Lives* medium roast coffee, stood up and walked over to the silver balloon, with the pink words GAIA INNER SECRETS TOUR, which had cost her sixty pounds, and which was floating on its string, just below the ceiling. It was starting to look a little wrinkled, and sagging. She tugged it down and lovingly gave it a long, steady top-up burst of helium from the cylinder she kept here for that purpose, and released it.

Then she sat down, breathing in the smells of this room. The scents of cardboard, paper, vinyl and polish and the faint trace of Gaia *Noon Romance* fragrance that she sprayed daily. She picked up her laptop and returned to the eBay auction page she was on.

It was for a bottle of Gaia organic Pinot Noir, from her own Napa Valley vineyard, the label bearing her tiny Secret Fox logo, like all her merchandise, and personally signed. All proceeds of the original sale of this bottle, auctioned at a charity, had gone to support a school in Kenya called Stahere. Yet another example of what a wonderfully kind and human person Gaia was. It was being sold by a Gaia fan in the UK, who had outbid Anna three years ago when it had originally been auctioned on eBay. Another Gaia collector had told her, confidentially, on a Gaia chatroom site, that this collector had lost his job and needed to raise cash.

Anna didn't have any of the Gaia Special Cuvée Pinot Noir wine. It was one of the glaring gaps in her collection. There were known to be only twelve bottles with signed labels in the whole world. At this moment her pockets were feeling deep. She would bid high on this. Oh yes! No one out there was going to beat her today. Let them try, she thought, darkly.

When she met Gaia next week it would be good to tell her about this bottle. Maybe she'd even take it with her and get her to initial the date on it!

Twenty-eight minutes remaining on the auction time. She saw another bid pop up: £375! That was £100 more than the last one. The activity was hotting up.

But regardless, whoever it was stood no chance against her. Not in the mood she was in today. Her *very deep pockets* mood. Not many people beat her at auctions when she was in one of these moods. Only one in the last year. Ha.

There was a lot of anticipation about this new film the icon would be starring in, *The King's Lover*. All the Gaia fan sites were buzzing with it. If the film became as big a hit as everyone was anticipating, the value of all her memorabilia would soar even higher.

Not that Anna would ever sell. She was a buyer, always a buyer. Always would be. She hated it when people started bidding stupidly against her. It was like people were trying to take something away that was rightfully hers. A coil of anger spiralled through her as she stared at this new bid, again.

*You don't know who you are messing with.*

# 24

Roy Grace drove straight from Tom Martinson's office into Lewes, to his favourite flower shop, the Riverside Florist, and was pleased to see the proprietor Nicola Hughes there, cutting a display of blooms for a client. He waited until she had finished, then asked her for a massive bouquet for Cleo, wanting to cheer her up when he eventually got home.

While she was putting it together, he noticed she was limping. 'I hope the other fellow came off worse!' he joked.

'Ha bloody ha!' she replied. 'Just had an ankle fusion. Ruddy well hurts but hey, you didn't come here to listen to me complain!'

He carried the flowers out and put them in the boot of his car. Then before driving off to his appointment with Glenn Branson in Brighton, he stared at the photograph on his BlackBerry that Cleo had texted through to him. At the words carved on her car.

*COPPERS TART. UR BABY IS NEXT.*

There was no mistaking its provenance. Amis Smallbone's signature was all over it. No doubt, as before when the words had been carved on their lawn while Smallbone was securely banged up in a remand cell, he hadn't carved them himself. A man like Smallbone would rarely get his hands dirty – except when he was having fun torturing someone, by cutting off their fingers or their ears or their genitals. But he was thinking hard about the significance.

In his view, if Smallbone had genuinely intended Cleo

to be harmed, he would have had her attacked, not simply left a message on her car like that. He needed to think hard about her security, but at this moment, he did not believe she was under any direct threat. It was more a message of defiance. Amis Smallbone wanting to worry him. Letting him know he was out of prison and had not forgotten. And it was typical of the creep to breach his release conditions, taunting the authorities, seeing how far he could push them.

He was going to be very sorry, Grace vowed.

*

The premises of Gresham Blake occupied a modest corner frontage on Church and Bond Streets, not far from Cleo's house. Grace had passed the place many times, glancing with curiosity at the flamboyant displays of men's clothes, but had never gone inside. It always looked way beyond his price range – and lifestyle. It wasn't until Glenn Branson had started nagging him to try to look younger and more cool, that he'd ever taken any interest in clothes at all. Like most detectives, he tended to wear the same functional, sober business suits, because you never knew where you were going, or who you might meet, in the course of a day.

At a few minutes to 11 a.m., he walked down from the Church Street multi-storey car park, the cost of which always made him wince, to see Glenn Branson standing outside the shop like he owned it, phone clamped to his ear. In the blazing sunshine, hordes of people were milling along the pavement. A marked police car screeched up the hill, siren howling, lights flashing, the sound so familiar in the city that few heads turned to look.

'Any developments?' Grace greeted him when he had ended the call and the din of the siren had faded.

Branson pocketed his phone. 'Nothing so far.' Then he

glanced at his watch. 'The post-mortem's starting in the mortuary at midday. Are you coming along?'

'Thought I'd leave that treat to you, if it's all the same. I'm *chickening* out.'

Branson groaned. 'That's truly terrible.'

Grace grinned, although he was not in a humorous mood. The news about Amis Smallbone's release and the vandalism of Cleo's car preyed heavily on his mind.

'Oh, there is one thing, chief, Bella's mum had a stroke this morning, apparently. She's been rushed to hospital, and I've let Bella go and see her.'

Grace nodded. Normally he never let anything personal interfere with work on an investigation, and particularly not during the crucial first days. But Bella Moy's mother, he knew, was everything to the highly competent Detective Sergeant. The virtually bedridden woman was the reason why, in her mid-thirties, Bella was still living at home, caring for her, without any life of her own, so far as he was aware. 'Sorry to hear that,' he said.

'She's very upset.'

Grace followed Branson into the shop, which had a sumptuous, if higgledy-piggledy, feel. Clearly business premises that had been outgrown by success, he thought. There were shelves of shirts; racks of shoes crammed in a corner; a display of cufflinks. Their feet sunk into the deep carpet, and the air was filled with the scent of a dense, masculine cologne. Branson gave their names to a young man with topiaried hair, behind the counter, then fondled a bunch of ties hanging from a rack and turned to Grace. 'You need a few of these, old timer. All your ties are rubbish. And we'll definitely have to sort you out a new suit here.' He pointed at a loud, chalk-striped blue jacket on a mannequin. 'That would well give you an air of authority. Would make you look like a proper chief.'

Grace looked at it doubtfully; it was far too showy for his taste. The last time Glenn had taken him clothes shopping he'd managed to spend over £2,500. He wasn't about to be suckered into that again, especially with the looming costs of a baby.

Glenn then pointed at a white jacket. 'You'd look good in that, too. Remember that Alec Guinness film, *The Man In The White Suit*?'

Before he could reply, a pleasant but harassed-looking man in his mid-thirties, with brown hair that gave the impression of being perpetually untidy, came down a short flight of steps from an adjoining room. He wore a tweed suit that looked too warm for this early summer day, a soft shirt, a tie at half mast, and was perspiring slightly.

'Hello, gentlemen, I'm Ryan Farrier.'

'Glenn Branson, we spoke earlier.' The DS stretched out his hand and shook the tailor's, then said, 'This is my guvnor, Detective Superintendent Grace.'

Grace also shook his hand. Then they were ushered up two flights of narrow, uneven stairs, into a room lined with rows of suits on racks, some of them only partly completed, with stitching visible on them, and an antique full-length mirror. There was a rich smell of new fabrics and polish. Then Farrier led them through into a smaller room, containing more suits on rails, another mirror and a curtained-off changing area. Roy Grace suddenly felt decidedly shabby in his navy blue Marks and Spencer suit that he'd bought in a sale more years ago than he could remember.

'So, gentlemen, tell me how I can help you?' the tailor said, turning to face them, and clasping his hands in front of him. To his embarrassment, Grace saw Farrier give his clothes a disapproving once-over. He himself had no idea how you could tell a cheap suit from an expensive one, but no doubt a man like Farrier could spot the tell-tale signs in two seconds.

Branson removed the plastic evidence bag from his pocket and held it up for Farrier to see. 'These pieces of fabric were found yesterday in the vicinity of a body we need to identify. We're wondering if you might be able to tell us something from them.'

'Can I take them out of the bag?' Farrier asked.

'I'm afraid not,' Branson said. He handed the bag over. 'Sorry, we didn't get a chance to take them to the dry cleaners.'

Farrier grinned awkwardly, as if uncertain whether Branson was joking, then studied the contents carefully. 'It's a suit fabric,' he said. 'A tweed of some kind.'

'Would it be possible to tell which tailor made it from what you have?' Grace asked.

Ryan Farrier studied the material again, with a frown, for some seconds. 'These samples are really too small. If you are trying to find out who made the jacket or suit these pieces originated from, I think you'd have a better chance from the cloth itself. It's very high quality, heavy tweed.'

'A winter fabric?' Grace said.

'Very definitely. Quite a bit heavier than the material I'm wearing myself. It's the sort of fabric you might have a suit made in for wearing for outdoors pursuits in the countryside – perhaps for going on a formal shoot – except, not in this colour! It really is a bit bold, you'd have to be a bit of a show-off to wear this.'

Heavy fabric meant it was likely the victim was killed during the winter months, Grace thought.

'I think it's a Dormeuil cloth,' Farrier added. 'I can check with them on Monday. Are you able to leave me the tiniest cutting?'

'I'm sorry,' Grace said. 'We can't risk contaminating the evidence – we've brought you photographs we can leave with you.'

'How many tailors would a company like Dormeuil supply cloth to?' Branson asked him.

Farrier thought for a moment. 'Gosh, hundreds, maybe thousands. Any good tailor will have swatches of their material – they are top quality – but also top prices. But this is quite flamboyant material – I can't imagine too many people having a suit made out of this. Dormeuil should be able to give you the names of all the tailors they've supplied bolts of this cloth to in recent years.'

'This is very helpful,' Branson said, then turned to Grace. 'Although of course the victim's not necessarily the person this was originally made for. He could have bought it second-hand,' he said, mindful of the number of second-hand clothes shops in Brighton.

Farrier looked pained. 'I don't think many people go to the expense of buying a suit made from Dormeuil cloth and then give it away or sell it. A quality suit tends to be for life.'

*And in this case, death*, Grace nearly added.

# 25

He sat in semi-darkness, in his cramped seat in coach, with the constant faint thrashing roar of air in his ears, feeling the occasional judder as the plane bumped through a patch of turbulence. Most people were asleep. Like the shithead beside him who'd drunk four disgusting Coke and whisky mixes and now had fits of snoring loudly every few minutes.

People shouldn't snore on planes. It was like people who let babies cry on planes. Those babies should be flushed down the toilets. He was tempted, very tempted, to pull a plastic bag down over the man's head. No one would see in the darkness.

But he had to control his anger.

Which was why he had the book open on his lap. It was titled *Managing Your Inner Anger*.

The problem was that just reading the book was making him angry. It was written by some fuckwit psychologist. What did any psychologist know about anything? They were all nuts themselves.

*Chapter 5. Develop your personal Action Plan (Devised by Lorraine Bell)*

*Develop your own personalized plan for managing and reducing anger, and carry it around with you,* he read.

Right, carry it around with me. In what? A carrier bag? A suitcase? A bowl on my head? An appendage to my scrotum?

*Write down the times you are likely to get angry, such as after a stressful day at work, or an alcoholic drink.*

Or after life craps on you yet again, from a great height?

He felt his rage building again now. The man beside him was snoring again, as loud as a chainsaw. The noise was so damned deafening he could not think. He jabbed him hard, really hard, in the ribs and turned to him, glowering. 'Shut the fuck up, you hear me?'

The man blinked at him, dazed and bewildered.

He curled his finger and thumb in front of the man's face. 'Snore again one more time, and I'm going to pull your tongue right out.'

The man stared at him for a moment, was about to say something, then seemed to think better of it. He looked nervous now, as if he could sense it wasn't an idle threat. After some moments of hesitation, he unbuckled his seat belt, stood up, and walked away down the aisle.

He returned to his book.

*I know when I'm getting angry because of the following early warning signs. Such as feeling shaky, clenching my fists.*

He was feeling shaky now, and he was clenching his fists. The thing was, he knew, he would actually have liked to pull that snoring man's tongue out, the way they did in olden days, with red-hot tongs. He deserved it. People had no right to snore like that.

*When I'm angry I have the following thoughts, or say to myself:*

There was a blank space for him to fill in. But he didn't need to fill anything in. He knew what thoughts he had when he was angry.

*The reasons I would like to change are:*

- *The consequences of losing my temper?*
- *Because I feel bad after?*
- *Because I am unwell and my anger is not helping my recovery?*

He slammed the book shut, feeling the anger inside him. Once the anger was out there was nothing he could do until it settled again. It was like snakes, hundreds of dormant venomous snakes inside him that had woken, were uncoiling, flicking their tongues, waiting to strike.

The thing was, he liked that feeling.

His anger liberated him. It gave him power.

Too many people listened to the words of that idiot Matthew in the Bible. *Whosoever shall smite thee on thy right cheek, turn to him the other also.*

That wasn't the way, that was just a bully's charter. He didn't have any truck with all that namby-pamby New Age New Testament liberalism. He believed in the Old Testament. That was The Word.

*And thine eye shall not pity; but life shall go for life, eye for eye, tooth for tooth, hand for hand, foot for foot.*

No messing about.

He'd promised to read the book and to fill in the questions. That was one of the suggestions his doctor had made. Try to refocus his anger into something positive. Ha! What was the point? He'd done bad things in the past, he knew that, but he couldn't help it, that was the snakes. It wasn't his fault if people woke the snakes.

And they had been awake for several days now.

# 26

The predictability of some villains was one of the few things that made his job a little easier, Roy Grace thought. The old-school ones tended to be territorial, creatures of habit, sticking to their manors for their criminal activities, and their drinking.

But like everything in life, nothing stayed still, he mused, and the old style of rogue, with whom canny police officers could develop some form of a trusting relationship over drinks in a pub, and glean invaluable intelligence, was fast becoming a relic, a dinosaur. They were being replaced with a nastier, meaner and altogether less sociable breed of crook.

Grace found the particular relic he was looking for in the fourth pub he entered, shortly before midday. Terry Biglow was hunched alone at a table, studying a racing form, in the gloomy, empty establishment. An empty half-pint glass stood in front of him, and a walking stick was propped against the wall beside him. The only other occupant was a tattooed, shaven-headed man behind the bar, wiping glasses.

Like Amis Smallbone, Biglow had been a scion of one of the city's biggest crime families. During the first three decades after the war, the Biglows carved up much of Brighton with the Smallbones. They ran one of the major protection rackets, controlled a large slice of Brighton and Hove's drugs scene, as well as laundering money through a string of antique furniture and jewellery shops. Biglow

PETER JAMES

wasn't a man you messed with back in those days, if you wanted to avoid a razor scar on your cheek or having acid thrown in your face. He used to be a sharp dresser, with expensive tastes, but not any more – not for a long time.

Roy Grace had last seen him some months ago, and Biglow had told him then he was terminally ill. He was shocked to see how much the old villain had deteriorated since. His face was almost skeletal, his hair, once so immaculate, was now wispy and unkempt, and his shabby brown suit and cream, tieless shirt buttoned to the top, looked like they belonged on someone three sizes bigger.

He peered up with eyes like a frightened rodent as Grace loomed over him, then his moist, thin lips broke into an uneasy smile. 'Mr Grace, Inspector Grace, nice to see yer again!' His voice was weak and reedy, and he wheezed, as if the very effort of speaking had drained him. Grace noticed his tiny hands were so emaciated they looked more like birds' feet, and the bracelet of his gold watch dangled loosely around his wrist.

'It's *Detective Superintendent* actually, Terry,' Grace corrected him, and sat down in the chair opposite him. The man smelled musty, as if he had been sleeping rough.

'Yes, you was promoted. Yeah, I remember now, you told me, yeah. Congratulations.' He frowned. 'I did congratulate yer, right?'

Grace nodded. 'Last time.' Then he pointed at the beer mug. 'Can I get you another?'

'I shouldn't be drinking. I'm sick, you see, Inspector – sorry – Detective Superintendent. Got the cancer. I'm on all this medication and stuff, not supposed to drink with it. But it ain't going to make much difference, is it?' He peered into Grace's eyes as if hoping for some reassurance from his old adversary.

Grace was not sure how to react. If he had to put money on it, Biglow had just weeks, or a month or two at best, to go. 'They always say medicine's a very inexact science, Terry. You never know.' He gave him a wan smile. Biglow just stared back. He's afraid, Grace thought. The man's actually afraid.

You weren't afraid of much when you ruled the roost in this city, were you, Terry Biglow? he thought. What will you be thinking in those last moments as your life ebbs away? Will you be thinking about all those people whose lives you ruined by selling them drugs? The innocent shopkeepers whose premises you torched because they wouldn't pay your protection money? The elderly, vulnerable people that your teams of knocker boys stole treasured heirlooms from? Are you going to feel happy heading off to meet your Maker with only that to show for your life?

'So how can I help you, Mr Grace?' Biglow wheezed. 'You ain't come in here for the quality of the beer or the congenial company.'

As he spoke Grace watched the man's eyes carefully for any tell-tale flicker. 'I hear Amis Smallbone's out.'

There was no reaction from Biglow at all, for some moments. Then he said, 'Released, is he? He's been away a long time. Good riddance, I say.'

Grace knew there'd never been any love lost between the two rivals. 'I need to find him.' Watching his eyes closely again he asked, 'Don't suppose you have any idea where he might be?'

His eyes didn't move, they stared rigidly ahead, the fear in them still palpable. 'Did yer know Tommy Fincher?'

Grace nodded. Fincher had plenty of past form in the Brighton underworld as a fence. 'Haven't heard of him in years.'

'Yeah, good old Tommy. He just died. Had a stroke. His funeral's next Tuesday, up at Woodvale. He and Smallbone was thick together.'

'They were?'

'Smallbone was married to his sister. She died of the cancer, years ago. He'll be going to the funeral for sure. You'll find him there.'

'You've earned your half!' Grace said.

'Make it a whisky, will yer, Detective Insp— Superintendent. Not that Bell's stuff, they got a nice Chivas, sixteen year, I'll have one of them if yer buying.'

For the information he had just been given, Roy Grace considered it a bargain. He made it a double.

# 27

Gaia Lafayette, dressed in blue jeans and a loose black top, sat numbly on the edge of the white sofa in her Bel Air home, as the two detectives left, then began crying again. It was her third interview with the police in the past three days. They had no suspect, but they had a fuzzy CCTV image which had been sent for enhancement. Ballistics tests had been carried out, but so far there was no match to any weapons on police files.

The detectives had run through possible motives, and talked again with her about any possible enemies she might have. Among the list of motives for murder, they told her, were money, jealousy, vendettas or a random, crazy person. Their feeling on what little they had to go on so far was that this was not random. They felt there was a high probability she was the intended target, and it was mistaken identity.

Her assistant Sasha came back from seeing the police officers out, her hair short and dyed black. There would be no more mistaking her assistants. She'd ignored the advice of her head of security Andrew Gulli, who felt that the murder of Marla was all the more reason to have her assistants dressed as doubles, and Todd, her current hunk, said the same thing.

But Gaia refused to put them through that risk. Having them dressed like herself had been a joke, a bit of hubris. She had never intended it to end in death.

'Why are you crying, Mama?'

Roan, a towel draped around him, his hair still wet from the pool, padded up to her.

'Mama's sad, honey.'

'Are you sad because Marla's not coming back?'

She hugged him and kissed his forehead. Originally she had planned to leave him here, but now that was unthinkable. She wanted him with her in England, where she could see him and protect him.

Her agent and her manager and Todd had all been trying hard to persuade her to pull out of the movie. How could she be properly protected in England, where her bodyguards couldn't carry weapons, they argued? But that was the point, she told them, reversing her decision to quit the film. She would feel safer right now in a country that didn't have a gun culture. And besides, her style had never been to hide away from her public. She was *Gaia*, the earth goddess! Mother Earth would protect her the same way she protected it.

And on a more practical level, the production was all set and depending on her, ready to go next week. If she pulled out now, it would collapse. The producers had made it clear it would be impossible to relocate the production to LA. Besides, how long would she have to remain in hiding? If someone out there wanted to get her, they could wait. Weeks, months, maybe even years. She just had to get on with it.

She hugged Roan. 'You know Mama loves you more than anything in the world?'

'I love you too, Mama.'

'So we're cool, right?'

He nodded.

'Looking forward to going to England?'

He shrugged. 'Maybe.' Then he frowned. 'Is that a long way?'

'It is. We're going to a place by the seaside. They have a beach. You want to play on the beach?'

His eyes brightened. 'I guess.'

'You guess?'

'Will Marla be there?'

'No, hon, she won't. It will be you and me. Taking care of each other. Will you take care of Mama there?'

He stared at her for some moments with round, trusting eyes. And in those moments she had never loved him more, nor felt more scared for him – and for herself. She hugged him tightly, tenderly, pressing her face against the soft young skin of his cheek, smelling the chlorine from the pool on his skin and in his hair. Tears rolled uncontrollably down her face.

# 28

Roy Grace had met a few coppers who were counting down the years to their retirement day, and the lucrative pension package that came with it, particularly with all the recent budget cuts that were demoralizing much of the force. But he knew far more who, like himself, lived in dread of that day.

With twenty years of service clocked up, he still had ten years in front of him, which might be extended to fifteen if the changes that were under discussion by the powers-that-be went through. But there were times when he worried just how fast time seemed to be passing.

Those were the occasions when he cut a moment's slack to take stock, and count his blessings, as he did now while waiting for the last of his team to file into MIR-1 for the Saturday evening briefing.

Some days he couldn't truly believe his luck, that he was doing a job he loved so much. Sure there were people he disliked, such as his former ACC, Alison Vosper, and there were bureaucratic processes that at times got him down, but when he looked back on his career so far, he could honestly say there had been no more than a handful of days when he had not looked forward to going to work. And one of the things he especially liked about his job was that few days were ever the same.

And right now he was doing what he loved best of all, the thing that really got his adrenalin pumping: the early days of a murder enquiry.

'The time is 6.30 p.m., Saturday, June the fourth,' he read out from the notes in front of him, prepared by his trusted Management Secretary, Eleanor Hodgson. 'This is our third briefing of *Operation Icon*. I'll summarize where we are to date.' He glanced down at his notes, then around at his team. Apart from the honeymooning Emma-Jane Boutwood, the only one who was absent was Bella Moy, still at the hospital with her mother. Then he gestured to Glenn Branson.

'Could you bring us up to speed with the findings from the post-mortem?'

'The information I have so far, chief, from the pathologist Dr Nadiuska De Sancha, and from the forensic archaeologist Joan Major, is that the victim is male, Caucasian, aged mid- to late forties. The broken hyoid and the cut mark further around the top vertebra indicate the likelihood of strangulation by a thin wire. There has been considerable degradation of the stomach contents, as would be expected. But chemical analysis reveals a fragment of oyster shell as well as the presence of ethanol, which indicates he had been drinking wine.'

'Er – do we know if it's red or white?' asked Norman Potting.

'Does that matter?' Nick Nicholl asked.

'It would tell us if he had a bit of class or not,' Potting commented, with a grin. 'We'd know we're dealing with rubbish if we found he'd been drinking red wine with oysters.'

Ignoring him, Branson continued. 'We took fragments of cloth found in the torso's immediate proximity for analysis and showed them to the Brighton tailor Gresham Blake. They believe it is a heavy tweed man's suit material, and are now helping us to identify the manufacturer. It's an unusual colourway, so we are hoping once we get the manufacturer we can get a list of retailers who might have sold suits made from it – or a bespoke tailor who may have made one to measure.'

'Such as Gresham Blake?' DC Emma Reeves asked.

'Exactly,' Branson said.

DC Nicholl raised a hand. Branson nodded at him.

'Just an observation, Glenn, but it seems strange that if the killer went to the trouble of dismembering his victim, presumably to hinder identification, that he would have left him in his clothes.'

'I agree,' Grace said. 'I've been thinking the same. It could be a deliberate attempt at laying a false trail. Or, as I think more likely, the perp thought that the clothes, along with the body, would be completely destroyed by the corrosive environment – and miscalculated. I've had previous cases where there has been dismemberment of the victim still in their clothes,' Grace went on. 'It's not uncommon, if you have a panicking perpetrator.'

DC Jon Exton raised a hand, looking first at Glenn Branson then at Roy Grace. 'Sir, if we're dealing with a chaotic offender he might, as you say, have killed in panic. Perhaps he went too far in a fight, and didn't give it any thought that the victim was still wearing clothes when he cut him up to remove the head and the limbs, thinking that would stop identification?'

DS Guy Batchelor, a burly, avuncular detective with a cheery smile, shook his rugby ball-shaped head. 'Surely if he was going to dismember his victim, the perp would have removed his clothes first. It would have made his job much easier.'

'I'm inclined towards the chief's opinion,' Glenn Branson said, then turned towards the Crime Scene Manager, David Green. 'What do you think?'

Green was a solidly built man in his late forties, with short grey hair, dressed in a sports jacket and grey trousers. He always had a cheery no-nonsense air about him. 'Those clothing remnants seem unlikely items to be found in a chicken shed,' he said. 'The farmer, Keith Winter, has no explanation for how they came to be there. Not something he feeds his hens on,' he said with a grin.

'Unless they were dressing up for a hen party,' Norman Potting said.

There was a titter of laughter, silenced by an icy glare from Roy Grace. 'That's enough, thank you, Norman,' he said.

'Sorry, chief,' Potting grunted.

Branson looked down at his notes, then continued. 'The best estimates of time of death are six months to one year. The condition of the body indicates that it was covered with quicklime – better known these days as calcium oxide. An amateurish attempt at accelerating its decomposition and an unsuccessful attempt at destroying its DNA. Joan Major has recovered DNA from the bones, which has been sent for fast-track analysis. We hope to have results back by Monday. In the meantime an enquiry team headed by Norman Potting will look into mispers.'

He paused and took a sip from a bottle of water. 'The Chief and I have set a parameter of missing persons within Sussex and the Surrey–Kent borders. In order to allow for errors in the pathology estimates, we are looking at all misper reports – as well as serials from concerned persons reporting someone possibly missing. Do you have anything to report?' He nodded respectfully at DS Annalise Vineer, the manager for the analysts, indexers and typists on the enquiry, who handled the computerized HOLMES System data.

A studious but good-humoured woman in her mid-thirties, with long black hair and a fringe covering her forehead, and dressed all in black, she had a dramatic appearance, counterbalanced by a quietly efficient air. 'We decided to extend our search time frame parameter – after discussions with DS Potting – to a range of three to eighteen months, to allow for time of death errors. 'We have three hundred and forty-two mispers who have been missing permanently within this period. Of these, one hundred and forty-five are male. So far we have eliminated eighty-seven, from their age and build.'

Grace made a quick calculation. 'This leaves us fifty-eight?'

'Yes, sir,' she replied.

He turned to Potting. 'What progress are you making on these, Norman?'

Potting gave the kind of smug grin he always gave, puffing his chest out self-importantly, like an understudy who has suddenly had the starring role thrust upon him. 'If we could find his skull – that would give us a head start.'

There was another round of laughter. This time Grace smiled, too. As he and everyone else present knew, Potting's comment was less frivolous than it sounded. Dead bodies could be identified in a number of ways. Visual identification from a family member was the most certain of all. DNA was as effective, also. As were fingerprints or dental records. Sometimes footprints, too, in the absence of anything else to go on.

With this torso, they had only DNA analysis to rely on at present. If the victim's DNA was not on the national database, they would be faced with a big problem. Expensive analysis of the isotopes in enzymes in the DNA might give clues as to the corpse's home country, or even county. Forensic scientists had learned recently that food – in particular its constituent minerals – is sufficiently localized to get a region of origin, if not an actual country. The information was of only limited value. For a murder enquiry to be able to make any progress, identification of the victim was paramount.

David Green raised a hand. 'The search team has completed work in the chicken sheds and no further remains have been found. Following a scoping exercise, I've now widened the search parameter to likely deposition sites in the entire area of the farmland, and a one mile radius of the countryside in all areas around it, using Ground Penetrating Radar.' He pointed to an aerial photograph that was pinned up on the large whiteboard at one end of the room. It showed the farm, outlined in red marker pen, and the surrounding fields, road and ponds. 'Divers are scanning or searching all the ponds and ditches this evening and tomorrow.'

Grace thanked him, then said, 'DS Branson will report on the press conference he held at 5.30 p.m. today. Before we get to that, I want to say something to all of you, and I want you to listen carefully. Earlier today I had a phone call from our good old friend Kevin Spinella at the *Argus*. Yet again, as he has done for the past year, he is ahead of all of us – despite the fact that he's currently in the Maldives on his honeymoon.'

'You mean the little shit found someone to marry him, boss?' Guy Batchelor exclaimed.

'Incredible as it may seem, yes. Now, I don't want to make false accusations about anyone, but these leaks to him are coming from someone with insider information. It could be one of you, or it could be someone in another division or department entirely. I just want you all to know that I'm determined to find this person. And when I do – ' he paused, waiting for his words to sink in. 'When I do,' he repeated, 'that person's going to wish they'd never been born. Everyone understand me?'

There was an uncomfortable silence. Grace stared briefly at each of them in turn. Twenty-seven people, some, such as Potting, Branson and Nick Nicholl, he had worked with many times previously. Others, such as the new DCs on his team, Emma Reeves, Shirley Rigg-Cleeves and Anna Morrison, he had no idea about. They all looked like good, decent people, but how could he tell?

Besides, at this moment, that was not his biggest problem. Kevin Spinella was more like an irritating sore that got worse the more he scratched. The man at least had his uses, and understood the game, which was more than he could say for a lot of today's generation of reporters. The real issue at this moment was to decide how wide a net to cast in trying to identify this body, and his killer. He looked down at Eleanor Hodgson's notes, and his own late additions handwritten in the margins.

'We need to research Stonery Farm. I'm setting an initial five-year parameter on this. I want the entire history of the place, and its owner, Keith Winter and his family. Have there been any reported incidents in the vicinity? Break-ins? Poachers? If cause of death is strangulation by wire, could Winter or any of his family have done this? Has he or any of his family ever studied martial arts? What kind of rivalries are there in the free-range chicken business?'

He paused as a ripple of laughter went around the room. Then he glared. 'I'm sorry, did I just say something funny?

Would any of you find it funny that a relative you loved had been found dismembered in a four-foot deep quagmire of shit?'

No one answered.

# 29

Glenn Branson followed Roy Grace out of the Conference Room and along the maze of corridors back to the open area where some senior members of the Major Crime Branch had their permanent offices.

'How did I do?' he asked.

'Good,' Grace said and patted him affectionately on his back, as they entered his office. He saw the winking message light on his BlackBerry, which he had left on his desk. 'We need to identify that body pronto.'

'How?'

Grace slipped behind his desk, sat down and picked up the phone, glancing through the fifteen new emails that had come in. 'I think you should contact the NPIA,' he responded, 'and see if we can get any insight from them about what kind of offender this might be.'

The National Policing Improvement Agency had a range of profilers on their books, who between them had experienced just about every conceivable method of murder, every variation of motive.

'Good thinking. Do they operate over weekends?'

'Not at full strength, but they'll have someone on call twenty-four seven.'

Branson eased himself into a chair opposite Grace's small desk. 'You got something on your mind? You seem distracted.'

Grace continued scrolling through the emails. There was one from Graham Barrington, the Chief Superintendent of

Brighton and Hove Police, who had been appointed the Gold commander for protecting Gaia during her stay in the city. No messages from Cleo, which was always a relief, after her recent collapse.

Graham Barrington was asking him if he could attend a risk assessment meeting on Gaia Lafayette at 10 a.m. the following morning, Sunday, at his office.

'A few things,' Grace said, typing a quick reply to Barrington that he would be there. 'I'm worried about Cleo – I just heard earlier that Amis Smallbone's been released. Her car was vandalized during the night.'

'By him?'

Grace shrugged. 'His style, yes.'

'Shit, what are you going to do?'

'Sort him out, when I can find him. Now I've got a new problem. Gaia. The Chief's put me in charge of her security while she's here in Sussex.'

Branson's eyes lit up. 'I want to meet her! I so want to meet her! Awesome! I can't believe she's coming to town!'

'Wednesday,' Grace said.

'Will you introduce me?'

'If you promise to keep my house tidy!'

'You've got it! Wow! Gaia. She's like – like – ' he raised his hands then dropped them in his lap – 'like incredible!'

'I thought you were only into black music.'

Branson beamed. 'Yeah, well, she sings like she's black! And the kids would die to meet her! How involved are you going to be?'

'I'll know more later.'

'I *have* to meet her. Got to get her autograph for Sammy and Remi!'

'They like her music?'

'Like it?' He rolled his eyes. 'They go nuts when they see

her on television. Every kid in England loves her. You know how big she is?' Then he grinned. 'Actually I suppose you don't, you're too old.'

'Thanks.'

'I mean it. At your age, you're probably dreaming about Vera Lynn. Everyone younger than you is dreaming about Gaia.'

'Yep, well I'm going to be dreaming about her too, from now on. Nightmares.'

'She's awesome. I'm telling you. Awesome!'

Grace nodded, thinking to himself. Gaia was truly awesome. Awesome news for Brighton. A megastar. The film would be a massive global boost to the tourism so much of this city depended on.

And he knew that if anything happened to her here, on his watch, it wouldn't just be the city of Brighton that would forever be tainted. He would be too.

# 30

His moist lips closed greedily around the fat soft tobacco leaf of the Cohiba Siglo. He sucked the dense smoke into his mouth, blew it out towards the ceiling, then picked up the crystal tumbler and drained the last of the thirty-year-old Glenlivet.

This was the life. A great deal better than prison, oh yes. You could get most stuff that you wanted inside, if you knew your way around the system and had influence, the way Amis Smallbone did. But nothing compared to being free. One of the girls – a redhead, naked except for her ankle bracelet – stood up from the sofa to get him a refill. The other stayed closely at his side, massaging his crotch through his trousers, slowly bringing a part of him back to life again.

He tried to keep his focus on his pleasures tonight. Saturday night. His first taste of freedom in a decade and a quarter. A porn movie was playing on the home cinema screen in front of him. Two blonde lezzies. Yeah. He liked a bit of girl-on-girl action. He liked this big room in this fuck-off mansion set back behind electric gates in Brighton's swanky Dyke Road Avenue.

He'd lived in a place even bigger than this once upon a time, just a few streets away. Before a certain Brighton copper took it all away from him.

The pad's owner, his old mate Benny Julius, with his pot belly and dodgy toupee, was down in the basement Jacuzzi with the other three girls. This was a *welcome home* party. Benny always did things in style, always liked living it large.

He winced as the girl slipped her hand inside his zip. Then she whispered into his ear, 'Oooh, it's quite small – but it's ferocious, isn't it?'

'Yeah, ferocious,' he whispered back, before his mouth was smothered by hers.

That was how he was feeling. Ferocious. His focus was slipping from his pleasures. *Ferocious.* He barely felt the girl's hand on his shaft any more. *Ferocious.* Twelve years and three months. Thanks to one man.

Detective Sergeant Roy Grace.

Been promoted a few times now, he'd read.

He was stiff as a rock.

'Like a pencil,' she breathed, huskily, into his ear. 'Like a tiny little pencil stub!'

He smashed her across the face with the flat of his hand so hard she fell to the floor. 'Fuck you, bitch,' he said.

'You couldn't if you tried,' she retorted, rubbing her cheek, looking dazed. 'It's not big enough to get it in.'

He staggered to his feet, but the drink had got there first. His natty grey suede loafers embedded themselves in the deep pile of the carpet and he fell flat on his face, snapping the cigar in half, showering dark grey ash across the white tufts. As he lay there he stabbed a finger at her. 'Remember who you fucking work for, bitch.'

'Yeah, I do. I remember what he told me and all. About why you're called *Small* bone.' She held up her forefinger and thumb and curled them, with a sneer.

'You fucking—' he climbed to his knees and lunged at her. But all Amis Smallbone saw, for a fleeting instant, was her left foot coming out of nowhere towards his face. An elementary kickboxing manoeuvre. Striking him beneath his chin, jerking his head upwards and back. It felt, as his consciousness dissolved into sparking white light, as if her foot had gone clean through his head and out the back of his skull.

# 31

As he drove his silver police Ford Focus from the Sunday morning briefing meeting on *Operation Icon*, down the London Road, heading towards the monolithic superstructure of Brighton's John Street Police Station, Roy Grace was deep in thought, with a lot weighing on his mind, and trying to organize his priorities.

His biggest worry was Cleo, who'd had a restless night with the baby kicking, and was not feeling well this morning. She was still very shaken from the vandalism of her car, and he wanted to get back to her as soon as possible.

There had been no developments on 'Berwick Male', as the headless, armless and legless torso had been named. Their best hope was pinned at the moment on a DNA hit, and they should hear from the lab in the morning.

Tomorrow he had to go to London, to Inner Temple, for a meeting with the prosecuting barrister on the Carl Venner snuff movie case. He needed to find time today to meet with the Case Officer DC Mike Gorringe and financial investigator Emily Curtis, to review their evidence files and go through his Policy Book. They would be grilled tomorrow as if they were in the dock, and needed to have all their answers ready. And right now he had to attend a meeting with Chief Superintendent Graham Barrington.

His phone rang, and he answered it on hands-free.

'Mr Grace?' said an unfamiliar, chirpy voice.

He answered with a hesitant 'Yes?'

'It's Terry Robinson, from Frosts Garage. You popped in a few weeks ago looking at an Alfa Brera?'

'Right, yes,' he said, remembering vaguely. There was a strange and irritating clicking sound on the line for some seconds, similar to the noise he heard before. Either a bad connection or something wrong with his phone, he thought.

'You asked me to let you know if any four-door Alfas came in. Are you still in the market for one?'

'Um, yes, I am.'

'We've got a year-old Giulietta. High spec, it's a beautiful car. Got a bit of mileage on the clock, but you said you didn't mind that, didn't you?'

'How many miles?'

'Forty-eight thousand. One owner. In Etna black. It's a stunning looking vehicle, sir. We've already got enquiries on it. I'd recommend you come and take a look as soon as possible.'

'Doesn't black show the dirt badly?'

'Black always looks best when clean, but it's the most popular of all colours. And it suits this car very well. It looks stunning.'

Grace did a quick mental calculation. 'I could try and get over early afternoon. What time do you shut today?'

'Four o'clock, sir. But I can't guarantee the car will still be there. If someone puts a deposit on the vehicle, that will be it.'

'I'm afraid I'm up to my eyes. I'll try to get over, but I'll just have to risk it.'

'I'll be here until four. Terry Robinson's the name.'

'Terry Robinson, thank you. I'll do my best.'

He halted at traffic lights. One of his favourite buildings, the ornate, absurd but beautiful Brighton Pavilion, was over to his right, the city's own faux Taj Mahal. Two yobs in a purple Astra pulled up alongside him, music pounding in deep bass through their open windows, shaking the air, shaking his brain. For an instant he wished he was back in uniform; he'd have leapt out of his car and had a go at them. Instead, as the lights turned green he watched them blast off into the distance, twin exhausts as big as drainpipes; probably the size of their arseholes.

Keeping his cool, he turned left at the next junction and up the steep hill, and made a right into the lower car park of John Street Police Station, the five-storey modern slab of a building that was the second busiest police station in the UK, and the place that had been his home during the early years of his career. Much as he enjoyed his job, the CID HQ at Sussex House, where he worked, was a soulless building. He missed the downtown buzz of this place.

Marked police cars were parked in long rows, as well as half a dozen police vans, but being a Sunday, many of the bays were empty, and he had a wide choice. He reversed into one, then phoned Cleo, who told him she was feeling a little better, and was loving his flowers.

Relieved, he let himself into the rear door, then climbed up three flights of stairs, with their familiar battered walls and institutional smell, and walked down the corridor of the Command suite, passing several empty offices, and then a small canteen. On his right, sticking out from a closed door, was a sign reading SUPERINTENDENT and on the left, CHIEF SUPERINTENDENT, whose door was open.

He went in. The office, which he knew well from many previous visits, was of a practical size befitting the rank of its occupant. To the right was a substantial desk and, directly in front of him, a large round table at which a group of people were seated, with three vacant chairs. All of them, except one, he noted, were formally dressed, like himself, as if this were a weekday.

On the wall to his left was a large whiteboard, on the bottom of which were three messages, written in marker pen, from Barrington's triplets. One said: *My dad's the world's best copper!*

With a twinge, he wondered if the baby Cleo was carrying would one day write something similar about himself.

Graham Barrington, in his mid-forties, was a tall, slim, athletic-looking man with short, fair hair. He was wearing a uniform short-sleeved white shirt with epaulettes, black trousers and shoes. Grace had known Barrington from when they were both in the CID together. The officer had told him then that the job he most coveted on which to finish his career was to be back in uniform as the Divisional Commander of Brighton and Hove – or 'the sheriff' as he jokingly called it – the job he held now. Grace was pleased for him. It was good to know it was possible to have ambitions and dreams fulfilled.

Next to Barrington was DI Jason Tingley, boyishly handsome, with brown hair brushed forward into a fringe, dressed in a navy suit; his only concession to the weekend was allowing his tie to be slack and his top shirt button open. Greeting him with a warm smile was the extremely competent press officer, thirty-two-year-old redhead Sue Fleet, wearing a dark suit and a blue blouse. Two other women he did not recognize, one in her late twenties in police uniform, the other in her late thirties wearing a white blouse, were also present, as was a solidly built, shaven-headed Sergeant from the Close Protection Team, Greg Worsley, dressed in a rumpled blue T-shirt, jeans and trainers. Completing the gathering was Chief Inspector Rob Hammond, a Tactical Firearms Commander.

Graham Barrington stood up to greet him. 'Roy, thank you so much for giving up your Sunday!'

'I can't remember the last time I actually had one!' he replied, then smiled at each of the others. He was pleased to see Jason Tingley, with whom he had worked years back on a brutal rape case. Tingley was a very smart detective. He also went back a long way with Graham Barrington; like most of the force, he had a great deal of respect for the man who had been credited with very substantial crime reductions in many areas of the city.

Barrington introduced him to the two women, then Grace sat down. All of them, he noticed, had Starbucks containers in front of them. He could have killed for a coffee right now – he cursed himself for not thinking ahead and getting one on the way here.

They chatted informally for some moments before Barrington cut across them. 'Right,' he said. 'The situation is I've had telephone contact with the Threat Management Unit of the Los Angeles Police Department and with Gaia's security chief, a former police officer called Andrew Gulli. The first issue I've had to deal with is explaining to Mr Gulli that his bodyguards are not permitted to carry guns in the UK.'

DI Tingley cut in. 'The threat is global, and we know our target is capable of using a firearm. Are we going to have any Armed Response Unit members active?'

'We are, Jason,' Barrington assured him. 'Chief Inspector Hammond and Sergeant Worsley are here to give us their plan for protecting Gaia and her son Roan.' He indicated to the two men to proceed.

Sergeant Worsley went first. 'Gaia Lafayette and her entourage are flying in to London Heathrow Terminal Five at 7 a.m. on Wednesday,' he said. 'We have suggested putting out a false trail that she is flying in to Gatwick via a private jet, but I understand she has had her press secretary inform the entire UK press of her actual plans. It looks like we have a case of the *ego* is about to land.'

Grace suppressed a grin. This was so typical of major stars. They claimed to hate the paparazzi, yet always tipped them off where they would be. 'Where is she staying? In Brighton, or outside?'

'In Brighton, sir,' Worsley replied. 'In The Grand Hotel. Her entourage has booked the Presidential Suite and all the other rooms on that floor – so we can at least make that floor a sterile area.' He looked down at his notepad. 'One of our big issues is budget, sir. The Chief has told me to offer every resource I have to her, but she's going to have to pay for anything beyond what we would consider a reasonable level – the kind of security we'd give to minor royalty.'

'You're aware of the attempt on her life last week?' Grace asked.

'That is very largely why were are here,' Hammond said.

'We're also aware that she will probably make some kind of pilgrimage to her childhood home in Whitehawk,' Worsley added.

'Another problem is she likes to jog, Roy,' Barrington said. 'Apparently she has her minders jog with her, but that's another area of security risk.'

Worsley nodded. 'We're planning on putting a ring of steel around her, sir. No one's going to get near her without us checking them first.'

Grace nodded. 'Good.' But he knew that no matter how much security you laid on, it was impossible to protect anyone totally. He asked Barrington for the name of his contact in Los Angeles and wrote it down, intending to speak to him directly.

They were all experienced officers in this room. And they all knew the reality. You could protect someone as much as you liked, but if they insisted on moving around freely, they were always going to be at risk from a lone nutcase.

He could not stop the chill of unease that coiled inside him.

# 32

The gaunt, cadaverous-looking American was dressed in a weary checked jacket, tieless gingham shirt buttoned to the top, grey trousers, leather sandals and grey socks. He peered down through unfashionably large glasses, his Adam's apple throbbing, reading her name badge. *Becky Rivett.* Worried that he was about to kick off at any moment, the receptionist at The Grand Hotel glanced up from her screen to give him a quick, reassuring smile, then moved the cursor up the page, searching desperately for his reservation.

He had thinning hair the colour of ash, cut in a pageboy fringe – a style that looked slightly absurd on a grown man in his fifties, she thought. His fists rested on the counter, clenching and unclenching, and he was perspiring slightly.

When Becky Rivett later tried to give the police a description of him, she told them he had reminded her of the actor Robin Williams, when he played that creepy role in *One Hour Photo.*

'I have a confirmation,' he insisted. 'I have your email.'

She smiled at him again, then frowned at her screen. He hated the way she smiled at him. It was a meaningless smile. She smiled at him not because she wanted to, but because she had to. He felt the anger rising; snakes uncoiling. He wanted to tell her she didn't need to smile at him, and that if she smiled at him again, with those neat little white teeth, he—

*Calm down.*

Then he remembered. Stupid fool! It was the jet lag.

Then doing his recce when he should have gone to bed and rested. You made mistakes when you were tired. 'I – ah – you know – gave you the wrong name.'

'You gave me Mr Drayton Wheeler?'

'Yuh uh – you'll find the reservation's under Baxter. Jerry Baxter.' He had decided using a fictional name might come in useful.

She looked down her list, frowned, tapped her computer, then saw it almost instantly. 'Ah yes, a single room for two weeks?'

'Correct.' He took several deep breaths.

She handed him the check-in form and a pen, and he filled it out. 'Do you need a parking space, Mr Wheeler – sorry – er, Baxter?' she asked.

'Why would I need a parking space?'

'I wasn't sure if you had a car.' She smiled again and his anger rose further. 'May I take a credit card imprint, please?'

'I'll be paying cash.'

She frowned. Guests who paid cash were a rarity these days. Then she smiled again, breezily. 'That's fine, sir. But we will need you to pay for incidentals as you go, if that's all right?'

'I will pay incidentally.' He grinned at her for some moments through stained teeth, then the smile slipped from his face as she failed to get his little joke.

She tapped away at her keyboard then, after some moments, handed him his plastic key card in a small folder. 'Room 608.'

'Do you have anything a little lower? I'm rather nervous of heights.'

She looked back at her screen, and tapped again on the keyboard. 'I'm afraid not, sir, we are fully booked.'

'Ah yes, you have that singer staying, Gaia?'

'I'm afraid I cannot comment on other guests.'

'I heard it on the news. It's in the newspapers.'

She feigned surprise. 'Really? I wonder where they got that from.'

'I wonder too,' he said, a tad too petulantly, taking the card.

'Do you need any help with your luggage.'

'Well,' he said, 'I would if I had any. But thank you, British Airways, they've managed to lose it.'

This time her smile was genuine. 'Poor you.'

'They tell me it will turn up later today.'

'We'll bring it up to you as soon as it arrives.'

*Really*, he nearly said. *I thought you might just put it in the middle of the lobby and have all your staff perform a rain dance around it.* Instead he replied, stonily, 'Yes, I would appreciate that.'

Then he walked away towards the lifts, clutching the little plastic room key in its paper folder, taking deep breaths to calm himself down.

He was here. Checked in.

He'd reached first base of his very sketchy plan. Following his anger, unsure where it would lead.

The thing was, there was no point in suing those slime-ball producers Brooker and Brody, for stealing his story. Lawsuits like that took years, he knew, he'd sued other pondlife in this goddamn viperous movie industry, and each time it was five years minimum and sometimes ten, with no certainty of winning. He didn't have the luxury of time any more. Six months, tops, the oncologist had said. Maybe a little longer if he could control his anger, and stop that from eating him up. Pancreatic cancer, inoperable, secondaries spread too far around his body. He was riddled with the stuff.

No point in suing with that time frame. But at least he could get even. Hurt a couple of total shysters big time, before the final cut. Before he himself got flushed out of this shithole toilet called earth.

# 33

'Unexpected item in bagging area. Remove item from the bagging area.'

Glenn Branson stared, bleary-eyed, down at the self-service machine in the Tesco Express in Hove.

'Please remove item from the bagging area,' the imperious, robotic female voice commanded. Glenn looked at the display on the screen, wondering what he had done wrong. The people either side of him did not seem to have any problems at all.

'Unexpected item in bagging area,' she proclaimed again.

He looked around for help, and yawned. It was 8 p.m., Sunday evening, and he felt exhausted. Since yesterday morning when Roy Grace had made him deputy SIO on *Operation Icon*, he had taken his duties seriously, staying up for most of the night working on his Policy Book, reading through the *Murder Manual,* and ensuring all the lines of enquiry that Grace had suggested he make were being covered.

He looked down at the bagging area, trying to figure out what the offending item might be. The quart of skimmed milk? The low-calorie moussaka that he was planning for his supper along with the mixed leaf salad? The aerosol can of spray polish? The packet of absorbent cloths? The box of goldfish food? The six-pack of Grolsch lager?

For months now he had been lodging in Grace's house, thanks to his mate's kindness. Roy Grace had effectively moved in to Cleo's home, so he felt a sense of responsibility for looking after the place and keeping it neat and tidy, especially since it was now on the market. He knew that in his first few months of living there he had let the place become a tip; he was so cut up over his marriage break-down, he had at times been finding it hard to focus. He was still cut up, but he was getting through it – largely thanks to Roy's support. The least he could do to repay him was keep his house in good order.

'Can I help you, sir?'

A young, Indian man in a blue Tesco top and black trousers was smiling at him.

*Yes, you can, you can tell me the identity of a headless, armless, legless corpse found at Stonery Farm yesterday,* he would have liked to have said. Instead he replied, 'Yeah, thanks. I can't figure out why she keeps shouting at me.'

The young man held a card on a chain over the barcode reader, then tapped several buttons. 'Okay, sir, enter your credit card, please.'

Two minutes later, Glenn left the store and walked across the expanse of tarmac towards his car. As he did so he passed a young couple unloading the contents of their trolley into the boot of their car. His heart tightened. A year ago – less – that would have been Ari and himself.

Sunday evening. They would have put the kids to bed and settled in front of the television with a simple, healthy snack. Hummus and pitta bread and olives was Ari's favour-ite Sunday evening meal. And *Top Gear*, of course. He glanced at his watch.

Shit.

*Top Gear* was on tonight and he'd forgotten to record it. He broke into a run.

# 34

Anna only found out by chance, by a Google alert she had signed up to which picked up all online mentions of her idol, that Gaia was a guest on *Top Gear* tonight. Her *Star in a Reasonably Priced Car*, according to the alert, had been filmed earlier in the year, when she had last been over here.

Cars were not Anna's thing. She had watched the show once before to see what all the fuss was about, and had turned it off in a huff when Jeremy Clarkson had been rude about Nissan Micras. That was the car she owned and liked, in an attractive shade of orange. It was a good car, easy to park, perfect for driving around this city. She did not need a Ferrari, even if she could afford one. Nor an Aston Martin. Or a Bentley. Although she had to admit that Gaia's sports Mercedes was a bit special. She could see herself in that.

With Gaia, seated beside her, driving.

Now, on Sunday night she was glued to the screen, and suddenly, there, on the horrible old pea-green car seat, sat Gaia! Tonight's *Star in a Reasonably Priced Car*!

Jeremy Clarkson, in blue jeans, an open-neck white shirt and a jacket that looked like he had borrowed it from someone much smaller, was interviewing her, or rather at this moment, in her soft Californian accent, she seemed to be interviewing him.

Gaia was dressed all in black. Her signal! The one they had agreed in their last telepathic communication. Gaia's special colour worn just for her.

Black T-shirt. Black, figure-hugging leather jacket. Black leather skirt. Black tights. Long black suede boots.

*Gaia, you are so good to me. So good. We are old spirits, you and I. We've met before in past lives. We've been lovers before, we both know that. Now sit sideways, please, to show me that you love me!*

As she mouthed the words, Gaia suddenly obliged, uncrossing her legs, and turning provocatively sideways, her skirt sliding up her thighs. She threw Anna a direct glance. Looking with her wide blue eyes directly into her soul. Then she winked.

Anna winked back.

Jeremy Clarkson laughed at some joke Gaia had cracked and that Anna had missed. He was fawning over Gaia. But Anna didn't care. She wasn't jealous of Jeremy Clarkson. She wasn't interested in what Gaia Lafayette and Jeremy Clarkson said to each other, nor was she interested in what either of them said to the millions of viewers.

She was only interested in Gaia's responses to her. And her idol was responding just the way she had asked her to.

'So you got your interest in cars from a very special lover, it says on your website,' Jeremy Clarkson went on. 'A Formula One driver. Could it have been the Stig?'

Gaia laughed. 'We don't know who the new Stig is, right?'

'Not until he sells his story to the press like the last one, no.'

She pointed at her chest. 'I'm not with him on that. People should not sell secrets.' Then she raised her right hand, pressed her thumb, middle finger and ring finger together and raised the other two fingers in the air. 'Secret fox! Right?' It was her signature image, a shadow boxing image of a fox, mimicking the design which was on all her merchandise.

Clarkson laughed again.

But Anna didn't laugh. Fury suddenly burned inside her. *Secret fox.* Gaia never did the gesture in public. That was *their* secret code to each other.

What did Gaia think she was doing?

Secrets were sacrosanct. Did she not understand? You didn't share a secret gesture with the whole damned world.

She would damned well tell her that.

# 35

'The time is 6.30 p.m., Monday, June the sixth,' Roy Grace read out from his notes, to his team seated in MIR-1. He'd only been back a short while from London, where he'd been closeted for several hours in the chambers of the prosecuting barrister on the Carl Venner snuff movie trial. Along with the Crown Prosecution solicitor, he had run through a seemingly never-ending series of questions that he and his fellow officers who might be called by the defence could be asked. The trial, which would have a lot of media attention, was now due to start the following Monday.

'This is our seventh briefing of *Operation Icon*,' he continued. 'I'll review, in conjunction with my deputy SIO, DS Branson, where we are to date. Our primary task at this stage remains the identity of the victim, "Unknown Berwick Male". DNA results back from the lab this afternoon show no matches on the national DNA database. So at the moment unless we can find the head or hands, to give us dental records or fingerprints, we're faced with a lot of good old-fashioned detective slog, I'm afraid.' He turned to Branson. 'Glenn, you have something to report on the suit fabric found close to the victim's remains?'

Detective Sergeant Branson pointed at the photographs of the checked suit fabric tacked to a whiteboard. 'I've had a report back from Brighton tailors Gresham Blake,' he said. 'They tell me this is a fabric manufactured by the cloth company Dormeuil and sold widely, despite it being so garish, both to bespoke tailors and off-the-peg manufacturers around the world. They have been producing this particular design for over forty years.'

'Glenn, wouldn't different batches of the cloth have variations?' Norman Potting asked. 'Might we be able to narrow the search down if they could identify the batch?'

Branson nodded thoughtfully. 'Good point. I'll ask them.' He made a note, then went on, turning to Emma Reeves. 'DC Reeves has been in contact with Dormeuil and is working with them on identifying all possible tailors and clothing retailers in Sussex – and further afield if we need – who may have used this cloth in recent years. But I do have one significant development to report on this, I'm pleased to say, which may give us significant help. *Crimewatch* have agreed to feature it on their monthly show, which by chance is next on tomorrow night. They will be interviewing Detective Superintendent Grace tomorrow shortly before the show is broadcast.'

'No,' Grace corrected him. 'They'll be interviewing *you*.' He sipped his coffee.

Branson's sudden look of panic provoked a titter in the room. 'Um – ' he mumbled, frowning at Grace. 'Me?'

'You.'

'Right.' Thrown, Branson took a moment to recover.

'A bit of advice, Glenn,' Norman Potting said. 'Don't wear that tie.'

'You're a great one to give sartorial advice,' Bella Moy snapped at him, huffily.

As if he hadn't heard her, Potting pointed at Branson's multi-coloured op-art design. 'I mean it Glenn, it will distract people, and it'll make you look less serious.'

Branson looked down at his tie, a little hurt. 'I like it, it's cheerful.'

Grace nodded. 'I have to agree with Norman; that won't look good on television.'

Nodding reluctant assent, Branson continued. 'We have some more information about "Unknown Berwick Male" from the forensic archaeologist.' Reading from a document in front of him he said, 'His age is estimated at between forty-five and fifty. From his bone density and body mass, he would have been of slight build, five foot, six or seven inches tall, weighing in the region of one hundred and forty pounds. He has suffered two broken ribs, either from an accident or being in a fight. From the healing in the bones I estimate this to have been at least ten years ago.' He looked at Potting. 'Norman, that should help with your mispers. What do you have for us so far?'

Potting read out a list of missing persons that fell into the approximate range, which came to twenty-three people. 'So far we've been focusing on Sussex and Surrey/Kent borders, and I have the outside enquiry team looking into each of these, collecting toothbrushes and hairbrushes to take DNA from. With your permission, chief – ' he looked at Branson, then at Roy Grace – 'I'd like to widen the parameters to the whole of Sussex, Surrey and Kent.' He turned to the indexer Annalise Vineer, who nodded, making a note on her terminal.

Good indexers were vital to a major enquiry. Grace knew from his experience at working on cold cases just how many of them might have been solved very much sooner – and in the case of serial killers, preventing the deaths of some of the victims – if more methodical referencing and cross-referencing across both the county and other police forces had taken place.

Missing person enquiries were like peeling off layers of an onion skin in reverse. With each layer you removed, you widened the search parameters further. Firstly to cover your entire county, then the neighbouring counties, and then the entire country. If that produced nothing, you started looking at continental Europe. 'Okay,' he said. 'Let's hope *Crimewatch* tomorrow throws up something. That material is distinctive, people will remember it.'

'Not as distinctive as Glenn's tie!' Potting chuckled.

Branson looked down at his notes. 'The proprietor of Stonery Farm, Keith Winter, has been very co-operative as have all members of his family. Nothing in any background checks done so far gives me any cause for suspicion. His finances are in good order, he is a respected man in his community and he has no apparent enemies. We are not at this stage regarding him as a suspect. But having said that, in my view, with the elaborate security system at Stonery Farm, it's unlikely that a stranger could have entered to dump – or plant – this body. Which makes me feel either we are looking for an employee of Stonery Farm, or someone who had access to the place and good knowledge of it.' He turned to the Crime Scene Manager. 'Any progress to report, David?'

'I've had the Specialist Search Unit, as well as a large number of uniform and Specials from East Downs Division covering the area since Friday afternoon, boss, looking for the head and limbs,' Green said. Like Potting, he looked first at Branson then Grace. 'We've covered the entire area of Stonery Farm, as well as the immediate surrounding areas with human cadaver dogs and archaeologists doing a visual search for soil disturbances, and the SSU have covered all ditches, streams and ponds.'

DC Jon Exton raised a hand. 'Chief,' he said, 'I'm trying to work out what the perpetrator might have been trying to achieve by removing the head and limbs. I don't understand why he wouldn't simply have cut the torso up, as well. It can't have been easy to have put the body in the chicken shed, unless he worked at Stonery Farm. So why did he?'

'Do you have a hypothesis you'd like to share with us?' Grace asked.

'Well, something keeps going around in my head.'

'Unlike the victim who doesn't have that luxury,' Potting interjected with a smug grin.

Ignoring him, Exton said, 'I'm putting myself in the perp's shoes. If I'm going to dismember my victim, why would I stop at cutting off his head and limbs, and leave his torso intact? Why not cut everything into little pieces? Much easier to dispose of.'

'What about someone who has a grudge against the farmer?' Nick Nicholl said. 'He doesn't want to get caught, so he removes the head and hands, but puts the body there to try to frame the farmer?'

A possibility, Grace thought, but that didn't strike him as likely. There were many kinds of murders, he knew from experience, but most of them fell into one of two categories: those cold psychopaths who planned carefully, and others who killed in the heat of the moment. The psychopaths who planned were the ones who often got away with murder. He remembered a conversation he'd once had with a Chief Constable some years back, when he had asked the Chief if in his experience he believed there was such a thing as the 'perfect murder'. The Chief had replied that there was. 'It's the one we never hear about,' he said.

Grace had never forgotten that. If someone devoid of all human emotion were to plan an execution killing, with the disposal of the body carefully thought out, he or she had a good chance of getting away with it. When you found a body, or body parts, that usually indicated carelessness by the killer. Carelessness tended to be caused by panic. Someone who had killed in the heat of the moment and had not thought it through.

This headless, limbless torso smelled of the latter to him. It was a hurried, amateurish body dump. When killers panicked, they made mistakes. And the kind of mistake a killer usually made was to leave a trail, however tiny. His job was to find it. Invariably, it involved getting his enquiry team doing painstaking work, turning every stone – and hoping, at some point, for that one small piece of luck.

He turned to the analyst, Carol Morgan. 'I want you to look back through the serials covering the winter months – let's set an initial parameter of February the twenty-eighth going back to November the first of last year – for any incident reported in the Berwick area. Someone behaving strangely, someone driving recklessly or just speeding; attempted break-ins; trespass. Take a three-mile radius around Stonery Farm as your starting point.'

'Yes, sir,' she said.

He let Glenn Branson run the rest of the briefing by himself. Although Grace kept track of all that was said, he was multi-tasking, running through the security strategy he had agreed with Chief Superintendent Graham Barrington, and which the Chief Constable had signed off. Gaia was arriving in this city the day after tomorrow. But he was also running through something that was happening tomorrow. Something he could not stop thinking about. The old rogue Tommy Fincher's funeral. And one particular mourner who would be attending.

Amis Smallbone.

Just the thought of the creep caused Grace to clench his fists.

# 36

To those few people acquainted with Eric Whiteley, he seemed a creature of habit. A small, balding, mild-mannered man, with a wardrobe of inoffensive suits and dull ties, who was always unfailingly polite and punctual. During the twenty-two years since he had joined the Brighton firm of chartered accountants Feline Bradley-Hamilton, he had never taken a day off sick and had never arrived late. He was always the first in the office.

He would dismount his sit-up-and-beg bicycle at the New Road offices, directly opposite the Pavilion gardens, at precisely 7.45 a.m., rain or shine, with a tick-tick-tick sound as he scooted the last few yards balanced on one pedal. He would chain the machine to a lamp post which he had come to regard as his own, remove his bicycle clips, let himself into the premises and enter the alarm code. Then he would make his way up the staircase and along to his small back office on the second floor, with its frosted-glass borrowed-light window that was partially obscured by a row of brown filing cabinets and stacks of boxes. In winter he would switch on the heater, in summer, the fan, before sitting at his tidy desk, booting up his computer terminal, and settling into his tasks.

One thing his colleagues had learned about him was that he was something of a self-taught computer expert. He was normally able to fix most software problems that occurred in the company.

Eric Whiteley liked computers, because he was happier

interacting with machines than people. Machines didn't bully you or make fun of you. And he liked figures, because there was no ambiguity about numbers; there was always a satisfying precision. His job was to audit the accounts for clients of his firm, from the figures supplied to him, to do the company payroll, and occasionally to visit the firms to assist one of the accountants going through the books. He had been doing this job for twenty-two years, and expected to continue for at least another thirteen years until he reached the retirement age of sixty-five. Beyond that he had no plans. 'We'll see where the wind blows,' he replied to work colleagues, on the rare occasions, such as the Christmas party, when someone asked him that question.

He did not like the Christmas party, always stayed the minimum amount of time he needed in order not to appear rude, and avoided conversations with his colleagues. After two decades of working with many of the same people, none of the other employees or partners of Feline Bradley-Hamilton knew any more about Eric Whiteley's private life than they had on the day he first joined the firm.

He bought his lunch from the same sandwich shop in Brighton's Bond Street every day of the week, and his menu never varied. Tuna mayo with sliced tomato on wholegrain, two twists of the pepper grinder, one shake of salt, a Twix bar, an apple and a bottle of sparkling water. Then he would buy a copy of the *Argus* from a newsagent and scurry back to the sanctuary of his office, where he would spend the remainder of his lunch hour eating and reading the paper all the way through – except for the sports pages, which did not interest him – and ignoring the phone if it rang.

Today, his eyes were suddenly drawn to the top-right column on the third page. It was an advertisement.

FILM EXTRAS WANTED!
EARN UP TO £65 PER DAY TO APPEAR IN
"THE KING'S LOVER",
STARRING GAIA & JUDD HALPERN.
PRODUCTION STARTS IN BRIGHTON NEXT WEEK.

There was a phone number, an email address and a website.

He carefully cut out the advertisement and placed it in the middle drawer of his desk. Then he returned to his lunch.

*

The advertisement caught the eye of a number of other people in the city at the same time as Eric Whiteley. One was Glenn Branson, who was sitting on a train with Bella Moy, heading to the *Crimewatch* studio in Cardiff. He was eating a banana and scanning through the newspaper. He wrote down the details excitedly. Sammy and Remi were nuts about Gaia! His estranged wife Ari was doing her best to poison his kids against him. Maybe he could get them roles as extras on the set – how cool would that be? And it would have to be worth a lot of brownie points in his relationship with them.

*

Another person reading the advertisement with interest was the occupant of room 608 in The Grand Hotel in Brighton, who had been going through the newspaper's small ads in search of a hooker.

He was feeling tired and jet-lagged, and was hyper with too much caffeine, but he didn't care, he poured himself another cup now, then reached for the phone, checked how to make a local call, and dialled the number given in the advertisement. Moments later he heard the tell-tale delay, after the call was picked up, that he was through to a voicemail recording.

His anger surged. He hated that system, that whole culture of voicemail. That was how people fobbed you off, how they screwed you.

'*If you're phoning to register interest in being an extra in* The King's Lover, *please leave your name, age and a number we can call you right back on. Alternatively you can email us your details, together with a recent photograph and a contact number. Thank you for calling Brooker Brody Productions!*'

For an instant, gripping the receiver hard, he felt the urge to tear it free of its cord, and half the guts of the phone out with it. But then he calmed a little. He hadn't come all this way to trash a hotel telephone.

Not that he knew, at this moment, precisely what he had come to do. Something, that was for sure. Something a lot of people were going to regret.

He left his name and number and hung up.

# 37

Roy Grace liked the design and location of Brighton's Wood-vale Crematorium. In his experience, the typical urban crematorium was a soulless and charmless place, because it existed for one grim function only. Unlike a church, no one got married there, or christened there, or worshipped there, or simply popped in when they were feeling low. But Woodvale, nestling in lush, well-tended grounds on a hill to the north of the city, had a sense of history and a good deal of charm. The central building of twin chapels with a bell tower between them, in Gothic Revival style, had the appearance of a village parish church.

Although his work revolved almost entirely around the deaths of other people, he tended to avoid dwelling excessively on his own mortality. He still had not come to any decision about what he believed in, and kept a totally open mind. On a few occasions, working with psychics in the past, he'd had astonishing results – but many failures too. When he used to discuss it with Sandy, and more recently with Cleo, he would say what he truly felt – that there was a spiritual dimension to existence, and he believed there was something beyond this world, but not in a Biblical sense. In his heart, he profoundly hoped there would be something else. But then he would see some terrible atrocity on the news – or get called out to one himself – and on those occasions he'd think gloomily that maybe it was better for the human race to restrict all its evil to this planet and the mercifully short lives of its inhabitants.

One decision he had not yet made was his own funeral. Sandy had said she wanted a woodland burial, in an environmentally friendly coffin, but he had always shied away from dwelling on the subject: it disturbed him too much to think about it. Although, after a case he had been on some months back involving the trafficking of human organs, he had finally taken the plunge and done something that Sandy had urged him to do years ago. He'd signed up as an organ donor. But that was as far as he'd got with confronting his own mortality.

He looked out at the scene through the driving rain that conveniently turned his windscreen opaque, concealing him. A black hearse and a cortège of limousines waited some distance from one chapel, like planes stacked on a runway.

A sudden chill rippled through him, making him jump. *Someone walking over your grave*, his mother used to tell him. He smiled, sadly and fondly for a moment at her memory, and felt a guilty twinge that he had not been to either of his parents' graves for a long time.

People were coming out of the chapel from the previous service. The usual mix of ages. No one hung around in the late afternoon rain. One group climbed into the back of an undertaker's limousine, the rest all hurried off to their cars.

The waiting hearse, followed by the cortège, moved to the chapel door. The doors of the first limousine were opening. People stepping out, ducking under umbrellas that the undertakers held for them. He gave the wipers a quick flick to clear the screen – and saw him almost immediately. Stepping out of the first limousine.

Amis Smallbone was here, just as Terry Biglow had predicted.

He would have recognized the runt from a hundred

miles away, he reckoned. Smallbone's ramrod straight posture and his elevator heels made him seem a bit taller than his five feet, one inch. Although masked a little by the rain, he didn't seem to have changed much in the past twelve and a bit years since Grace had last seen him, across a courtroom, where he had given the evidence that had played a crucial role in putting him away.

Evil was too big a word to use for Amis Smallbone. To have called him *evil* would have been to flatter him. He wasn't smart enough to be truly evil. He was just nasty. A very *nasty* little man.

After a few minutes, the pall-bearers opened the rear door of the hearse and slid out the coffin containing, Grace presumed, the body of the dead fence Tommy Fincher. He grinned irreverently at the thought that the old rogue might have some last stolen item with him, that he planned to offer to God at a knockdown price.

He saw Terry Biglow emerge from the second limousine, a frail-looking figure, heavily reliant on a stick, and couldn't help feeling sad for the man. It wouldn't be long before the former racketeer's funeral would be taking place, and he must be thinking about that now, very acutely, Grace thought. At least Biglow had something endearing about him, despite being a total scumbag, which was more than he could say about Smallbone. Biglow was a man he had always been able to do business with when he wanted information, and he would miss him.

An entire rogue's gallery of Brighton's underworld hurried by in front of him, through the rain, and in through the chapel entrance. Grace recognized almost all of the faces. Most of them were male, but there were a couple of significant females, too, notably brothel queen Gloria Jouvenaar, and alongside her an elderly lady on a stick, Betty Washington, who in her time had been the wiliest of all the city's madams.

While he waited in his car for the cremation service to be over, he called Glenn Branson to wish him luck at the *Crimewatch* recording. The DS sounded nervous as hell. Grace did his best to calm him down.

'Can I ask you a favour?' Branson said.

'Try me.'

'The movie with Gaia. I don't suppose there's any chance of my getting a few days off – like – taking some annual leave – so I can take my kids – and be extras? I've no idea if we could even get to become extras, but it would mean an awful lot to them.'

'Matey, just think that through, will you? You're the deputy SIO in the early days of a brutal homicide enquiry, and you're suddenly stepping away to become a film extra? Hello?'

There was a long silence. 'Yeah, thought you'd say that,' he replied finally.

Grace felt his friend's pain. He knew just how shitty life had been for him this past year, but if you wanted a career in Major Crime, your work was always going to have to come first. 'Look, tell you what I'll do – no promises – but I imagine I'll be meeting her sometime in the next couple of days to review her security here. I'll see if she'd be willing to meet you and your kids for a couple of minutes. What do you think?'

Branson sounded elated. 'You know, old timer, sometimes you're not at all bad – for a white man.'

'Sod off!' Grace replied with a grin.

Then people began to emerge from the chapel. The service was over fast. Clearly not too many eulogies for Tommy Fincher. He ended the call and sat watching, waiting.

Smallbone came out holding the arm of a woman he did not recognize.

He watched them climb back into the black limousine, then after some moments the car moved off. Grace started his engine and began to follow, keeping a safe, discreet distance behind.

# 38

He couldn't believe it! They were calling him back from the production office of *The King's Lover*, less than an hour after he had phoned. A young woman with an irritatingly cheerful voice, like she wanted to give him the impression she was his *new best friend*.

'Jerry Baxter?'

He did not like her tone one bit. He was tempted to ask her if she had seen the news today on television, about the famine in Africa. Heard it on the radio? Read it in a newspaper? He wanted to ask her how she could sound so happy with the knowledge of that terrible thing happening out there in the world.

Our world. Everyone's world. Was she totally stupid?

The snakes were rising. Stuff was getting all tangled up inside his head as it often did when he got angry. He needed to focus, remember why he was here, why he had phoned the production office in the first place.

'That's me!' he said.

'Thanks for calling us. We're casting for extras now. We start shooting on Monday and we'd need you every day next week until Saturday evening. Would you be free?'

'Absolutely,' he replied.

'We're shooting crowd scenes outside the Pavilion, weather permitting. I'll give you the address to come for costume fitting.'

'Are you filming inside the Pavilion, too?'

'Yes, a lot, but there won't be any requirement for extras there.'

'Ah, right,' he said, slightly disappointed. But the information was helpful, he decided, although he wasn't sure why. He filed it away. Sometimes his brain felt like a junk room where the light bulb had blown and no one had replaced it. You had to root around with a torch for stuff you wanted; and each year as he got older the torch got smaller and the batteries dimmer. There was stuff he'd filed away in there that he had long forgotten about and probably never would retrieve now. Mostly the place was guarded by the snakes that rose, their tongues flicking, each time he looked in there.

After he ended the call, he went down into the lobby of the hotel and approached the reception desk. He asked for information about the Brighton Pavilion: what time did it open and close, were there guided tours, did you have to book?

The man behind the desk, who was wearing a smart grey uniform, opened a leaflet and showed him the hours of opening, and the times of the guided tours.

Drayton Wheeler thanked him. It was pelting with rain outside; he decided this would be a good afternoon to spend doing something cultural indoors. What could be better than a visit to Brighton Pavilion?

# 39

'Goddamn rain! Goddamn English weather. Shit!' Larry Brooker, huddled beneath an umbrella, stood on the lawn of the Royal Pavilion, his Gucci loafers sodden from the wet grass. He checked the weather forecast on his iPhone for the tenth time today, as if somehow, miraculously, at any moment the grey images of rain that filled all six days were suddenly going to turn to sunshine. The cameras didn't start rolling until next Monday, but they were on a tight schedule for these final days of pre-production and this lousy weather was not a help.

The film's director seemed impervious to the stuff plummeting down from the sky. Unshaven, with a shoulder-length mane of white hair and a perpetual worried frown, Jack Jordan was wearing a long-peaked baseball cap and an old flying jacket over jeans and sneakers. The two-times Oscar nominee, as well as a BAFTA winner, stood like some ancient soothsayer who had just foretold the end of the world, staring up at one of the onion domes framed by minarets, with his group of acolytes around him – the Location Manager, the Line Producer, the Production Secretary, the Production Designer, the Director of Photography, the First Assistant Director, his Personal Assistant – who it was an open secret he had been shagging for years – and two other people Larry Brooker didn't know, but had no doubt he was paying for.

Jack Jordan pointed out something on the rooftop; the

DP nodded and his PA wrote herself a note. Jack Jordan raised a small camera and took a picture.

Brooker hadn't slept last night. There was another big hiccup with the production finance. Gaia was arriving in town tomorrow from London, so was their male star, Judd Halpern; they were in full pre-production, building sets up at Pinewood for some of the interiors, ninety-three people on the payroll burning through cash. His partner Maxim Brody had called him from Los Angeles last night, very kindly at 1 a.m., to tell him about the new problem.

Quite a big problem, actually.

The whole production was going to fall over in three days' time if their backer, Californian internet billionaire Aaron Zvotnik, didn't come up with the money he had promised. And Zvotnik, it was all over the news, was in trouble himself, with a big lawsuit launched against his company by Google for some infringement; his stock had plunged. He had warned Brody he was facing cash calls for his own stock purchases and could no longer guarantee to honour his commitment.

And just how great was that, thought Brooker? At this late stage his and Maxim's only option was to dig into their own pockets to save the production until they could find a replacement for Zvotnik's cash. Brooker was almost broke, but Maxim Brody, luckily, had deep enough pockets to keep them going for a few weeks. Long enough, with a star of Gaia's stature on board, to find someone to bail them out, but it would almost certainly mean going cap in hand to one of the major studios, and being royally screwed.

He stared moodily at the building. It was one of the most extraordinary places he'd ever seen, and as an inveterate traveller, he'd seen a lot. It was the only building that measured up, in his memory, to the Taj Mahal. Although, to be fair, he'd only seen that at 6 a.m. with a blinding hangover and stomach-cramps from diarrhoea.

The Pavilion was designed in the style of an ornate Indian temple, completely over the top, like some vast, garish wedding cake. Yet it worked, it was quite stunning and majestic, and the interior, decorated with an equally exotic and lavish chinoiserie, was even more extravagant. Developed from a farmhouse in 1787 by the Prince Regent as a seaside retreat for trysts with his mistress – and later his secret wife – Mrs Maria Fitzherbert, the Royal Pavilion was designed and expanded for several decades afterwards by John Nash. It was *the* defining icon of the city of Brighton and Hove, and one of England's most famous landmarks.

To his relief, Jack Jordan and his entourage were now moving inside, out of the rain. When Larry Brooker had put his first movie together, twenty-five years ago, he'd seen himself living the LA dream. Within a few years, he had planned, he would have his mansion in Bel Air, his fuck-off yacht on the French Riviera, and his private jet. But it hadn't worked out that way. He'd made a decent living so far, and would be a rich man if such a big chunk hadn't gone up his nose and an even bigger chunk to his ex-wives. He felt like he was on a constantly nerve-racking ride, but as yet he was not playing in the league he'd hoped for, and if this film did collapse his and Brody's reputations would be in tatters. They had to keep it going somehow.

A security guard nodded at them. Brooker followed his director and crew along a corridor and into the Banqueting Room. As he looked around him, he decided that if this movie became the global smash hit they anticipated, he would build himself a dining room in that Bel Air mansion that was a replica of this one. It was on a scale that was even more opulent than it looked in the photographs, and so beautifully ornate. He stared in awe at the painted canvas walls, and up at the domed ceiling with its massive centre-piece of plantain leaves in bas-relief, from which hung several immense and fabulous chandeliers.

The central one, the biggest of all, reminded him of a sky-burst firework. It was a good thirty feet high, seemingly held in the claws of the dragon in the apex of the dome. It hung high above a dining table, laid for thirty people, with elaborate candelabra, gold vessels, fine china and crystal goblets.

'I guess this is where George and Maria had their intim-ate little dinners,' the Production Assistant said, with a grin, to Jordan.

Several of them laughed, but not Brooker who was too wrapped up in his thoughts. He was extremely glad they had decided to shoot here on location and that they hadn't attempted to replicate this room in a studio.

'Actually, no it isn't!' a tall man in a business suit said, walking across to them. 'I'm David Barry, the Curator of this building. It's very interesting, but George wasn't at all happy sitting at this table – he was always terrified the chandelier was going to come crashing down.'

All of the team looked up at it. 'I don't think there'd be much left of anyone that landed on,' Jordan said.

'Quite!' the Curator agreed. 'It weighs just over a ton and a quarter!'

'How do you keep it clean?' someone asked.

'It's done every five years,' he replied. 'It has fifteen thousand individual glass drops, or lustres, each of which has to be removed, washed, polished and put back.'

'Hope it's – ah – well supported,' Brooker said, only half in jest.

The Curator nodded. 'It is indeed. Queen Victoria was

concerned about its safety, and had new supports constructed in what was one of the first introductions of
aluminium to this country – it was the strongest material
in the world at that time.'

No one noticed the tall, gaunt man in a wet mackintosh,
with a camera slung around his neck, carrying a small
umbrella in one hand and a Royal Pavilion brochure in the
other, who appeared to be admiring a painting on the wall.
But he wasn't remotely interested in the picture. He was
listening to their conversation.

# 40

Tommy Fincher's wake had been going on for over three hours now in the upstairs private room of the Havelock Arms. But Roy Grace didn't mind the wait. He sat patiently in his car across the road from the pub, in the pelting rain and failing light, making calls and emailing on his Black-Berry. And watching. He hoped it would continue for a couple of hours yet. The darker the better.

It was no surprise this establishment had been chosen for the wake. It was one of the city pubs where villains were known to hang out. He'd recognized at least fifteen familiar faces arriving, all of them frequent fliers with Sussex Police. A couple were huddled half in and half out of the door-way now, having a smoke. Inside they'd be drinking their respects to Fincher – and no doubt networking. None of them trusted each other, but the turf wars of old, slugged out in the streets and alleyways of this city with knuckle dusters, razor blades and bottles of acid, had for decades now been a thing of the past. These days the local villains had bigger problems to worry about than each other. Encroachment by the Chinese triads and the Albanian and Russian Mafias was already hitting the pockets of British criminals hard. The drugs trade, prostitution, porn, contra-band booze and cigarettes, fake designer goods, and the growing business in internet scams, were all markets being taken over by invisible poachers with even more brutal reputations than their local counterparts, and mostly off-shore bases.

In that respect, Brighton and Hove had been fortunate. The city did not have the gun and knife crime that blighted so many places in the UK. But Grace was ever wary that nothing stayed the same, and you could never afford to be complacent.

He couldn't afford this time he was spending tonight either, but in truth he was rather enjoying himself. This was taking him back to his early days in the CID, when he'd spent two years on a surveillance team, much of that following and watching known local drugs dealers – several of whom were here today. He'd once spent thirty-six hours sitting inside a specially converted fridge in the back of a rusty old delivery van. It was made to look like it had been abandoned, but had actually been carefully sited a short distance along the street from a suspected drug dealer's house in Moulsecomb. Grace had been there round the clock, with a supply of food and water, unable to step out, having to relieve himself into metal containers, filming the comings and goings through a spy hole in the side of the vehicle.

It was in that fridge that it had first occurred to him that being a detective was like fishing, that you needed a lot of patience to land a big fish, an analogy he used today whenever he did training work with student detectives.

He looked at his watch. 8.35 p.m.

Among the faces he had not been surprised to see was a real old lag, Darren Spicer. A career burglar, in his early forties but looking a couple of decades older. There weren't many night-time – or *creeper* – burglars left these days, fortunately, Grace thought. They could make more money far more easily as drug dealers or internet fraudsters. In recent years Spicer would probably have been one of Tommy Fincher's best customers – when he wasn't inside.

He was distracted from his thoughts by a track that had begun playing. 'Mr Pleasant' by the Kinks. He had long thought this group wrote some of the greatest lyrics of all time, and this particular song was one of his favourites. It had a sinister, nasty undertow that perfectly suited the assembled company across the road, behind that steamed-up first-floor window. And in particular, one man. Small-bone.

*Mr Pleasant.*

Or rather, Mr *Unpleasant* . . . Grace thought. He could smell sweet whiffs of the cigarette smoke from across the road, and suddenly really fancied one himself. And a drink to go with it, a malt whisky – or maybe a cold lager because he was thirsty. But no chance of either; he daren't risk leaving the car and missing his target, and he hadn't any cigarettes with him.

He was also hungry, having missed lunch because he'd worked flat out on preparing some extra documents the prosecuting counsel had requested for the Venner trial, needing to get them despatched before heading to the funeral. The only thing he had in the car was a KitKat which had been in the glove locker for months; the chocolate had gone all lumpy from having melted several times in the sun, and was covered in white speckles. He took the wafer bar out, removed some of the foil and bit a piece off. It tasted stale and crumbs dropped in his lap. But he needed to eat something, and he could be here a long while yet, so he forced it down, grimacing with each fresh bite, and cursing for not having planned ahead.

But in reality he'd had no plan, other than cancelling tonight's briefing on *Operation Icon* because of Glenn's absence, and to free himself up. He had just intended turning up at the funeral to find Smallbone, but without having decided how he would confront him. Anger at the man was pent up inside him. A deep rage at what he had done – or had arranged for someone to have done – to Cleo's car. He was in danger of doing something stupid and he knew he needed to keep a lid on it somehow. But he wasn't sure, when he finally met Smallbone face to face tonight, whether he would be able to. No one was ever, ever, ever going to threaten or scare his beloved Cleo.

A young couple hurried past, both of them laughing at something, and disappeared up the street. He glanced at the car clock then at his watch. In just over twenty minutes' time, the live *Crimewatch* broadcast would be starting at the dedicated BBC studio in Cardiff. At some point during the hour, Glenn Branson would be speaking on air, presenting the case. Immediately afterwards Glenn and Bella Moy would man the phones in the studio, on the number Glenn had given out. They would remain there until midnight following the live update programme at 10.45. Then they'd be staying at a hotel in Cardiff and taking the train back to Brighton in the morning. Grace knew the procedure, he'd done it several times. It was one of the best possible resources for an enquiry, almost always yielding an immediate response from the public and, frequently, positive leads. He dialled Glenn's number, but his phone was off.

He left him a voicemail wishing him luck. He knew how Glenn would be feeling right now. He'd be in the green room, with Bella and the other guests on the show, throat dry, nervous as hell. That was how he always felt himself before going on live television. It was impossible to feel any other way – you had one chance and blowing it was not an option, and that feeling of responsibility always got to you.

He dialled Cleo. When she answered he heard furious barking. 'Hi, darling!' she said cheerily over it. Then she said, her voice raised, 'QUIET!!!'

'What's he barking at?' Grace asked, apprehensive suddenly.

'Someone just rang a doorbell on television!'

He smiled with relief. 'How are you feeling?' Across the road he watched the two smokers go back inside.

'Tired, but a lot better. Bump's been very active. Treating me like I'm a football!'

'God, poor you!'

'What time do you think you'll be home?'

'I don't know.'

'Have you had supper?'

'A stale KitKat.'

'Roy!' she said, admonishing him. 'You have to eat properly.'

'Yep, well there's a bit of a limited menu where I am at the moment.'

'Where are you?'

'I'll explain when I see you.'

'I'm going to bed soon. Did you get my message about food?'

'Message?'

'I left you a message, earlier this afternoon – I couldn't get through. Asking what you were doing about food tonight.'

'I didn't hear any message.' Strange, he thought. Had she dialled a wrong number? He doubted it.

'Shall I leave you something in the fridge? I've got some nice lasagne.'

'That would be great, thanks,' he said.

'I've made a salad – I want you to eat it, okay?'

'I promise! Hey, Glenn's on *Crimewatch* tonight.'

'I know, you told me earlier, I'm recording it for you.'

He was about to ask her more about the message she'd left, when the pub door opened and a figure stepped out into the rain, looking a little unsteady on his pins. Although it was across the street, in a rain-lashed dusk, there was no mistaking him.

Hastily ending the call, he watched Amis Smallbone, nattily attired in a brown Crombie coat with a velvet collar, popping open an umbrella. Then, with his head held arrogantly high and a slightly swaying gait, he strutted along the pub's short forecourt towards him, then stopped on the pavement, as if looking around for a taxi.

Grace was astonished the man was unaccompanied. And could not believe his luck. He stepped out of the car, and strode quickly and decisively over to him, noting the street seemed empty of people in both directions. Good.

Diminutive and perfectly formed, like a bonsai version of a much bigger thug, Smallbone looked as neat and tidy as a carefully gift-wrapped package. He spoke with a small sharp voice, perfectly matched to his stature, but imbued with phoney grandeur. It was as if he imagined himself having the appearance of a respected country squire, whereas to the outside world he looked like a racetrack spiv, or a sleazy character on a street corner selling fake wristwatches.

'Amis Morris Smallbone. Fancy bumping into you here! Roy Grace – remember me?'

Amis Smallbone stopped in his tracks. He blinked through the gloom, as if he were having difficulty in focusing. Then, his voice a little slurred but as unpleasant as ever, he said, 'What do you want?'

'Don't you know what it means when someone uses all three of your names?'

Smallbone squinted, puzzled, then momentarily lost his balance. Grace gripped his arm to steady him, and kept hold of it. He could smell the booze on the man and he reeked of tobacco. 'No,' he said sullenly.

'Think!' Grace said.

'I have no idea.'

'It means you're being arrested.'

# 41

Anna sat in her Gaia shrine, dressed in the turquoise, feathered ball gown Gaia had worn on stage in her *Save The Planet* tour. She had showered before putting it on earlier this evening, not wanting any of her own body smells to contaminate her idol's perfume and perspiration, which she believed she could still detect in the ten-year-old garment.

She was busy revising. Re-reading parts of Gaia's authorized biography, after having spent the first part of this evening testing and re-testing herself on Gaia's song history, to make sure she had absolutely every single title, and in the right order, and the date it was first performed. It really would not do, when they finally met tomorrow, for her to make a silly mistake. She wanted to be perfect for her idol.

And she was pretty confident she did have them all right. She was good at dates, always had been. She'd excelled at history at school – she could remember the dates of every king and queen of England; and every battle; and just about all the other important dates. Some of her fellow pupils had called her a swot. So? She didn't care. What did they know about the world? How many of them today, all these years later, had a Gaia collection like this?

Huh?

'How many do you think, Diva?' she said to the cat.

The cat sat at the foot of a glass display cabinet, which contained framed concert tickets and racks of programmes. It did not respond.

She checked her watch. 8.55 p.m. It was time to go downstairs to watch one of her favourite programmes, *Crimewatch*.

True crimes. With luck there would be a murder on the show; perhaps a reconstruction. She replaced the cat litter on a couple of pages torn from *Sussex Living*, a free magazine that she never bothered reading but was good for this purpose. Then she went into the living room and switched on the television.

She liked the filmed reconstructions, the more violent and gruesome the better. So much more powerful than in a TV drama or a movie, because you knew they were for real. She could close her eyes and imagine the victim's fear; the pain; the desperation. It aroused her. Sometimes Gaia played around with bondage in her stage acts. She loved that. That really aroused her too.

Maybe Gaia would tie her up tomorrow? She could suggest it to the star, couldn't she? She shivered, deliciously, at the thought.

*

Twenty minutes into the show the presenter Kirsty Young introduced a tall, black detective dressed as if he had just come from a funeral. On the screen appeared the caption, *Detective Inspector Glenn Branson, Sussex CID*.

Anna took a delicate sip of her Gaia mojito. Sussex. Something local, even better! In the *Argus* and on the radio and television news there had been coverage about a body found on a chicken farm in East Sussex. Not much had been said about it so far, but it sounded very sinister. Deliciously sinister. She hoped he might be going to talk about that now.

Moments later there was a film clip of the detective

standing by a metal gate, with a sign beside him saying STONERY FARM. He looked very nervous.

*Yes! Oh yes! Thank you, Detective!* She was so excited she slopped some of her mojito over the rim of her cocktail glass.

'Sussex police were called to this free-range chicken farm last Friday morning, where a male torso was discovered by workers cleaning out the waste tank of the chicken shed,' Kirsty Young said.

The film cut to show a huge, single-storey shed, a good hundred yards long, with clapboard walls and a row of roof vents, and tall steel silos beside it. The television camera pulled back to reveal this was on a screen in the studio; the detective pointed, saying, 'The body was found in here, and we believe he had been here for between six and nine months, could be longer. We have no DNA, no fingerprints and no dental records. We need to identify this man. There is no case colder than the one in which the victim is unidentified. And tonight we are asking for your help.'

Anna sipped her drink and watched eagerly. Oh yes, this was her kind of stuff!

'The man is estimated to have been between forty-five and fifty years old, five feet six or seven inches tall, of slight build,' the detective continued. 'At some point in the past he suffered two broken ribs, either from being involved in an accident – could have been a sporting injury, or sustained in a road accident, or indeed a fight.' He smiled, but it could just as easily have been a nervous twitch, Anna thought.

'Help from the public is vital to us in this case. We cannot start a murder investigation in earnest until we know who that body is. One thing that may be significant in helping to jog the mind of someone out there is the gentleman's stomach contents. He ate a last meal which probably included oysters and wine.'

*What kind of oysters? Tell us?* Anna urged, silently. *Colchester? Whitstable? Blue Point? Bluffs? What kind? Tell us, tell us! Colchester? Colchester are the best!*

Now the detective was pointing at two ragged pieces of fabric that were stuck to a whiteboard. Next to them was a complete male suit in the same material, on a shop-window mannequin. 'Something that may be significant to our enquiry is these two pieces of cloth found in the vicinity of the body. We believe they come from a suit similar to this one.' He pointed at the mannequin.

The screen filled with a blow-up photograph of the two pieces. It was a distinctive yellow ochre and red and dark-brown check. Anna listened to the detective's voice, taking another, larger sip of her drink.

'This is a tweed suit material, in a heavyweight cloth from the quality manufacturer Dormeuil,' DS Branson said. 'You can see this is a very bold and distinctive design. You'd remember if you saw a suit of this pattern, or if you knew someone who had a suit like this.'

Anna did. She drained the rest of her drink in one gulp then set the glass down. The numbers to call for the Incident Room and the anonymous number for Crimestoppers came up. But Anna did not call either of them.

Instead she made herself another drink.

# 42

'This isn't the way to the nick,' Amis Smallbone slurred, as the car bumped and jolted over the grass.

'Woken up at last, have you?' Grace said, watching him in the rear-view mirror, although in the growing darkness, it was getting harder to see him. He'd been good as gold for the past twenty minutes, out for the count. He'd hardly needed the handcuffs, one of which was clamped around Smallbone's right wrist, behind his back, the other to the rear passenger door handle, which had been made inoperable from the inside by the child lock.

Smallbone's mobile phone, which Grace had removed and placed on the passenger seat beside him, rang for the third time.

'Hey, that's my phone ringing.'

'Crap ringtone,' Grace said as it stopped. He was out of his comfort zone, doing what he was now doing, but he didn't care. He was going to teach this little shit a lesson he would not forget. He drove for several hundred yards towards an old fort, long abandoned, at the top of the Devil's Dyke, Brighton's highest landmark. It was where he used to come and play as a child, and where he used to bring Sandy when they were courting. The lights of the city were some miles behind them across farmland.

In his first couple of years as a uniformed copper, before he'd joined CID, and before the force had today's level of public scrutiny and accountability, they used to scoop up aggressive drunks on a Friday or Saturday night in a police van, drive them up here, and toss them out on the grass, leaving them with a five-mile trek back to the town centre. No better way to sober them up!

He climbed out of the car, and carefully checked all around him, peering through the driving rain. It was deserted. Then he opened the rear door and peered in. Smallbone glared at him. He slid in beside him and pulled the door shut. The smell of booze and cigarettes coming off the man was much stronger, mixed with a sickly cologne.

'What the fuck do you want?'

Grace stared at him and gave him a cheery smile. 'Just a little chat, Amis, then I might release you without charge, if we come to an understanding.'

'Without charge for what?'

'Breaching your prison release conditions, by not staying at the hostel where you were instructed to reside, and failing to report to your probation officer. I can of course read you your rights and formally charge you on both these counts, and you'll be straight back inside, if you'd prefer. Five more years, maybe? That sound good to you?'

Smallbone said nothing for some moments. Grace continued to stare at him. He'd aged noticeably, he thought. His face, which once had cold, boyish good looks that used to remind him of one of those perfect, soulless young men in Hitler Youth posters, now had the leathery, lined texture that prison and heavy smoking did for you. His hair was still immaculate, but the blonde colour had gone and instead was the gingery colour of bad dye. But he still exuded the same arrogance from every pore of his skin. 'I didn't do it.'

'Do what?'

'What you said I done.'

'Vandalize my lady's car?'

'I didn't do it. You're making a mistake.'

Clenching his fists, and having to work hard to control the anger that was steadily building inside him, and his hatred for this scumbag all the more intense now he was so close to him, Grace said, 'Your handwriting's all over it.'

Smallbone shook his head. 'You can think what you like, Grace, but knowing your reputation in this city, I don't think I'm the only person who isn't signed up to your fan club.'

Grace leaned closer, his face right up against Smallbone's. 'Twelve years ago, just after you were sent down, someone burned almost identical words on to my lawn. Don't even try to deny that was you, because that will make me even angrier. All right?'

He leaned back a little. Smallbone said nothing. Then Grace leaned forward again, pressing his face even closer, so their noses were almost touching. 'You're out on licence, a free man, Smallbone, free to do anything you want. But I'm warning you now, and I'm not ever going to warn you again. If anything happens to my lady and the child she is carrying, anything at all, *anything*, I won't be locking you up again, understand? I won't be locking you up because there won't be enough bits of you left to fill a matchbox, by the time I've finished with you. Do you understand?'

Without waiting for any comment, Grace climbed out and walked around to the other side of the car, then jerked the door open as hard as he could. Smallbone, his right arm twisted behind his back and hooked by the other end of the cuff to the door handle, was jerked out and fell on his back in the grass, with a pained grunt.

'Oops, sorry,' Grace said. 'Forgot you were holding on to the door.' Then he knelt and frisked him for a second time. When he was satisfied he didn't have another phone, he unlocked the cuffs, and pulled him to his feet. 'So, we understand each other, do we?'

Smallbone stared around him, in the almost pitch darkness now, the pelting rain matting his hair to his head. 'I told you, I haven't touched her car. It's not my doing. I don't know anything about it.'

'In that case,' Grace said with a smile, 'you've got nothing to worry about. Have a nice walk home. It should sober you up nicely!'

'Hey – what do you mean?'

Grace walked round to the driver's door and opened it.

'You're not leaving me here?'

'Actually, I am.'

Smallbone patted his pockets. 'You've got my phone!'

'Don't worry, it's safe!' Grace climbed in, shut the door and hit the central locking. Then he started the engine.

Smallbone pounded on the roof, shouting, 'Hey!' He tried to open the front passenger door.

Grace lowered the window a fraction. 'I'll drop your phone off at Brighton nick – oh, and your umbrella too!'

'Don't leave me here like this . . . please,' Smallbone said, trying politeness for once in his life. 'At least give me a lift back to town.'

'Sorry,' Grace said. 'It's an insurance thing. Not allowed to take passengers unless on official police business. You know how it is these days. Health and Safety, all that shit. Bummer.'

He drove off, slowing down for a brief instant to flick on the rear spotlight, and enjoy the sight of the forlorn, bewildered-looking figure stumbling across the grass after him.

# 43

Apart from one night here during happier times with Ari, when they'd toured around Wales before Sammy was born, Glenn Branson did not really know Cardiff at all, and he wasn't sure of his exact whereabouts in the city right now. Except it was a nice, swanky hotel, and the bar was still open and busy. He sat at the counter with Bella Moy next to him. He was buzzing, on a high from having been in the TV studio, feeling a faint sense of anticlimax that it was all over.

He grabbed a handful of nuts in exotically coloured coatings and crunched them, then lifted his pint glass. 'Cheers,' he said.

Bella raised her Cosmopolitan and they clinked glasses.

'Well done, star!' he said.

'You were the star,' she returned with a sweet smile.

She was dressed in a navy trouser suit with an open-necked white blouse and elegant high-heels. He wanted to tell her how lovely she looked, but he didn't quite have the courage, unsure how she might react, knowing from past experience that she had a very brittle side to her. And besides, he thought regretfully, in today's politically correct police world, the slightest innuendo taken the wrong way could have you up before a disciplinary tribunal for sexual harassment.

But what a transformation, he thought, from the normally drab attire she wore at work, and her messy mousy hair. She'd had it done especially for tonight, an elegantly layered cut, and for the first time since he had known her, he was looking at her as an attractive woman. He noticed the fine gold chain with a tiny cross around her neck, and wondered how religious she was. He realized, despite having worked closely with her for the past two years, how little he knew her. 'Must be tough with your mum being in hospital,' he said.

She nodded sadly. 'Yes.' She shrugged, and in that gesture he saw, through that sadness, what might have been a hint of relief.

'How long have you been looking after her?'

'Ten years. I lived away from home for a few years, then my dad was sick with Parkinson's and Mum had a minor stroke and wasn't able to look after him, so I moved back in with them. He died and I – I sort of stayed on, looking after her.'

'That's dedication.'

'I suppose.' She smiled wistfully and he sensed even more strongly her deep inner sadness.

She drained her glass and he ordered her another, downing his own too and getting a pleasant buzz from the alcohol. He was enjoying himself. It was good having some company. And he had to admit it, he'd really, really enjoyed being on television. Live television! Roy Grace had called him twenty minutes ago telling him he'd just watched the recording and congratulating him on giving a command performance – even if he had stolen his line about cold cases and the identifying of the victim!

There had been a flurry of calls but no positive leads so far. They'd agreed Grace would take the morning briefing so that he and Bella didn't have to rush back at dawn.

Which meant he could enjoy himself for a while longer. Away from Brighton and for the first time in a long while not feeling all chewed up inside about Ari and his kids. And suddenly he found himself staring at Bella not as a colleague, but as a guy out on a date would. He didn't want this evening to end just yet. Instead he found himself wondering what it might be like to sleep with her.

Their eyes met. She had big, soulful eyes. A pretty nose. He liked her slender neck, although that crucifix bothered him some. Was she a prude? Why had she got divorced? He needed to know more about her. 'Do you have – you know – like – a fella?'

She smiled evasively. 'Not really. No one – you know – that I'm an item with.'

'Oh?' His hopes rose. There had been several times in the past when he had looked at the DS in briefings, munching away almost obsessively on her Maltesers as if they were a Freudian substitute for something else, and thought to himself that with a makeover she could be really attractive. And now here she was, smelling of an alluring scent, and with just that makeover. Although he could improve on her further, if she gave him the chance. And, he decided, emboldened and increasingly amorous from the drink, he was going to try to persuade her to give him that chance.

Roy Grace had told him, on a couple of occasions recently, that he needed to accept that his marriage was over – had been, in reality, for a long time – and that he should start seriously considering a new relationship. Well, he thought, this just might be it.

They chatted on for a while, and she finished her second Cosmopolitan.

'Have another!' he said, draining his second beer – or was it his third? A cheesy song was playing in the background, 'Lady In Red'. Not normally his kind of music, but it was doing it for him at this moment.

'I have to go to bed,' she said, slipping off her bar stool, suddenly, surprising him with her abruptness. 'It's been a great evening!' She gave him a quick, damp peck on the cheek and was gone.

He sat there, reflectively nursing his empty glass, then ordered another pint. He listened to more cheesy songs, savouring that soft, wet touch of her lips, and thinking, for the first time since Ari had told him their marriage was over, that maybe it was possible to find a new life.

And that he might have found the person to start it with.

# 44

Like all police officers, Roy Grace had long been conditioned to arrive early for meetings of any kind, at any level. The Wednesday morning *Operation Icon* briefing had been short, with little progress to report in the past twenty-four hours. Their best hopes of a breakthrough, at this stage, were pinned on a positive response from Glenn Branson's appearance on *Crimewatch*.

At a quarter to ten, he showed his warrant card to the security officer on the gates at Malling House, then drove through the barrier. He was still privately smiling after his encounter with Amis Smallbone last night. He couldn't help it. He had no doubt the creep was swearing and cussing, and that his head was full of all kinds of retribution, but he had equally no doubt that Smallbone would not go within ten miles of Cleo ever again.

He parked and stepped out of his car into a fresh, warm, early summer morning. He walked across the complex of buildings towards a modern, functional building that housed the visitors' reception desk, entered the large waiting area, and gave his name to one of the uniformed receptionists.

Then he sat down and picked up a copy of the Police Federation magazine and began idly flicking through it, scanning with interest several articles mentioning officers he knew. After a few minutes a shadow fell over him and he looked up.

It never mattered what the nature of his business was

with officers from PSD – the Professional Standards Department – he always felt a tad nervous dealing with them. They
were, essentially, the force's own police force, whose job
was to investigate both public complaints and any internal
misconduct of their fellow officers. It didn't matter that
they might once have been colleagues, as Detective Superintendent Michael Evans had indeed been; they now played
for a culturally different team. They were perceived by some
as the enemy, even when you were seeking their help or
advice.

'Good to see you, Roy. Long time!'

Grace stood up. It had been several years since they'd
last met. A sprinter with the Sussex Police Athletics team,
the Detective Superintendent was a wiry forty-five-year-old,
with a shaven head and a slightly world-weary cynicism in
his eyes. 'Good to see you too.'

Evans frowned. 'Did things ever get resolved about your
wife – Sandy, wasn't it?'

He clearly wasn't up to speed, Grace thought. 'Nope.
It'll be ten years in a couple of months. I'm going through
the process of having her declared legally dead. I'm planning to get married again.'

Evans pursed his lips and nodded, like some inane troll
on a toy counter. For some reason his expression reminded
Grace that he needed to buy a birthday present for his
god-daughter, Jaye Somers, who would be ten in August.
Then he said, 'Word of advice, Roy, make sure you get all
that buttoned up. You know, just in case . . .'

'I know.'

Compliance was a big current issue in the police force.
There had been too many scandals over expenses and
police relationships recently. They were all walking on egg-
shells these days.

He followed Evans a short distance to the modern block where the PSD was housed, then along a corridor and into a small, box-like office, and took one of the two chairs opposite his desk. The office was that of a man who lived a neat, orderly life. Tidy desk, tidy shelves, regulation framed photos of a perfect-looking wife against a blank, blue background, and cute kids against beige backgrounds. Nothing to give any hint of any interests. It was, he imagined, like a KGB member's office during the height of the Cold War.

'So how can we help you, Roy?' he asked, settling down behind his desk and not offering any drinks.

'You may remember I mentioned to you a while ago I've been concerned about leaks of key information on a number of murder enquiries I've been running during the past year,' Grace said. 'It's still going on and I need advice from you on dealing with the situation.'

Evans opened a lined notebook, identical to the Policy Books that were maintained during Major Crime enquiries. He jotted down the date and Grace's name. 'Right. Can you give me details?'

For the next thirty minutes, Grace talked him through the cases, during the past twelve months, where Kevin Spinella always seemed to have privileged information on what was happening, long before any press officer had circulated it. Sometimes, Spinella had called him only minutes after he himself had been informed of a murder. All the time he kept an eye on the notes Evans was taking – he had long been skilled at reading upside down.

When Grace had finished, Evans said, 'Well, so far as I can see there are three scenarios. The first is someone in your team is providing the information. The second is another member of police staff, perhaps even the press office. If you can let me have this Kevin Spinella's phone number, we'll run a check on all outgoing calls made from police phones to see if that picks up anything. We can also run a check on work computers to see if there's any communication between him and any police staff. It could be he has a hold on someone in the Force – either on an officer or a member of civilian staff. And of course the third scenario, which is a hot topic at the moment, is that someone's hacked into your phone. What do you use?'

'My BlackBerry, mostly.'

'My advice to you is to take the phone to the High Tech Crime Unit, and get them to see if it's clean, in the first instance. If it is, come back and we'll see what the next step is.'

Grace thanked him for the advice. Then he hesitated for a moment, Michael Evans's friendly attitude making him wonder whether he should say anything about Amis Smallbone, to head off any possible complaint by the creep. But he decided against. Smallbone, out of prison after a long sentence, was going to concentrate on building his crime empire up again; he wouldn't risk further wrath from himself by making an issue out of last night. He might seek some kind of revenge against him, down the line, but he would have to deal with that as and when.

He drove back to Sussex House, then wound his way along the corridors of the ground floor to the rear of the building, and entered the High Tech Crime Unit. To the casual observer, most of it didn't look any different to many of the other departments in the building. An open-plan area, densely packed with workstations, on several of which stood large server towers, and on some, the entrails of disembowelled computers as well.

A plain clothes Sergeant was in charge of the unit, and

many of the people working there were civilian computer experts. One of them, Ray Packham, hunched over a computer on the far side of the room, he knew well, and had worked with on a number of recent cases. A pleasant-looking man in his forties, neatly dressed, he had the quietly efficient air of a bank manager. On the screen in front of him were rows of numbers and digits that were meaningless to Grace.

'How long can you spare it for, Roy?' he asked, taking the BlackBerry.

'I can't spare it at all,' he said. 'I'm in the early days of a new murder enquiry. And I have to help safeguard Gaia, who's arriving today. How long would you need it?'

Packham's eyes lit up. 'Could you do me a big favour, Roy? Get her autograph for Jen? She's crazy about her!'

'I'll be getting her autograph for half of Sussex Police and their beloveds at this rate! Sure, I'll try.'

'I've got to finish an urgent job I'm on – I wouldn't be able to start looking at it until later today at the earliest. But I can clone it, if you give me an hour, and keep that, so you can have the phone back.'

'Okay, that would be great.'

'Where are you going to be?'

'Either in my office or MIR-1.'

'I'll bring it up to you as soon as I can.'

'You're a good man.'

'Tell Jen!'

Grace grinned. Packham doted on his wife and his new, crazy beagle puppy, Hudson. 'How is she?'

'Good. Her diabetes is much more under control, thanks for asking.'

'And Hudson?'

'Busy trashing the house.'

Grace grinned. 'He should meet Humphrey. Actually, on second thoughts, better not. They might swap ideas on new ways to eat a sofa.'

# 45

At 12.30 p.m. Colin Bourner, the doorman of The Grand
Hotel, stood proudly outside the handsome portals of the
historic building he loved so much, sharp and elegant in his
black and grey uniform. Built in 1864, its swanky interior
had once boasted the first lifts in England outside of London. A darker chapter of its history came in 1984, when the
IRA blew it up in an unsuccessful attempt at killing the then
Prime Minister, Margaret Thatcher.

The hotel had been lavishly rebuilt, but in recent years,
under different management, had lost much of its kudos.
Now under a passionate new manager, Andrew Mosley, it
was steadily climbing back to its former glory. As testament
to that was the quality of cars parked outside in the cres-
cented driveway, for which he had the keys in his safe
keeping. A black Bentley saloon. A red Bentley coupé. A
silver Ferrari and a dark green Aston Martin. Also parked
outside, less conspicuously, an unmarked silver Ford Focus,
with two police officers from the Close Protection Unit
inside.

And the surest endorsement of all for any establishment
with high aspirations, a large cluster of paparazzi crowded
the pavement outside and some, with long lenses, across
the street. Accompanying them were outside broadcast
units from both local television stations and Radio Sussex,
along with a growing crowd of excited onlookers, as well as
a cluster of Gaia fans, several holding record sleeves, CD
booklets, or copies of her autobiography. A number of them

were dressed wildly, in homage to some of their idol's more outlandish stage appearances.

Bourner was excited too. High-profile celebrities were good for his hotel's image. And, with luck, he might get Gaia's autograph himself! For the next month this place was going to be fizzing with excitement. Brighton had its share of star visitors, but rarely the calibre of the one they were expecting at any minute.

After the vile weather of yesterday, there was a clear sky, and beyond the promenade on the far side of the busy road in front of him, the flat sea was deep blue. Brighton looked its glorious best; a fitting welcome for the star.

Suddenly a convoy of three black Range Rovers swept into the drive and pulled up in front of him, in perfect synchronization, leaving a large gap between each of them.

Bourner stepped forward towards the first one, through a strobing blaze of camera flashlights. But before he reached it, the front and rear doors opened, and four scowling heavies emerged. All of them were north of six feet tall, wearing identical black suits, white shirts and slim black ties, with headsets hooked over their ears and wrap-around sunglasses. None of them seemed to have a neck.

A matching set of besuited giants emerged from the second car. From the third climbed a white man in his mid-thirties, of average height, dressed in dark suit and tie, accompanied by three hawk-eyed, power-dressed women, also in their thirties, the doorman estimated.

'Hello gentlemen!' he said to the first group.

One of them, who made King Kong look like a circus midget, peered down at him and in a thick American accent said, 'This The Grand?'

'It is indeed, sir,' Colin Bourner said breezily. 'Did you have a pleasant journey?'

The white man in the sharp suit strode up to him. He had slick, jet-black hair and spoke out of the side of his mouth with a whiney accent. He reminded Bourner of one of his favourite old Hollywood movie stars, James Cagney. 'We're the advance security team for Gaia. Can you take care of the baggage?'

'Of course, sir.'

A bunch of bank notes was pressed into his palm. It was only later, when he checked them, that he realized they totalled £1,000. Gaia had a policy of tip big and tip early. There was no point in tipping on your last day, in her view. Tip on your first, to make sure you get good service.

Instead of entering the hotel, the eight bodyguards lined up, four either side of the revolving doors.

Moments later there was a cheer from the crowd across the road and another eruption of flashes. A black Bentley saloon swept into the driveway and, clearly pre-rehearsed, pulled into the space between the first and second Range Rover, right in front of the doors.

Colin Bourner leapt forward but was outflanked by four of the bodyguards who got there before him, blocking his view, and opened the rear door of the car. They were joined by another two. The star and her six-year-old son stepped out to a barrage of flashlights and shouts from the paparazzi: 'Gaia!' 'Gaia, over here!' 'Gaia, this way!' 'Gaia! Hi!' 'This way, Gaia!' 'Gaia, darling, over here!'

She was dressed in an elegant camel two-piece, and smiling; the little boy in baggy jeans and a grey Los Angeles Dodgers T-shirt was scowling. Her flaxen hair glinted in the sun as she turned and gave a sunny wave to the photographers and the crowd across the road. Moments later she vanished from view as the security guards closed around her, cocooning her and the boy and sweeping them through into the hotel lobby, past more hopefuls clutching record sleeves and CD booklets, and straight to the lift.

None of the entourage paid much attention to the gaunt, cadaverous-looking man in a drab, grey sports jacket over a plain cream shirt, who was reading a newspaper and apparently waiting for a friend or a taxi.

But he was paying a lot of attention to them.

# 46

'Did you fall off your bicycle?' Angela McNeill asked, clutching ... folder in her hand.

... in his tomb-like back office, was in
... right today, at all. He
could leave the office early, but instead, for the first time in
all the years he had worked for this accountancy firm, he
had arrived late.

And now he was being interrupted while eating his
lunch – which was something he hated. He considered
eating a private function.

His tuna mayo sandwich, with sliced tomato on wholegrain, and one bite taken from it, lay in its opened wrapper
on his desk. The Twix bar, apple and bottle of sparkling
water lay beside it. In front of him was the front page of the
*Argus*, with its headline: **Gaia fever hits Brighton!**

'No, I did not fall off my bicycle; I've never fallen off my
bicycle, actually, well not for a very long time.' He eyed his
meal, anxious to return to it.

This woman was new to the firm. A professional book-
keeper, widowed two years ago, she had been trying for
some time to strike up a friendship with Eric, the only single
man in the firm. She didn't find him attractive, but she
sensed he was lonely, like herself, and that perhaps they
could be occasional companions, go to plays or concerts.
But she could not figure him out. From the brief conversations they'd had, she knew he wasn't married, and he

didn't appear to have a girlfriend. But she didn't think he was gay, either. With her finger she traced a line down her cheek, mirroring the mark on his face. 'What happened?'

'My cat,' he said, defensively.

Her face brightened. 'You have a cat? So do I!'

He glanced down at his sandwich again, hun~

he had missed breakfast, and wished sh~

he said.

'What kind of cat?'

'One that scr~ 'You're funny!' She squeezed her way
She grinned. 'You're funny!' She squeezed her way through the narrow gap between the filing cabinets and his desk and put the folder down. 'Mr Feline asked if you could do the monthly management accounts on Rawson Technology as soon as possible. Any chance of looking at them today?'

Anything for peace, he thought. 'Yes.' He nodded.

But she didn't leave. Instead she said, 'Do you like chamber music? There's a concert on at The Dome on Sunday and a friend gave me some tickets. I just wondered – you know – if you weren't doing anything?'

'Not my thing,' he said. 'But thank you.'

She glanced down at the newspaper. 'Don't tell me you're a Gaia fan?'

He was silent for some moments, thinking about a reply that would get rid of her. 'Actually, I love her, I am a huge fan.'

'Seriously? So am I!'

Inwardly he groaned. 'Well, there we go, who would have believed it?' he responded.

She looked at him through fresh eyes. 'Well, well, you're a dark horse, Eric Whiteley!'

Inside, he was tightening with irritation. How could he

get rid of this bloody woman? He gave her a thin smile. 'We all have our guilty secrets, don't we?'

'We do,' she said. 'That's so true. So true. We do, don't we?'

He raised a finger to his lips. 'Don't tell anyone!'

'I won't,' she said. 'I promise. Our secret!'

She left the room and he returned, relieved, to his sandwich. He flicked through the pages of the paper. On the fifth page the headline caught his eye. **Sussex murder mystery on Crimewatch**.

He read the article slowly and intently while he finished his lunch. Then he returned to the front page story. *Guilty secrets!*

He smiled.

# 47

'I think I may be in love!'

Roy Grace looked up as Glenn Branson entered his office, swung around one of the chairs in front of his desk, and sat astride it like he was riding a horse.

'So do I!' Grace held up a printout of a Frosts Garage fact sheet and photograph of a shiny black Alfa Romeo Giulietta. 'What do you think of her?'

'Awesome!'

'A year old, high mileage, but she's in my price range!'

Branson took the details out of courtesy and glanced through them. 'It's only got two doors!'

'Nope, four – the rear door handles are hidden.'

'So you could put the baby in the rear seat, right?'

'Exactly!'

'Go for it. Treat yourself, you deserve it. And hey, at your age, it could be the last fun vehicle you buy before your mobility scooter.'

'Fuck off!' Grace retorted with a grin. 'So what or who are you in love with?'

'Well, you're probably not going to believe it but – um – ' He looked uncharacteristically coy, suddenly. 'You know – Bella is actually a very attractive lady when she puts her mind to it!'

'I thought she was looking quite foxy on *Crimewatch*, actually. Only saw her in the background, but she looked better than I've ever seen her. So did you pull?'

'Not exactly. But I'm working on it.'

'Good man, I'm pleased. It's about time you started getting a life again.'

'She's a sweet lady.'

'She's smart, I've a lot of time for her. And well done you on your television debut – you were brilliant!'

Branson looked genuinely thrilled. 'You think so, really?'

'Really!'

There was a knock on the door.

'Come in!' Grace called out.

Ray Packham entered, holding Grace's BlackBerry. He looked at both detectives, then hesitated. 'Sorry to interrupt, chief. Just bringing this back.'

'Any joy?'

'I've cloned it – I'll study it as soon as I have a moment.' He handed over the phone.

Grace thanked him, and saw the red message light winking furiously. He began a perfunctory scroll through the messages of the past hour. Then, moments after Packham had shut the door, the BlackBerry rang.

It was Chief Superintendent Graham Barrington, the Divisional Commander for Brighton and Hove. 'Roy, just to let you know Gaia has arrived at The Grand. I've arranged with her security chap, a fellow by the name of Andrew Gulli, for a meeting to discuss her security in Brighton in an hour's time, in the Presidential Suite at the hotel. Are you able to make that?'

Grace told him he was. Just as he ended the call his internal phone rang. He answered, and heard the excited voice of one of his new team members, DC Emma Reeves.

'Sir,' she said, 'I've just taken an interesting call from someone who saw *Crimewatch* last night!'

'And?'

'It was from a member of an angling club near Henfield.

He's just seen a piece of cloth that matches the one DS Branson showed on television.' Henfield was a village ten miles north-west of Brighton.

'How sure is he?'

'He's sent me a picture from his mobile phone. It certainly looks like a match. He says he was there yesterday and he's certain the fabric wasn't there then.'

'You're in the Incident Room?'

'Yes, sir.'

'I'll be straight down.'

He ended the call then stood up. 'Want to go fishing?' he asked Branson.

'Never been fishing in my life.'

'Now's the time to start, before you get too old.'

'You can sod off, too!'

'Remember the actor Michael Hordern?'

'*Sir* Michael to you! *Passport To Pimlico. Sink The Bismarck! El Cid. The Spy Who Came In From The Cold. Where Eagles Dare. Shogun. Gandhi.* He was well brilliant!'

'Know what he said?'

'I've a feeling you're about to tell me,' Branson said with a grin.

'*Of our allocated lifespan of three score years and ten, time taken out for fishing does not count.*'

'That's how you stay young, old timer?'

'Haven't fished in years,' said Grace. 'I just have the gift of natural youth.'

'In your dreams.'

'No, in my dreams I'm even younger, and pushing you around in a wheelchair.'

# 48

Ten minutes later, Roy Grace stared at the blow-up of the photograph that had been texted through to Emma Reeves's phone. It was a jagged piece of fabric, snagged on what appeared to be a branch of gorse.

'Looks a pretty close match,' Glenn Branson said, looking over his shoulder.

'It's the same pattern,' Grace agreed.

'This chap is absolutely certain it wasn't there yesterday.'

Grace nodded, thinking hard. 'Significant it appears the morning after you show it on *Crimewatch*? Could be that the perpetrator still had most of the suit – and possibly our missing body parts, and was panicked into disposing of them.'

'That's what I'm thinking.'

'Okay, send one of our detectives down to the fishing club with the Crime Scene Manager, taking the piece of cloth we have, and see if the fabric matches. If it does, get the whole area sealed off as a crime scene and get a forensic strategy in place right away. We'll need a land and water search. It sounds like a potential deposition site.'

Leaving Grace in his office to finish off some urgent paperwork on the Venner case, before heading to the security meeting on Gaia, Glenn hurried back to MIR-1. He despatched DC Emma Reeves, together with David Green, the Crime Scene Manager, to the angling club.

Then he sat at his workstation and began checking

through the large number of other calls that had come in following his *Crimewatch* appearance. But there was nothing else of interest. A handful of the usual crank calls, and a couple from people who had called the Crimestoppers line anonymously to report suspicious neighbours. He delegated various members of his team to follow up each call, but at this moment, none seemed as positive as the one from a man called William Pitcher.

An hour later Emma Reeves phoned Glenn Branson in great excitement to tell him that the fabric did appear to be an exact match. Also she said there were fresh-looking tyre tracks that had not been made by the vehicle belonging to the angler who had made the call. Feeling a thrill of excitement, he appointed her as the temporary scene guard. Then he asked her for the directions, and told her he would be on his way in a few minutes.

He ended the call and looked around the Incident Room, wondering who else to take. He saw Bella Moy finishing a call and walked over to her. 'Fancy a drive out into the countryside?'

She shrugged, and gave him a strange look, followed by a hesitant 'Okay, yes.' She grabbed a handful of Maltesers from the box on her desk and stood up.

She had been quiet during the early morning train journey back from Cardiff, and Glenn wondered whether he'd said something to upset her the previous night. She had appeared for breakfast wearing a top he had never seen before: although conservative it was far more modern than her usual style, and he wondered if it had been for his benefit.

Disappointingly, she seemed strangely subdued in the car now, updating him as he drove with the latest bulletin on her mother, who was not doing well in hospital. Every few minutes the TomTom, clipped to the top of the dash-board, interrupted their conversation, barking out the route.

For the final mile, Bella took over, reading aloud from the directions Emma Reeves had given them, then lapsing into her own thoughts. They headed down a narrow country lane, then turned left at a sign which read WEST SUSSEX PISCATORIAL SOCIETY, crossed a cattle grid, and drove down a steep, single-track road with tall hedgerows on either side.

'Ever lived in the country?' Glenn asked, trying to break the rather awkward silence that persisted between them. He wondered again, had he upset Bella in some way last night? He didn't see how.

'Doesn't appeal,' she said.

'Nah, nor me. I'm a born townie. Too many inbred weirdos in the country, if you ask me.'

'I grew up in the country,' she said. 'My parents were tenant farmers. They moved to Brighton when they retired.'

'Ah,' he said, trying to think of a way to recover from that. 'Of course, I don't mean *everyone.*'

She said nothing.

There was another sign to the angling club, pointing left, through an unfinished building development in a farm-yard that looked as if it had been abandoned. There was a large, derelict-looking farmhouse, a half-finished barn conversion with a sign outside that read, DANGER, DO NOT ENTER, a grey breeze-block structure with no glass in the windows or doors, and a row of ancient, windowless flint cottages with a half-filled skip outside. Bags of sand and ballast lay around the area, along with a length of drainpipe and a large wooden reel of electrical cabling.

Ploughing through a muddy puddle just beyond, they saw a white Scientific Support Unit van. It was parked on concrete hardstanding alongside a large, navy-blue off-roader. A strip of blue and white crime scene tape was secured across a narrow entrance which had a sign fixed to a post, NO VEHICLES BEYOND THIS POINT.

Emma Reeves, a stern, good-looking blonde-haired DC, sensibly gowned up in a white oversuit, wellington boots and blue gloves, and holding a crime scene log, was acting as scene guard. Next to her stood Crime Scene Manager David Green, also gowned up, together with a smiling man in green waterproofs and waders, holding a fishing rod in a pose like a sentry.

Glenn hefted his Go-Bag out of the boot of the car, silently cursing that he had not come in boots; mud oozed over the tops of his immaculately polished loafers as he and Bella Moy approached them.

'Sir,' DC Reeves said, 'this is William Pitcher who phoned in – he's actually a retired paramedic.'

Turning to him, Glenn said, 'Thanks for your call. You're sure this fabric wasn't here yesterday?'

'I'm certain – but I hope I haven't brought you on a wild goose chase,' William Pitcher said, looking at David Green, then Emma Reeves and then Glenn. 'But that cloth was not here yesterday, I'm certain. I left here at nine last night, and I've checked the register, and no members of this club came after me, nor did anyone come this morning.'

Through dense woodland terrain beyond them, Branson saw the glint of water. He looked at Emma Reeves then the Crime Scene Manager. 'Do you want us in oversuits?'

Green shook his head. 'Not necessary – unless you want to go exploring?' He looked dubiously down at Branson's shoes. Bella more sensibly had gum boots on.

'I just want to see the suit cloth.'

Green led him up to the snagged strip of fabric, being

careful not to tread on any footprints or tyre marks. There was a gap in the hedgerow and trees through which Branson could see a wooden jetty and some decking. The lake was roughly an oval shape, overhung in parts by trees and bushes, and several wooden fishing platforms had been built around its shore. At the far end it narrowed to little wider than a river, then opened up beyond into what appeared to be another oval lake. It was an idyllic spot.

William Pitcher turned out to be extremely chatty, a mine of information about the club and its members. Glenn Branson had never considered that there might be a distinction between what defined a pond and a lake. Now, thanks to William Pitcher who enlightened him, he knew. Any body of inland water larger than half an acre was a lake. And what he was looking at was close to three and a half acres of prime trout water, although, Pitcher explained, it had a weed problem.

Weeds, it was shortly to turn out, were the least of this particular stretch of water's problems.

# 49

Amis Smallbone had fury boiling inside him. He padded towards the edge of the turquoise water of the swimming pool, every step with his blistered feet utter agony, stared at the four green cylindrical conifers in metal tubs at the far end, and puffed hard on the Cohiba.

It wasn't just fury. It was a maelstrom of rage. The eye of a tornado spinning inside his guts.

He sat in the swing sofa and took a slug of his drink. Focused so hard on his thoughts, he barely even noticed the icy, peaty taste of the vintage Jameson's Irish whiskey. There was blue afternoon sky above him. A jet made a vapour trail across it. Wednesday; coming up to his first week of freedom. Although, since his encounter with Grace, he'd resentfully checked in with the hostel and with his probation officer, not wanting to give the bastard another hold over him.

Years ago he had lived in one of the finest houses in this city, worth three million pounds; plus he'd had a villa in Marbella; an eighty-foot yacht; a Ferrari Testarossa. Now what did he have? Forty-six quid given him on his release from prison, plus his weekly benefit, which was a pittance.

What would that buy him?

Not even a round of this whiskey he was drinking now in a London hotel bar.

And one man was responsible for taking it all away from him. Not content with that, he'd made it clear he wasn't leaving him alone now that he was out of jail. The bastard had taken him to the top of the Devil's Dyke and utterly humiliated him – for something he hadn't done.

He had one small stash of money that Grace's team hadn't found. It was enough to tide him over for a few months in some comfort, but he needed to get back into business fast.

Henry Tilney, big and muscular, with a shaven head, black goggles over his eyes, was swimming laps in the kind of confident crawl that said *I ain't just the meanest sonofabitch in this pool, I'm the meanest sonofabitch in the world.*

How had this man evaded conviction, Smallbone wondered, while he had got a life sentence? Out on licence after twelve and a half years, sure, but he'd be straight back in again if he screwed up his licence conditions.

Had Tilney, as he'd long suspected, grassed him up? Was that why he was taking care of him now? To keep him sweet and stop him prying?

He watched as Tilney finished his swim, strutted into the pool house, water running off his skin, his balls and dick twitching visibly in the crotch of his budgie smuggler trunks, and came back out with a can of lager in his hand. He popped it open with a sharp hiss and raised it to his mouth as froth foamed out. After taking a deep swig he said, 'You should take a dip, twenty-nine degrees, mate – it's glorious!'

Smallbone scowled. 'Not my thing. Never liked water, you can't trust what's in it – or been in it.'

Tilney gave him a smile that masked unease. 'Yeah, well, I ain't pissed in it, in case you're worried.'

Smallbone shook his head. 'Not worried about you pissing in it, I'm more worried that Roy Grace pissed in it.'

Tilney frowned. 'What the fuck do you mean by that?'

Smallbone shrugged, noting Tilney's awkward body

language. 'He's pissed on my life. You're lucky if he hasn't pissed on yours, too.'

Tilney sat down in a sunlounger opposite him. 'Let him go.'

'Let him go? After what he did to me back then? And what he did to me last night?'

'He's a dumb-fuck copper on fifty grand a year and that's all he's ever going to be. You're sixty-two, Amis. Most people are thinking about retirement at your age. You don't have a pot to piss in. You want to spend the next few years making serious dough for your retirement, or hitting back at the police? You know where antagonizing Roy Grace'll get you? Spending your last years in some shitty Housing Association bedsit like Terry Biglow. That what you want? To be the next Terry Biglow?'

'I want Roy Grace,' Smallbone replied, his skin tightening so hard around his face that Tilney could see his skull beneath it. 'I've got information about him. Apparently the Chief Constable's made him personally responsible for looking after Gaia while she's in town. You know what I'm going to do? Piss on his parade, that's what. I'm going to make him look very stupid.' Then he gave a leer. 'I'm going to have her hotel suite burgled.'

'And where's that going to get you?'

Smallbone gave an oily smile. 'Revenge, all right? And a bit of money. I've spent twelve years dreaming about paying him back. You know what he did to me last night?'

'You told me twice already.'

'Yeah, well, I ain't Amis Smallbone for nothing.'

'You sure about that?'

'I thought you was my friend.'

'I am, mate, so let me give you some straight talking. The world has changed in the last twelve years, in case you was too busy to read a newspaper. Burgling's a mug's game, too much hard work, too high risk. Drugs and the internet's where the dough is – and with minimal risk. And you need to remember something.'

'What?' Smallbone asked, sullenly. He had the feeling he was being put in his place.

'You were never as good as you thought you was. Your dad – now there was a class act. Everyone feared your dad, and everyone respected him. You've always lived on that, traded on being your dad's son, but you was never half the man he was.'

'Shut the fuck up.'

'You need to hear this,' Tilney went on. 'You've always been small time, talking the big talk. You had all that flash stuff, the fancy houses, the cars, the yacht, but did you ever actually own any of it? It was all rented, wasn't it? All smoke and mirrors, that's why you ain't got nothing now.' He took a swig of his beer and wiped his mouth with the back of his hand. 'You know what I do? I look forward. You and Roy Grace, that's history. Forget about it. Forget Gaia – she's going to have bodyguards coming out of her jacksie while she's here.'

Smallbone glared at him.

'Grab yourself a beer, sit down, relax, chill out a little. In fact, hey, while you're about it grab two beers – one for yourself and one for your ego.'

# 50

David Green's strategy was to start a ground search of the area around the lake by Scenes of Crime officers, supervised by himself, and an underwater search of the lake by divers from the Specialist Search Unit, supervised by Police Search Adviser Sergeant Lorna Dennison-Wilkins, who had managed the search of the chicken farm.

The large yellow SSU truck was parked behind the growing collection of vehicles along the track which, to Glenn Branson's relief, so far did not include any reporters – one positive about this remote location.

Lorna Dennison-Wilkins was an elfin, attractive woman of thirty, with short brown hair. Glenn always found it hard to believe how ably she coped with the tough, grim jobs her unit faced almost daily. The SSU had to do all the tasks that were considered beyond the remit of ordinary police officers. These ranged from recovering decomposing corpses from sewers, wells, drains, the seabed and from lakes like this one, to crawling on their hands and knees doing fingertip searches in mud or excrement, such as in the chicken farm, to conducting the same kind of searches for body parts or murder weapons in waste tips. When they weren't doing that, they searched through the homes of drug dealers, risking at every moment being spiked by hidden hypodermic needles.

One image that had never left him was Lorna's description, a year or so back, of how she and her team had had to recover, from a frozen tree, fragments of the face, skull and brains of a man who had stuck a twelve-bore shotgun under his chin.

The silence of the lake and surrounding woodland was broken by the rasp of the outboard motor of the Specialist Search Unit's grey inflatable dinghy. Two of the team were in the boat, in scuba gear but minus their masks and tanks, one helming, the other studying the screen of the sidescan sonar. Glenn stood watching on the jetty. The smell of spent petrol from the outboard's exhaust suddenly reached his nostrils, momentarily blotting out the pleasant tang of muddy water and plants. As there was no permanent boat on this lake, they restricted the search area to what they estimated to be throwing distance from the bank.

The dinghy suddenly slowed, and there was a splash as a pink marker buoy was dropped into the water, marking the spot where there was an anomaly – something on the screen that looked as if it did not belong on the lake bed.

Over the course of the next forty minutes three more marker buoys were dropped – two in the far section of the lake. Then the dinghy returned to the jetty, and Glenn followed the two men back to their truck for a debrief.

The interior of the vehicle smelled of rubber, plastic and diesel. They sat around the small table, and Glenn was grateful for the mug of tea someone pushed in front of him. Jon Lelliott, one of the most experienced members of the unit, well able to read accurately the often indistinct images on the screen, said, 'There are four anomalies. Wrapped up, I think, corresponding in shape and size to human limbs.'

*

Outside, twenty minutes later, Crime Scene Photographer James Gartrell had finished taking photographs of the strip of suit cloth, which had now been bagged. He was now positioning his camera on a tripod directly above a muddy footprint that had been found in close proximity to where the fabric had been snagged on the gorse bush. A plastic yellow marker, stencilled with a black number 2, was wedged into the ground beside it, and a ruler lay alongside the footprint. This would enable him to make an exact size photographic print of it later. Working with precision, he was using a spirit level to ensure the camera was exactly perpendicular to the footprint, before setting up lights to ensure the camera recorded all the intricacies of the footprint as clearly as possible.

Five SOCOs were working through the dense, wooded surrounds of the lake in line formation. To avoid further contaminating the area by treading anywhere unnecessarily, Glenn returned to the observation post on the wooden decking of the jetty, where he had stationed himself, watching and waiting, on his phone most of the time, getting updates from members of his enquiry team. He also took a call from his solicitor, which ended with him shouting down the phone at the woman who was informing him that Ari had now changed her mind about the agreed custody arrangements for their children. In the meantime Bella was having a hard time back at the entrance gate, explaining to several club members who had turned up anticipating a quiet day's fishing, that their lake was now a cordoned-off crime scene.

Glenn ended the call to his solicitor, and glared out across the water for some moments. *Bitch. Bitch. Bitch.* Dappled sunlight was beaming down through the overhead branches from a clear sky. A pair of coots paddled jerkily out of a tall screen of reeds, curious but seemingly unconcerned about the divers. He watched a water boatman, about an inch long, sculling along just beneath him. Startled by a light splash from a fish rising, he looked back towards the middle of the lake and saw the concentric ripples where it had been.

Two divers were entering the water, one on the right and one on the left, each holding a black and red underwater recovery bag. They were in scuba outfits, with bright yellow harnesses from which a green and yellow cord trailed up to a spool held by an attendant, also in a dry suit, for each of them. A dive supervisor stood observing. Glenn, standing near him, watched as they sank below the surface in a maelstrom of bubbles.

This was a beautiful, peaceful place, he thought. There were worse places to spend a day. A fly-fishing club – William Pitcher had explained the difference between fly fishing and coarse fishing. As Branson now understood, anglers would only cast their feather trout flies on the surface; there were no weights to drag them down to the bottom. Whatever lay beneath could remain undiscovered for years, perhaps for ever. Making this a smart choice for a deposition site?

Behind him, he heard rubber-soled footsteps clumping along the wooden boards, then Bella's voice. 'This is so beautiful!' she said.

'Yeah,' he replied, with a grimace, still very churned up from the phone call. He could understand at this moment how people could murder their spouses.

Bella stood beside him and nodded, with a strangely sad smile. 'Ever fished?' she asked him.

'No, not my thing. Not sure I'd have the patience. You?'

'I prefer to catch mine already battered, with plenty of chips.'

He laughed, and then they began to chat more easily, although she still seemed more distant and less responsive today than last night. Perhaps it was him who was distracted, by his troubles with Ari and his constant longing for his kids – or perhaps she was fretting about her mother?

After some minutes, Jon Lelliott began wading out of the water towards them, holding a recovery bag with strands of weed hanging from it. He carried it across to the small SOCO tent which had been erected close by the SSU lorry.

Watched by Glenn and several others, he unzipped the bag very carefully. It contained what looked at first like a thin, dark-coloured log. It was only when Glenn looked closer that he could see clearly exactly what it was. A black bin bag, tied with fuse wire, wrapped around a long, narrow object, with something white protruding from the end.

A hairless human hand.

Glenn flinched in revulsion, but Bella stared at it with professional detachment. 'Left hand. It doesn't look at all decomposed, I would say it's not been in the water very long,' she stated with certainty in her voice.

Although he'd attended a number of grim crime scenes, Glenn had not, to his relief, had to deal with many dismembered corpses before. Even so, it didn't require any expertise to tell that this was not the work of someone with surgical skills. The partial limb looked like it had been hacked off with a blunt blade – the bone was splintered and there were tendrils of muscle and skin hanging around the end like a ragged fringe. It could almost have been a theatre prop, he thought. Or something from a joke shop. There was no smell of decay coming from it, another indicator that Bella was probably right that it had not been long in the water.

In which case, he thought, disappointed, it was unlikely to be connected to the torso from the chicken farm which had been there many months.

'Twenty-four hours, tops,' David Green said, joining them around the table. 'I would say much less. Otherwise crayfish, rats, voles or pike – if there are any – would have started taking nibbles from the exposed flesh. I'm actually surprised nothing's had a go at it already – crayfish are normally present within a couple of hours.'

'Unless there are more body parts down there which are keeping them happy,' Bella said.

'Quite,' Green agreed.

There were indeed more down there.

During the next hour and a half, the police divers recovered the rest of the left arm up to the shoulder, the lower right arm and hand, also severed at the elbow, and the rest of that, too. As well as both legs, each chopped into three parts. But no head.

Each body part had been wrapped in a bin-liner, weighted with a rock and tied with fuse wire.

Also, around the muddy and partly boggy shore of the lake, there were some footprints identical to the one close by the strip of cloth that had been spotted by William Pitcher, each in a position corresponding with throwing distance of where one of the body parts had been located. A numbered yellow marker lay beside each of them.

At the same time as the last of the body parts was being recovered, the SOCO team, in their line search, followed a trail of footprints leading away from the lake. At the end of this trail, in a shallow and evidently hastily dug hole, covered in branches, lay suit trousers and a jacket, matching exactly their sample strip of fabric.

A few minutes later, back at the rear of the Specialist Search Unit truck, each of the body parts lay wrapped in white plastic sheeting, tagged and dated. Glenn, sipping a mug of coffee, examined the suit through the plastic bags. But to his disappointment, whatever labels had once been sewn in had been removed.

Turning to Bella he said, 'So, what do you think?'

She shrugged. 'That there's a sodding Great White in there that ate the head and torso. The dive team must have missed it.'

He grinned. 'Yeah, my thoughts exactly.'

'Failing that, we might have some of the missing bits of our human jigsaw puzzle. Except the body is months old and these aren't.'

'With powers of observation like that, you could make a fine detective!'

'Flattery will get you anywhere,' she replied, and gave him a warm smile.

She seemed so vulnerable, he thought. She was a tough detective but a lost human soul. He wanted to put his arms around her and hug her, but this was not the time or place.

But, he decided, at some point in the very near future he would find the right time – and place.

# 51

Amis Smallbone decided he would find the right time and place, too. He stood alone on the terrace steps of Brighton's Grand Hotel, a Chivas Regal on the rocks in one hand, a cigarette in the other. He dragged hard on it, staring with small, hateful eyes out across the busy traffic of King's Road at people strolling along the promenade on the far side, and at the flat blue sea beyond.

He was dressed nattily but in dated style: blue blazer with shiny brass buttons, open-neck white shirt with a paisley cravat, blue chinos and blue and white Sebago deck shoes. He looked like he might have just stepped off a yacht. Like the sodding great one he was staring at right now, a showy motor cruiser, powering through the sea at a fast lick, a tall, mare's tail wake arcing behind it.

That could have been him on that yacht, he thought, taking another drag. If it had not been for Detective Roy Grace.

Henry Tilney was right, he knew. Leave it, put it behind him. But that had never been his way. People needed to be taught lessons. Grace had wiped him out. He'd lost everything. Twelve fucking years of his life locked up in shithole prisons, surrounded by losers.

Gaia was here in this hotel. Up in the Presidential Suite, having a cosy chat with Roy Grace at this moment, together with Chief Superintendent Graham Barrington and a bunch of other cops. He smiled as he crushed out the cigarette, drained the whisky and contemplated going back inside to order another. At least he still had some of his old sources. And one of them could give him access to any room in this hotel, twenty-four seven.

He could listen to the conversation in the Presidential Suite, too, at this moment, if he wanted, thanks to his old contact. But there was no need. He pulled another cigarette pack out of his left-hand jacket pocket. A tiny light winked on it – so faint it was almost impossible to see in this bright daylight. He returned it to his pocket with a smug smile. He would listen to the recording later, at his leisure.

\*

One floor above Smallbone, in the imposing, eau-de-nil, deep-carpeted sitting room of the Presidential Suite, Roy Grace, who was never normally star-struck, had to pinch himself. He was sitting on a sofa next to Gaia! And she was nice – she was warm, friendly and funny, not at all the diva he had been anticipating; but her presence was mesmerizing.

She was dressed in a man's shirt, white with the sleeves rolled up, ripped blue jeans and black suede ankle boots with buckles similar to a pair that Cleo had, except these looked more expensive. Her blonde hair had the freshness of someone who has just stepped out of the hairdresser's salon, and her face looked closer to thirty than the thirty-seven years she was carrying; she had a radiant complexion and not a single wrinkle. She was far more gorgeous in the flesh than in her photographs. And she smelled of an amazingly sexy, musky scent.

Glenn Branson would have killed to have been here, he thought, trying to avoid staring at her too much. But that was hard, especially with several top buttons of her shirt undone, revealing an erotic glimpse of her cleavage.

Lying on his tummy on the carpet, a short distance away from them and absorbed in an electronic game, was her son Roan, in jeans, a yellow T-shirt and sneakers, his hair awry.

'Presidential Suite' was a fitting name for this collection of rooms, he thought, sneaking another surreptitious glance at her. They were traditionally furnished in a sumptuous but traditional Regency style and had a regal air about them. Also seated with them in the room were two of Gaia's power-dressed female personal assistants, and her security chief Andrew Gulli, a dry, serious man, dressed in a business suit, white shirt and sombre tie. The police officers present were Chief Superintendent Graham Barrington, who was in uniform, DI Jason Tingley who was running the security operation for Brighton and Hove, and Greg Worsley from the Close Protection Unit, like Tingley wearing a suit and tie. All three of them seemed a little star-struck, Grace thought, like himself.

Outside on the landing, two of Gaia's man-mountain bodyguards stood sentry, and two other pairs covered each of the two fire escape doors from the five-room suite. In here, she was as safe as in Fort Knox.

And that was the problem.

All the time she was in here, they could keep her safe. But she had made it very clear she did not want to be a prisoner – she wanted to go jogging early morning every day, and more importantly to her, she did not want her son being brought up in a cocoon. She insisted on being able to take him to the beach, walk around the city freely with him, take him to a pizza place, or anywhere else he fancied.

It would have been a problem to protect a star of her calibre under normal circumstances, Grace knew, and these were far from normal. Someone had tried to kill her, and the perpetrator was still at large. That person could be here in this city right now. For all he knew, he – or possibly she – could even be in this hotel. The Threat Management Unit of the Los Angeles Police Department, who had been in close contact with Graham Barrington, were deeply concerned.

At least the Chief Constable, Tom Martinson, had had the good sense to throw the rule book – which restricted armed protection to royalty and diplomats – out of the window and sanction round-the-clock Armed Response Unit officers to protect her, provided the total cost did not fall on budget-restricted Sussex Police. Two of them had shadowed her car down from Heathrow Airport, and another two, in plain clothes, were in the hotel lobby. Close protection of this kind was expensive, but as Martinson had reasoned, the alternative, of something happening to Gaia while here in this city, would in the long term be far more expensive in terms of damage done to the city's image, and the fear it would instil in every potential visitor.

That Gaia was receiving this level of protection gave Roy Grace some comfort, but not enough. The Chief Constable had made it clear to him that, because of the attempt on her life and the homicide that had resulted, ultimate responsibility for Gaia's safety while in Brighton rested on his shoulders. But he insisted Gaia was going to have to contribute to the costs and in a phone call to him earlier, he had given Grace responsibility for negotiating this important aspect.

Brighton was a city riddled with alleyways, nooks, crannies, forgotten tunnels and secret passageways. If you were a killer lurking in darkness, you could find few darker places than here. The only way he could guarantee Gaia's safety, in his view, would be to ship her around from door to door in an armoured car, with a cordon of police surrounding her when she emerged. And that wasn't going to happen.

He turned and looked at her, and their eyes locked for a ~~nt~~. Hers were an iridescent metallic blue. They were ~~t~~ famous eyes in the world; they'd appeared ~~hs~~, and had been written about in a ~~trashy~~ magazine Cleo had ~~ed~~ they might actually be the ~~orld~~.

~~have~~ any quibble with that. Cleo ~~man~~ he had ever met in his life – not only stunningly beautiful, she ~~Gaia~~, for all her humour, for all her ~~hard~~ carapace. She'd be terrific for a ~~she'd~~ spit you out in the morning the ~~ow~~ spider eats her male after mating with him – and then excretes his remains.

Gaia suddenly leaned towards him. Embarrassingly close; and for an instant she was so close he feared she was about to kiss him. Then in her gravelly voice she said, 'Detective Superintendent Grace, you have eyes just like Paul Newman's. Did anyone ever tell you that?'

He blushed. Actually, yes, someone had. Sandy.

He shook his head, and with a coy smile said, 'No, but thank you!'

Across the room he saw Jason Tingley winking at him.

Trying to suppress a grin, Roy Grace addressed Andrew Gulli, as he reviewed the situation to date. He finished by saying, 'Although we appreciate the seriousness of the threat level in the USA, Mr Gulli, we are a long way away here. In our view, in the UK the threat to your client is low to medium.'

Gulli raised his arms in the air, in disbelief, and in his

James Cagney voice said, 'How can you guys say that? Anyone can buy a gun in this country for a few bucks. Don't try to kid us with that kind of bullshit!'

'With respect, we've delivered your client and her son safely here, and we've offered twenty-four-hour protection around her in this hotel.' He gave Gaia an apologetic look before turning back to Gulli. 'But what we cannot do is provide the budget to maintain security if she wishes roam freely around the city. The Chief Constable is wi to sanction armed protection, but you will have to c ute to the cost.'

'This would not happen in any other cou world!' Gulli said. 'Don't you realize the value ing to this city?'

'We're very privileged to have her here

'Hey, Andrew,' Gaia interrupted. 'I d lem. I think what Officer Grace is saying is fair. We'll contribute – why shouldn't we?'

'Because that's not how it works!' Gulli retorted petulantly.

'With respect,' Graham Barrington said, very politely and diplomatically, 'it is how it works in our country.'

'This is bullshit!' Gulli said, raising his voice almost to a shout.

Grace stood up, towered over him and said to him, 'Can you and I go and talk in private somewhere, for a minute?'

'Anything you have to say, you can say here.'

'I want to talk to you privately,' Grace said, in his sternest don't-mess-with-me voice. People often made the mistake of thinking, because Roy Grace was polite, that he was a pushover. Gulli was suddenly seeing another side to the detective. He stood up, a tad huffily, and pointed to an interconnecting door.

Grace led the way through into a room that had been turned into a makeshift office, and perched on the edge of a maple desk, signalling Gulli to close the door behind him. Through the window, Grace could see the derelict remains of the superstructure of Brighton's West Pier rising from the flat blue sea. He felt, as he always did, a twinge of sadness for the loss of this pier he had so loved as a child. Then he turned to face Gulli.

'How much is your client being paid to make this movie, Mr Gulli?'

'You know what? I don't think that's any of your business, Detective.'

'Detective *Superintendent* actually,' he corrected the man.

Gulli said nothing.

'Everything connected to this city is my business,' Grace said. 'I happened to read that Gaia's being paid fifteen million dollars – approximately ten million pounds – for four weeks' production here, and three in a studio.'

'She's one of the world's biggest stars, that's the kind of money they make,' Gulli said, on the defensive now. 'She's actually doing this for a lower fee than usual because this is an independent production and not a studio.'

'I'm sure she's worth every penny,' Roy Grace said. 'She's terrific, I'm a fan. But you need to understand something. Because of the financial crisis in this country, every police force has had to cut twenty per cent from its budget – Sussex Police has to lose fifty-two million pounds. That means that loyal officers are being forced into retirement after thirty years' service, when many of them had been counting on staying on for many years longer. Some of them will face real hardship as a result. Many of them joined the force in their late teens, which means approaching their fifties – still young by today's standards – they're going to be out of work. Some will not be able to pay their mortgages and will lose their homes. You might not think that's your problem.'

'You're right, it's not my problem.'

Grace pulled out his mobile phone. 'Tell you what I'm going to do. I'm going to call Michael Beard, the editor of our local paper, the *Argus*, and I'm going to tell him I'm standing here with you, and that although your client Gaia Lafayette is earning ten million pounds for this movie, she's not prepared to pay one penny towards the costs of her security while she's in this city. Are you okay with that? I guarantee you within twenty-four hours that will be on the front page of every newspaper in this country. Happy with that?'

Gulli gave him a sullen stare. 'What kind of contribution are we looking at?'

'That's better,' Grace said. 'Now, as you say in your country, we're on the same page.'

# 52

'And this is the master bedroom,' the young estate agent said. He was a cocky twenty-five-year-old, toned and muscular, with mussed-up hair, dressed in a charcoal suit and snazzy loafers.

'It's a good size,' he continued. 'Much more generous than you get with today's new-builds.'

She looked at the Mishon Mackay estate agency particulars, then stared around the room, taking in the ornate king-size brass bed, a mahogany dressing table, on which sat various bottles of perfume as well as make-up items, and next to it an Art Deco-style chaise longue. A silver framed photograph sat on the dressing table. It was of a couple in swimsuits, lying on the deck of a boat on a calm blue sea. He was smiling, his face tanned, with crow's feet around his clear blue eyes, as if squinting against bright sunlight, his short, fair hair ruffled by the wind. She was a good-looking woman, with long blonde hair, also flailing in the wind, a happy smile on her face, a slender body in a turquoise bikini.

That was the thing with photography, she thought. Those captured moments. The woman might have scowled ten seconds later, but the memory in that photograph would always be of her smiling. Like a poem by Keats she had read and memorized once, at school, 'Ode On A Grecian Urn'. It was about two lovers, in bas relief on the side of a Grecian urn, about to kiss. That moment frozen in time. They never would kiss, never consummate their relationship, and for that reason, that relationship would last for ever.

Unlike reality.

With a twinge of sadness she turned away and walked over to the window. It had a view of the back garden, and the rear of a neighbour's house in the next street along. She stared down at a wide strip of lawn, dominated by a Zen water feature in the centre – a cluster of smooth stones, with a dried-up channel around them and a fountain which was not switched on. The grass had recently been mown, but the beds on both sides and at the far end were choked with weeds.

'I'm afraid we'll have to keep moving,' the agent said, more arrogantly than apologetically. 'We have another viewing in twenty minutes. This kind of house is in big demand.'

She lingered for a moment before following him, staring around at the room again. It was too tidy, the bed not slept in, nothing lying around. It had an unaired, unlived-in feeling.

She followed the agent out, across the landing into another room, gently steering her small son, who was absorbed in a hand-held computer game. 'This is the larger of the spare bedrooms,' the agent said. 'It's a good size. Make a nice room for your son, I'd say.' He looked at the youngster for approval, but the boy did not take his eyes off his game, concentrating as if his life depended on it.

She looked around with interest. Someone was living in this room – a grown man. She noticed a row of highly polished, expensive-looking shoes lined along part of the skirting board. Several suits in dry-cleaner cellophane hanging haphazardly, for lack of a wardrobe. An untidily made bed. Then they went into the bathroom. A row of colognes, aftershave lotion, skin balm, an electric toothbrush and several luxurious black towels on the heated rail. There were moisture droplets inside the shower cabinet, indicating it had been very recently used, and a strong, lingering smell of a man's cologne filled the room.

'What is the owner's reason for selling?' she asked.

'He's a detective, I understand, with Sussex Police.'

She said nothing.

'This was his marital home,' he went on. 'I understand he's separated from his wife. I don't know any more, really. I can find out for you if you're interested?'

'I'm not interested.'

'I've got a cousin in the police,' he went on. 'He said the divorce rate's very high among coppers.'

'I can imagine.'

'Yeah. I suppose it's their lifestyle. Lot of shift work. Late hours, stuff like that.'

'Of course,' she said.

He led them downstairs, into the narrow hallway and through into the sitting room, which was decorated in a minimalist style with futon sofas, and a low, central Japanese table. In one corner stood an antique jukebox, and on the floor in front of it was a mess of old vinyl records, some out of their sleeves, and several untidy piles of CDs. 'This is nice, big windows and a working fireplace,' he said. 'A good family room.'

She stared around, while the boy continued playing his game, an uneven *beep-beep-beep, beep, beep-boing* coming from his device. In particular she stared at the jukebox. Casting her mind back to her life of ten years ago. Then they walked through into a large, open-plan kitchen-dining room.

'I understand this used to be two rooms which the owner knocked into one. It could of course be kept like this, or changed back to a separate kitchen and dining room,' he said.

*Of course it could!* she thought. And then she noticed the goldfish. It was in a round bowl on the work surface close to a microwave, with a tall plastic hopper for dispensing food, clipped to the side.

She walked over and pressed her face close to the bowl. The fish looked old and bloated, opening and closing its mouth in a slow, steady, gormless rhythm. Whatever golden orange colour it had once had was now faded to a rusty grey.

The boy suddenly looked up from his game, followed his mother over and peered into the bowl, too. '*Schöner Goldfisch!*' he said.

'*Wirklich hübsch, mein Schatz!*' she replied.

The estate agent watched her curiously.

'Marlon?' she whispered.

The fish opened and closed its mouth.

'Marlon?' she repeated.

'*Warum nennst du ihn Marlon, Mama?*'

'Because that's his name, *mein Liebling!*'

The agent frowned. 'You know its name?'

Could a goldfish live this long, Sandy wondered? Over ten years? 'Maybe,' she replied.

# 53

'Larry, we have a bit of a problem with the script,' the film's veteran director Jack Jordan said, peering up at the massive chandelier in the Royal Pavilion Banqueting Room. The craggy, world-weary film director, a few days shy of his seventieth birthday, seemed even more gloomy than usual. His eyes, shrouded by the long peak of his baseball cap, looked like two reluctantly prised-open molluscs.

Having forked out his last $100,000 to keep the production going, Larry Brooker was in no mood for yet another tantrum from this chronic worrier. He ended his phone call to their sales agent, who had the great news that he had just managed to sell Romanian rights in *The King's Lover* for 50,000 bucks. The agent assured him this was a very good price for Romania. Yeah, right, it might be, but at their current rate of cash burn, 50,000 bucks was barely enough to keep the pre-production going for four more days; and that was before deducting the 20 per cent sales commission that would be sliced off the top.

Brooker was feeling particularly spaced out and irritable today – a combination of jet lag, and the sleeping pill he had taken to counteract it which felt like it was only kicking in now, some fifteen hours after he had popped it. Problems. There were always problems on productions. As the producer, you had to keep the whole thing together, and you were always up against the wall of the schedule, with every conceivable event you could imagine conspiring against you to get less footage in the can each day than you needed – and as a consequence to send you soaring over budget. Production on any movie became a morass of many different, simultaneous problems melded into one giant motherfucker. Weather, accidents, tantrums, local bureaucracy, script lines that did not work when you tried to film them, neurotic actors, jealous actors, bitchy actors, egotistical actors, drunk actors, slow actors; God love them all.

In his experience the movie directors themselves were among the worst offenders. He'd never worked with one who hadn't moaned about the length of time he had to get a crucial scene in the can, or about the lack of budget for special effects, or the shooting schedule he was meant to stick to. Why did every fucking film director he'd ever worked with need a wet nurse?

'What kind of a problem, Jack?' he responded.

'Well, a bit of a technical problem with the script.'

Just from the way Jordan spoke, Brooker got the sense he was about to be mightily pissed off. In his baggy black T-shirt, even baggier jeans and his signature black Gucci loafers, he looked his director squarely in the eyes. 'What technical problem, exactly?'

All of Jordan's acolytes stood around him, like he was some kind of deity. The Location Manager, the Line Producer, the Production Secretary, the Production Designer, the Director of Photography, the First Assistant Director, and his Personal Assistant.

'With the script? What kind of *technical* problem?'

'Looks like whoever researched it has screwed up, big time.'

'Perhaps I could explain, Mr Brooker,' said Louise Hulme, the Royal Pavilion's resident historian who had been assigned to the production. She was a pleasant, academic-looking woman, with long fair hair clipped back, wearing a pink summer dress and sensible white shoes. 'You have this scene in your script which is a key moment in the relationship between King George and Maria Fitzherbert. It's when he ends their relationship by telling her he doesn't love her any more.'

Brooker squinted at her, not liking her school-marmy manner. 'You gonna tell me their relationship never ended?'

'Not at all, it did indeed end. But in your script, George tells Maria when they are seated next to each other at a banquet at this table.'

'Uh huh,' Brooker said. His phone vibrated. He pulled it out of his pocket, glanced at the display. INTERNATIONAL was all that was there. Probably someone calling about money he owed. He killed the call and turned his focus back to Louise Hulme.

'Well, the first problem is one of historical fact, Mr Brooker. You see, during the time when George the Fourth and Maria were lovers, this building was only a modest farmhouse. All the grand building works, such as this Banqueting Room, weren't started until a considerable time later. This room was actually completed five years after their relationship ended, so it is impossible that that conversation could have happened in here.'

She delivered the information with an assured, know-all smile that profoundly irritated Brooker. This room was stunning, it looked a fitting place for a king to dump his mistress. Who cared about historical accuracy? A handful of academic pedants, that was who. No one in a movie theatre in Little Rock, Arkansas, or Springfield, Missouri, or Brooksville, Florida was going to give a shit whether this room had been built then or not.

'I guess we'll have to take a bit of artistic licence there,' he said. 'This is a movie, it's entertainment, not a documentary.'

'Quite,' Louise Hulme said, with a smile that masked a frown of disapproval. 'But you do have another historical inaccuracy in your scenario.'

'What's that?' He shot a glance at Jack Jordan, whose gloom seemed to have deepened further, as if the world were now in the final seconds of countdown to self-destruct.

'Well, the thing is,' Louise Hulme continued, 'George did not have the courage to end the relationship face to face. So he did it in what I suppose would be the contemporary equivalent of an email, or even a tweet.'

'What did he do?'

'Well, he held a very important banquet in honour of the King of France – and did not invite Mrs Fitzherbert. In the court etiquette of the day, that was as formal a signal that a relationship was at an end as you could give.'

'Lady, I respect you know your history,' Brooker said. 'But that's just not something that translates cinematically. This is one of the biggest scenes in our movie. It's the emotional climax of our whole story! They're seated, centre stage at the table, surrounded by all these grand people, his friend Beau Brummell just opposite, and he drops the bombshell.'

'It's just not how it happened,' she said.

'Yeah, well, it's how it's gonna *have* to have happened! Just look at this room; look around it! This is one of the most stunning rooms I've ever seen. I can just imagine the light from the candles on the table and the chandelier playing on her face as she turns from delight to abject misery!'

'There's another problem, Mr Brooker,' she said, her tone becoming increasingly acid. 'About Prinny.'

'Prinny? Who's *Prinny*?'

The woman looked at him reproachfully. 'That was King George's nickname – the name everyone called him by.'

'Ah, okay.'

'You don't seem to have done your research very well,' Louise Hulme said. 'If you don't mind my saying.'

Keeping a lid on his anger, Brooker replied, 'Lady, you need to understand this is a movie, okay? I'm not a historian, I'm a movie producer.'

'Well, the thing you should know is that Prinny became very nervous about the chandelier – he refused to sit directly beneath it.'

He stared up at the vast crystal sculpture, suspended from the claws of a dragon beneath the domed ceiling. It was wonderfully dramatic. This was going to make an amazingly visual scene. 'Yeah? Well in my movie, he's gonna sit beneath it,' he said, defiantly.

Across the room, on the far side of the blue ropes that kept the public to a restricted route through the building, a lanky, cadaverous man in a baseball cap, who seemed like just another of the hordes of tourists that passed through this building daily, and was listening to the altercation, looked up at the chandelier, studying it intently.

# 54

'The time is 6.30 p.m., Wednesday, June the eighth. This is the tenth briefing of *Operation Icon*,' Roy Grace said to his team in the packed Conference Room in the Major Incident Suite. 'I will now summarize where we are.'

He was feeling in a good mood. He'd had a call from the estate agents, Mishon Mackay, to say they'd had some viewings of his house today. One, a woman, with a small boy, had seemed interested.

Looking down at his notes, he began his summary. 'Four limbs – two arms and two legs – were recovered in separate locations from the West Sussex Piscatorial trout lake near Henfield, West Sussex, this afternoon. They are currently at Brighton and Hove City Mortuary, awaiting examination tomorrow by Home Office pathologist Nadiuska De Sancha. DNA from each of them has been sent for analysis to see if there is a link with the torso recovered from Stonery Farm.'

'Good to know our investigation might now have a leg to stand on,' quipped Norman Potting, who was immediately silenced by a forbidding glare from Grace; but only for a brief moment.

'Sorry, Roy, didn't mean any 'arm.'

There was a titter of laughter, and Grace himself grinned, too. 'Shut it, Norman, okay?' He noticed an exchange of glances between Potting and Bella Moy, and waited for some withering comment to Potting from her, but she stayed silent so Grace pressed on.

'Darren Wallace at the mortuary, who has more experience than any of us in these matters, told me that the limbs seem very cold – far colder than they should be even allowing for the fact that they have been immersed in lake water. He surmises that they may have been frozen. I'm sure all of you who can cook know how long it takes to thaw a frozen leg of lamb?'

There were several nods.

'All I can say at this stage, from the initial mortuary report,' Grace went on, 'is that the jagged nature of the severed bones of the limbs bears a visual match with the corresponding areas of the torso, which gives us a timeline problem. It is possible that they've been kept refrigerated until now. This is far too early to be sure that we have found the missing limbs, but we could be looking at this lake as a second deposition site.'

'And if we haven't, chief,' Nick Nicholl said, 'then we have another murder enquiry on our hands?'

'Exactly,' Grace said. 'But I don't want to go there at this stage. My personal hypothesis is that the perpetrator got panicked by the appearance of the cloth on *Crimewatch* last night and decided to dispose of the remains in his possession. But at this stage this is highly speculative.'

'And does not explain the victim's head, which is still missing,' said DS Lance Skelton, the Office Manager for the investigation.

'Why would the perpetrator have retained the limbs, chief?' DC Jon Exton asked.

'I have no idea. That's our job to find out.' He looked down at his notes again. 'Right, missing persons. Norman, anything to report?'

'I have the outside enquiry team working through all mispers in Sussex, Surrey and Kent who correspond to the estimated date "Unknown Berwick Male" was killed, and to his build and estimated height. But I have nothing to report so far, boss.'

Grace thanked him then moved on. '*Acting Detective Inspector* Branson,' he said with emphasis, 'what can you tell us about the suit recovered at the lakeside?'

'I had to make a decision, boss, between leaving it with the tailor, Ryan Farrier at Gresham Blake, to see what we can learn about its owner from its size and construction, or sending it to the lab for immediate DNA analysis. But I thought in the interests of preserving any possible DNA it should go to the lab first.'

'That's the right decision,' Grace said. 'Maybe you could take this tailor up to the lab and he could examine it there.'

'I've arranged that already, for tomorrow morning!' Glenn said, with a grin.

Grace smiled back. He was so proud of his protégé. In his methodical manner, eye for detail and the way he thought for himself, Glenn was demonstrating more and more that he had all the makings of a very fine detective. He glanced back down at his notes. 'A substantial number of quality footprints were found at the site, some in the vicinity of the piece of cloth found on the gorse bush.' He paused to point to the blow-up and the sample strip pinned to the whiteboard at the end of the table. 'In particular several matching footprints were found around the perimeter of the lake, and beside the deposition site of the suit.' He turned to DC Exton. 'Jon, there were casts and photographs taken; I'm tasking you to find the manufacturer of this footwear. I suggest you start with the National Policing Improvement Agency – their National Footwear Reference Collection.'

'Right away, chief.'

'I've asked a forensic podiatrist, Dr Haydn Kelly, who is

one of the country's leading forensic gait analysts, to attend tomorrow evening's briefing – giving him time to analyse the footprints.' He looked up. 'Right, *Crimewatch*. Do we have any further leads from that?'

'Nothing significant, chief,' DC Nicholl said. 'We've had seventy-five calls so far, and three names. And a load of crank calls. The usual drunks calling in. One said his dad did it – and then went on to say his dad died five years ago. Another said that Kirsty Young did it. We graded the calls, as usual, A, B and C. The only Grade A was the angler, William Pitcher, this morning.'

Grace thanked him then asked, 'Does anyone have anything else to add?'

Several heads shook.

'See you all tomorrow at 8.30 a.m.'

As he left the briefing room and headed back along the corridor towards his office, he encountered the figure of Ray Packham, from the High Tech Crime Unit, walking urgently towards him.

'Roy! I've just had a chance to take a look at your Black-Berry.'

'Oh?'

They stopped beneath a large red noticeboard on which was a flow chart headed, *MURDER INVESTIGATION MODEL*.

'You were right to be concerned. You've been hacked.'

Grace stared back at the analyst, suddenly feeling profoundly uncomfortable. 'I have?'

Packham nodded.

'By whom?'

'I'm not sure you're going to like this. Perhaps we should go to your office?'

Grace led the way.

# 55

It was a warm evening and the breeze had dropped. Colin Bourner, the doorman of The Grand Hotel, stood proudly outside the front entrance. Across the clogged traffic of King's Road, and the people strolling or biking along the promenade on the far side, he stared at his favourite view of the sea, flat as a millpond, bathed in the early evening sun. The tide was far out; a handful of fishermen were digging for lugworm bait, and one man combed the wet sand with a metal detector.

On the pavement, closer to the hotel, a dozen paparazzi hung around, and a few fans strung out alongside them, all hoping for a glimpse of Gaia.

A turquoise Streamline taxi turned into the driveway and pulled up. One of the many things Bourner loved about this job was that you never knew who might be arriving. All kinds of celebrities – actors, broadcasters, sports stars, politicians and even royalty sometimes. The hotel was bristling with security – and buzzing with excitement – because they had a big celeb here at the moment, Gaia, who had arrived earlier today. Who knew who might be arriving in the back of this taxi?

He opened the rear door with the same welcoming smile he gave to all visitors to this hotel, and a blonde-haired apparition, caked in far too much make-up, stepped out in a cloud of musky scent. She was dressed in a short black dress that was too tight for her, a silk shawl and dark, wet-look leggings, and stood a little unsteadily on her ludicrously high black suede ankle boots, as if she were having difficulty with them.

'Good evening, madam, welcome to The Grand Hotel!'

She smiled back and trilled a lipsticky falsetto, 'Thenk yew.'

She paid the taxi then tottered across the pavement very slowly, fluttering her arms, as if she were being careful not to slip on ice, a bling handbag hanging from a shoulder chain. Then as she entered the revolving doors, she adjusted discreetly, but not that discreetly, the hem of her skirt, pulling it down in an ungainly manner.

Mutton dressed as lamb, Colin Bourner thought, watching her, trying to figure her out. She was dressed like a tart, but he knew all the regular ones who came in here, and this one was too old and too ugly. *Blimey!* he thought. Twenty-five years at this hotel, broken by a brief stint at another around the corner, and he'd seen it all. Every day provided him, at some point, with a new and fresh freak show. This was definitely today's highlight in that department.

Anna walked through into the cavernous hall, feeling very nervous all of a sudden. She had felt fine at home, preparing herself for this moment, thinking of all the signals her idol had given her on *Top Gear*. But now she was actually here, passing the front desk, looking at the signs ahead pointing to various functions – BRIGHTON BUSINESS CLUB . . . CRIMESTOPPERS GOLDEN HANDCUFF CLUB DINNER . . . BRIGHTON AND HOVE MOTOR CLUB . . . she was feeling the enormity of this place.

People everywhere. Hotel staff. Couples milling around, men in tuxedos, women in their evening gowns and finery. She felt almost underdressed.

Would Gaia approve?

Should she go home and change?

She paused and took a deep breath. Her hands were shaking, her throat felt dry, everything seemed suddenly to be in a haze, all in soft focus. She needed a drink, she decided. Dutch courage. Something strong but which wouldn't leave her breath reeking of alcohol. That would not make a good first impression on Gaia.

She walked through into the bar, and eased herself, very carefully, up on a stool, then ordered a double vodka with tonic. Moments later she changed it to a treble. There was a bowl of peanuts in front of her on the bar. She reached out a hand to take some, then hesitated and withdrew it. She'd brushed her teeth before leaving home, and Gaia might not like the smell of peanuts on her breath.

'Good decision!' said a portly, rather drunk-looking American sliding on to the stool beside her. 'Y'ever see that analysis on bar peanuts?' His voice was slurred and he reeked of tobacco.

She gave him a dismissive smile, then focused on the bartender who was mixing her drink.

'Urine and faeces,' the drunk continued. 'Yup. Analysis shows the average bowl of free peanuts on a bar top has twelve different traces of urine and three of faeces. People are goddamn disgusting, they don't wash their hands properly after using the bathroom.'

'Will you be running a tab, madam?' the bartender asked.

Anna shook her head and paid with cash. As she took the change, the American asked, 'You have dinner plans?'

'I do have plans,' she said very smugly. She reached for her drink and downed some gratefully, waiting for the buzz. It started coming on fast. She drank some more.

'Thirsty lady!' her new, unwelcome companion said. 'Let me buy you another.'

She looked at her large Panerai Luminor wristwatch, an exact copy of Gaia's. Except Gaia's was real, costing many thousands, and hers was a fake she'd bought on the internet for fifty pounds. It was coming up to 7.15 p.m. 'I don't have time,' she said.

'Cool watch!' he said.

'Thank you.'

'Perhaps we could meet later?' he persisted, then gave her a wink. 'Know what I mean? For a nightcap?'

She grabbed a handful of nuts and shovelled them into her mouth. When she had finished chewing and swallowing them she turned back to him, briefly flashed her teeth at him and said, 'Thank you, but I don't think you'd want to kiss me now!'

She drained her drink, feeling much more courageous, and slid carefully and as elegantly as she could down from the stool, with a contemptuous flick of her Cornelia James shawl. Then she made her way towards the front desk. She would have the receptionist phone up to Gaia that she was here.

# 56

Roy Grace sat behind his desk in his office and looked at the High Tech Crime Unit investigator Ray Packham, who took a seat opposite him. 'So, tell me?'

Grace liked the guy a lot, but always felt, because he looked so much like a bank manager, that he should be asking him for a loan, rather than for the deeply sensitive information that Packham, who was a technology genius, seemed to be able to mine from the innards of any computer or phone.

'Well, Roy, we found a suspicious code embedded within your BlackBerry's software. It did not correspond to any of the apps you have downloaded. We reverse engineered it, and found it's a sophisticated form of data logger. It encrypts all calls you make or receive, and texts – and sends them via email using your phone's 3G.'

Grace felt a chill ripple through him. 'All my calls?'

Packham nodded. 'I'm afraid so. I've checked with Vodafone, who are very co-operative these days.'

'Where've they been sent to?'

Packham smiled nervously. 'I did warn you that you're not going to like this.'

'I'm not liking this.'

He gave him the number, and Roy Grace wrote it down on his desk pad. He looked at it, thinking hard. It looked familiar.

'Recognize it?'

'Yes, but I can't immediately place it.'

'Try entering it in your phone,' Ray Packham said, with a wry smile.

Copying the numbers off the pad, Grace tapped them in. As he entered the last digit, a name appeared on the display of his BlackBerry.

Grace stared for some moments in disbelief. 'That fucking little shit!'

'I could not have put it more eloquently myself, chief!'

# 57

A smart man in his early thirties, flanked by two equally smart women, stood behind The Grand Hotel's wooden reception desk. He smiled warmly as Anna approached.

'I've come to see Gaia Lafayette,' she said.

His demeanour changed, very subtly, from warm to defensive, and he studied this rather strange-looking woman more closely. She looked weird enough, certainly, to be a friend of the star. 'Is she expecting you, madam?' He had a slight foreign accent, perhaps French, Anna thought.

'Yes, she is,' she said, the vodka giving her a lot of confidence and a calm, assured manner. *Actually she gave me the signal on Top Gear*, she nearly added, so confident was she feeling, but she held that nugget back.

'May I have your name, please?'

'My name?' For an instant, Anna was thrown. 'She will of course know it's me!'

His smile faded. 'Yes, but I will need your name, please.'

'Right!' She nodded assertively. 'Tell her Anna. Anna is here.'

'Anna?' he waited patiently.

'Anna.'

'Your last name?'

'My last name?'

She didn't like the way he was looking at her. *Last name.* Maybe she shouldn't have had that vodka. The haze was returning. She had to blink hard to bring him back into focus. 'Just tell her that Anna is here,' she said, impatient now.

He put his hand on the phone receiver. 'I will need your last name,' he said. 'For Security.' He glanced down. 'I have a list and don't see your name, Anna, on it. Perhaps your last name?'

'Galicia,' she replied.

'Galicia?'

'Yes.'

She could feel herself perspiring. Her armpits were damp. She hoped she had applied enough Gaia Nocturne Roll-On.

He looked down at the list and shook his head. Then he dialled a number, and after a few moments said, 'I have Anna Galicia in reception to see Ms Lafayette.'

While he waited for the reply, Anna took the opportunity to try to read the names on his list, upside down. She saw *Daily Mail*.

The receptionist turned back to her after some moments, and said, 'I'm sorry, you are not on their list.'

She reddened. 'Um, yes, well, that's probably because I'm a freelancer on the *Daily Mail*, not on staff, but I'm here from the *Mail* – to do a feature on Gaia.' She fumbled inside her handbag and produced the false press card she'd made herself some years ago; it was useful for getting into the VIP areas of Gaia concerts.

That made sense to him; she looked a little kooky, the way some female journalists did; he'd seen plenty of journalists interviewing stars in here, and in the Lanesborough, where he worked previously, in London.

He took the card and read it, then said, 'They're expecting someone with a different name.'

Anna shrugged as if butter would not melt in her mouth. 'I was asked to substitute at the last minute.'

'Please go up to the first floor.'

As she turned away, knowing this had all been pre-planned by Gaia – just a little test for her! – she saw a group of people, three women and two gay guys she knew, fellow serious Gaia collectors, seated on a pair of sofas, all clutching record sleeves and CD booklets.

'Anna, come and have a drink!' one of the guys, Ricky – whose eBay identity was *Gaia Slave* – called out to her.

'Thank you, but I'm actually on my way to meet Gaia,' she replied, very smugly.

'Never!' said the youngest of the group, a girl in her early twenties. Her name was Kira Ashington, and she had purple streaks in her hair. Kira had a dog-grooming business and, to Anna's fury, frequently outbid her in online auctions for Gaia memorabilia. It was delicious now to be able to take such sweet revenge.

'I actually have a personal invitation from Gaia,' Anna said, trying to look nonchalant.

'How – how – how did you get that?' Ricky was so chewed up with envy he could barely get the words out.

'Because I'm her number one fan! She recognizes that.'

'God, you are so lucky! Couldn't her number two fan come with you?' Kira asked.

'Not tonight, Josephine.' Anna blew her a kiss.

'Have a wicked time!' Ricky said.

'Thank you.' With her head held very high, Anna walked towards the lifts. She had never felt so proud in all her life.

\*

Some moments later, as the lift doors opened, Anna stepped out on to the carpeted corridor. Two hulks, each wearing an earpiece attached to a cord, stood either side of a door, backs to the wall. They gave Anna a hostile look, like she was a herpes virus.

Walking up to them, feeling decidedly unstable on her heels now, thanks to that vodka, she announced herself and produced her press pass.

'You ain't expected, lady,' the one on the left said, his lips barely moving.

'Oh yes, I am expected. I'm Anna Galicia. Gaia's expecting me.'

He looked down at her with big eyes, as expressionless as barren planets. 'Not tonight, lady, she ain't. She ain't taking no more interviews.'

'She is expecting me, she most definitely is!'

The giant on the right stared at her morosely. The one on the left said, 'The boss is tired, she's just flown the Atlantic. She's done with interviews tonight. You want to make an appointment to interview her, call her in the morning.'

'You don't understand!' Anna said. 'I'm not interviewing her – we – we're having a drink together! She invited me!'

'You Anna Galicia?'

'Yes I am!'

'Your name ain't on the list, lady.'

Anna felt frustration building inside her. 'Fuck the list!' she said.

He shrugged. 'You wanna see the boss, you have to be on the list.'

'There's been a mistake! Really, a mistake. Please, ask her! Tell her Anna is here! Anna Galicia! She will know me! She's expecting me. She'll be mad at you if you don't let me in, I promise you!'

He spoke quietly into his mouthpiece. Anna lip-read what he was saying. He was asking for confirmation. Her chest was heaving with frustration. Gaia was in there! The other side of that door. She was just feet away from her number one fan. For God's sake, just feet away! Gaia wanted to meet her, she'd made that very plain, and now these morons were stopping her!

'Sorry, lady, they're telling me they don't know who you are.'

Anna began drawing shorter and shorter breaths as her anger surged. 'I'm not just another reporter, I'm her number one fan!' she said. 'Her number one fucking fan! If it wasn't for me she'd probably be turning tricks in a seedy massage parlour – and you'd be totally somewhere else! She wants to see me. Now!'

The two guards exchanged a glance. Then the one she was talking to said, 'I'm sorry, lady, I'm going to have to ask you to leave.'

'Over my dead body,' Anna said.

Then, to her astonishment, she saw a door open along the corridor and a woman, wearing a baseball cap, dark glasses, a crimson jogging suit and fancy trainers, emerged.

It was her!

'Gaia!' she called out, and began stumbling towards her. 'Gaia, it's Anna!'

Moments later both her arms were seized, gently but firmly, and her idol was engulfed by a platoon of body-guards also in jogging suits and baseball caps, who swarmed out of the door.

'Let me go!' Anna shrieked at the two hulks restraining her.

The lift pinged and she saw the entourage enter.

Anna wriggled furiously. One of her shoes came off. 'You have no right to do this. Let me go!' she yelled.

The lift doors closed, and then they released her. Anna's brain was racing. There must be an exit! Doors! Fire doors! Staircase! She saw it down to her right. A green FIRE EXIT sign. She knelt and grabbed her shoe, but without wasting time putting it back on, she broke into a hobbling run, holding the shoe in one hand, along the corridor, through the fire exit door and down the concrete stairs.

LOBBY LEVEL, she read, in small letters, and pushed open the door. She was in an unfamiliar part of the ground floor, with a sweeping staircase right behind her leading up to what looked like a conference level. Where was the lift she'd gone up in?

Then she saw the entourage stepping out across the hall. The cluster of jogging bodyguards, and in their midst she caught a glimpse of Gaia. She ran forward, still holding her shoe, calling out, 'Gaia! Gaia! It's Anna! Wait!'

She dodged past a small group of Japanese men, each towing a wheeled suitcase, and caught up with the entourage yards from the revolving door. 'Gaia! It's me, Anna!' she called out again, racing to reach the door ahead of them, but two of the guards elbowed her aside.

'Hey!' she said indignantly, and pushed back, almost getting past them, and suddenly Gaia was right in front of her! Her face inches from her own. So close she could smell Gaia's perfume, and was a little surprised it was not her idol's own brand. 'Gaia! It's Anna! Hi—'

For a fleeting instant, Gaia raised her sunglasses, gave her a hard, blank, icy stare, then turned away and was gone, through the revolving door.

'Secret fox!' Anna called out desperately. 'Gaia, it's me, Anna! Anna! Secret fox!' She lunged towards the door, but two of the tracksuited guards grabbed her arms, holding her back.

'Let go of me!' she yelled.

They continued holding her, so hard they were hurting her arms. She dropped her shoe. She wriggled like a wildcat, broke free, lost her balance and fell backwards to the floor, right on top of her fallen shoe which dug painfully into the small of her back.

She looked up, dazed and confused for an instant, and saw the five fellow Gaia collectors all looking at her. Ricky – *Gaia Slave* – came over to help her, but a hotel porter reached her first, knelt and asked if she was all right, then gently held her arm as she got back to her feet. Everything was spinning inside her head. Somehow she got her shoe back on. She saw the five collectors staring at her.

'We thought you were her number one fan, Anna!' Kira, the girl with the purple streaked hair, said mockingly.

All five of them laughed.

Anna walked out through the revolving doors and stood on the pavement. She was breathing in short, hard, angry bursts. The paparazzi, she could see, were running across the road, chasing after the pack of joggers that was heading away along the promenade.

'Can I get you a taxi, madam?' the doorman asked.

'I don't want a fucking taxi,' she said, smarting with humiliation and shaking with rage, struggling to open the clasp of her handbag. Then she rummaged inside it and pulled out her mobile phone. 'I've been assaulted, I want the police.'

# 58

For the first time since Ari had thrown him out, Glenn Branson was in a sunny mood. He left MIR-1 feeling like a man on a mission. He would surprise Bella, he thought. Cheer her up. He knew that visiting hours at the hospital would be over shortly.

He drove to his local Tesco Express, bought a bunch of sweet-smelling flowers and a box of Maltesers. Then he stopped by an off-licence he favoured, Mullholland's Wines on Church Road, and selected a bottle of chilled Sauvignon Blanc from the cooler, which he remembered her telling him in Cardiff that she liked.

He drove down to his lodgings in Roy Grace's house off Church Road, had a quick shower, brushed his teeth and sprayed himself with his current favourite cologne, Chanel Blue. He fed Marlon and hurried back out to his car. Remembering Bella's address from having dropped her home once before, he entered it in the satnav stuck to the dash of his ancient Ford Fiesta, and was just reversing out of the drive when his phone rang. It was 8.25 p.m.

He stopped, debating for a moment whether to ignore it. But in his new, elevated status of deputy SIO he was on call round the clock. Ignoring it was not an option. 'Glenn Branson,' he answered, somewhat reluctantly, hoping to hell, just at this moment, that there wasn't an urgent new development on *Operation Icon*.

It was Roy Grace.

'Yo, old timer, you're up late for a man of your age!'

'Very witty. Not interrupting you, Glenn, I hope?'

'Nah, I was just discussing the meaning of life with Marlon.'

'He should get out more. Come to think of it, so should you.'

'I'm working on it.'

Grace's tone became more serious. 'Okay, we have a development.'

*Shit*, Branson groaned inwardly. 'We do?' he said, trying to sound enthusiastic.

'The Specialist Search Unit have located a human head. They think it might be Berwick Male's head.'

This time Branson's enthusiasm was genuine. 'Where?'

'It's in a shallow grave in a ditch, about a quarter of a mile west of the lake where they recovered the limbs earlier today. Because there's no Home Office pathologist free tonight, we have one coming tomorrow morning at seven, Ben Swift. Can you meet him at the site? I'll cover the morning briefing.'

'Of course, chief.'

Grace's voice sounded a little strange, a lot more formal than usual, as if he were considering his words carefully. 'Okay, I'm going to give you the compass co-ordinates. Got something to write them down on?'

Branson pulled his notepad out of his pocket. 'Ready.'

Grace repeated the directions, which Glenn already knew, to the West Sussex Piscatorial trout lake, near Henfield. He was a little surprised at the elaborate directions the Detective Superintendent gave him, as if Grace did not realize he had already been there for much of today. But all the same, he dutifully wrote them down, and the precise co-ordinates.

'We've been lucky so far that the press haven't cottoned

on. Hopefully we can recover the head before we have to worry about the next stage of our press strategy,' Grace said.

'Guess we're lucky that Spinella's away on honeymoon,' Branson said.

'Clearly there is a God!'

*

Worthing was the next coastal town west from Brighton and Hove. With its Victorian pier, faded Regency buildings and wide promenade, it had a generally calm air, compared to the edgy vibrancy of its racy neighbour to the east. Glenn Branson had always liked the place, despite its reputation as a major retirement centre and the sobriquet that went with that, of 'God's Waiting Room'.

The satnav took him on a route that bypassed the town itself, and down into a suburb, Durrington, and into a broad network of streets lined with postwar bungalows, two-storey houses and shopping parades. The kind of pleasant, utterly civilized open area, peppered with yellow Neighbourhood Watch signs in front windows where, you felt, nothing bad could ever happen to any of its residents.

He slowed to 28 m.p.h. as he approached a speed camera, then made a right, followed by a left, obeying the dictatorial commands of the woman's voice from inside his TomTom, then made another right on to Terringes Avenue. It was a quiet street of neat red-brick houses; he drove along, peering through the twilight at the house numbers.

'You have arrived!' the satnav announced.

He saw 280 on his right, 282, then 284.

He felt a sudden flutter of nerves. God, this was how he had felt – how many years back? – when he was first dating Ari!

Number 284 was on a junction. He drove past the house and turned right, drove a hundred yards then made a U-turn and parked.

*Calm down!*

He could smell the scent of the flowers.

*What the hell am I doing here?*

His insides were jangling, as if he'd stuck his finger into an electrical socket.

*Calm down!*

He took some deep breaths.

What if she was out?

What if she told him to get lost and made a complaint about sexual harassment?

For a moment, he was tempted, very seriously tempted, to twist the ignition key, tramp the accelerator and get the hell out of there.

*You're not even divorced, man!*

He ruminated on that for some moments.

Yeah, but.

He got out of the car, scooped up the bottle and flowers, and locked the doors. He walked the short distance up to Terringes Avenue, turned left towards Bella's home, and then froze.

A man was standing outside her front door, clutching a huge bouquet of flowers in his arms. A man he recognized.

He could not believe his eyes. No way, it absolutely could not be him! But it was.

The door opened, and Bella stood there, wearing a short dress, her hair looking like it had just been done, as it had last night.

She looked like she had been expecting him. He said something and she laughed. They kissed, just a fleeting peck. Two people comfortable with each other.

Norman Potting went inside and the door closed behind him.

Glenn stood there, gobsmacked. Then, slowly he walked back to his car, stopping on the way to jam the bouquet into a dustbin.

He drove off at speed, shaking his head in anger, astonishment and self-pity, the wine bottle rolling on the passenger seat beside him. Norman Potting. Incredible! Like, it did not make any sense. What the hell did she see in an ugly old lech like him?

Clearly something.

Or had he totally misread it?

# 59

'You bitch! You cut me dead!' Anna screamed at Gaia.

Her idol stared icily back.

'You humiliated me in front of so many people. You can't do that, you can't treat people like that, do you understand?' She was gripping the knife in her hand. It was an antique dagger with a scabbard that she had kept in her handbag ever since a man tried to attack her outside a nightclub in Brighton, a few years ago.

She had learned from an episode of *CSI* that it was dumb to use an ordinary household knife to stab someone. Invariably the knife would strike bone and when that happened your hand would slip forward along the handle, and the blade would slice into your hand. As a result you would leave some of your own blood at the scene. A dumb way to get caught. But if you used a dagger with a guard, that would stop your hand sliding forward.

'You think you can just treat people how your mood takes you? One moment sending them passionate signals and the next cutting them dead? How would you like to be cut dead?' She raised the dagger, the blade glinting in the overhead light. 'Do you think all of us who love you would still love you if your face was a mass of scars? How much value would you have then, do you think?'

She stared at her, hatred blurring her vision. 'All this stuff of yours, this tat, this grot, this rubbish we pay a fortune for on eBay. Do think we'd still pay the same if you had knife cuts all over you? Well, do you? Can't you speak?

Cat got your tongue? How would you like to try singing with your tongue cut out? People did that to their enemies in some countries once. If they got screwed. They'd use red-hot pincers to pull their tongues right out of their throats. You wouldn't look so damned great going on stage and trying to sing without your tongue, would you? You wouldn't make much of a lover for King George in this film, would you? You'd be pretty useless at kissing, and you wouldn't be that great at giving him oral sex. Have you thought about that?'

She waited.

'Have you?'

She waited again.

Then, screaming at the top of her voice, and shaking with rage, 'HAVE YOU?'

She slashed the knife forward, ripping across Gaia's face, right from the side of her forehead, across her right eye, down her cheek. The cardboard cut-out fell off the display stand and tumbled to the floor.

Anna stared down, dagger held high, gripping it even harder. Gaia stared up at her from the beige carpet, the rip clear and even across her face. 'Listen to me, bitch.' She knelt, staring down into Gaia's eyes. 'No one stays on a pedestal who doesn't deserve it – no one, not for ever. You'd better understand that. You'd better understand what you did tonight. Look at you now,' she sneered.

Mimicking 1950s sex idol Betty Page, Gaia had her hair died black, with a fringe, and was wearing a see-through black negligee. Bondage tape was wound across her mouth. There was Japanese writing on the front, below her face, and it was signed by Gaia. The poster came from her second Japanese tour and was one of only four in existence. Anna had paid £2,600 for it five years ago.

'We build you up, and we can smash you down just as easily. See? See what a worthless bit of cardboard you've now become, bitch?'

She put the knife down, raised her hand making their special sign. 'Secret fox!'

# 60

Glenn was still thinking about Norman Potting and Bella Moy at 6.45 the next morning, as he made the now familiar left turn at the West Sussex Piscatorial Society sign and crossed the cattle grid. Ominous clouds were thickening overhead and he didn't need the weather forecast on the radio to tell him a deluge was on its way. Rain was not good news for an outdoor crime scene.

In the city, the uniform division called it 'Policeman Rain'. The streets were always much quieter when it was raining, there were fewer street fights, fewer muggings and bag snatches, fewer break-ins, and fewer drug dealers lurking on corners. Villains did not like getting wet any more than anyone else. But for crime scenes, heavy rain was the worst news, because crucial evidence, such as tyre marks, footprints, clothing fibres and hairs could get washed away very rapidly.

He was excited by Roy's news last night that a head had been found. There was no guarantee it would turn out to be 'Unknown Berwick Male's', but if his clothes were here, and it matched the limbs, then it was highly likely. And if they had the head, they might be able to get a visual identification of the victim, and failing that, identification through dental records. Quite apart from anything else, the swifter this investigation moved forward under his stewardship, the better it would reflect on him.

It was strange, he thought. On all previous murder investigations he had been on, he – and every member of the enquiry team – developed empathy with the victims, and it became personal, a determination to bring the perpetrator to justice. But at the moment, although a man was dead, without knowing his identity he felt distanced from him.

As he drove through the abandoned farmyard development, he was a little surprised not to see the big yellow SSU truck in situ – if they had found the head last night, he would have thought they would have been out in force here from first light today, doing a fingertip search of the area around it. But it was possible they had been called out to an emergency operation somewhere else. The only vehicles here were a marked police car, its windows drenched in dew, belonging to the hapless officer on the last shift of overnight crime scene guard duty, standing forlornly in front of the tape, and a small blue Vauxhall Nova. It might be the Home Office pathologist's, he speculated, but he would have thought that covering the mileage he did, and carting around his equipment, he would have had a more substantial vehicle.

He pulled alongside it and, before switching off the ignition, checked the overnight serials on the car's computer, to see if there had been any incidents logged that might have required the SSU's attendance. But it had been a quiet night, just run-of-the-mill stuff. A car theft, two RTCs, a robbery at the Clock Tower, a smashed window at Waitrose, a boat set on fire at the Marina, two domestic fights. He climbed out and peered through the Vauxhall's window, but the interior of the car looked as pristine and impersonal as a newly collected rental.

He opened the boot of his car and struggled into a protective suit, then pulled on the gum boots he had brought, not making the same mistake as yesterday of ruining his shoes in the mire. Then he clumped his way carefully through the slippery mud of the track and up to the very young woman police officer, and held up his warrant card. Her name badge read PC Sophie Gorringe.

'I'm the deputy SIO – everything all right?'

She nodded and gave him a stoic smile. She looked in her late teens, and could have barely left college, he thought.

'Long vigil?'

'Two hours to go, still,' she said. 'Nicer since it got light – it was quite spooky when it was dark – kept hearing an owl.'

'Whose is that car?' He jerked a thumb over his shoulder.

Sophie Gorringe was about to speak, when he heard a familiar chirpy voice behind him.

'Mine, Detective Sergeant Branson!'

Glenn recognized the voice instantly. 'Aren't you supposed to be on honeymoon?' he said in dismay, as he turned.

The twenty-five-year-old reporter from the *Argus* smiled smugly. He was thin faced, with short, gelled-back hair, wearing a dark grey suit with a white shirt and a narrow tie, and chewing gum, as ever. His face was nut brown, except the tip of his ferret-like nose which was pink, from having peeled. 'Seems like I came back just at the right time.' He was clutching his notepad.

Glenn heard a car, and a moment later Roy Grace came into view, driving his unmarked silver Ford Focus estate.

Spinella's phone rang, and he turned away from Branson to answer it. It sounded like he was being given instructions for another job after he had finished here. Just as he ended the call Roy Grace strode up to them, in gum boots but not in a protective suit.

'Nice honeymoon?' he asked the reporter.

'Beautiful – ever been to the Maldives?' Spinella asked.

'No, I'm on a copper's salary not a bent reporter's.'

'Haha,' Spinella said. But his laughter was uneasy. There was a tenseness in Grace's demeanour that Glenn could sense, as, clearly, could the reporter.

'So, what exactly brings you here, Kevin?' Grace asked him.

Spinella grinned. 'You know me and my contacts.'

'So you got tipped off that we've found a head – possibly belonging to the missing torso?'

'Yes – so – I thought I'd better get straight down here and see what – er – what you'd like me to put in the paper.'

'You did, did you?'

Branson frowned. He knew Grace did not care for this reporter, but his attitude was considerably more hostile than normal. The reporter shuffled from foot to foot.

'Yeah, you know,' Spinella said. 'To help you with your enquiry – that's how we like to work with each other, isn't it, Detective Superintendent?' His eyes went shiftily from Grace to Branson and back to Grace.

'Who told you about the head?' Grace asked.

'I'm sorry, Detective Superintendent, I can't reveal my sources.'

'Perhaps that's because you don't have any,' Grace retorted.

'How – how do – I mean – I can't reveal them.' Spinella looked distinctly uneasy.

Suddenly, surprising Glenn Branson and Spinella, Grace lunged forward and snatched the reporter's phone from his hand. 'Kevin Spinella, I believe a criminal offence may have been committed. I'm arresting you on suspicion of illegal telephone hacking. You do not have to say anything; but it may harm your defence if you do not mention, when questioned, something that you later rely on in court. Anything you do say may be given in evidence.'

Spinella's eyes widened in shock. 'You – you can't – you can't do this to me – you – you . . .' He stared at the handcuffs Grace had suddenly produced.

'Can't I?'

Roy Grace rarely handcuffed people himself these days. But one technique he had never forgotten was how to speed cuff a villain. He snapped one, in one sharp, continuous movement, on Spinella's right wrist, jerked his left arm behind his back and snapped the handcuff on that, too.

'What's this all about?' Spinella demanded sullenly, but already the tone of his voice had changed and he was sounding anxious rather than insolent.

'There is no head that's been found,' Grace said. 'I made that up. You swallowed it, hook, line and sinker.'

Glenn Branson grinned. 'That's quite appropriate, chief, for this location.'

Grace smiled back grimly.

# 61

'Who's your fat friend?'

They all looked at the guide in astonishment. She was standing in the hall of the Royal Pavilion beneath a portrait of the corpulent figure of King George IV.

A knot of nineteen of the twenty visitors to the Royal Pavilion were gathered tightly around her, hanging on every word. Just one person, standing right at the back, had his attention somewhere else altogether.

'Oh my God!' an elderly American woman wearing a plastic rain hood exclaimed. 'He said *that*? To the *king*?'

The guide, a woman in her early fifties, had the authority of a school headmistress about her. 'He did indeed,' she said firmly. 'You see, Beau Brummell was a very well-known figure – a real Regency dandy. Tall, quite statuesque, always immaculately dressed and coiffed, whereas poor George just got fatter and fatter as he got older and looked less and less distinguished. Well, they had a bit of a falling out. Beau Brummell, Lord Alvanley, Henry Mildmay and Henry Pierrepoint were considered the prime movers of what Lord Byron styled the Dandy Club. The four of them hosted a ball in July 1813 at which George, still then the Prince Regent, greeted Alvanley and Pierrepoint but cut Beau Brummell dead. Getting his own back, Brummell turned to Alvanley and said, very disdainfully, "Alvanley, who's your fat friend?" '

Drayton Wheeler was grateful for the pelting rain, because it enabled him to wear a baggy mackintosh with the collar turned up, and a wide-brimmed hat low down over his face. This was his third visit here in three days, and he was concerned not to be noticed by any of the staff, especially the security guards, so on each occasion he had worn different clothing. As the guide continued talking about the rift between George and Beau Brummell, he stared nervously at the closed, ochre-painted half-gate at the top of a stone staircase that led down into the basement of the building.

He checked the inside pocket of his jacket, and felt the reassuring lump of folded papers – the set of plans for each floor of this building he'd purchased from the Planning Office yesterday. He'd spent much of the night studying and memorizing them. He looked over the gate and down the staircase again.

'Poor Prinny's obesity became a very big issue for him,' the guide droned on. 'There is an underground passage running from here to what was once the royal stables. Prinny had it built because he was so ashamed of how gross he looked that he didn't want the public to see him. He went up to twenty stone in weight. So he could come and go in private!'

Wheeler looked furtively around. There was no guard standing in the hallway. The people in front of him blocked the guide's view of him. This could be his best chance. He stepped back a few paces, peered over the top of the gate, and saw it was secured shut by a small brass bolt. He looked back at the crowd. No one was looking his way. He lowered his hand over the top, felt the bolt and tested it. It made a scraping sound as he slid it open. He froze, looked down the staircase, then at the crowd on the guided tour, then along the hallway in both directions.

Then he pushed the gate open, stepped on to the

staircase, rapidly closing the gate behind him, then crouched, for a second, listening, his heart hammering, his ears pounding. Then he hurried down the steps, still crouching, and turned right at the bottom, entering a long, narrow corridor with a brick floor that, in contrast to the immaculately maintained and presented public areas, was dusty and shabby and poorly lit. He walked past a decrepit green door, sagging on its hinges, with a yellow and black DANGER – HIGH VOLTAGE sign on it. A cobweb across the top left corner of the door showed it had not been opened in a while.

Perfect.

He pulled it open. The hinges shrieked and the bottom of the door scraped on the bricks. He looked around nervously, but there was no sign of anyone. He peered inside and saw a whole wall of fuses and electrical switchgear, and some pipework that looked like it was lagged in asbestos. But crucially, there was enough floor space for him to be able to sit down.

He entered and pulled the door shut again, with some difficulty. It smelled fusty and there was a faint humming sound, as well as a steady, rhythmic ticking. It felt as warm as an airing cupboard. He took out the torch he had brought along, and his Kindle from the bag of provisions he had concealed beneath the mackintosh, which he folded to use as a cushion, then squatted down on the floor for the long wait until this evening, when the whole place would be locked and deserted.

He fired up his Kindle, then at the same time pulled his wallet out of his coat pocket, and flipped it open. A small boy in a grubby T-shirt, with messy hair either side of his *LA Lakers* baseball cap, grinned cheekily back at him. Six years old, standing in the back yard of their old home in

Pasadena, in front of a row of sunflowers, taller than he was. Taller than he would ever be.

His only son. Wearing his thick glove, holding a ball he was pretending to be about to pitch.

Two days after that photo was taken, Ferdy was mauled to death by the neighbour's Rottweiler, when he'd climbed over the fence to retrieve that ball.

# 62

There were two levels of post-mortem carried out in the Brighton and Hove City Mortuary, as in all other mortuaries throughout the country. The standard one was for victims of accidents, sudden deaths, or when people had died more than fourteen days since they had last seen their doctor and cause of death was uncertain.

With the bodies prepared in advance by Cleo and her assistants, the actual post-mortem itself, carried out by one of a rota of local pathologists, took about half an hour, with further analysis of fluids carried out later in the labs. But for suspicious deaths, a specialist Home Office pathologist would be called in, and the post-mortem would last many hours.

Brighton and Hove City Mortuary processed an average of 850 bodies a year, the vast majority being standard post-mortems. These were carried out in the mornings, and by mid-afternoon, most days, work was finished for the mortuary staff – unless they were called out to recover a body.

A few weeks ago, Cleo had collapsed at work, suffering internal bleeding and had been rushed into hospital. The consultant gynaecologist had kept her in for several days, and then released her with strict instructions that she was to do no heavy lifting and to take a rest at some point during every working day. Grace knew she was ignoring both of these edicts and he was increasingly worried. When she had collapsed previously, she had been lucky that her assistant, Darren, had been there to drive her straight to hospital. But she was often alone in the mortuary and he worried what might happen if she collapsed again when she was the only person there. So he made a point of phoning her around 3.30 p.m. every afternoon to check she was okay, and again just before the evening briefing, to check she was fine at home.

He was truly terrified of losing her. Perhaps, he reflected, it was because after Sandy had gone he had believed he would never be happy again. And always Sandy's shadow was present. Some days he was convinced that she was dead. But more often, he believed she was still alive. What would happen, he sometimes pondered, if she were to turn up again now? If she had some completely rational explanation for her disappearance? One scenario he played over often was that she had been kidnapped for this past decade and finally escaped. How would she feel to find him married with a child?

How would he feel, if he saw her?

He tried not to dwell on that, to push it from his mind. Sandy was in the past. Ten years ago, in almost another life. He would be forty years old very soon. He had to move on. All the legal processes for having Sandy declared legally dead were under way, with advertisements placed here and in Germany, where there had been a reported but unsubstantiated sighting by a police officer friend, who had been on holiday in Munich. As soon as the ink was dry on the formalities, he and Cleo would marry. He longed for that day.

Cleo sounded tired this afternoon, and he put the phone down at the end of the call, worried. God, there seemed to be so much that could go wrong with pregnancy – and they never told you that at the outset. His joy and excitement that she was carrying their child was tempered by his fears of what might happen to Cleo, and the awesome burden of responsibility of bringing a human being into this world.

*What the hell do I know about the world and about life? Am I a fit and wise enough person to teach a child anything?*

Every villain he had ever locked up had been a baby once. Any human life could take so many twists and turns. Like the face staring at him now from the photograph in the court file he was working on. A grossly overweight American, in his early sixties, with little piggy eyes and a ponytail, who made big money from selling videos of people being murdered to order – and who had shot Glenn Branson with a handgun while resisting arrest. He despised this man with all his heart and soul, which was why he was putting so much work into the trial documents, to make sure there was absolutely no chance the creep got off on any technical flaws that a brief could find in the prosecution's case.

What kind of a baby had Carl Venner been? What kind of upbringing? Did he have parents who loved and nurtured him and had high hopes for him? How did you stop a child turning rotten? Maybe you couldn't, but at least you could try. Giving a child a stable upbringing had to be the starting point. So many of the villains in this city came from broken homes, lone parents who either could not cope, or had long since given up caring. Or parents who sexually abused them. But he knew that wasn't always the answer. There was always going to be an element of lottery about it, too.

And an enormity. Sometimes the sense of responsibility rose up and almost overwhelmed him. There were so many books to read on pregnancy, on the baby's first months, those vital early years. And always the fear that the baby might have something seriously wrong. You never knew. Tests gave you some reassurance, but they couldn't tell you everything. He just hoped their child would be healthy. They would do their very best to be good parents.

He looked down again at Venner's face. *What did your father think about you, in those months before you were born? Was he around? Did he even know your mother was pregnant? Is he alive? If he is, do you think he's proud of you? Proud of having fathered a revolting monster who traded in pornography and murder for profit?*

How would he feel if he had a son who did that? Would he be angry? Would he feel he had failed as a parent? Would he write him off as evil, beyond redemption?

'Evil' was a word that always bothered him. It was an easy word to apply to terrible things human beings did to one other. Roy had no doubt in his mind that there were some people, like Venner, who did things that were totally and utterly evil for financial gain, just to line his pockets and his fat gut and to put a Breitling watch on his fat wrist. But many others who did bad things were victims of poor parenting or fractured society or religious zeal. That wasn't to say you could forgive them for their crimes, but if you could understand what led them to commit them, then you were at least doing something to try to make the world a better place.

That was Roy Grace's own personal philosophy. He believed that everyone who was born into a decent life had one price to pay for that. No one person was ever going to change the world, but all of us should try to ensure we leave the world a slightly better place than when we came into it. That, above all else, was what he strove to do with his life.

# 63

'The time is 6.30 p.m., Thursday, the ninth of June. This is the twelfth briefing of *Operation Icon*,' Roy Grace announced. 'I'm pleased to welcome Haydn Kelly to our team.' He indicated to the smiling man seated opposite him in the Conference Room of the Major Incident Suite. Kelly was in his mid-forties, sturdily built, with brown hair cropped short, and a tanned, amiable face. He was conservatively but elegantly dressed in a smart navy suit, cream shirt and a red patterned tie.

Grace looked around his assembled team, which had now grown to twenty-six people, including the MIR-1 Office Manager – Detective Sergeant Lance Skelton – two indexers and two crime analysts. 'Okay, a bit of housekeeping before we start.' He broke out into a broad smile. 'I'm very happy to tell you all that the mole who has been blighting our major enquiries for most of the past year has been outed.'

He instantly had the rapt attention of the entire room, broken only for a moment by a sudden burst of ringtone from a mobile phone. A blushing DC Emma Reeves hastily silenced it.

'I'm very pleased and relieved to tell you that it is not anyone within the police service. It is none other than our good friend, Kevin Spinella from the *Argus*.'

'Spinella?' DS Guy Batchelor said, astonished. 'How, chief – I mean – I thought the mole was feeding him? What did he do?'

'He hacked my phone.' Grace held his BlackBerry up for

all to see. 'He did it electronically. He installed some form of data logger software. It made a recording of every single phone call I received or made, and all texts, and immediately sent them electronically to his own phone.'

Several of the team were frowning. 'But how did he get access to your BlackBerry, to install it, boss?' Nick Nicholl asked.

'He didn't need to,' Grace replied. 'Ray Packham at the High Tech Crime Unit said that all he would have needed to do was to stand within a few feet of me. I keep the Bluetooth option switched on all the time. He could have simply uploaded it from his phone to mine in a matter of seconds.'

'But that little toerag's a newspaper reporter, not a tekkie boffin, boss,' DC Exton said.

'He would have needed a tekkie friend,' Grace said. 'I imagine we'll find whoever that is. At this moment Spinella's in custody and his phone's being taken apart. But I need the High Tech Crime Unit to check all your phones – and my strong advice is to keep your Bluetooth switched off all the time you don't need it.'

'So, do we know how far this goes up the chain of command at the *Argus*, sir?' Dave Green asked.

'I spoke to the editor, Michael Beard, earlier. He sounded very genuinely shocked, and said if that were the case, the reporter was totally out of line and acting in a rogue manner, completely alien to the paper's policy. I subsequently received an email from him a few minutes before I came in here, telling me that Spinella has been suspended with immediate effect. I get the sense Spinella was acting alone – the editor wouldn't do that to him if he were acting on official policy.'

'So what happens to Spinella's career now?' Norman Potting asked.

Bella Moy rounded on him. 'What? You care?'

Glenn Branson watched the exchange, intrigued. Until last night he thought that Bella couldn't stand the man. Now, he realized, it was more like the bickering of an old married couple. He was still in shock from seeing them together, and had not told Roy yet. He looked at the two of them now. Surely she was capable of attracting someone a lot better than Norman?

Such as himself.

Then again, he knew, his collapsed relationship with Ari showed just how little he understood women.

'I think I'd be lying,' Roy Grace went on, 'if I said I was going to be losing any sleep over harming Kevin Spinella's future career prospects.'

There was a ripple of laughter.

'Has he been charged yet?' Jon Exton asked.

'What, like his phone?' Potting riposted and chortled, oblivious to the raised eyebrows around him.

Grace ignored him. 'Yes, he has. With a bit of luck he could be looking at three to five years.'

'Couldn't happen to a nicer guy,' Nick Nicholl said sarcastically.

'He'll like being inside,' Potting said, on a roll now. 'He thrives on inside information!' He chortled again.

'Very witty, Norman,' Grace said. Then he turned to the press officer, Sue Fleet. 'You'll need to liaise with the *Argus* and find out who will be our new principal contact there.'

'Yes, sir.'

'Okay, let's move on, down to business.' He looked at his prepared notes. 'Glenn, what do you have for us from the post-mortem today?'

'We hope to have the DNA results on the four limbs back tomorrow, boss. But from their well-preserved condition the pathologist Nadiuska De Sancha was able to match them up pretty well to the torso. She was unable to find anything under the nails, skin scrapings or anything else which might indicate a struggle and perhaps give us the perp's DNA.'

'What about fingerprints?'

'Yes, boss, we got a complete dead set.'

'Good.'

'We also got good plantars, too.' Plantars were toe prints. 'The fingerprints indicate the hands – therefore the arms – are probably from the same body, but there are no hits from the database, so we're no further forward with identification.' He turned to the forensic podiatrist. 'Do you have anything to add on the legs, Haydn?'

'At this stage,' Kelly said, 'the right and left leg appear to belong to the same body – I'm as near to one hundred per cent certain as I can be. I fully expect the DNA analysis will confirm this for us.'

'So all we need is the head, and we'll have a complete assemble-it-yourself human cadaver in kit form,' Potting said.

There were several sniggers. Bella Moy gave him a reproachful look.

'What do you have for us on mispers, Norman?' Grace asked.

'We now have thirty-seven male mispers from the three counties, chief, who fit the age and build profile of the victim. The families that we have been able to contact have been asked to provide items we might be able to obtain DNA from. There are five mispers where we have been unable to find any relatives, and another six with relatives who can't provide us with anything at all.'

Grace thanked him, and turned to DC Nick Nicholl.

'Nick, how are you getting on with the list of people who've had access to Stonery Farm?'

'We're pretty much complete, sir.' He turned to the indexer Annalise Vineer. 'Annalise has been making up a database for us to cross-reference against.'

'We have everyone in it who has been to the farm in the last twelve months – at least the names that the Winter family have given us,' she said, with a slight toss of her head which sent her fringe flicking left, then right, over her forehead. 'Tradesmen, friends, professionals. I'm also cross-referencing them against the Police National Database to see if there are any matches with known criminals.'

'Good work,' Grace said. He looked down at his notes. 'Right, I understand we have some development regarding the suit fabric.' He looked at Glenn.

'I had a long conversation with a very helpful woman at Dormeuil, the cloth manufacturer. They've confirmed it is their fabric, and, no surprise, that it is not one of their major sellers. One problem we have – but it could be much worse – is that a relatively new specialist manufacturer of men's fashion suits, called Savile Style, bought a large quantity of the material three years ago, making over nine hundred suits from it, which they've supplied mostly to individual men's clothing stores around the country – as well as some overseas. They're putting together a list of all stockists – definitely one or two in Brighton – who bought the suits. Dormeuil are also letting me have a list of all tailors who've bought bolts of this cloth too, which would have been for made-to-measure suits – tailors like Gresham Blake.'

'What we need to do,' Grace said, 'is to get the names of every individual we can who bought a suit in this fabric and then, Annalise, check against the visitor list to Stonery Farm and see if that throws up anything.' He turned to Bella Moy. 'Did we get any more leads from *Crimewatch*?'

'No, sir,' she said. 'A steady volume of calls – forty-eight in the last two days – but nothing else of significance, so far.'

'Right, the footprint.' He turned to the Crime Scene Manager. 'David, what have you got for us so far?'

'We have actually got five matching footprints from the scene, boss. Three of them correspond to the sections of the lake where limbs were recovered, which is a good indication they might be the perp's. The tread is over an inch deep, which means almost certainly a boot of some kind. Hard to be precise about the size – often shoe and boot manufacturers use the same sole over several sizes and the fit is in the uppers. But this appears to be smallish – probably a man's size eight.'

'Can you give us an indication of the perpetrator's height from that, Haydn?' Grace said. He looked quizzically at the forensic podiatrist.

'Not really, there are too many variables. Some leading experts say the normal height range for this size would be from five foot five inches to five foot nine. But that is making a number of assumptions, including that he was wearing footwear correctly sized for him. People often wear gum boots a size larger than their normal shoe size – and if he's a smart crim, it's possible he wore padded-out boots to deceive us about his true size. If he's really forensically aware, he may have even bought a new insole, to wear a bigger size boot in an attempt to also mask his footprint.'

'So,' Glenn said, 'assuming the scrote's not a size nine or ten squeezed into these boots, which would be pretty difficult to walk with, would it be a reasonable assumption we are looking at someone no taller than five-eight?'

'Reasonable but not certain,' Kelly replied. 'I would not be comfortable telling you that you could eliminate taller people than that from this enquiry.'

'Haydn,' Grace said, 'I'd like you to explain one of your particular skills, which could become relevant at a later stage in this enquiry. Am I correct that you would be able to recognize whoever left these footprints, from watching him walk and studying his gait?'

'A human gait is as distinctive as a fingerprint,' Kelly said. 'Gait is a person's style or manner of walking and divided into two phases: Stance and Swing. In the stance phase, the person's heel contacts the ground, body weight is transferred through the foot to when the toes leave the ground – technically this is called heel contact, mid-stance and propulsion. The swing phase begins immediately after the toes leave the ground, the whole of the lower limb swings forward, and ends at the point when the heel re-strikes the ground. This is unquestionable. How the foot, lower limb and the rest of the body behave in achieving this is distinctive to each individual. Equally that same lower limb can have a posture – or shape – that contributes to its individuality. In some cases this is quite pronounced.'

Grace's phone, on silent, vibrated. On the display it read, INTERNATIONAL.

Excusing himself he stepped away from the table and out of the room into the corridor, answering it as he walked, 'Detective Superintendent Grace.'

From the other end he heard an American voice he recognized from their conversation on Monday. The man had been serious and to the point then, and was the same now. 'Sir, it's Detective Myman, from the LAPD.'

'Good to hear from you, how are you?'

'We're doing fine,' the American said. 'We got a piece of

good news for you. We have a suspect in custody for the murder of Marla Henson, assistant to Gaia Lafayette.'

Grace's spirits soared. 'You do? Fantastic!'

'I thought you should know right away, so you can maybe lighten up on your protection of her.'

'How certain are you this is the right person?'

'Oh, he's the perp, no question about that. Got the gun in his house that matches up with the ballistics, got his computer with the two emails he sent on it, and there's a whole stack of newspaper cuttings about Gaia in his den with some damned strange wording and symbols written all over them. He's a screwball, but he's pretty much admitted it.'

'What was his motive? He just hated her?'

'He's got a woman he lives with, she was kind of a bit part actress some years back. Plenty of them in this city. She waits tables in a small place in Santa Monica. Seems like he thought it was unfair Gaia got the part and she didn't, so he kind of figured in his dumbass mashed-up brain that if he eliminated Gaia, his girl would get the part instead.'

'This is very good news that you've got him,' Grace said.

'I'll let you have any more information as the situation develops.'

'I'd appreciate that.'

'You got it.'

# 64

'Who's your fat friend?'

Crouched at the bottom of the steps, staring warily around him, as well as constantly looking up, Drayton Wheeler heard the woman's voice with relief. The first guided tour of the day. It was his cue.

He had spent much of the night prowling around, avoiding the guards, exploring up in the roof spaces. When he had tried to sleep in one, it had been impossible, with images of being caught invading his mind and the sound of pelting rain drumming on the copper roof above him.

He had found the perfect hideout at the top of the building. Well, so long as you didn't mind an icy draught and the constant patter and scratching sounds of rats. The creaking of floorboards, like the whole place was haunted with a thousand ghosts. Not that that mattered. He just hoped to hell there were ghosts, because in that case he'd be one soon and, boy, did he have a few scores to settle when he came back. Before dawn, he'd returned to the quiet of his basement lair.

He scrambled silently up the stairs and listened.

'He did indeed say that to the king. You see, Beau Brummell was a very well known figure – a real Regency dandy.'

Drayton watched the attentive audience who were facing away from him, blocking the guide from view, their anoraks and mackintoshes dripping water. He slid the bolt, opened the gate, slipped through, and closed it behind him, securing it again.

'Well, they had a bit of a falling out. Beau Brummell, Lord Alvanley, Henry Mildmay and Henry Pierrepoint were considered the prime movers . . .'

He eased his way around the back of them, moving so slowly he was barely noticed. On the far side was a uniformed guard, but he was looking down at his phone, texting. Pulling his baseball cap low over his face, Drayton Wheeler followed the exit signs, which took him through the gift shop. But there was nothing in here for him. One of the many liberating things about dying, he thought, was that you didn't need to waste money buying souvenirs.

He stepped outside into the pelting rain. Smelled the aroma of wet, recently mown grass, breathed in the salty tang of the air. It was 10.20 a.m., Friday, 10 June. He felt great. He'd never felt better or happier in his life! Maybe it was the drugs he was on, or maybe it was just the fact that in six months, give or take, he'd be out of here. He didn't care, he felt liberated.

And he had a shopping list!

# 65

It didn't take much persuasion for Roy Grace to accept an invitation to morning coffee with Gaia in her suite at The Grand, to discuss the latest development. He actually had butterflies in his stomach when he arrived, a few minutes before 10.30. He was never normally nervous in his work – even in the most dangerous situations his brain was always focused on the task ahead. But he had to admit to himself he had the collywobbles now.

He had encountered a few famous people in the course of his work, inevitably, because Brighton was home to a huge and diverse number of celebrities, but Gaia was in a different league to all of them. Standing dwarfed by the two bodyguards, he was expecting the door to be opened by one of her assistants, and was surprised that it was Gaia herself who greeted him. She was wearing a denim shirt, white jeans, high-heeled espadrilles and a dazzling smile. 'Detective Superintendent Grace – thank you so much for coming!' She sounded genuinely grateful, as if most people might kowtow instantly to her every whim, but not police officers.

He did a double-take, looking at her again, then entered the room, which smelled of freshly brewed coffee and a dense perfume. Her hair was completely different from a few days earlier – it had now been cropped short in a boyish cut. Pointing her fingers at her head she asked, 'What do you think?'

'Nice,' he said, and in truth it did suit her. But then again, he thought, she had such striking looks she'd have looked good in a bin-liner with a rusty bucket on her head. Behind her, a woman in her late twenties, dressed in black jeans and a black T-shirt with a small, gold Secret Fox logo on it, strode across the room with a script in her hand, and put it down on a table beside the sofa. Grace noticed that although most of the pages were white, some were blue, pink, yellow, green, and cherry.

'Latest changes,' the assistant said, and walked out again.

Gaia acknowledged her with a briefly raised hand, then turned her attention back to Roy Grace, pointing at her own head again. 'You think so?'

'Yes, I do,' he said, although his personal preference had always been for long hair.

'Gotta wear a goddamn wig for the production – this huge heavy Maria Fitzherbert thing – it's so hot – feels like I'm wearing a rug on my head. The hair falls all around my face, I can hardly see a goddamn thing when I'm wearing it.'

Grace grinned. 'I believe in her time women only used to wash their hair a couple of times a year.'

'Yuh huh – Marie Antoinette actually had birds in her hair.'

'Very hygienic.'

'So,' she said. 'I got saved by your colleague – Chief Superintendent Barrington?'

Grace frowned. 'You did?'

'My hairdresser didn't get over to England – she travels with me everywhere, now she's pregnant and she went down with complications. So he's found me this great hairdresser – actually she's a police officer's wife!'

'She is – who?'

'Tracey Curry. Chief Inspector Steve Curry's wife.'

PETER JAMES

'I know him – I didn't realize his wife was a hairdresser.'
'She's a genius!'
'I'm glad to hear Sussex Police are turning out to be a full service agency!' he said.
'Just keep me alive and look after my kid – that's all the service I need.' She indicated an armchair opposite the sofa, and he sat down.
'We have some good news on that front,' Grace said. 'I imagine you've heard?'
The voice of James Cagney said, 'We sure did!' Her security chief Andrew Gulli strode into the room, dressed as before in a dapper suit. 'Detective Superintendent Grace, it's so good to see you again.' He sat in the chair next to him.
Another young female assistant materialized out of the ether and asked Grace how he took his coffee.
Gulli raised both his hands in the air, as if holding up an imaginary football, then lowered them, still with the ball, to his lap. 'The thing is, Detective Superintendent, they may have caught this guy, but I don't want us relaxing our guard on Gaia and Roan. You have a lot of crazy people in your city, right?'
'We have our fair share,' Grace admitted. 'But no more than anywhere else in this country. Brighton's a pretty safe place.'
'I read you normally have around fifteen to twenty homicides a year, but you've already had sixteen, and we're only halfway through this year. So your homicide rate has doubled.'
Gaia, who sat herself down attentively on the edge of the sofa, was staring at Grace. He could see, beneath her beauty, the crease lines of fear.

'It's a statistical blip,' he replied cheerfully, and instantly knew he had said the wrong thing.

'Yeah, right,' Gulli said, his Cagney accent even more pronounced now. 'So tell me, how did those people lying in body bags in your mortuary feel about being a statistical blip, Detective Superintendent Grace?'

Grace was momentarily distracted by the arrival of his coffee, and waving away the offer of sugar, said, 'If it's any comfort, most of the murders were low-life criminals on criminals or domestics.'

Gulli scratched behind his left ear. 'I've been reading a lot of history on your city. In the 1930s Brighton was known as the "Crime Capital of the UK" and the "Murder Capital of Europe". You know, it doesn't seem like much has changed.'

Grace was starting to feel annoyed with the man. But he kept his patience. 'I'll talk to the Chief Constable and pass on your concerns.'

'I'd be very grateful,' Gulli said. 'In the meantime I'd appreciate it if you maintained the current level of officers.'

'I can't make promises but I'll do all I can.'

'Thank you,' Gaia said. She was smiling at him sweetly, and with an almost mesmerizing concentration, staring into his eyes. Was he imagining it, he wondered, or was he getting the come-on from her?

'Mom, I'm like so bored!'

Roan walked across the room, barefoot, in baggy jeans and an orange T-shirt, a Nintendo console hanging from his fingertips.

She patted the side of the sofa and he sat down grumpily beside her. 'He's not too impressed with the weather, are you, sweetie?'

He peered at his Nintendo screen.

'Is that the new one?' Roy Grace asked. 'The 3DS?'

The boy studied the screen and gave him a reluctant nod.

'He wants to go on the beach, but nothing doing with this weather.' She pointed to the window at the pelting rain. There was a sudden change in her expression. 'Do you have kids, Detective Superintendent?'

'No, I don't. Just a goldfish.'

She laughed. 'I figured it would be nice for Roan to meet some kids his age. Do you know anyone who has some who might be willing to play with him, hang out with him a little?'

His eyes widened. 'Actually, I do, yes!'

'I would so appreciate that.' She kissed her son's cheek, but he barely noticed, he was so focused on his console. 'You'd like that, wouldn't you, hon? Someone to play with?'

He shrugged. 'Whatever.'

'I could make a quick call – Roan's six, right?'

'Just had his sixth birthday party three weeks ago.'

'This person's got two kids – I think they're about six and nine.'

'Perfect!'

He dialled Glenn Branson's number.

'Yuh, old timer, what's up?'

'I have someone who wants to speak to you.'

'Who's that.'

'I'll put her on!' He handed Gaia the phone and said, 'His name's Glenn.'

'Hi, Glenn!' she said in her huskiest voice.

Grace smiled. He was trying to imagine his mate's face at the other end of the line.

# 66

'What do you mean, you don't have any?'

The man hunched over the counter in a white coat was the kind of miserable jerk who should not have been there at all. He should have quit or retired long before he'd decided he hated doing this job so much he wasn't ever going to be pleasant or helpful to anyone who came in here. With his frayed grey hair and his thick, round bottle-lensed glasses he looked like a Nazi geneticist who'd had a career change. He spoke like one, too.

'Ve don't haf any.'

'You're a fucking pharmacist; all pharmacists sell thermometers.'

The man shrugged and said nothing.

Drayton Wheeler glared at him. 'You know where there's another pharmacist?'

He nodded. 'I do.'

'Where?'

'Vy should I tell you? I don't like you. I don't like your attitude.'

'Fuck you.'

'Vuck you too.'

For an instant, Wheeler was tempted to punch his smug, evil face. But there were all kinds of potential repercussions from that. Not smart. He mustn't get side-tracked, had to keep focus. Focus. Focus.

He walked out of the shop in a rage and collided with a woman pushing a shopping trolley. 'Stupid old woman!'

he shouted at her. 'Watch where you're going!' Then he stormed off up the street, everything a blur, his rage playing havoc with his eyes. He was tired. He was grungy. He was hungry. He needed food. He needed a bath.

But most of all he needed a thermometer.

# 67

As he walked through The Grand Hotel shortly before mid-day, threading his way along the corridors towards the car park, Roy Grace's phone rang. It was Glenn Branson for the second time. The first had been to thank him for putting him on the line to Gaia; he had seemed totally blown away.

'Darren Spicer, right?' the Detective Sergeant said.

Glenn was a movie buff and half his references in life involved movie titles. In his current star-struck mood, Grace's first reaction was to wonder what film he was referring to.

'Darren Spicer?' Then he realized.

'Remember him, chief?'

'He's about the most forgettable person I've ever remembered. Yes, I do.' He refrained from adding he'd seen him arriving at Tommy Fincher's wake a couple of days ago. 'What about him?' Then he had to wait for a moment as an ambulance screamed past before he could hear Glenn's voice.

'He just belled me. He wants to speak to you.'

Darren Spicer was one of the local villains who was also an occasional informer for Sussex Police. A career burglar, with form that stretched back to his early teens, he was a true recidivist, or what they colloquially called a 'revolving door prisoner'. He was a man who had spent more of his working life behind bars than free. Earlier in the year, in a stroke of luck – in Grace's view totally undeserved – Spicer collected a £50,000 reward put up by local millionaire philanthropist Rudy Burchmore, for information leading to the arrest of the man who had attempted to rape his wife. It was his biggest financial result to date in a long second career of acting as a police informant, both from inside jail and out.

'What did he want?' Grace asked.

'He wouldn't say. Just told me it's urgent and you'd want to know.'

'What reward is he after this time?'

'I dunno. He sounded anxious and gave me a number.'

Grace jotted it down on his pad, then entered the car park, stopped and dialled it.

It was answered almost instantly with a furtive, 'Yeah?'

'Darren Spicer?'

'Depends who's calling him.'

*Fuckwit*, Grace thought. He gave his name.

'Got something for you.'

'What's it about and what do you want?'

'I want a monkey.' A monkey was £500.

'That's big money.'

'This is big information.'

'Want to tell me?'

'We need to meet.'

'What's it about, generally?'

'That movie star you're protecting.'

'Gaia?'

'Know the Crown and Anchor in Shoreham?'

'That's a bit upmarket for you, isn't it?'

'I'm a rich man these days, Detective Superintendent. I'll be here for another thirty minutes.'

*

Shoreham Harbour was a major port at the western extremity of Brighton. A village that had long since grown into an annexe to the city was spread along it. The Crown and Anchor pub, with its outside terrace overlooking the harbour, had one of Shoreham-by-Sea's most attractive and best value restaurants. He had eaten there many times in the past with Sandy, and more recently with Cleo.

Whatever else he might think about Spicer's sad and generally scuzzy lifestyle, there was no denying the villain was well connected, and his information tended to be reliable. True, £500 was a lot, but the police had funds set aside for payments like this.

Thanks to new levels of public accountability, all police officers, unless attending an emergency, had to comply with public parking regulations. Which was why he wasted ten minutes of his day driving around the narrow streets of the old village part of Shoreham, in the pelting rain, trying to find a parking space.

Spicer was seated on a bar stool, nursing an almost empty straight glass of stout. A tall, gangly man in his early forties who, thanks to his many years spent in prison, looked upwards of sixty. He wore a yellow polo shirt, baggy jeans and brand new trainers. His head was shaven to a brown fuzz, his face was grizzled, with dead eyes.

'Get you another Guinness?' Grace said by way of introduction, as he slid on to the stool next to him. It was still early and the bar was almost empty.

'Thought you wasn't coming,' Spicer said without even looking at him. 'I need a fag. Bring my pint out on the terrace.' He climbed down from his stool and ambled across the bar. Grace watched him. He had the posture of a bent crane.

A few minutes later, Roy Grace pushed his way through the glass patio door and out on the wooden decking overlooking the Adur, the river which fed the harbour. It was low tide, and mostly mudflats, with a narrow stream of water flowing through the middle. Dozens of gulls were foraging in the mud. Across the far side was the permanent moored community of houseboats, which had been here ever since he could remember.

Spicer was sitting beneath a large umbrella, rain falling all around him, holding a roll-up between his forefinger and thumb.

Grace handed him his pint of Guinness and set down his own glass, containing Diet Coke, and pulled up a chair. 'Good weather for ducks!' he said.

The smell of Spicer's cigarette was tantalizing. But he had made a resolve, many years ago, never to smoke in the daytime, and only one or two, occasionally, in the evening.

Spicer took a long drag and inhaled deeply. 'Are we agreed it's a monkey?'

'That's a lot of money.'

'I think you'll find it a bargain.' He drained his glass, then lifted the one Grace had bought him.

'And if I don't?'

Spicer shrugged. 'No skin off my nose. I'll just do the burglary, and I'll net a lot more than a monkey, yeah?'

'What burglary are you talking about?'

He drank deeply from his new pint. 'I've been offered good money to burgle Gaia's hotel suite.'

Grace's whole body clenched tight. He felt a shiver ripple through him. Suddenly, £500 did seem a bargain. 'Tell me more?'

'We have a deal?'

'I'll get the money to you in the next couple of days. So, first thing, why didn't you take the job?'

'Don't do burglary no more, Detective Superintendent. The police made me a rich man. Don't need to do no burglaring.'

'So what are you into now? Drugs? I guess a wedge like fifty grand could make you a bit of a player.'

Spicer shrugged evasively. 'I in't here to talk about myself.'

Grace raised his hands. 'Don't worry, I'm clean, no recorder! So tell me who's offered you this job?'

Even though the terrace was deserted, Spicer still looked cautiously around, before leaning across the table and, in a very low voice, said, 'Amis Smallbone.'

Grace stared back at him. 'Amis Smallbone? Seriously?'

Spicer nodded.

'Why you?'

'I used to work at The Grand after I come out of prison, down in the maintenance department. Know my way around the place with me eyes shut. I know how to get into any room there. Smallbone had heard that, that's why he come to me.'

'I don't suppose you'd like to go on the record with this?'

'Yer having a laugh!'

'If you made a statement I could get his licence revoked. He'd be back inside for a good long stretch.'

'I know I'm not that smart,' Spicer said. 'But I'm still alive. If I go public and grass up Smallbone, I'd have to watch me back for the rest of my life. No thanks.' He looked worriedly at Grace. 'This is not – you know?'

Grace shook his head. 'It stays with me. No one will ever

know we had this conversation. So tell me more? I didn't think burglary was Smallbone's game.'

'It ain't. He just wanted to fuck you over. Embarrass you.' Then Spicer gave a wry smile. 'I don't think he likes you very much.'

'That's a shame. My mantelpiece will look very bare this Christmas without my usual card from him.'

# 68

'No I don't need help, thank you. Do I look that fucking frail?'

The doorman of The Grand Hotel was taken aback, but outwardly kept his composure. 'Very good, sir, just trying to be helpful.'

'When I want your help, I'll tell you.'

Drayton Wheeler walked on through the lobby, perspiring heavily, struggling from the weight of the sealed brown box under his left arm, and his two heavily laden carrier bags.

He passed a couple of photographers and the same oddball group of people occupying a bay of sofas, several of them holding CD booklets and record sleeves, who seemed to be camped out here, sad fans of that superbitch cow actress. How wrong was she for the part? *His* part. The one *he* had written. He pressed the button and waited for the lift. His anger was all over the place, he knew. He had shouted at two different pharmacists, the idiot on the checkout desk in the Waitrose supermarket, the cretin in Dockerills hardware store and the total asshole in Halfords.

He got out at the sixth floor, walked down the corridor, then struggled to get his key card out. He pushed it in then removed it.

The light flashed red.

'Shit!' he shouted. He rammed it in then pulled it out again, the weight of the package under his left arm killing him. He put it in again, the right way around this time, and the light flashed green.

He half kicked, half pushed open the door and stepped into the small room, staggered over towards the twin beds and dumped his packages down on one, with relief.

He needed a shower. Something to eat. But first he needed to check everything, to make sure the fuckwits hadn't sold him the wrong stuff.

He hung the DO NOT DISTURB sign outside the door, turned the security lock, then ripped open the first package, took out the car battery and set it down on top of the *Sussex Life* magazine that lay on the small round table. Then he dipped into one of the carrier bags and pulled out a heavy metal tyre bar, and then six thermometers which he placed next to the battery. Then he removed the bottle of hydrochloric acid, labelled as paint stripper, which he had bought from Dockerills. He placed that on the table, on top of another magazine, *Absolute Brighton*. Then he added a bottle of chlorine. He opened the last carrier bag, which was from Mothercare.

He stood back for a moment, clasped his hands together, and smiled. The great thing about dying, he thought, was that you no longer had to be worried about anything. A quotation was spinning around in his head and he tried to remember who said it.

*To dream of death is good for those in fear, for the dead have no more fears.*

That was right, oh yes. *Do you know that quotation, Larry Brooker? Maxim Brody? Gaia Lafayette?*

*Know who you are dealing with?*

*A man who has no more fears!*

*A man who has the chemical components to make mercuric chloride. And who knows how to make it!*

He was a successful industrial chemist long before he became a screwed screenwriter. He remembered all this stuff from a long time ago.

Mercuric chloride is not a salt but a linear triatomic molecule, hence its tendency to sublime.

*Did you know that, Larry Brooker? Maxim Brody? Bitch queen Gaia Lafayette?*

You will soon.

His phone rang. He answered it aggressively, not in any mood to be disturbed.

An irritatingly cheery young woman said, 'Jerry Baxter?'

He remembered the voice. 'Uh huh.'

'You didn't turn up for your costume fitting today. Just wanted to check if you were still interested in being an extra on *The King's Lover*?'

He held his temper. 'I'm sorry, I had an important meeting.'

'No problem, Jerry. We're shooting crowd scenes outside the Pavilion on Monday morning, weather permitting. If you're still interested, could you come tomorrow?'

He said nothing for some moments, thinking hard. Then he said, 'Perfect.'

# 69

Cleo found a parking space two streets away from her home, shortly after 5 p.m. on Friday evening. The rain had stopped and the sky was brightening. As she climbed out of her little Audi she felt leadenly tired, but happy. So incredibly happy, and with the weekend to look forward to ahead. As if responding to her mood, the baby kicked inside her.

'You happy too, Bump?'

She lifted her handbag off the passenger seat, locked the car and started walking home, totally unaware of the two pairs of eyes watching her from behind the windscreen of the rented Volkswagen that had been following her from the mortuary.

'*Warum starrst du die dicke Frau an?*' the boy asked.

In German, she replied, 'She's not fat, my love. She's carrying a baby.'

In German, he asked, 'Whose baby?'

She did not reply. With hatred in her eyes she watched the woman.

'Whose baby, Mama?'

For some moments she said nothing, feeling deep turmoil inside her. 'Wait here,' she said. 'I'll be right back.'

She left the car and walked up the street for some yards past the Audi. Trying to appear nonchalant, and not to draw any attention to herself, she turned around until she could see the front of Cleo's car.

There was a patina of dust on the bonnet, and several

spatterings of seagull droppings, one lying on the duct-tape repair to the roof. But the wording she had carved was still there, clearly visible.

*COPPERS TART. UR BABY IS NEXT.*

# 70

Anna paced around her Gaia museum, her Gaia shrine. A Martini glass in her hand. She was drinking – deliberately drinking – a cocktail that was so not Gaia. It was a Manhattan. Two parts bourbon, one part red Martini, Angostura bitters and a maraschino cherry on its stalk, in a Martini glass.

She was drinking it to spite Gaia.

She was drinking it to get drunk.

It was her third Manhattan of the evening. Friday evening. She didn't have to go to work tomorrow. So she could get totally smashed.

She had never been so humiliated in her life as she had been on Wednesday. Her face was still burning. She could hear the silent laughter of all the other fans on the sofas.

Standing in front of a life-size cardboard cut-out of her idol, she stared into those blue eyes. 'What went wrong? Hey? Tell me? I'm your number one fan and you turned away from me? Tell me why? Hey? Tell me? You found someone else? Someone who's more into you than me?'

Not possible.

No way.

'You've made my life worth living, don't you know that, don't you care? You're the only person who's ever loved me.'

In her left hand she held a knife. A kukri. The knife one of her father's ancestors had taken from a dead soldier way back during the Gurkha wars. Gurkhas were brave people. They did not care about dying.

*If a man says he is not afraid of dying, he is either lying or is a Gurkha.*

What do you think about that, Gaia? Are you lying or a Gurkha?

Or just a parvenue from Whitehawk in Brighton who thinks you are too big to bother to acknowledge your fans?

She strutted very slowly down the steep wooden stairs, went through into the kitchen and filled her glass with the remainder of the drink that was in the silver cocktail shaker. Then she went back upstairs to her shrine.

'Cheers, Gaia!' she said. 'So tell me, did it feel good cutting me dead yesterday? Hey? Tell me about it? Who put you on your platform? Did you ever think about that? Did you ever think about me? You stared at me so often. I watched you watching me on *Top Gear*. And on so many other shows. So what do you think gave you the right to treat me like – like – scum – shit – like – like – trash? Tell me, I'm really interested. Your number one fan needs to know.

'I do really.

'Tell me.

'Tell me.

'Tell me?'

# 71

For the Friday evening briefing, Glenn Branson chose a seat that gave him a clear view of Bella. He noticed that, as usual, she and Norman Potting sat well apart so that eye contact between them was difficult. Experienced detectives, he thought, they'd clearly planned this between them. So just how long had their relationship being going on? It wasn't that long ago that Potting had married for the fourth time, suckered by a Thai girl who'd been bleeding him dry of money.

He watched her pop a Malteser into her mouth. She wasn't in any sense beautiful, but there was something about her that he found very attractive. Warmth and a vulnerability that made him want to scoop her up into his arms. Just a short while ago he'd thought he might be able to offer her something better than the life of drudgery she had looking after her ailing mother. Now it was a different challenge altogether. Potting was so not right for her. He looked at him. At the smug grin on his face.

*Come on, Bella, how on earth could you fancy him?*

'Glenn? Hello? Glenn?'

With a start, he realized Roy Grace was speaking to him, and he had no idea what about.

'Sorry, chief, I was somewhere else.'

'Welcome back from Planet Zog!'

There was some sniggering in the room.

'Long day?' Potting queried. His words were like a knife twisting inside him.

'I asked you about the DNA results on the four limbs,' Grace said, glancing briefly down at his notes. 'You said you were expecting them back from the lab today?'

Branson nodded. 'Yep. I have the results.' He opened a plastic folder. 'I can read you out the full lab report if you want, chief?'

Grace shook his head. To most police officers, himself included, DNA reports were a mysterious, arcane art. He had always been rubbish at science at school. In fact he had been rubbish at most things at school except for rugby and running. 'Just summarize for now, Glenn.'

'Okay. So all four limbs are from the same body and it's a millions-to-one certainty that they belong to the torso of "Unknown Berwick Male",' he said.

'Good work,' Grace said. 'Right, so we have another piece of our jigsaw in place. All we are missing now is his head.'

'Could be we are looking for a man who lost his head to a woman,' Potting said, and guffawed.

'You should know!' Bella rounded on Potting. Potting blushed and looked down. To everyone else present her remark was a barb about his marital failures. Only Glenn knew the truth behind it.

'Not very helpful, actually, Norman,' Grace said.

'Sorry, boss.' He looked around with a sheepish grin, but no one responded.

Roy Grace stared at Potting. He was a fine detective, but sometimes he could be so damned irritating with his bad jokes, and on this enquiry he seemed to be worse than ever.

'The issue we have is the timing difference between the torso and the limbs,' Glenn said, pushing his mess of thoughts to the back of his mind, and fully focused again now. 'We know that the torso was deposited many months ago and is in a highly advanced state of decomposition. The limbs are relatively fresh.'

'Which would indicate that Darren Wallace's opinion that they had been frozen is probably correct,' said the Crime Scene Manager, David Green.

'Is that not something the pathologist can determine?' Bella Moy asked.

Green shook his head. 'Not easily. Freezing will cause cell damage, but it is going to take a while to establish that.'

'So what does this tell us?' Grace said, addressing the entire team. 'Why was the torso dumped months ago and the limbs only in the past couple of days?'

'Someone playing games with us, chief?' suggested Nick Nicholl.

'Yes,' Roy Grace said. 'That's a possibility. But let's apply our old friend Brother Ockham's razor.'

William of Ockham was a fourteenth-century friar and logician. He believed that the simplest answer was usually the right one.

'You're suggesting a link between *Crimewatch* and the limbs, boss?' said Guy Batchelor.

'I think we're dealing with someone either very cunning or very nervous,' Grace replied. 'It's possible that he left the torso and the suit fabric in the chicken farm as one clue for us. Then the limbs and the piece of suit fabric at the trout lake as another clue. In which case at some point we'll find another piece of fabric and the head. Or, as I think more likely, *Crimewatch* spooked the perpetrator into getting rid of some – and possibly all – of the rest of the evidence. Lorna's team are continuing to search for the head.'

'Or maybe that's the one trophy he can't bear to part with?' Potting said.

Grace nodded. 'Yes, that's possible.' He looked at his notes. 'For the moment we have no option but to work with what we have. Right, the suit fabric.' He looked up at Glenn Branson. 'What is the situation with that?'

'DS Batchelor's been on to this, boss.'

Batchelor nodded. 'I've got the outside enquiry team going through the list that Dormeuil supplied us. All men's clothing stores and tailors within our three counties' parameter who bought sufficient quantities of this cloth to make suits from, including Savile Style. I gave a list of eighty-two people who bought one of the suits – or had one made – to Annalise Vineer at midday today.' He turned to the indexer. 'What do you have for us, Annalise?'

'There is something interesting,' she said, flushing a little, as if not used to being in the limelight. 'There's a men's clothing store in Gardner Street, Brighton, called Luigi, which sold a suit in this material to a man called Myles Royce two years ago. It wasn't bespoke, but the proprietor, Luigi, remembers making a number of tailoring alterations to make a better fit. Myles Royce is on our mispers list. DS Potting is following up.'

Grace turned to Potting. 'Have you progressed this?'

'Yes, chief. Luigi had an address for his customer in Ash Grove, Haywards Heath, which I went to this afternoon – a pleasant detached house in a decent neighbourhood. There was no answer and the place looked in a state of neglect. I come from a farming background and I know a little about grass. In my view the lawn hasn't been cut this year. The garden's overgrown with weeds. I found one helpful neighbour at home, an elderly lady opposite, who told me he lived alone. She's been looking after his cat for several months. Apparently he had some investments – some kind of family trust that he lived on – and he'd told her he was going off to do a bit of travelling for a few weeks, and never returned.' Potting paused and shuffled through the mess of papers in front of him.

'Now here's the interesting thing – well – maybe not that interesting.'

Grace stared at him, waiting patiently, wishing he could get to the point. But that wasn't Norman Potting's style and never would be.

'I got the name and phone number of his mother from this lady,' Potting said. 'So I went round to see her, in a care home in Burgess Hill. She told me her son used to call her at seven every Sunday evening without fail. She hasn't heard from him since January. She's very distressed – apparently they were extremely close.'

'Did she report him as a misper?' Bella Moy said.

'In April.'

'Why did she wait so long?' Nick Nicholl asked.

'She told me he was often travelling,' Norman Potting replied. 'She said he was a very big fan of Gaia, obsessed by her. He'd a small trust fund, and made a bit of money, apparently, dabbling in the property market, and that enabled him to travel the world following her.'

Grace frowned. 'A wealthy, grown man, travelling the world for Gaia? What was all that about?'

'I'm told she's a huge gay icon,' Potting replied.

'Is – was – Myles Royce gay?' Branson interjected.

'The neighbour said she saw a few young men turn up at his house, but never any ladies,' Potting said.

Grace thought hard. Something didn't quite add up. A Gaia fan butchered. Gaia in town. A recent murder attempt on her in Los Angeles. Coincidences?

He didn't like coincidences much. They were too convenient. Easy to explain something away as *coincidence*.

Much harder to drill down beneath the surface to see what was really there.

'Has his mother got anything we might get his DNA from, Norman?' he asked.

Potting shook his head. 'No, but I got the neighbour to let me into his house. I removed one of his suits. He fits our size profile exactly. And I brought back a hairbrush and toothbrush – I've already had them sent to the lab.'

'Well done,' Grace said. Then he lapsed into thought.

*Gaia.*

Was there a connection?

Why should there be?

He'd been a detective for too long to dismiss anything. A Gaia fan had possibly been murdered. Gaia was in town. But if he had been murdered, that had been long before anyone knew she was coming to town.

He continued thinking for some moments. Deposition sites tended to be ditches beside quiet roads, or woodlands alongside them. He turned to Glenn Branson. 'We need to get a list of all the members of the trout-fishing club and have them interviewed – see if any of them saw anything – or react suspiciously to being interviewed. It's a pretty remote place – I'm not sure any member of the general public would find it by accident. Whoever used this as a deposition site must have had prior knowledge of it. We should also work on a list of anyone who might have had reason to visit it – like maintenance workers clearing the weeds, or working on repairs—'

'I'm there, boss!' Glenn Branson interjected, and looked at the indexer. 'Annalise is already liaising with the trout club secretary.'

'He's being very helpful,' Annalise Vineer said. 'He's given me the full membership list, and he's working on a wider list of names of all people the club has dealings with who might have reason to have visited, or at least know its location. Such as people from the Environment Agency who handle fishing licences, their fencing contractor, the company they use for weed control, their driveway maintenance people, their printers and their solicitors. I hope to have the full list by tomorrow.'

Grace thanked her. Then he turned to another of the detectives on his team, Jon Exton. 'Anything to report from the National Footwear Reference Collection, Jon?'

'Yes, boss!' Exton said. Glenn liked the young man because he was always brimming with enthusiasm.

'I've found an exact match,' Exton continued. 'It's good news and – er – not such good news.'

Grace frowned. This wasn't the time or place to start talking in riddles. 'What do you mean?' he said, a tad snappily.

'Well the good news, boss, is that the print is from a wellington boot, rather than a trainer.'

Many prisons issued prisoners with trainers when they left, if they had no other shoes. Partly as a result of that, there were more trainer footprints at crime scenes than any other kind of footwear; the vast numbers of stockists and quantity of trainer manufacturers made it hard to trace the source.

'The footprint is from a Hunter wellington boot,' Exton went on. 'The style is one of "The Original" range. I'm afraid the bad news is that this brand is one of the most popular manufactured in this country. There are sixty-four stockists in Sussex, Kent and Surrey. And of course you can get them online.'

Roy Grace absorbed the information, thinking hard. How many of these were self-service stores like garden centres? What was the possibility of the staff remembering who bought these boots? In every murder enquiry he had to balance the costs of deployment of officers against the probabilities of achieving any result. Sixty-four stockists would consume a lot of the outside enquiry team manpower, if he wanted to get a result quickly. How many a day could any individual cover? In his experience, having to wait for staff they needed to interview to come back from breaks, and the like, was time consuming. Six retail outlets a day would be good going. It would take two officers a good week to cover every shop and store.

DC Reeves put her hand in the air. 'Sir, Hunter is a very expensive brand – I know because I recently went shopping for some wellies. Do you think there is some significance in this? That it tallies with the expensive suit material from the victim? What I mean by this is it tells us the perpetrator might be financially well off.'

Grace nodded. 'Good point, Emma.' He made a note. Then he instructed Jon Exton to proceed and have all stockists interviewed. Although, in his heart, he knew there was a slim likelihood of a result from that effort. At least it would cover his backside when he wrote it up in his Policy Book, should his investigation get questioned at a later date.

He turned to the forensic podiatrist Haydn Kelly. 'Anything to add at this stage, Haydn?'

Kelly shook his head.

'Okay. I don't think we are going to achieve a lot more overnight. The next meeting will be at 6.30 p.m. tomorrow,' Grace said. 'Glenn and I will be holding a press conference at eleven o'clock, so if there are any significant developments that come in before then, let me know.'

As he stood up, Emma Reeves asked, 'Any chance of Gaia's autograph, chief?'

Grace smiled.

# 72

NOT DEAD YET

Cleo lay in bed, her laptop propped in front of her on the duvet, logged into Mumsnet, her coursework papers for the Open University degree she was taking in Philosophy spread all around her. She was leadenly tired, but it was only 7.30 p.m., far too early to go to sleep. Laura Marling, one of her current favourite folk singers, was playing on her iPod.

The baby was going wild tonight – it felt like it was dancing inside her. She lifted the duvet, hitched up her nightdress and watched, fascinated, as her belly looked like it was dancing too, its shape shifting from round to square, with little pointy bits sticking out.

She wished Roy was here to see this. He'd promised to be home soon. She hoped the baby would still be active when he got here.

'You're going to be amazing, Bump. You know that? You're going to be the most loved baby in the whole world!'

Bump danced even more wildly, as if in acknowledgement.

She left Mumsnet and logged on to Amazon to look up prices of car seats. With the birth of the baby imminent, she was focused on all the stuff she needed to get. She had a list compiled by her best friend Millie, who had two daughters, and another list compiled by her sister Charlie, an interior designer, who had insisted on decorating the baby's room herself.

Cot; crib linens; mattress pad; waterproof mattress pads; blankets; baby wipes; nappies; changing pad; nappy bag;

nappy-rash cream. The list just went on and on. Everyone had told her that her life would change, but only now was it really starting to dawn on her how right they were. She went on through the list. Six bottles and sterilizing equipment; bottle brush; bottle warmer; infant formula milk; nipple cream; breast pads; nursing bras; a breast pump in case Roy had to feed the baby when she wasn't there.

And just how often would Roy be there? That was one of her biggest concerns. She knew just how wedded to his work he was. In her job at the mortuary there was a constant stream of sudden deaths, which police officers had to attend. Whenever the name Roy Grace came up, she heard nothing but positive comments. He seemed universally liked and respected. He was a good man, she knew that – just one of the countless reasons why she loved him.

But there was one shadow to their relationship. He was a great copper, but would that mean he'd be a great father?

Would he be there for their child's first Nativity play – or would he be tied up on a murder investigation? And on Parents' Evening? Sports Day?

When they talked about it he always dismissed her concerns, reminding her that his father had been a police officer, yet had always managed to find the time to attend the things that had mattered. But he had not been a homicide SIO who didn't know what was going to happen in thirty minutes' time, let alone thirty days'.

Roy constantly assured her that their life together was more important than his work. But was that true? And did she even want that to be true? Would she really want a murder enquiry to suffer because Roy was more interested in spending time playing with his child?

One of Cleo's friends was married to a high-flier and she hardly saw him, particularly after the second baby was born.

He would arrive home after both infants were asleep, eat dinner, and then crash out in the spare room so he wasn't woken by the baby's constant demands for food.

Did the baby actually know yet she had a father?

Another worry that she had right now was the vandalization of her car.

Roy had told her he knew who had done it, and that he had ensured it would never happen again. But there was always going to be the danger of retribution against any police officer by an aggrieved criminal. That was something she knew she would have to live with – and be a little bit vigilant all of the time.

But she had another, even deeper, worry. Roy's missing wife Sandy.

Cleo found it hard to get him to talk about her, and yet she felt the woman's presence all around her. During the early days of their relationship, Roy had invited her back to his house. They'd made love in his bedroom and she'd stayed the night, but had barely slept a wink. She had fully expected the door to fly open at any moment, and this attractive woman to appear, staring at them contemptuously.

Sure, Roy had assured her that his relationship with Sandy was long dead, and that's how she regarded it. But there was always the nagging doubt in her mind.

'What if?'

'If?'

It gave her some comfort that Roy was having his wife declared legally dead. Ten years on. But that would not stop her reappearing if she were still alive. And how would Roy react then?

He claimed that it was over, and nothing would change that.

But what, Cleo wondered, if she had been abducted by some crazy guy. How would Roy react if Sandy appeared now, escaped from some deranged kidnapper? Surely he would be morally obliged to take her back? Regardless of what he said . . .

Cleo was not a person who would normally wish anyone dead, but sometimes she fervently wished that Sandy's body would turn up. So at least Roy would have closure. And they could move on with their lives free and clear of any shadows.

# 73

She sat in the shadows on the shaded side of the street, where she had been parked for over two hours. But at least darkness was falling, finally. It was 9.30 p.m. Once she used to love these long summer days. But today the daylight was just a major nuisance.

The interior of the small rental car reeked of cheese-burger and greasy fries. Through the windscreen she had a clear view of the entrance to the gated townhouse development where Cleo Morey lived. On the radio, the sound turned low, the Rolling Stones were singing 'Under the Boardwalk'.

The song took her back to one of their many disagreements about so many things. She preferred the version sung by The Drifters. They had argued over who wrote it. She claimed it was Kenny Young and Arthur Resnick, who were part of that group. But Roy insisted it was The Rolling Stones.

'*Mama, mir ist langweilig,*' said her son, in the passenger seat beside her. He had red all around his mouth, and was busily dipping a cluster of French fries into the mess of ketchup at the bottom of the carton.

'*Mein Schatz, wir sind jetzt in England. Hier spricht man Englisch!*' she said.

He shrugged. 'Yah? Okay. I'm bored.' Then he yawned.

She stroked his forehead, affectionately. '*Sehr gut!*'

He turned his head and looked at her quizzically. 'You said people speak English here, now you speak German yourself. Huh!' He picked up the huge carton of Coke and sucked noisily through the straw.

Sometimes, when the boy made her really irritated, she would think – although never say to him – *I left Roy for you? I must have been crazy.*

But that was the truth. Or at least part of the truth. She had left Roy Grace because she had found out she was pregnant with their child. The child they had both wanted so badly; the child they had been trying to have for almost eight years. It was so ironical. She had found out she was pregnant, finally, just days after she had made the decision that she did not want to spend the rest of her life married to Roy Grace. Married to Sussex CID. Subordinate to Sussex CID.

She knew that the moment Roy found out she was pregnant, she would be stuck; for a long time; for a life sentence; even if they parted, she would have to share the child with him for ever. As a result of a windfall inheritance from an aunt, which she did not tell Roy about, she was independently well off. She could afford to leave. And she did.

She didn't say a word to her parents, whom she despised. Did not tell anyone. Instead she went into hiding with the only people who had ever given her a feeling of self-worth. The only people who, she felt, regarded her as someone in her own right, and not someone defined by who had given birth to her, or who had married her.

For the first time in her life, she had been her own person. Not her parents' daughter, Miss Sandy Balkwill. Not her husband's wife, Mrs Roy Grace. She had her new name, which she had borrowed from her maternal, German grand-mother. Her new identity. Her whole new life ahead of her.

Sandy Lohmann.

Sandy Lohmann was a woman who had cleared everything from her head: the husband who constantly let her down because he had to go to a crime scene; the father who let her down because he could never tell the truth about a damned thing in life; the mother who'd never had an opinion of her own.

The Scientologists operated the *Clear*, under their universal banner, THE BRIDGE TO TOTAL FREEDOM. They had helped her to clear the past out of her mind, and look at the world through fresh eyes. And they had helped her to look after the baby.

It was while living in their headquarters near East Grinstead in Sussex that she had met Hans-Jürgen Waldinger. He had subsequently persuaded her to move with her infant son to Munich, where he introduced her to the organization he had helped to establish, called the International Association of FreeSpirits. The organization offered similar mental regeneration to the Scientologists, but in what she felt was a less aggressive – and costly – process.

She had found Waldinger very attractive. And still did. But living with him had not worked out. She rapidly ended up arguing and rowing with him just as much as she had done with Roy. In the end she had moved into an apartment of her own.

So what the hell was she doing back here?

A damned advertisement in a Munich newspaper she had just happened, by chance, to see a month ago. That was why.

SANDRA (SANDY) CHRISTINA GRACE
Wife of Roy Jack Grace of Hove. City of Brighton
and Hove, East Sussex, England.
   Missing, presumed dead, for ten years. Last
seen in Hove, Sussex. She is five feet, seven

inches tall (1.70 metres), slim build, and had
shoulder-length fair hair when last seen.

Unless anyone can provide evidence that she
is still alive to Messrs Edwards and Edwards LLP
at the address beneath, a declaration will be
sought that she is legally dead.

Of course, at some point Roy was going to move on with his
life, what did she expect? But all the same it hurt like hell.
She couldn't help it. It was his damned fault she'd had to
leave in the first place. Now it seemed he was trying to
dismiss his past with a single wave of his hand. Having
herself declared dead could only be for one reason: so he
could be free to marry again.

Marry his pregnant bitch.

She pulled the particulars of the house out of the glove
locker. The house where they had once been so happy.
Their home. It was on the market now, and it might never
come back on the market again for the rest of their lives,
because it was the kind of house people lived in for years.
The kind of family home where people could grow old
together.

The two of them could have grown old there together.
That had been the plan. She and Roy. What would that have
been like? What kind of an old couple would they have
made?

'How long do we have to stay here?' Bruno asked suddenly in German.

She looked at him, the son Roy had always wanted, and
was about to reply, but then stiffened. A man was striding
down the street towards them, dressed in a dark suit, and
carrying a bulky attaché case. It had been ten years since
she had last seen him, but in this fading light it could have
been just twenty-four hours. His trim figure was just the

same and his face had barely aged. Only his hair was different, cropped short and gelled. It suited him.

He looked happy, and that sent a deep twinge of sadness spiralling through her.

She knew there was no chance he would recognize her in the falling darkness, wearing large sunglasses, a baseball cap pulled low over her forehead, and with her hair dyed black. But even so, she tilted her face down. A thousand thoughts were going through her mind. *Was the woman carrying a boy or a girl? How happy was he with her? How long had they been seeing each other? Did they argue all the time?*

*What do I do next?*

She waited some moments then took a cautious peep. Just in time to see him tapping the entry panel keypad. Then he pushed the wrought-iron gate open and entered. Moments later it swung shut behind him, with a clang.

Swung shut on her.

Locking her out of his new life.

She kept looking until he had walked out of sight.

Then she twisted the key in the ignition, so hard that for a moment she thought she had snapped it. The engine fired. She checked her mirrors, then accelerated up the road, squealing the tyres, sending Coke spurting over her protesting son.

# 74

'Goddamn lucky it ain't raining,' Drayton Wheeler said. He turned, as if for confirmation, to the awkward-looking woman standing behind him in the long line of people stretched back from the main entrance to Brighton Race-course; the building had been commandeered by the film production as the assembly point for the extras.

She looked up from the copy of the *Argus* she was reading, staring for some moments at the rather odd man in front of her in the queue to register as film extras. 'Very lucky.'

'You're fucking telling me.'

He was definitely a weirdo, she thought. Tall and gangly, with a grey pageboy fringe poking out beneath a wash-faded baseball cap. He was all twitchy, his face screwing up in frown lines, as if filled with pent-up anger, and had a sickly, sallow complexion. There were fifty people in front of them, all shapes and sizes, waiting to sign on and be fitted for costumes. They had been standing for over an hour, in the blustery wind high up on Race Hill. White rail posts marked the race track, and there were fine views across the city and south, over the Marina and the English Channel.

Suddenly, from the front of the queue, a cheery woman's voice called out, 'Are family Hazeldine here? Paul Hazeldine, Charlotte Hazeldine, Isobel Hazeldine and Jessica Hazeldine? With their dog, Benson? If you are here, could you make yourselves known to us please! Come forward to the front of the queue!'

Wheeler looked at his watch. 'Gonna be another hour at least.' He looked at the woman, who was about his age. She had an angular face, with blonde hair styled like Gaia's from a photograph that was in a large spread about the shooting of the movie in today's edition of the local paper.

His movie.

His script they had stolen.

He could do with sex. She wasn't attractive, but she looked like she was single and she wasn't a paper bag job. No wedding band. Great legs. He was a legs man. Maybe she was up for sex? Maybe, if he played it right, he could get her back to his room for a screw afterwards? He could focus on her legs, and not her face. His apparatus still functioned – one of the side-effects of the happy pills he was on to help him forget that he was dying. She looked lonely. He was lonely.

'Done this before?' he asked, trying to break the ice.

'Actually,' she said, 'that's none of your business.' She lifted her newspaper, to block him out of sight, and continued reading the spread on Gaia and on the filming which was starting on Monday.

*Bitch.* She was thinking. *Oh you bitch, Gaia. I'm going to think about giving you one more chance. Understand? One more chance. And that's only because we love each other.*

She could tell, from the contrite expression Gaia had, that she was trying to send her a signal. An apology.

*It's almost too late. But I might give you one more chance. I haven't decided.*

She lowered the paper. 'Actually I'm only doing this because I'm a personal friend of Gaia.'

'No shit?' he said.

She smiled back proudly. 'She's wonderful, isn't she?'

'You think so?'

'She can do no wrong!'

'You think so? Jesus!'

'Well, from what I've read about this film, the script is crap, but she will make it something special.'

'Crap? Lady, did you say the script is crap?'

'Whoever wrote it has no idea at all about the truth between George and Maria. But that's Hollywood, right?'

'I don't like your tone.'

'Fuck you.'

'Fuck you, too,' he said, glaring at her. He wanted to tell her he wrote it, that *his* version of events was correct, regardless of what abomination those assholes at Brooker Brody had made it into. Instead he turned away. Fighting to bring his anger back under control.

They stood in silence for the next ninety minutes. Finally it was his turn to sign on. He gave his name as Jerry Baxter. He was given a copy of the production shooting schedule and the Monday call sheet, and was then sent through to the upstairs room for male costume fitting. As he left, the fresh-faced young woman behind the desk smiled up at the next in line. 'Your name, please?'

'Anna Galicia,' she said.

'Do you have any acting experience?' the woman asked her.

'Actually, I'm a personal friend of Gaia.'

'Really?'

'Yes, really.'

'You should have asked her to contact us – save you queuing.'

'Oh, I would hate to bother her while she's rehearsing. She likes to get into the zone before acting.'

'I've heard that.'

'She does, it's true.'

Anna Galicia signed the release form, and entered the details requested from her. She was given the production schedule, a call sheet for Monday, and was then directed through to the female costume room.

It was full of fat women, slim women, young women, middle-aged women, squeezing into ridiculous costumes and ornate wigs. They were there for the money, the sixty-five pounds a day. They were there for vanity. For fun.

None of them was there for the same reason as herself.

None of the others was there because Gaia had personally asked them to be there, like she had asked her. To make amends for her behaviour at The Grand. She had been stressed out with jet lag. She was deeply sorry for her behaviour.

Anna was big-hearted. She knew how to forgive.

She'd forgiven her.

# 75

After his costume fitting, Drayton Wheeler took the extras'
courtesy bus down to the centre of Brighton, then walked
along to the Royal Pavilion, checking that one part of his
purchase from Mothercare was safely in his pocket. He paid
his entrance fee and went in. It was half past one. Over four
hours before the place closed to the public.

More than sufficient time, with luck.

He made his way straight to the Banqueting Room, and
was pleased to see it was packed with people, all slowly
moving around the edge of the room, restricted by the ropes
on their brass posts which kept them well away from the
banqueting table. He was even more pleased to see there
was only one security guard in here at the moment.

He stopped only a short distance along, pretending to
admire a handsome mahogany side table, laden with silver-
ware. A couple with two bored children shuffled past, followed by a group of Japanese tourists, who stopped right in
front of him. On the far side of the room the security guard
was momentarily occupied preventing someone from taking
a photograph. Now was perfect!

No one noticed him slip his hand beneath the side table,
and press something small and hard against the underside,
holding it until he was certain the glue had taken. It took
only a few seconds, during which the Japanese tourists had,
very obligingly, not moved either.

Then he shuffled on forward, going with the flow.
Mission accomplished!

# 76

'The bitch won't let me!' Glenn Branson said, storming into Roy Grace's office shortly before 8 a.m. on Monday. 'Can you believe it? The chance of a lifetime, something they could tell their children about one day, and their grand-children!'

Grace looked up from the notes his MSA had prepared for this morning's briefing. 'Won't let you what?'

'Take Sammy and Remi to meet Gaia's kid, right?'

'You're joking!'

'I am so not joking. I am seething. She said no. I asked them both when I took them out on Saturday afternoon, and they were thrilled to bits. I told you they're both massive Gaia fans. So I told her they wanted to go, when I took them back.'

'So, she can't stop you. Just take them.'

'She says Gaia is a symbol of sex and bad language and she's not having her corrupting them.'

'That's ridiculous! Her little boy is six years old!'

'You want to phone Ari and tell her?'

'I will, if you like,' Grace said, with false bravado. Not many things scared him in life, but Glenn Branson's wife did.

'I spoke to my solicitor over the weekend. She advised me not to force the issue, that Ari could use it against me.'

'How?'

'I don't know.' He sat down in front of Grace, looking dejected. 'How was your weekend?'

322

For a change, Grace had had a peaceful weekend. Just two short briefings on *Operation Icon*, and the rest of the time he had spent with Cleo. They'd gone shopping on Saturday and bought stuff for the baby's room, had a takeaway curry on Sunday, watched a couple of movies, and in between read some of the papers. One of Cleo's extravagances, which he liked, was that she had virtually every English Sunday paper, from lowbrow to highbrow, delivered every week.

It was a fine day, and she had insisted they go out for fresh air to their favourite place, the undercliff walk at Rottingdean, and she had managed the entire length of it. It really seemed the problems with a sudden bleed that she'd had a few weeks ago were a thing of the past. Just a few more weeks to go before she was due.

She would stop work at the end of this week. Most of the rest of Sunday he'd spent on the sofa with her as she worked on her Philosophy studies, and he'd gone through all the trial papers on the Carl Venner case, which opened at the Old Bailey this morning.

He reached out and took his friend's massive black hand. It was hard as a rock, like gripping a piece of ebony. All the same, he squeezed it. 'Don't let her get you down, matey. Okay?'

Glenn squeezed back.

Grace said nothing. He could see the big, tough guy he loved so much was close to tears.

# 77

'The time is 8.30 a.m., Monday, June the thirteenth. This is the seventeenth briefing of *Operation Icon*,' Roy Grace said to his team in the Conference Room. 'Does anyone have any progress to report since our briefing of yesterday morning?'

Annalise Vineer raised her hand. 'Yes, chief. I've been going through the list of members of the West Sussex Piscatorial Society supplied to me by their secretary, and the list of all people who had any involvement with this club. I've found someone with a link to Stonery Farm.'

'You have?' Grace said. 'Well done – tell us!'

'I don't know if it's of any significance, but Stonery Farm and the West Sussex Piscatorial Society use the same firm of Brighton accountants, Feline Bradley-Hamilton. There's one name in particular that's common to both, which is an auditor employed by this firm, a man by the name of Eric Whiteley. He has carried out the annual audit for both the farm and the club for several years.'

Grace wrote the name down. 'I'm not familiar with how auditors work,' he said. 'Would he have been to the premises of both?'

'Well, he goes to the office at Stonery Farm each year. The Piscatorial Society secretary was unable to tell me whether Whiteley has ever actually been to the lake that the Piscatorial Society own. But he is their principal contact.'

'How many employees are there at these accountants, Feline Bradley-Hamilton?' Grace asked.

'Fourteen, sir,' Annalise Vineer replied. 'There are four partners, the rest are employees.'

'So anyone from this firm would have access to information about Stonery Farm and the Piscatorial Society, presumably?' Grace quizzed.

'Presumably, sir, yes,' she replied.

Grace felt excited; at last he had something concrete to work on now. And his instincts were telling him that while the perpetrator was not necessarily part of this accountancy firm, there was the possibility of a lead coming from here. 'So we can't be sure Eric Whiteley would be the only one in the firm who knows where the lake is?'

'No, sir. But certainly he's the only one who visits Stonery Farm on a regular basis.'

'And that's the only match you have? The only person common to both?'

'Yes, it is, sir.'

'Is the club secretary able to tell you anything about this Eric Whiteley?'

'Not much, sir. Says he's a quiet, unassuming man who just turns up at the secretary's house every year, by appointment, to get the paperwork signed off. He doesn't talk much, apparently.'

'Okay, first things first, we should interview everyone in the firm who's been there more than six months. I want two trained interviewers – ' He looked at the faces around him.

Glenn raised a hand. 'Boss, I'd like to suggest Bella and I do the interview. Big *if*, but, *if* this Eric Whiteley, or anyone else at the accountancy firm, should turn out to be the perp, he might react – and be thrown a bit – by having seen us on *Crimewatch.*'

Grace nodded assent. Both detectives were trained Cognitive Suspect Interviewers. 'He doesn't sound a very likely candidate, but the link between the two places is interesting.'

He looked down at his notes, then at Norman Potting. 'Myles Royce, Norman? You're expecting DNA results back from the lab later today?'

'I am indeed, boss.'

'Let me know as soon as you hear.'

'I will indeed.'

Glenn Branson stared at Potting, still trying to figure out what on earth Bella Moy could see in the man. Twenty years her senior, charmless and, despite his recent makeover, not in any way physically appealing. At least not in his view. Although to be fair, he had been married four times, so presumably he had *something* that was not immediately apparent.

David Green, the Crime Scene Manager, reported on the progress that SOCOs and the Specialist Search Unit were making, looking for the missing head in the area around the West Sussex Piscatorial Society. Or rather, the lack of progress. This morning he had instructed them to widen the search parameters.

That was not good news, Grace thought. Although, from experience, he knew that there was always the possibility that the head, if buried on dry land, could have been carried off by a fox or a badger. Perps often spent hours digging deep graves for their victims. But these tended to preserve the bodies quite well. It was shallow graves that caused much bigger problems for murder investigation teams, because all kinds of animals would carry the remains away, for food and nests, dispersing them over a wide area.

He drew a circle on his pad around the name *Eric Whiteley*. So far their only suspect. He looked forward to the interview report.

After the meeting ended he headed back to his office and phoned Victoria Somers, the mother of his god-daughter, wondering if Jaye might like to play with Gaia's son. She was a few years older than Roan Lafayette, but from the tone of her mother's voice, that did not matter remotely. She sounded thrilled to bits.

One very small problem sorted.

And brownie points for himself all round.

# 78

He felt ridiculous. He had a pretty good idea that he looked ridiculous too. And he was perspiring heavily. He was in goddamn agony. The waist of the jacket was far too tight for him; the crotch of the cream pantaloons was crushing his balls, and the boots the idiot wardrobe woman had crammed his feet into were at least two sizes too small, and crippling his toes. His wig felt like he was wearing a straw bird's nest.

He should be spending his last days on a sunlounger on a yacht in the Caribbean, drinking mojitos, surrounded by nubile young women. This was so wrong. The story of his fucking life. Screwed all the time. The goddamn movie business, goddamn television. Screwed by each of his agents. And now this final insult. Brooker Brody Productions stealing his story. The best damned thing he had written in his life.

And instead of basking in glory, he was sweating in tights and an itchy wig.

*You're going to be sorry. So sorry. All of you. Oh fucking yes.*

That bitch who had been rude to him on Saturday was going to be sorry, too. He was looking around for her but had not seen her so far. He had plans for her. That was the great thing about dying – you no longer had to give a shit!

But first he had to focus. The task ahead. He had a copy of the production schedule. It gave him every day's shooting on location in Brighton. Inside and outside the Pavilion, depending on the weather. Outside during the daytime, weather permitting. Inside when it was closed to the public.

Tomorrow after it was closed they were starting shooting the scene in the Banqueting Room when George IV ended his relationship with Maria Fitzherbert, telling her she was history.

The king would tell her while they were sitting beneath the chandelier that he was always scared of. Hollywood stars Judd Halpern and Gaia seated beneath that chandelier. How great would it be to have it crash down on both of them?

He could imagine the headlines around the world the next day. Two legends dead!

*How are you going to feel about that, Larry Brooker? Maxim Brody? Bet you will be sorry you ripped off my treatment, won't you? All your dreams shattered like the crystals of the chandelier.*

*See? I'm pretty poetic, really. Know what I'm saying?*

The bus, packed full of costumed extras, moved off, pulling out through the gates of Brighton Racecourse, and on to the road. It turned left, down the hill, heading towards the sea, and then the Pavilion.

Drayton Wheeler clutched the small rucksack tightly. It contained his change of clothes; drinking water; food; torch; a glass San Pellegrino bottle filled with the mercuric chloride acid cocktail he had very carefully mixed; and a towel from the hotel bathroom.

When he focused on the task ahead, and forgot all about his outfit, he felt a lot better. Oh yes.

He felt extremely happy.

# 79

The bloody woman was pestering him again. Angela Mc-
Neill was managing to find an excuse to come into Eric
Whiteley's office almost every lunchtime now, on some
pretext or other. He tried ignoring her, but she was not the
kind of person who would even notice she was being
ignored.

Today she was holding a clutch of bound annual
accounts for Stonery Farm, which had been returned by a
Sussex Police financial investigator called Emily Curtis,
wanting to replace them in their correct filing cabinet. There
was no urgency on this, Eric knew, she could have done it
at any time, but she chose his lunch hour. Deliberately.

Angela McNeill stood over him, looking down at the
tuna mayo sandwich, Twix bar, apple and bottle of sparkling
water. 'My, you're a real creature of habit, aren't you, Eric
Whiteley?'

He concentrated on reading the *Argus* newspaper, open
in front of him. They had conveniently printed the entire
production shooting schedule, so that the public could
know where to go and watch. The production was still
appealing for more extras for some crowd scenes.

They had asked him to turn up this morning, but of
course he couldn't, not today, not during a weekday, except
in his holidays. But the next days off he had booked were
not until September.

'You always have exactly the same lunch.'

He wasn't sure whether it was a question or just a

comment. Either way he didn't care and it was none of her business. He didn't like her voice, it was a charmless, flat monotone. He didn't care for the way she smelled either. She wore a scent that smelled like toilet air freshener. He hated the way she stood over him, watching him feed like he was some creature in a zoo. He could imagine her being the kind of woman a husband would want to murder.

'It's what I like,' he mumbled without looking up at her, and realized he had now re-read the same sentence three times.

'It's important to vary your diet, you know, Eric. There's a lot of mercury in fish. Too much fish is bad for you.'

'I'm a bit of a fishy character!'

'Oooh, you've got a wicked sense of humour, haven't you? I can tell!'

He wished he'd kept his mouth shut. Then he silently prayed that if he were ever in his life unfortunate enough to get stuck in a lift with someone, it wouldn't be her.

His phone rang.

Saved by the bell, he thought, picking it up.

It was the receptionist. Her voice sounded strange. 'Eric, there's a gentleman and a lady who'd like to speak to you in the Conference Room.'

'Really? What about? I don't have any appointments today.'

In fact, he very rarely had appointments. He mostly worked alone, crunching numbers; it was other people in this firm who regularly dealt with the clients. The only meetings he ever had were the occasional ones with inspectors from the HM Revenue and Customs probing into the finances of clients, and when he was auditing.

'They are police officers – detectives. They're interviewing everyone in the firm.'

'Ah.' He frowned. 'Shall I come down?'

'Right away, if you could, please.'

'Yes, good, right.' He stood up and put on his jacket. 'I'm sorry,' he said to Angela McNeill. 'I – my appointment's here – I have to go to the Conference Room.'

'Aren't you going to finish your lunch first?'

'I'll have it afterwards.'

'Would you like me to put your sandwich in the fridge? You shouldn't leave it out, you could get salmonella.'

'A bit of salmonella would go rather nicely with tuna,' he said, and escaped from the room, leaving Angela to laugh at his joke.

As he walked along the corridor he wondered what this could be about. Had they found the bicycle he'd had stolen two years ago? Somehow he didn't think they'd be interviewing everyone in the firm about that.

He entered the small Conference Room, with its eight-seater table, with a breezy smile but feeling nervous. A tall black man in a flashy suit and even flashier tie stood there. Next to him was a rather plain-looking woman in her mid-thirties, with tangled brown hair, wearing a white blouse, black trousers and utilitarian black shoes.

'Good afternoon!' he said. He could feel beads of sweat popping on his brow. Police always had that effect on him. He noticed the male officer peering down at his feet for a moment.

'Eric Whiteley?' The man produced a warrant card. 'I'm Acting Detective Inspector Branson and this is my colleague, Detective Sergeant Moy. Thank you for taking the time to talk to us.'

Eric studied his warrant card for some moments because he felt he should, to look like he was taking this meeting seriously. Then he said, expansively, 'Please have a seat. Can I offer you any refreshments?'

'Thank you,' the Acting DI said. 'We've already been looked after.'

'Good!' Eric said. 'Well, that's good, isn't it!'

He noticed a quick exchange of glances between the two officers. The two detectives sat on one side of the table, with their backs to the window with its view out across the Pavilion grounds, and he sat opposite them. Immediately he realized he was in a bad position, because the strong afternoon light from the brilliant blue sky was directly behind them, making it hard to see their faces clearly.

He felt intimidated. Like sitting in front of two school bullies. 'Erm, I don't suppose you've come about my bicycle?'

Both of them looked at him strangely. 'Bicycle?' the woman said.

'I had it stolen from outside – a long time ago now. The bastards cut through the padlock.'

'No, I'm sorry,' Branson said. 'That would be local uniform or CID – we're from the Major Crime Branch.'

'Ah.' Eric nodded approvingly.

The detective was staring very hard at his face, eyeball to eyeball, which made Eric feel even more uncomfortable. As if at any moment he was about to say Ubu! Useless, Boring, Ugly! Instead he said, 'Mr Whiteley, we're making enquiries regarding the murder of an as yet unidentified body. The torso which was found at—'

'Stonery Farm?' Eric interrupted.

'Yes,' Bella Moy said.

'Correct,' Branson confirmed. 'There were also body

parts which belong to this same body recovered from the West Sussex Piscatorial Society trout lake near Henfield.'

Eric nodded. 'Yes, yes, I thought you'd be getting round to me eventually!' He gave a nervous laugh, but neither detective smiled.

'How long have you worked here, Mr Whiteley?' Glenn Branson asked.

He thought for a moment. 'At Feline Bradley-Hamilton? Twenty-two years. Well, it will be twenty-three in November.'

'And what exactly is your role here?'

'I do company audits, mostly.'

The detective was still eyeballing him, without blinking. 'Would I be correct in saying you carried out the audits this year on Stonery Farm and on the West Sussex Piscatorial Society?'

'Something fishy about the West Sussex Piscatorial Society, is there, Detective?' He giggled nervously at his joke.

Neither of them smiled, which made him even more nervous.

'Nothing fishy at all, Mr Whiteley,' he replied, levelly. 'Could you tell us how long you have been auditing these two?'

Whiteley thought for some moments. 'Well, some years.' He looked down. He was feeling increasingly intimidated. 'Yes. Ten years, at least. I can check if you would like? With Stonery Farm I could tell you egg-zactly!' He giggled again, and was met with stony glares.

'We're investigating a murder, Mr Whiteley,' Glenn Branson said. 'I'm afraid we don't quite share your humour on this. Have you ever been to the premises of Stonery Farm, Mr Whiteley?'

'Every year. I do some of the accounts work on site.'

'And you've been to the West Sussex Piscatorial Society trout lake?'

'Only once, just to familiarize myself with the location – it's the club's main asset. But I carry out the audit work for the club here – it's very straightforward.'

'Does anyone else from this firm accompany you when you audit Stonery Farm?'

He shook his head. 'No, I get on very well with Mr Winter, the owner; it's a job for one person, really.' His armpits were damp. He was sweating profusely now and still could not see their faces clearly. He wanted to get back to his office, to his solitude and his lunch and his newspaper. 'This murder is a terrible thing,' he went on. 'I mean, there could be a bad impact on Stonery Farm's business. I mean, would you want to eat free-range eggs from hens that had been feeding in an area where there was a corpse? I'm not sure I would.'

'Or eat fish that had been feeding where human body parts were found?' the woman detective asked.

Whiteley nodded. 'Very creepy, if you ask me.' He giggled again, then looked at the two faces glaring at him. At the two bullies. Two unsmiling bullies. 'I'm very careful what I put in my mouth – what I eat. My body is my temple.'

'*Kramer vs. Kramer*,' Branson said.

'Pardon me?'

'Dustin Hoffman said that in the movie.'

'Ah, right.'

There was a brief silence, which Eric Whiteley found increasingly awkward. The two detectives stared at him as if he were a book they were reading. Clearing his throat he said, 'Um, so how do you feel that I can – you know – assist in your enquiries?' He grinned again, from nerves.

'Well,' Glenn Branson said, 'it might help if you stopped finding this so funny, Mr Whiteley.'

'Sorry.' Eric ran his fingers across his lips. 'Zipped!'

There was a long silence again. He felt the two detectives just simply staring at him. As if their eyes were full of unasked questions. He squirmed in his chair. He was hungry. He wished he had eaten his sandwich now. And the Twix. But at the same time, his stomach was feeling unsettled. He glanced at his watch. His lunch hour was running out. Ten minutes left.

'Got a bus to catch?' Glenn Branson asked. 'Or a train?'

'I'm sorry, I'm not with you.'

'You keep looking at your watch.'

'Yes, well, I am a bit worried about salmonella. You see, you need to be careful with sandwiches in this heat.'

Once more he clocked the two detectives exchanging a glance. Like some secret code.

Like school bullies.

Branson looked directly at him again, staring into his eyes. 'Does the name Myles Royce mean anything to you?'

He did not like the bullying stare from the detective and looked down at the table. 'Myles Royce? No, I don't think so, why?'

'You don't think so?' Glenn Branson asked. 'You don't *think* so or are you certain?'

The detective's manner was making him agitated. He was feeling flushed again, his face getting hot. He wanted to be out of this room and back in the sanctuary of his own office. 'How certain can any of us be of anything in life?' Eric replied, eyes still fixed on the table. 'I don't want to give you a wrong answer. This firm deals with lots of clients and each of them in turn employs lots of people. The name doesn't mean anything to me today, but I can't guarantee

I've never met someone of that name. I wouldn't want to be accused of misleading you.'

'I'm not exactly clear,' Glenn said, speaking very slowly and firmly. 'Are you saying you've never met someone by the name of Myles Royce? Myles Terence Royce?'

Eric closed his eyes for some moments. He was shaking. Then he glared defiantly back at Branson. 'I will not be bullied. Do I make myself clear?'

# 80

As Drayton Wheeler clambered down the steps of the coach into the blazing June sunshine, he was perspiring heavily and his wig had become even itchier. A young man, wearing a yellow tabard over a T-shirt and ripped jeans, was bellowing through a megaphone.

'All extras proceed to the assembly area opposite the front entrance of the Pavilion!'

The street was lined with production trucks and there were heavy-duty cables trailing everywhere. A camera mounted on a dolly sat on a long length of track on the Pavilion lawn. There were gantries of lights high up off the ground; harassed-looking grips and gaffers were working feverishly. The Director of Photography was standing near the camera, taking light measurements and issuing instructions to his crew. To the left, on the tarmac area in front of the Dome, was a cluster of large motorhomes with slide-outs, and it was easy to spot Gaia's, which was the size of a house, and Judd Halpern's, only marginally smaller, parked alongside it, power cables and water hoses trailing from each. A huge crowd of onlookers was gathered behind a tape cordon manned by several security guards.

Gathered to watch the filming of scenes he had suggested and which Brooker Brody Productions had stolen.

Oh, they were going to be sorry.

The young man, the third, fourth or fifth Assistant Director, continued to bellow instructions.

Drayton scowled. He shuffled along in the line of extras in their equally hot and uncomfortable costumes.

A hawk-eyed young woman came running up to him, her hair in a messy ponytail, a headset with earpiece and microphone clipped to her head. 'Sorry,' she said, holding out her hand. 'You can't have that rucksack with you!'

'I'm a diabetic!' he snapped back. 'It has my medication.'

'I'll look after it for you – if you need anything in it, just let me know – I'll be around.' She reached for the bag and he gripped it tightly.

'I'm not letting this out of my sight, young lady. Okay?'

'It's not okay. People in 1810 did not carry rucksacks!'

Wheeler pointed at the building. 'Yeah? Let me tell you something. You see that building?'

'The Pavilion?'

'Uh huh. You're telling me rucksacks didn't exist in 1810?'

'That's right!'

'Yeah, well let me tell you something else. This goddamn fucking Royal Pavilion didn't exist in 1810 either.'

'Well,' she said, smiling, unfazed. 'This is a movie – we have to cut a little slack here and take some licence with exact dates.'

Gripping his rucksack tightly in his fist he said, 'Yeah, right. Well, that's what I'm doing too, I'm cutting a little slack. So fuck off.'

They glared at each other for some moments. 'Okay,' she said. 'I'll be right back!'

He watched her hurry off. Then he hastily pushed his way past the long line of costumed extras in front of him and reached the front entrance of the Pavilion. A security guard stepped into his path. 'Sorry, sir, ticket holders only.'

'I have to use the toilet,' Drayton Wheeler said.

The guard pointed to his left, towards the catering truck and the cluster of motorhomes. 'The toilet facilities for extras are over there, sir.'

He pointed to his rucksack. 'The AD told me I could put my rucksack inside. I'm a diabetic you see. She said I could store it in the back room where the wheelchairs are. I need to take a shot.'

The guard frowned. Then, conspiratorially he said, 'Okay, be quick.'

Wheeler thanked him, and hurried inside. The corridor was deserted. He stopped by the closed, ochre-painted half-gate at the top of the stone staircase that led down into the basement of the building, and looked around. No one in sight. He slipped the bolt as he had done previously, closed the gate behind him, then descended the steps and hurried along the underground brick-floored corridor. He stopped outside the decrepit green door, with the yellow and black DANGER – HIGH VOLTAGE sign, and yanked it open. He stepped inside, into the familiar fusty smell and pulled the door shut behind him.

Then he flicked on his torch. He checked out the wall of fuses and electrical switchgear, and the pipework that looked like it was lagged in asbestos. A pair of bright red eyes shone back.

A rat, the size of a small cat. Then with a scratching, scurrying sound it was gone.

'Fuck you!'

He shone the torch around, checking every crevice. Listening to the humming sound and the rhythmic click-tick-click-tick of the electrics. It felt even warmer in here than before. He shone the torch around again, warily. He hated rats. He hated spiders. He hated enclosed spaces.

In six months' time his body would be in an enclosed space. A coffin.

He smiled.

The last laugh, oh yes. He would have that all right.

He'd left instructions in his will for his ashes to be flushed down the toilet of Brooker Brody Productions offices on the Universal Studio lot.

As he pulled off his horrible wig, and wriggled out of the rest of his clothes, he just hoped there was an afterlife, so that he could get to witness it.

Particularly to see the face of that bitch, his not quite *ex*-wife, when she heard about those instructions.

He opened his rucksack and started to take out his normal clothes and provisions. Okay, so this wasn't the greatest place to spend the next twenty-four hours, and they didn't do room service. But compared to the coffin awaiting him in six months' time, this was a suite at the Ritz Carlton.

# 81

'The time is 6.30 pm, Monday, the thirteenth of June. This is the eighteenth briefing of *Operation Icon*,' Roy Grace said to his team. 'We've made some good progress since this morning.' He turned to Potting. 'Norman?'

Potting had a smug smile on his face that made him look like a gross Buddha, Glenn Branson thought, staring at the old warhorse, still unable to believe this man was now, unknowingly, his love rival.

'We have a report back from the lab,' Potting said, smugly, in his rural burr. 'The DNA from the hairbrush and toothbrush I took from the home of Myles Royce matches the DNA from the torso recovered from Stonery Farm, and the limbs recovered from the West Sussex Piscatorial Society. No question, it is the same person.'

The atmosphere in the room changed perceptibly.

'Good work, Norman,' Grace said. 'Okay, we need to do our background on the victim. Norman, as you've already met the mother, you should take a Family Liaison Officer with you and break the news. See what further information you can find out from her about his friends and associates. Get the mother's permission to search his house. In particular let's see if he left a computer or mobile phone – and hopefully both. If his mobile phone isn't there, ask his mother for his number, and we can still get most of what we need from his service provider. We can get cell-site analysis done on his movements, and we can see who he talked to.'

He paused and made a note. 'If he owned a car, let's get its movement history over the past eighteen months off the ANPR network. Also see what photographs he has in his house of other people – who his friends were and who he admired. I'll get the High Tech Crime Unit to hunt on social networking sites – see if he tweeted, had a Facebook page, Linked-In, any of those. We need to know everything about him. Who he engaged with, where he went to socialize, what hobbies or kinky perversions he was into, what clubs he was a member of. In particular I want to know more about his Gaia obsession and any fan clubs he had joined. Okay, Norman, that's your action.'

'Yes, chief.'

Glenn looked at Potting, then at Bella. She looked so sad today, yet he knew how he could make her happy. If he could get that prat Potting out of the way.

Was he being ridiculous? His own life was a total mess, and maybe it was totally wrong to start thinking about messing with someone else's.

'Glenn?'

'Right, boss, me and Bella interviewed all fourteen staff members of the chartered accountancy firm Feline Bradley-Hamilton today. This is the only company we've found that has links with both Stonery Farm and the West Sussex Piscatorial Society; the firm's made a specialist accountancy practice in farming and outdoors pursuits – and it's created its own software package for farmers. During this process we encountered one person we are not happy about, and we feel should be looked into further.' He glanced at his notes. 'His name is Eric Whiteley.'

'Tell me your reasons,' Grace said.

'I used your right-eye, left-eye technique that you taught me.'

Grace nodded. Human brains were divided into left and right hemispheres. One contained long-term memory storage, and in the other, the creative processes took place. When asked a question, people's eyes almost invariably moved to the hemisphere they were using. In some people the memory storage was in the right hemisphere and in some the left; the creative hemisphere would be the opposite one.

When people were telling the truth, their eyes would swing towards the memory hemisphere; when they lied, towards the creative one – to *construct*. Branson had learned from Roy Grace to tell which, by tracking their eyes in response to a simple control question such as the one he had asked Eric Whiteley earlier, about how long he had worked for the firm – to which there would have been no need for him to have lied.

'And?' Roy Grace asked.

'It's my view he was lying to us.'

Grace turned to Bella. 'What did you think?'

'I agree, sir. Whiteley's an oddball. I wasn't at all happy with how he responded to our questions.'

Grace made a note on his pad. *Eric Whiteley. Person of Interest?* 'Did you get his home address?'

'Yes,' Bella said. 'With difficulty.'

Grace raised his eyebrows. 'Oh?'

'He kept trying to tell us we were invading his privacy,' Branson said.

'I think you two should go to his house and talk to him again there. Sounds like we need to either bring him in or eliminate him from our enquiries.'

The problem, he knew, with not having a time or date of Royce's death was that all the team were working in a vacuum. When there was a clearly established time of death, alibis were often a fast and efficient way to eliminate people like Whiteley – or incriminate them. He turned to his HOLMES – Home Office Large Major Enquiry System – and Intelligence researchers. 'I want you to check the serials going back two years, and see if any of Whiteley's neighbours have ever complained about him. See if he's been involved in any incidents. We need more information on him.' Then he said to Bella, 'I think you should have a word with Whiteley's senior partner and find out what kind of employee he is.'

'I have a call in to him already, sir.'

'Good!' Then he turned to DC Exton. 'The Hunter wellington boots – anything to report from the stockists?' He pointed up at the trio of whiteboards. One board showed a photograph of Stonery Farm, circled in blue marker ink, and a photograph of the West Sussex Piscatorial Society trout lake, also circled in blue, with a line connecting them. A second showed photographs of a Hunter boot, and three photographs of the actual-size prints found around the edge of the trout lake. The third board had photographs of the torso and limbs of Myles Royce, and now, just added today, his face.

'I've obtained a list of online retailers,' Exton said. 'We've been working through these, compiling a list of names of customers they've supplied in our parameter area of Sussex, Surrey and Kent in the past two years. But the problem as we know with many stockists, like garden centres and outdoor wear shops, is many don't keep customer records. We're getting as much as we can through credit card records, but that is slow and incomplete. I've been feeding names as they come through to the indexer.' He looked at Annalise Vineer.

'Nothing so far,' she said. 'I've names from sixteen

stockists of people who've made recent purchases, but no hits, and that includes Eric Whiteley.'

Grace had worked with her on several murder enquiries and knew just how thorough she was. If she said no hits, she meant it. He looked at his notes. 'Haydn – how are you doing on gait analysis?'

'I've completed my computer modelling. I won't bore you with the technical data but analysis of these prints shows our perp has a very unusual gait. I'm confident I could pick him out in a crowd. I could spend a few days in the CCTV control room at John Street, if you like?'

Brighton and Hove had one of the most comprehensive CCTV networks of any city. This was helped by the fact that the English Channel bordered the south, giving a relatively narrow arc to the east, north and west. But the problem, as Grace saw it, was *which crowd*? Haydn Kelly was on an expensive daily rate; he couldn't just sit him down in front of a bank of television monitors and have him observe real-time footage in the hope of spotting the perp, when there were no guarantees that Myles Royce's killer was even in the city.

He looked up at the dead man's photograph. Royce was fifty-two, his mother had told Potting. He looked a little younger, in Grace's view. The unfortunate man had not been blessed with great looks. He had a rather weak, flaccid face with bulging eyes, as if he had a thyroid problem, protruding lips, a squat nose and a shapeless mop of dark-brown hair with the unnatural flat tones of a bad dye job.

A trustafarian. Modest inherited wealth. Never had to do a day's work in his life. Just dabbled in property from time to time. From the expression he wore in his photograph, he sure as hell did not look happy, Grace thought.

*So how did you end up like this? Your torso covered in*

*quicklime and immersed in chicken shit? Your limbs in a trout lake? And your head missing?*

'You know what, chief?' Norman Potting said, as if reading his mind. 'If we could just find his head, maybe he could tell us who did it!'

There was tittering in the room. Roy Grace did his best to keep a straight face, but after some moments he allowed himself a grin.

In all the murder enquiries he had attended, and more recently had run, he could not remember a single one where there had been less information about the victim or the suspected perpetrator.

In two hours' time he had to attend a press conference with Glenn. If they put over their messages correctly, it could lead to a crucial witness either phoning the police directly or the Crimestoppers line anonymously. The enormity of his responsibility never escaped him. Myles Royce was his mother's only child. He was her life. For over thirty years after leaving home, he went to see her every week, and phoned her every Sunday evening at seven, without fail. Now he hadn't phoned for almost six months. And he wouldn't be phoning ever again.

What had he done to deserve ending up dead, and with such appalling lack of dignity? Who had done this to him – and why? Was the motive sexual? Jealousy? Robbery? Homophobia? A random psychotic attack? Revenge? An argument that turned into a fight?

He looked at his team. 'Which of you are Gaia fans?'

Several hands shot up. He looked at Emma Reeves, who seemed the keenest. 'Am I right that Gaia includes a bit of S&M in her work, yes?'

'Yes, chief – but only in a fun way in one of her acts, and on one of her album covers.'

'Are we missing something very obvious here? Did she ever write a song about dismemberment? Or have some sick art about it that someone might have copied?'

'I know everything she's done, sir,' Emma Reeves said. 'That makes me a bit sad, doesn't it?'

Grace smiled. 'Not at all.'

'But there's nothing I can think of in her work that would send some sicko off to dismember someone.'

\*

After the briefing ended, Grace returned to his office and made a new entry into his Policy Book.

*Homophobic murder?*

*Blackmail of a gay lover?*

*Criminal involvement? Witnessed something? Drugs deal at a gay cruising site?*

His phone rang. He looked down at the display and did not recognize the number. He stepped out into the corridor as he answered it.

The voice of the caller was low and furtive. 'Detective Superintendent Grace?'

Grace didn't need to ask who was calling. He recognized the voice of the recidivist and informer, Darren Spicer. 'Yes, how can I help you?'

'Got some more information for you. You can have this for free.'

'That's very generous.'

'Yeah. Thought you'd like to know. That deal I was offered, what we discussed?'

'Uh huh.'

'Your friend's just come back to me and doubled it, for me to do that job.'

# 82

Drayton Wheeler lay, curled up on the floor, listening to Mozart's *Figaro* overture on his iPod earphones. It was Mozart's music which had sustained him through all the shit in his life. Mozart lifted him to the heavens. When the time finally came, he didn't want some fucking priest holding his hand, he wanted to be alone, listening to this.

He looked at his watch, munching on the cheese sandwich he had selected from his rations. Midnight. It would be safe to move into position now – he had figured out the security guards' rota in here during the small hours.

He finished eating, switched off the iPod and drank some water. He removed the iron tyre lever from his rucksack, and scooped everything else back into it apart from the torch, then stood up and hauled it on to his shoulders, shaking the cramp from his legs. Then he relieved himself in a corner.

When he had finished, he slowly and cautiously pushed open the heavy door and stepped out, looking in both directions. Just darkness. No one there. Holding the tyre lever in his right hand and the torch, switched on, in his left, he made his way along the passage, passing old pipework, a modern red firehose reel, and three rickety old antique chairs with broken wicker seats. He felt nervous. So close now. He had to succeed. *Had to*. He switched the torch off, held his breath then, knowing there would be security guards prowling around above him, inched his way up the steps in the darkness until he reached the half-gate.

Footsteps.

*Shit.*

He crouched, heart pounding, pulse tugging at the base of his wrist as if it were a small creature trying to get out. He gripped the tyre lever tightly.

Rubber-soled shoes clumping along. The sound of jangling keys. Then whistling 'The Harry Lime Theme'. The whistle of someone who was nervous. Whistling badly, missing several of the notes. Was the guard nervous of this place at night?

*Just don't come down here.*

To his relief the footsteps faded into the distance and were gone. But he stayed crouched for several more seconds, listening. A walk of twenty feet, not covered by any sensor, would take him to the door which opened on to the stairs up to the long-deserted apartment beneath the dome. He slipped the bolt, pulled open the gate and stepped out into the hallway, holding his breath. Listening intently. Total silence. He pulled the gate shut and slid the bolt back into place, flicked on the torch for an instant to get his bearings and then off again. He walked on tiptoe, passing a sign which pointed to TOILETS, pulled open the door, stepped inside and pulled it shut behind him.

Then, switching on the torch and guided by the beam, he climbed up the long, steep spiral staircase with the rickety banisters, pausing for breath halfway up. Shadows jumped around him. This place was probably full of ghosts. So what, he'd be one soon, too. The dead had never bothered him. Ghosts weren't scumbags like some of the living.

He reached the top and entered the old, abandoned apartment beneath the dome. A door lay against a wall. There were dust sheets over uneven, angular shapes. Horrible mottled wallpaper, dusty oval leaded-light windows with views out across the street lights, shadows and orange permaglow of the city at night, and the vast black expanse of the sea. A mouse – or a rat – scampered away, feet scratching on the bare boards. The air smelled dusty and dank.

He felt tired. The coffee in his flask had long gone cold. He would have liked to lie down on the floor and sleep, but he didn't dare. It would be dawn in a few hours. He needed to get into place under the cover of darkness. He stepped carefully across the circular room, passing the trapdoor secured by two bolts, with the wording on it, DANGER – STEEP DROP BELOW. DO NOT STAND ON DOOR, accompanied by the image, in purple, of a falling man. He kept the beam of his torch low, just in case anyone was looking up in this direction, and walked through a doorway into what had once been another bedroom, with everything in here also shrouded in dust sheets. In front of him was a wall, covered in graffiti. One in swirly writing said, J Cook, 1920. There was a drawing of an owl. Another drawing of a shield. Another read, RB 1906.

To the left was a small door, barely bigger than a hatch. He knelt, slid the bolts and pushed it open. The cool, blustery night air with its fresh, salty tang, engulfed him, and he breathed it in, greedily, gulping it into his lungs, a relief from the stale air inside. He removed his rucksack and pushed it through, then eased himself out, hauled himself to his feet, and carefully pushed the door shut.

He was standing on a narrow, steel platform with a handrail, with the wind tugging at him. A long way below, directly in front of him, was the dark area of the Pavilion grounds, and the shadows of the motorhomes of the stars and the production trucks. In the glow of the street lighting, and through the swaying branches of the trees, he could see the Theatre Royal and the restaurants, shops and offices of

351

New Road, and beyond, the dark, uneven rooftops of sleeping Brighton.

Around him, up here on the roof, were turrets, minarets, chimney stacks and chimney pots, and a network of walkways and metal-rung ladders fixed to walls. There was enough ambient light here to see where he was going without using his torch. He set off, walking along a steel platform between two pitched slate roofs, with skylights along one side, carefully gripping the handrail. He had memorized the plans, but even so, now he was up here, he found it hard to get his bearings. There was a faint traffic hum below him. Then the distant doppler wail of a siren stopped him for an instant, in panic.

But it ripped on past and faded.

The dome above the Banqueting Room, which was his target, lay directly ahead of him. One more walkway, then he scaled a short metal ladder, and hauled himself up on to another walkway. His tiredness was evaporating and he was starting to feel really good. Invincible! *Yeah, though I walk alone through the shadow of the Valley of Death, I shall fear no evil. For I am the Meanest Sonofabitch in the Valley.*

*Oh yes!*

*No one messes with Drayton Wheeler.*

*No one messes with the Meanest Sonofabitch in the Valley!*

One more ladder. His rucksack swung right, pulling him over, but he hung on grimly. *Three limbs on a ladder at all times!* That was the rule you had to remember. One hand, two legs; two hands, one leg.

He climbed on to the narrow platform, and the dome curved up towards the sky, majestically, steep as a mountain, right in front of him now.

He switched on his torch for a few seconds, saw the tiny

inspection hatch door, and switched it off again. He opened it, again pushed his rucksack through in front of him, then he crawled forwards, and through it, on to the first two steps of a wooden staircase, into pitch darkness. Switching on the torch again, he pulled the door shut behind him. His whole body was pounding. He was shorting out with excitement.

*Oh yes, baby, oh yes!*

He could safely keep the torch on now. He crawled forward, up several more steps, then on to a wooden platform. The interior of the dome mirrored the exterior, like a second skin. The exterior was rendered in carved stone, but the interior frame was constructed from wooden slats, like a concave ladder.

There was no point in climbing it now, he knew from his previous recce, because it just got progressively steeper. He would be more comfortable staying here, on this platform.

If the production stuck to its schedule tomorrow, after the Royal Pavilion closed to the public, Brooker Brody Productions would start filming one of the key scenes in the movie. *His movie.* King George IV and Mrs Fitzherbert sitting at the banqueting table, directly beneath the massive chandelier that His Majesty was so nervous of.

The fixings supporting the chandelier were directly above him. A two-minute climb. From the top he could look down, through a tiny crack, at the top of the chandelier, and almost the whole of the room.

With luck if he got his timings right, Gaia Lafayette and Judd Halpern would be pulped.

That would put an end to the ridiculous travesty that Brooker Brody Productions had written into the script, about Maria Fitzherbert committing suicide after being dumped by the king.

Much better for her to die like this.

# 83

At 1.30 a.m. Roy Grace, snuggled up against Cleo, was woken by a solid kick in his ribs.

'Ouch!' he said, for an instant thinking it was Cleo giving him a dig with her elbow, which she did on the rare occasions when he snored. But she seemed to be sound asleep. Then he felt another kick.

It was the baby.

Then another kick.

Without moving, Cleo murmured, 'I think Bump's practising for the London Marathon. He hasn't stopped.'

Grace felt another sudden movement but gentler this time. He said quietly, 'Hey, Bump, do you mind, I need some sleep! We all need to get some sleep, okay?'

'Not sure I can remember what sleep is any more,' Cleo said. 'I've got terrible heartburn and I've been to the loo four times.'

'I didn't hear you.'

'You were well away.'

'I was? It didn't feel like it. I don't feel like I've slept a wink, either.' He kissed her on the cheek.

'I'm wired,' she said. 'I'm so wide awake I could do some studying.'

'Don't, try to rest.'

'I can't take sleeping pills. I can't have a drink. God, you're so lucky you're a man!' Then she felt the baby move again, and she smiled. She placed Roy's hand on her abdomen. 'It's amazing, isn't it? That's a mini *us* in there! I definitely think it's a boy. Everyone's telling me I look like I'm carrying a boy. You'd prefer a boy, wouldn't you?'

'All I want is for you and our child to be healthy. I'll love it just as much whether it's a boy or a girl.'

She slipped out of bed and padded to the loo. He lay there, his mind a tangle of thoughts suddenly. The enormity of what it meant to bring a child into the world. And tragic Myles Royce – an example of what could happen to a child.

He closed his eyes and concentrated on the case. With every major enquiry, he always fretted that he might be overlooking something vital and obvious. What was he overlooking here?

'I've found several baby car seats on the internet,' Cleo said, returning from the loo.

'Car seats?'

'We need one.'

'Of course.' Yet another thing to add to the never-ending list of stuff they had to have. And never-ending cost.

'Do you think we should get a new one, or buy one on eBay – be a fraction of the cost.'

He squeezed her hand. 'What are we talking about in potential savings?'

'One hundred and fifty pounds, maybe.'

'That's a lot of money.'

'It is.'

Back in his days in uniform he had attended some terrible car crashes. One he had never forgotten, where a baby, strapped into a car seat that had sheared from its mountings in a head-on collision, smashed into the back of his mother's head, breaking her neck and killing her instantly and then hitting the front windscreen.

'Let me ask you a question, darling,' he said. 'If you were going to jump out of an aeroplane, wearing a parachute, would you rather know that the parachute you had on your back had been bought because it was the cheapest available on the market, or because it was the best?'

She squeezed his hand. 'The best, of course.'

'So there's your answer. We're talking about our baby's life. It wouldn't be much of a bargain if it turned out to have stress fractures from involvement in a previous accident.'

'Being a detective makes you so suspicious, doesn't it?'

'I was born suspicious,' he said. 'Maybe I have my dad to thank. But that's my view.'

He lapsed back into his own troubled thoughts. Amis Smallbone's intention to rob Gaia. *Well, good luck, sunshine.* No one was going to get past the goons guarding her suite. He'd notified Chief Superintendent Barrington, and the number of officers guarding her had been increased as an extra precaution.

Then his brain switched back to Myles Royce. At least now they had a name. But one thing was going around and around in his mind. Royce had been a Gaia fan. Gaia was now here in Brighton.

Someone had tried to kill her in Los Angeles.

She'd been sent death threats through an anonymous email account.

The LAPD had the suspect in custody. They were convinced they had the perp.

Was he reading too much into Royce being a Gaia fan?

Every major crime enquiry was a hugely complex puzzle. Thousands of pieces to be fitted painstakingly together. Except, when the puzzle was complete, there were never happily smiling faces. Just the grim satisfaction of knowing they had achieved justice for the victim, and possibly some closure for the family.

Provided of course he got a conviction.

'There was a documentary on the box tonight about Gaia,' Cleo murmured suddenly.

'There was? Did you watch it?'

'Not really my thing, but I recorded it, in case it was helpful for you.'

'Thanks,' he said. 'I'll watch it tomorrow. You're an angel.'

'I know,' she said. 'Never forget that, Detective Super-intendent!'

He kissed her, then slowly fell into troubled sleep.

# 84

At 1.45 a.m. Anna Galicia walked along New Road, Brighton, across the street from the Theatre Royal, wearing a bomber jacket and jeans and a baseball cap pulled on tight against the blustery wind. She stopped by a low wall, screened by some shrubs, watching the activity in the Royal Pavilion grounds wind down for the night. Two police officers strode along the pavement and she turned her face away from them. There was a tantalizing smell of frying bacon coming from the catering truck that still appeared to be open.

A short while ago, burning with hatred, she had watched Gaia leave her swanky trailer and step up into the back of a black Range Rover. The car had swept out of the grounds in a presidential-style convoy of identical vehicles.

You don't care about the environment really, do you, Gaia? Anna thought, her anger tinged with sadness. Your whole persona, your act – and even your bloody name – is all a lie, isn't it? Do you really need five Range Rovers just to transport you less than half a mile from the set to your hotel and back?

Do you?

You are such a hypocrite.

Someone has to teach you a lesson.

Then Judd Halpern, Gaia's co-star playing King George IV, emerged from his trailer. He was looking the worse for wear from drink – or drugs, in all probability – and had to be helped down the steps by two minions, and guided into the back of a Jaguar. A security guard, standing outside the main entrance, lit a cigarette. She watched it glow bright red for an instant.

Several other vehicles also left, carrying away, presumably, some of the supporting cast and senior crew. A number of unit members were still working, switching off lights on stands and humping equipment around. She stepped forward and walked nonchalantly across the Pavilion lawns, being careful not to trip over any cables. No one appeared to take any notice of her. Good.

She made her way over to the cluster of trucks and motorhomes, heading as discreetly as she could towards Gaia's trailer, which was parked close to the gatehouse building on Church Street. Just in case anyone had noticed her, she meandered as nonchalantly as she could towards the archway, as if she were just Ordinary Joe taking a late-night stroll before bed. But just as she reached the shadows on the far side of Gaia's trailer, she ducked down, pulled her iPhone out of her handbag, then switched on the *Torch* app.

She could not believe her luck.

Legend had it that King George had had a secret underground passage built, connecting the Royal Pavilion with Maria Fitzherbert's house in the Old Steine, so that he and his mistress could have their trysts in secret. But this was not true, she knew from her research. There was a secret passage, but it was built by the king for a very different reason. It was because, an immensely vain man, he was embarrassed by how gross he had become – weighing twenty stone – and did not want the public to see him. He could walk to the stables out of sight, and enter his coach in privacy. All the public would see of him would be his face at the window.

The stable block had been rebuilt by Queen Victoria,

and moved several feet to the north. The original exit from the secret passage was now a sealed trapdoor, overgrown with grass. Gaia's trailer was parked, she could see from the slight marking on the grass, backed up almost on top of it.

Deliberately? To make it up to her? It had to be a signal. *How good was that?*

Then she walked stealthily around the vehicle. Rental mobile homes like this must have some kind of discreet advertising on them, she figured. Then she found it, on the front right, a square metal plate. AD MOTORHOMES LTD. Beneath was a website address, an email address and a phone number.

She wrote down the company's number and the registration plate of the vehicle.

# 85

At the Tuesday morning briefing of *Operation Icon*, Bella Moy reported on her conversation with Stephen Feline, the senior partner of the accountancy firm where Eric Whiteley worked. Feline said that Whiteley was a bit of an oddball who kept to himself, but an exemplary employee, hard-working and totally trustworthy.

'He's an oddball all right,' Glenn Branson said. 'We went to his house after the briefing last night. He was obviously in, we saw someone moving behind the curtains, but no one answered his door. We rang the bell several times. Then we dialled his home number. Someone answered – sounded like him, and we told him we were outside. He hung up without saying anything. We rang back and we could hear it ringing – and we saw curtains twitch upstairs. But it went to answerphone each time we tried ringing again.'

'The behaviour of someone who has something to hide,' Grace said.

'With his reluctance to see us, me and Bella decided it would be better to talk to his neighbours, see what we could find out about him before we tried him again.'

'And?'

'They confirmed he's one of those people who keeps himself to himself. A couple of them said they've never seen him. One said she's seen him several times go off to work on his bicycle and come home at night and he's nodded at her a few times, but that's all. One said she's seen a tarty-looking woman come to the house a couple of times.'

'Sounds like a call girl,' Grace said. 'He lives alone?'

Glenn Branson nodded. He looked down at his note-book, open on the first page of the interview with Whiteley. 'Well, the thing was, boss, we were focused on his work connection with Stonery Farm and the angling club. That was a hard enough struggle. We didn't get much into his private life. But yeah, definitely single.'

'So none of the neighbours ever talked to Eric Whiteley?'

'All the immediate neighbours we talked to are elderly, a couple of them pretty infirm. All pleasant enough but no one seems to know or care too much about anyone else. It's sort of a weird little enclave where he is.'

Grace made a note. 'This man is not making me feel all warm and fuzzy. I want to know more about him. Why would he hide from you, unless he had something to conceal?' He looked at Glenn then, pointedly, at Bella. 'Any thoughts?'

'I don't know, sir,' she said.

'This is a murder enquiry, Bella. "Don't know" is not an answer I want to hear. Go back to his office in the morning and get in his face. Is that clear?'

'Yes, sir,' she said, and blushed under his uncharacter-istically withering glare.

Grace turned to the indexer. 'Annalise, anything on your check on the serials about Eric Whiteley?'

'I have one thing, sir. Almost two years ago exactly, he reported a bicycle theft from outside his office.'

There were a couple of sniggers. One from a recent addition to the team, DC Graham Baldock, and the other from Guy Batchelor. Grace glared at them both. 'I'm sorry,' he said. 'I don't find having a bicycle stolen funny. It may not be the kind of major crime we deal with in this branch, but if you have a bike you love that gets nicked it's pretty distressing. Okay?'

Both detectives nodded apologetically.

'It sounds like Whiteley was pretty difficult then. I spoke to DC Liz Spence at John Street who was dealing with bicycle crime at the time. He was pretty aggressive towards her over it. Didn't feel the police were doing enough, that they should have made it their major priority. She was sufficiently concerned back then about his level of aggression to put background checks on him.'

'And?' Grace asked.

She shook her head. 'Nothing came up.'

'If you want my opinion, sir,' Bella Moy said abruptly, 'he's just a harmless saddo.'

Grace looked at her for some moments. 'You may be right, Bella, but you have to remember something. Criminals escalate. The sicko who starts off as a seemingly harmless flasher can turn into a serial rapist twenty years later.'

'Yes, sir, I understand,' she said. 'I didn't mean to be frivolous.'

Grace saw his BlackBerry was flashing red at him. New emails. He tapped to check them as he asked, 'Norman, anything back yet from the High Tech Crime Unit on Myles Royce's computer?'

'No, chief, not so far.'

He glanced through the emails. The second was from the Chief Superintendent of Brighton Police, Graham Barrington.

**Roy, call me urgently after your briefing.**

# 86

Drayton Wheeler looked at his watch. 9.03 a.m. Time was passing slowly. Ordinarily, with just six months or so left of it, he might have been grateful. But not up here, lying on this hard wooden floor inside the dome that supported the chandelier, surrounded by mouse droppings, and goddamn seagulls screeching outside.

The battery on his fucking Kindle was running out. In his calculations he hadn't figured that would happen, but he'd left the thing switched on to wireless, which ate up the battery life. Great. He had about nine hours to kill, and an hour of reading time left. So much for his ambition to finish *War and Peace* before he died. He laughed. His own private joke. With six months to live, he had to be choosy about what he read. Did it matter what he had and hadn't read in his life? In six months' time would anyone care that Drayton Wheeler had not read *War and Peace*?

Nor anything by Dostoyevsky. Nor Proust. He hadn't read much Hardy either. Just one Scott Fitzgerald. Two Hemingways. All people you were supposed to read to make you a more rounded human being. And the more rounded you were, the easier it was for some bastard to stick a pin in you and deflate you.

Well, he sure as hell would not be fretting about it in his grave. Fade to black. Good riddance.

At least today's *Times* had downloaded. He could cheer himself up with the last of the Kindle's battery life by reading all the shit that was going on in the world. Palestine.

Libya. Iraq. Iran. North Korea. *Hey, you know what, sort yourselves out, world, you're going to have to learn to get by without me.*

Dying. With every single one of his damned ambitions unfulfilled. Thanks to people like Larry Brooker and Maxim Brody who had screwed him. Everyone had screwed him. Life itself had screwed him.

He was a genius, he knew that. He always had the ideas first. And some other bastard always got there before him, or stole them. He'd had the idea of writing about a child wizard. Fucking JK Rowling got hers out first. He'd had the idea about a young teenage girl falling in love with a vampire. Some Mormon called Stephenie Meyer wrote her books ahead of him.

Now *The King's Lover*. This time, he knew, no one was there ahead of him. He had the surefire formula.

And it had been stolen from under his feet.

*Sue me.*

*Oh sure, Larry Fucking Brooker. I could sue you. If I had a million bucks in the bank and ten years to live, I could wipe your ass for you with legal paperwork.*

He munched angrily through his breakfast of a stale Marks and Spencer egg and bacon sandwich and an over-ripe apple, washed down by cold coffee. *Breakfast of Champions!*

He had that book on his Kindle. Written by one of his favourite authors, Kurt Vonnegut. Vonnegut was a cynic too. The book was all about a great visionary writer called Kilgore Trout who found one of his science fiction novels being used as toilet paper in a motel lavatory. That was pretty much how Wheeler felt about his own career. He was a genius constantly pissed on from a great height. *Well, smug little baldy Larry Brooker and fat toad Maxim Brody, you're about to get pissed on from a great height back! Hope you're looking forward to shooting the banqueting scene tonight.*

*I'm looking forward to it a lot.*

# 87

The opening day of the Carl Venner trial at the Old Bailey
had gone as well as could be expected, Roy Grace's Case
Officer, Mike Gorringe, who was attending for the whole
duration, had reported. The hearing was set to run for three
weeks and Grace would not be needed until the middle
of next week at the earliest, which suited him well. He
had plenty of other issues to deal with here in Sussex at
the moment. The most pressing one, as he sat at his desk,
staring at his computer screen, was the email Chief Superintendent Graham Barrington had just forwarded him.

It had been sent to Gaia's published email address last
night, read by an assistant who vetted all of her fan mail,
and immediately forwarded to her head of security Andrew
Gulli.

> I still cannot believe how you cut me dead. I thought
> your whole point in coming to England was to see
> me. I know you love me, really. You're going to be
> sorry you did that. Very sorry. You made me look a
> fool. You made people laugh at me. I'm going to give
> you the chance to apologise. You are soon going to
> be telling the whole world how much you love me.
> I will kill you if you don't.

He rang Graham Barrington's direct line. It was answered
instantly. 'What do you think, Roy?' Even though Barrington
had been a police officer for nearly thirty years, his voice
was still full of an infectious, boyish enthusiasm, and Grace

loved that, because it was how he felt, too – most days at any rate.

'I guess we need to assess whether this is a harmless nutter or a serious threat. In the first instance, are we certain this isn't from the perp in Los Angeles, Graham?'

'Well,' the Chief Superintendent replied, 'it's in a similar vein, but I spoke to our contact there, Detective Myman – I just woke him up, it's 1 a.m. local time – and he assures me that the man they have in custody has no internet access. I've forwarded it to the High Tech Crime Unit to see if they can find the source for us. What's your view, Roy?'

'Has anyone spoken to Gaia about this?'

'Not yet, she's still asleep, I understand.'

'Someone needs to talk to her as soon as she's up.'

'Maybe you should – I think she's quite sweet on you, Roy!'

'Probably a good reason why I shouldn't then!' Then, being serious again he said, 'We need to find if she has any idea who this could be. Has she had a confrontation with any of her fans since she's been here?'

'I've asked Gulli that question. There was a middle-aged woman in The Grand Hotel who tried to push past the security guards, and then made a complaint to us about their brutality.'

'Oh? How was it followed up?'

'Uniform attended. They took a statement from her and then interviewed a couple of the security guards later. Seems the woman lied about being a journalist to try to get into Gaia's suite, then chased after her. We're not taking her complaint any further.'

Grace wondered why no one had thought to notify him about this incident. Then he looked at the email again. One possibility going through his mind was whether this could be Amis Smallbone winding them up? He read the words and did not think so. There was something sad about them, a desperation. A wounded lover? A stalker deluded that Gaia was in love with him? Or *her*?

'I think we need to know more about this woman at The Grand, Graham. Can you get someone from your CID team to go and talk to her?'

'I'll get Jason Tingley on it right away.'

'What do we know about Gaia's current love life?'

'She has a lover in Los Angeles. A fitness instructor. Detective Myman said he was interviewed after her assistant was killed and cleared. Sounds like their relationship is fine.'

'I'd like to get this email analysed by a psychologist,' Grace said. 'There may be some subtext we're not aware of.'

'Good idea. Meantime I'm going to step up her protection.'

'Definitely,' Grace said. 'Do we know her movements today?'

'They're filming a big interior scene at the Pavilion tonight. She's free during the day. She's promised to take her son on the Pier and to the beach. I'll make sure we don't let either of them out of our sight.'

'I think my young god-daughter is going to join them,' Grace said.

'We'll have a ring of steel around them, Roy.'

Grace thanked him and hung up. Emails were tumbling into his inbox faster than he could read them. A whole bunch of stuff about the police rugby team he was running, and had to deal with, on top of everything else. And in twenty minutes' time he had to drive over to Sussex Police

HQ at Malling House, to brief his boss ACC Peter Rigg on *Operation Icon*.

Gaia would be fine, for now, in Graham Barrington's hands. He hoped.

# 88

The phone was answered on the second ring. 'AD Motor-homes.'

Putting on an American accent, because she thought it might sound more convincing, Anna Galicia said, 'I'm calling from Brooker Brody Productions. We have mislaid the key to the motorhome our star, Gaia, is using and need another one urgently.'

'Oh dear,' the woman said. 'We'll have to get a spare couriered to you.'

'You're in St Albans, Hertfordshire, right?'

'Yes.'

'We have someone up in that area picking up some props. I'll direct them to come to you for the key – they'll be there in about two hours.'

'Yes, okay, fine, it will be waiting in reception.'

Anna thanked her and hung up.

# 89

They began setting up for the big scene an hour before the Pavilion closed for the day. A call had been put out for extras, but Drayton Wheeler had not responded.

From his position right at the top of the wooden slats that formed a concave staircase up the inside of the dome, he could look straight down through a gap beside the metal shaft that supported the chandelier, into the Banqueting Room.

And he could listen. Thanks to the baby monitoring system he had bought in Mothercare. The radio microphone was underneath the mahogany table down in the Banqueting Room. The speaker was switched on beside him. He could hear everything perfectly, except for the occasional irritating whine of feedback.

It was 4.30 p.m. Nearing the end of the day that had felt like it would never end. He sat perched up here, watching stupid tourists shuffling around the exterior of the room. A plush rope prevented them from getting near to the actual banqueting table itself. He wasn't bored any more now.

It was remarkable how simple the fixings of the chandelier were. A cross-beam of four metal poles, attached to wooden struts, each secured by a large bolt. In the centre of the cross-beam was welded a single, thick aluminium shaft, three feet long, to which one and a quarter tons of chandelier, with its 15,000 lustres, was attached.

He tied the hotel towel tightly around the shaft.

Then he grinned.

Ready to rock and roll!

Down below he could see doubles for Gaia and Judd Halpern being seated at the banqueting table, for the Director of Photography to light them.

Etiquette had it that the king and his paramour were seated first. The rest of the guests would file to the table.

Timing was going to be the big issue. If he got really lucky, it might not be just Gaia and Judd Halpern that the chandelier landed on. It could be another ten people, either side of them and opposite. Some big names in the supporting cast. Hugh Bonneville, from *Downton Abbey*, was playing Lord Alvanley and Joseph Fiennes was playing the king's friend, Beau Brummell. Emily Watson was cast as the Countess of Jersey, who had for some years usurped Maria Fitzherbert, and was about to usurp her again in this ludicrous, totally historically inaccurate scene. None of them should have taken these roles; they were all conspiring to alter history. No one had any right to do that. For sure, they did not deserve to do that and live!

If luck really went his way, he might get all of them.

From his rucksack he very carefully retrieved the San Pellegrino screw-top bottle. Its contents looked like water. But if you were to drink it, death would be agonizing and not instantaneous. It contained mercuric chloride acid. A substance powerful enough, from the experiments he had already carried out, and his calculations that had followed, to eat through an aluminium shaft, six inches in diameter, in twenty-five to thirty minutes.

He could see Larry Brooker's bald dome. He was pacing around shouting at people so loudly, Drayton had to turn down the volume on the baby monitor. Crew were scurrying everywhere, frenetically busy. A dozen extras were seated around the banqueting table, which was laid out for a feast, doubling for the cast as the Director of Photography and his underlings were making final lighting adjustments. The sound boom was being manoeuvred into place.

All getting set for the big scene.

Gaia would be in her trailer. Having her make-up and hair done, and reading through her lines once more, no doubt.

*His lines.*

Judd Halpern would be in his trailer, staring at his lines, and doing several lines of a different kind – coke, washed down with bourbon, if past form was anything to go by.

Larry Brooker was saying something to a young man who looked like he might be the First Assistant Director, who was nodding vigorously.

*Do you realize why you are all here? It's because of a screenplay called* The King's Lover *that you are making. If I hadn't written it, none of you would have a job on this production.*

*Are you grateful to me?*

*You don't even know who I am, do you?*

*But you will soon.*

# 90

'The time is 6.30 p.m., Tuesday, June the fourteenth. This is the twentieth briefing of *Operation Icon*,' Roy Grace said to his team. 'We have some developments.' He looked at Potting. 'Norman, can you tell us about your search of Myles Royce's house?'

'I took DC Nicholl with me, as well as POLSA Lorna Dennison-Wilkins and Crime Scene Photographer James Gartrell to record our search. Royce's mother wasn't exaggerating when she said her son was a big Gaia fan. The place is so full of her stuff you can hardly move in there. I've never seen anything like it. Almost every room's crammed with cardboard cut-outs of her, dresses, records, souvenir programmes, piles and piles of press cuttings on the floor, and some of them pasted on the walls. In my view he wasn't just a fan, he was a total obsessive. Just to be clear, I'm talking about an oddball. You can't open the door fully to some of the rooms, there's so much stuff piled in there. If we need it, Lorna can bring in more of her team tomorrow to catalogue everything.'

'People like this bother me,' Grace said. 'Obsessives are fanatics, and unpredictable. The one thing that really worries me right now is that we have a Gaia obsessive dead, and Gaia is in town. It might be a total coincidence. But this has to be an important line of enquiry for us to find out which other Gaia fans Royce associated with.' He looked down at his notes, then continued.

'Right, from the High Tech Crime Unit's examination of

Royce's computer, so far, he would appear to have been one of a small group of obsessive Gaia fans who exchanged information and constantly bid against each other for everything that came up for auction. And it seems that he had one particularly acrimonious rivalry with a character called Anna Galicia. Which is where this gets interesting for us.' He looked down at his notes. 'This rivalry developed into an email slanging match with this woman. A really nasty, bitchy exchange over some item of Gaia's they had both been bidding for that she wore in one of her shows. The High Tech Crime Unit's still working through the email trail. But meantime I asked Annalise Vineer to run a name check on Anna Galicia, and she got a hit.' He nodded at her.

'Last Wednesday evening,' Annalise Vineer said, 'uniform attended a Grade 3 call at The Grand Hotel. It was a woman complaining she had been assaulted by two of Gaia Lafayette's security guards. She gave her name as Anna Galicia. Following the information of the link between her and Royce from the High Tech Crime Unit, two uniformed officers were sent to her address to interview her. But it doesn't exist. She gave a false address.'

Glenn Branson frowned. 'Why would she have done that if she was making a genuine complaint?'

'Exactly,' Roy Grace said. 'By all accounts she was pretty angry. So why give a false address?' He looked around at his team. 'Any ideas?'

'Doesn't make sense to me,' Graham Baldock said.

'Nor me,' Guy Batchelor said. 'If you're making a complaint, you're making a complaint. If you have something to hide you don't make a complaint in the first place. I mean, do you?' He shrugged.

'I'm not at all happy about this person,' Grace said. 'We need to find her quickly. Very quickly.'

# 91

'How can I make my multi-million-dollar movie with a goddamn lead actor who's off his goddamn face, for fuck's sake!' Larry Brooker yelled at the top of his voice, across the floor of the Banqueting Room, at the hapless Third Assistant Director, Adrián González. 'You wanna tell me?'

González raised his hands in a gesture of despair. His role was to deliver Gaia, Judd Halpern and the other principal actors to the set, and escort them back to their trailers when they weren't required. He was an earnest, fresh-faced twenty-eight-year-old, with a shock of short, unruly ginger hair, dressed in a blue T-shirt emblazoned in white with the words THE KING'S LOVER, tatty cargo shorts and trainers. He wore a headset with an earpiece and microphone, had a mobile phone and a pager clipped to his belt, and was clutching a call sheet. He shrugged helplessly at Brooker.

There was a pathetic ego thing going on between the two stars, who had taken an instant dislike to each other from day one. Halpern had already kept Gaia waiting twice, so now she refused to come out of her trailer, for any scenes she was doing with him, until it was confirmed to her that he was on set and ready.

The director, camera team and the rest of the crew watched Larry Brooker's latest tantrum. The bald, tanned producer, in a black Versace shirt open halfway down his chest, displaying his gold medallion, black chinos and Cuban-heeled boots, strode over towards González, like a pocket dictator, and gripped him by the front of his T-shirt.

'What the fuck's going on? Thirty minutes we've been waiting for this goddamn asshole. We have a schedule to keep to. We've got two busloads of extras sitting out there!' Still gripping González's shirt he turned to the Line Producer, Barnaby Katz, a short, tubby man in his early forties, with a barren dome rising from a sparse tundra of fuzzy hair, who looked close to a nervous breakdown. He was dressed in a shapeless lumberjack shirt, baggy jeans and old desert boots. 'What the fuck are you doing standing there with your thumb up your ass?' he shouted at him. Then he released González, who stood still for a moment, as if unsure what to do next.

'I'll go and have a word with him,' Katz said.

Brooker tapped his chest. 'No, I'm going. Okay?'

He stormed out of the Banqueting Room, left the building and strode across the grounds towards the trailers. Along the street, beyond the Pavilion lawns and the cordon manned by the security guards and the row of trucks, was a large crowd of people waiting to catch glimpses of the stars – mostly waiting for Gaia, he guessed.

*Judd Goddamn Halpern.* Jesus, how he hated actors. Judd Halpern didn't do public transport, his agent had informed them. Which meant they'd had to put in the budget 150,000 bucks to fly the jerk, his assistant, and some girl he was currently screwing, over to London in a goddamn private jet. Then, because he was, apparently, a *method* actor, he had demanded that there was unpasteurized milk on the plane, as King George would have drunk, so he could get himself into character.

Fuckwit.

He strode up to Judd Halpern's motorhome and banged on the door. Without waiting for an answer he pulled it open and stormed up the steps. Inside was a fug of cannabis smoke that took him back to his student days. Through it he could see Halpern, seated at his dressing table, staring bleary-eyed into the mirror that was lit all the way round with bare light bulbs. Today's script pages, lime green, lay fanned out in front of him, with markings all over them, like a corrected school essay. A bottle of bourbon sat on the desk, alongside a plastic ballpoint pen with the nib and ink tube removed.

Halpern was dressed in bulbous white pantaloons, a velvet, gold-braided jacket with a high collar and a cream neck ruff secured with an ornately jewelled brooch. His wavy black wig sat on the dresser in front of him. A female make-up artist was working on his face, while a joint burned in the ashtray. Standing in front of them, as if trying to block his path, was Halpern's effete personal assistant, and behind him, slumped over a table, with a cocktail glass in front of her, and a Grey Goose vodka bottle next to it, was a scantily clad girl of barely legal age.

By the relatively tender age of forty-two, Judd Halpern had already blown his career twice. The first time was after being the child star of a global hit US television series, *Pasadena Heights*, when he had become so impossibly arrogant, no one would work with him. Then, having recovered from that in his early twenties, helped by his almost absurdly handsome looks, which had been compared to those of silent screen star Rudolph Valentino, and his unquestionable acting talent, his career had been reborn with two successful movies. Then it hit the skids after a series of drug convictions ending in a four-year spell in jail, when once again he had become a Hollywood pariah.

Now, according to his agent, he was clean, over it, remorseful about his past, anxious to make a fresh start, and had just made a movie with George Clooney that was a slam-dunk to totally relaunch his career. Which was how Brooker Brody Productions had secured an actor with A-list history for only a couple of hundred thousand dollars above scale.

'Judd,' Brooker said, more civilly than he felt. 'Like, we're all waiting for you.'

'Ready when you are, CB!' Halpern said, staring back, with dilated pupils, at his own handsome, if borderline flaccid, reflection in the mirror. He reached for the joint, but before his fingers touched it, Brooker snatched it and crushed it out in the ashtray, stubbing it, snapping it, then stubbing it again for good measure.

'Hey, man!' Judd Halpern protested.

'You have a problem?'

Halpern glared at him. 'Yeah, I have a problem.'

'Yeah? Well I have a problem, too. My name isn't CB, it's LB. *Larry Brooker.*'

'It was a joke!' Halpern said. '*CB. Cecil B. DeMille.* Right? *Ready when you are, CB!*' He frowned. 'You don't know it?'

'If I'd wanted jokes, I'd have hired a goddamn comedian.' Brooker pulled out his handkerchief and folded the broken joint into it. 'I have a problem too. I suggest you take a look at your contract. The clauses on how you can be fired. Taking drugs is one of the first.'

The actor shook his head. 'I'm just smoking a cigarette, man. I like to roll my own.'

'Yeah? And you know what? I'm the fucking pope.'

The two men glared at each other, Halpern having a hard time focusing. Brooker tried hard to contain his rage. He had a movie to make and bring in on a tight budget, and it was getting harder every day as the schedule slipped. 'You want to tell me your problem?'

'Sure,' Halpern slurred. He picked up the pages, scrunching them. 'This is not what I signed up to.'

'What do you mean?'

'I took this role because I kinda liked the idea of King George the Fourth. He was an innovative dude. He had a great and tragic love affair with Maria Fitzherbert.' Halpern lapsed into silence.

Brooker waited patiently and then, as a prompt, he said, 'Uh huh.'

'I was assured the script was historically accurate.'

'It is,' Brooker said. 'George screwed Maria for several years then dumped her. What's your problem?'

'He was twenty-eight – I'm forty-two.'

'So why did you take the part?'

'Because I was told Bill Nicholson was doing a rewrite, that's why I agreed to this. He's quality, man.' He pointed at the script pages. 'He didn't write this, surely?'

Brooker shrugged. 'We had a bit of a problem at the last minute.'

'You mean you didn't want to pay his fees, right?' The star pulled open a drawer, lifted out a pack of cigarettes, pulled one out and lit it. 'The comedian who wrote these pages doesn't seem aware that this Pavilion wasn't even built at the time this scene was supposed to happen. That's another problem.'

'You want to know my problem?' Larry Brooker said.

Halpern shrugged at himself in the mirror. Then he watched himself draw on his cigarette. 'No,' he replied, finally, curling his lips, attempting – and failing – to blow a smoke ring.

'My problem,' Brooker said, coolly, 'is actors. You ask an actor to walk down the street, and he turns round and he says, "Why exactly am I walking down this street?" You know what I tell him?'

Halpern stared at him, clearly struggling to hold focus. 'No, what do you tell him?'

'I tell him, "The reason you are walking down this street, is because I'm fucking paying you to walk down this street." '

Judd Halpern gave him an uneasy smile.

'So listen to me good, Mr Big Shot Actor. You're trying to rebuild your busted career. That's fine by me. For the rest of this production, when you are called, you're going to come out of this trailer like a goddamn greyhound out of its gate, walk straight on set, and give the performance of your life. You know what will happen if you don't?'

Halpern looked at him a tad sheepishly. He said nothing.

'You'll be history. There won't be a production company in the world that's going to want to work with you by the time I've finished telling them about you. I promise you. You reading me loud and clear?'

'I am, but the script is still not right.'     .

'Then you'd better use your acting genius to turn it into something magical.'

'You think I can?' Halpern said, his demeanour changing.

'Sure you can, kiddo. You're the world's Greatest Living Actor! That's why I goddamn hired you.'

Halpern stiffened and preened. 'You really think so?'

'I don't think so, Judd. I *know* so.' He gave him a winning smile.

'Cool,' he said. 'Let's rock and roll!' He reached for his wig.

'On set in ten minutes, okay?' Brooker said.

'I'm there!'

'You're goddamn terrific, you know that?'

Halpern smiled and attempted a shrug of modesty. But he wasn't very good at modesty.

Brooker closed the door behind him and headed back to the set. *You total asshole*, he was thinking.

# 92

'That is so much better!' Gaia said, sitting wrapped in her silk dressing gown as her hairdresser, Tracey Curry, standing on killer black heels, finished cropping her blonde hair.

Gaia stared approvingly in the mirror at her new cut, which was even shorter than a few days ago.

'You'll find that a lot more comfortable under that wig,' the hairdresser said.

'You're a treasure!' She turned to her assistant, Martina Franklin. 'What do you think?'

'It kinda suits you!'

Eli Marsden, her make-up artist, nodded approvingly. 'It looks terrific!'

Gaia turned to her little boy, who was seated at a table further along the motorhome, watching a video on his iPad. 'Roan, hon, you like Mama's new hairstyle?'

'Uh huh,' he said glumly. 'I'm bored. Can I go take a look around the palace?'

'Sure, hon. Go take a wander, I'll be in soon. Ask one of the security guys to walk you over there.'

Roan, dressed in a baggy blue THE KING'S LOVER T-shirt, jeans and trainers, jumped down from the table and scampered out of the air-conditioned chill of the trailer into the warm, clouding over, evening air. Deciding to ignore his mother and explore alone, he walked jauntily across the Pavilion lawns and up to the front door. The security guard looked down at him. 'You're Gaia's son, right? Sloan?'

'Uh, Roan,' he corrected.

'Sorry, *Roan.*'

The boy shrugged. 'S'okay. Mama said I could take a look around.'

He gestured. 'Go right ahead, Roan. Turn right when you go inside and follow the corridor and you'll get to the Banqueting Room where your mum's going to be filming.'

'Okay.'

# 93

'Okay, everyone, clear the doubles, please, the cast are coming on set.' The voice came out of the baby monitor, loud and clear for some moments, then distorted by a feedback squawk.

Perched up at the top of the dome's wooden frame, watching and listening, Drayton Wheeler began trembling with nerves and excitement. *Now! Now! Have to do it now!* He was never going to know for sure exactly when the cast would all be assembled around the table. He was going to have to rely on a calculated judgement – and luck. But this moment now was, in his view, the best shot he was likely to get.

He picked up the San Pellegrino bottle, his hands shaking so much he was scared of slopping some of the mercuric chloride acid on himself. Pointing it away, he unscrewed the metal cap, and it slipped from his fingers. He could hear it tumble all the way down the wooden slats, rat-a-tat-tatting, then as it struck something metallic, a loud *ping*.

He held his breath. Listened. Static came through the baby monitor. Then Larry Brooker's voice, talking to the director. 'We gotta make some time up. We've lost two hours thanks to that asshole.'

'We can work on, Larry, keep everyone late,' Jack Jordan said. He had a soft and precious voice that Drayton Wheeler found particularly irritating.

'Don't go there.' Brooker was thinking about the budget and the overtime rates for some of the crew if they went over the maximum number of hours, Wheeler guessed. 'You'll just have to take some shortcuts,' Brooker commanded.

'Darling boy, this is not the scene to take shortcuts on.'

Wheeler could hear the disdain in the director's voice, and thought, *Don't have a fucking argument, not now!*

Another voice said, 'Are we ready to fill the table?'

'I want to see if Judd's compos mentis enough to film before I bring everyone else in,' Jordan said.

'He's fine,' Brooker said. 'I just spoke to him. He's gonna be a pussycat tonight.'

'He's just leaving his trailer now,' one of the Assistant Directors announced.

Wheeler listened to the words. Then very carefully, holding his breath, he tipped the entire contents of the San Pellegrino bottle on to the towel which he had wound around the single aluminium support shaft for the chandelier.

Instantly a wisp of smoke rose from the towel as it began to discolour into brown and grey blotches. Some of the acid ran further down the shaft. He continued to hold his breath, partly to avoid inhaling any of the fumes the acid released, and partly out of terror that it might drip down on to the table, way below, and get noticed.

More curls of smoke were rising. He moved down several slats, until he was below the level of the acid, then checked his watch. 7.04 p.m. If his calculations were right, at around 7.35 p.m. the acid would have eaten through enough of the shaft for the chandelier to plunge.

Through the monitor he heard the conversation between Larry Brooker and Jack Jordan continuing.

'I'm telling you, darling boy, I cannot possibly shoot tonight if he's wrecked.'

'He's fine, Jesus, I just spoke with him!'

'You said that he was fine last night. He couldn't remember his lines for more than ten seconds. You know who this is going to reflect on? I don't work this way, Larry. I just can't connect with him. Do you understand?'

'He'll be fine. Good as gold.'

'He was complaining to me yesterday that Gaia was chewing raw garlic before their kissing scene. I think I should go and talk to him off set, before everyone else arrives.'

*Shit, shit, shit*, Wheeler thought. *Just get the jerk on set. And everyone else!*

He watched Jordan walk out of the room. One of the Assistant Directors said into his microphone, 'Hold all cast.'

*No!* Wheeler urged, silently. *Bring them on, bring them on, get them into position!*

Suddenly he saw a small boy, with mussed-up brown hair, wearing a T-shirt and jeans, walk into the room, duck under the ropes and walk towards the table. Gaia's little brat, he recognized from earlier.

*Fuck off kid! Get out of here! Clear off, you little bastard!*

The boy wandered, curious, around the table. He peered, nosily, at the hams, chickens, haunches of venison, suckling pig, silver flagons of ales and wines, and bowls of fruits. Then he pulled up a chair at the table, sat down, and stared around him, with a regal air, as if imagining himself back in time.

*Clear off, kid!*

He looked just like his own son.

Suddenly there was a strange sound directly above him. A sharp hissing. He looked up, and to his shock, the entire interior of the dome above him had disappeared in a swirling mist of acrid smoke. He could feel it burning his lungs, parching his mouth.

Sudden panic gripped him.

There was a piercing, creaking sound.

He looked down for an instant, and the chandelier was trembling.

*No, no, no.*

His careful calculations had come out at thirty minutes. What had he got wrong?

It was shaking even more now, and the creaking was getting worse.

The damned boy was still sitting there, lifting a silver goblet as if pretending to drink from it.

He coughed, the acid fumes burning his eyes and searing his throat. Half blinded, tears were streaming from his eyes. He coughed again, a long, deep, choking, hacking cough. *Get lost, kid! Scram!*

His goddamn calculations were wrong. Had he screwed up on the acid strength? The calculations of the diameter of the aluminium?

There was a terrible screech of stressed metal, right below him. He looked down and to his horror could see the whole chandelier had moved, several inches, and was now off-kilter.

The shaft was about to snap.

The whole chandelier, as he had planned, was about to fall. But on to Roan Lafayette.

No.

'Kid!' he yelled. 'Get away! Get away! GET AWAY!'

But no one could hear him from up here.

The boy continued to play happily with his goblet.

Of course he could not hear him from up here.

There was another piercing metallic shriek.

Through his observation hole, he could see the chandelier was swaying now. Any moment it would plunge down. No one had noticed. It was going to kill the kid and that was never his intention.

*Oh shit, shit, shit, shit.*

This was screwing up all his plans. He launched himself down the rest of the wooden slats, knocking over and then accidentally treading on and splintering the baby alarm speaker, squeezed back out through the narrow hatch, and then clambered down the ladder.

He felt surprisingly energized and clear-headed.

*I am not killing a child. I am not killing a child.*

He sprinted along the steel walkway, ignoring the handrail this time, then clambered in through the hatch to the apartment beneath the big dome. He ran through the main room, past the dust sheets, over the trapdoor secured by the two bolts, then down the spiral staircase, keeping well clear of the rickety handrail. Then he burst out through the door at the bottom, into the central hallway.

Two security guards standing there looked at him in astonishment.

As Wheeler ignored them and sprinted down the corridor towards the Banqueting Room, the guards ran after him. 'Hey! Hey, you!' one shouted. 'Let me see your ID!'

Three grips, unwinding a cable drum, were blocking the entrance to the room. One guard caught up with Wheeler as he tried to barge past them, and grabbed him by the shoulder. 'Hey!'

Drayton Wheeler turned and punched him in the nose so hard he bust it, sending the guard reeling back, and at the same time agonizingly dislocating his own thumb. But he barely even noticed. He ran on into the Banqueting Room and looked up.

The chandelier was swaying as if suspended by a solitary, fraying piece of string.

At any second it was going to come down.

The stupid kid, in a world of his own, was now pretending to eat with a knife and fork. The rest of the crew in here were well clear of the table.

Wheeler clambered over the rope.

'Hey!' The other security guard shouted at him.

Wheeler ignored him. Ignored everything but the kid at the table and the looming, swaying shadow above him. He threw himself across the room and grabbed the boy, yanking him clean out of his chair by his arm, his knife and fork clattering to the ground.

'Hey!!' Roan shouted, furious and bewildered, moments before Drayton Wheeler, gripping him by the shoulder and buttocks, threw him, with all the force he could muster, across the polished wooden floor, sliding and spinning like a human curling stone.

Roan shrieked in protest as he crashed into a brass upright supporting the rope.

Then, before Drayton Wheeler had a chance to move, the chandelier dropped.

He sensed, fleetingly, the shadow, descending on him, enveloping him, far too fast for him to cry out. The full force of the chandelier struck him on the head, smashing him to the floor a split second before it demolished an eight-foot-long portion of the centre of the table.

The floor shook under the massive, splintering crash, as if a bomb had gone off in the room. There was a jangling, reverberating boom. Hundreds of the 15,000 glass drops shattered, sending a glittering, shimmering display of coloured light into the air, for an instant, like a firework. Lights in the grand room flickered. Goblets on the table crashed over, shattering, spilling their contents; plates, chandeliers and tureens slid down into the tangled mess of chains, gilded metal framework and glass. Then there was a gentle, almost absurd tinkling sound. As if someone had just dropped one single glass. That was all and nothing else.

It was followed by a brief instant of absolute silence. No one moved.

Then a male voice cried out in shock, 'Oh shit, oh no!'

A female voice screamed, 'There's a man under there! Oh my God, there's someone under there!'

There was another moment of stunned, awed silence. It was broken by a hideous, whooping, hysterical screaming from the film unit's continuity woman. Bug-eyed, she was standing, pointing at a dark red pool of blood spreading out from under the mangled wreckage where the centre of the table had been only moments ago.

A single streak of stark white light flitted across the scene. Someone had taken a photograph.

# 94

Several of the film unit's lights had been beamed on to the fallen chandelier. Under their glare, two paramedics in green uniforms, Phil Davidson and Vicky Donoghue, were picking their way through the shattered glass and twisted metal, trying to locate the victim's head, being careful not to put any additional weight on the wreckage that could crush the man further. There was blood everywhere beneath them, spreading slowly outwards, and a terrible stench like a bad drain. Both of them knew what that meant. That the man's stomach and bowels had been split open.

They could glimpse the man's clothes in a few places. Repeatedly, Vicky Donoghue asked, 'Sir, can you hear us? Help is on its way. Can you hear us, sir?'

There was no response. Outside, she could hear a cacophony of sirens winding down. Hopefully the fire brigade had arrived with lifting gear. Then she saw flesh. A wrist.

Carefully she eased her gloved hand in between the jagged leaves of glass palm fronds, and held the wrist lightly. It was limp. 'Can you hear me, sir? Try to move your hand if you can't speak,' she urged. Then she curled her fingers around the wrist, feeling for the radial artery.

'I've got a pulse!' she announced after some moments in a low voice to her colleague. 'But it's weak.'

'We've got to get this mess lifted off him. How weak?'

She counted for a few seconds. 'Twenty-five.' She counted again. 'Going down. Twenty-four.'

He mouthed the question at her without actually saying the words. He didn't need to. They'd crewed together for long enough to be able to read each other's signals. *FUBAR BUNDY?*

The words were an acronym for *Fucked Up Beyond All Recovery, But Unfortunately Not Dead Yet.* The gallows humour of the ambulance service that helped them cope with horrific situations like this.

She nodded affirmative.

\*

Jason Tingley, with his boyish mop of hair brushed forward, white button-down shirt with black buttons, and narrow black tie, every inch a twenty-first-century Mod, was at his desk in the CID department on the fourth floor of Brighton's John Street Police Station, nearing the end of his twelve-hour shift as the on-call Detective Inspector. At the forefront of his mind was yesterday's disturbing development of the emailed death threat against Gaia.

He yawned; it had been a busy day, starting at the beginning of his shift with a woman claiming she had been raped after having a row with her boyfriend, and leaving a party at 6.45 a.m. Who the hell partied until 6.45 a.m. on a Monday night – or rather, Tuesday morning – he wondered? Then at midday the Road Policing Unit had stopped a car in the city with its boot filled with bags of cannabis. And at 3 p.m. there had been an armed robbery on a jewellery shop in the city centre.

He was still dealing with the paperwork on that now, and was almost finished. He was hoping to be able to get home in time to see his two children before they went to bed, and enjoy a meal and a quiet evening in front of the television with his wife Nicky. Then his phone rang.

'Jason Tingley,' he answered.

It was the Ops 1 Controller, Andy Kille. 'Jason, there's been an incident at the Royal Pavilion just come in that I thought you, the Chief Superintendent and Roy Grace might want to know about.'

'What's happened?'

He listened with great concern to the sketchy details that Kille had been given. It seemed a strange coincidence that a chandelier which had been in situ for almost two centuries should suddenly fall down this week, of all weeks. Unless the film crew had been meddling with it and had damaged something?

'Do we know anything about the person under the chandelier, Andy?' he asked.

'Not at this stage, no.'

'I'm going to take a look,' he said. 'I'll keep Roy Grace and Graham Barrington informed.' He ended the call, stood up and hooked his jacket off the back of his chair. By the time he had reached the car park out the back, and belted himself into one of the grey Ford Focus cars from the detectives' pool, he had notified the Chief Superintendent of Brighton and Hove, who was away for the day attending a course, but had not managed to get through to Roy Grace.

Five minutes later, as he turned left and drove under the archway into the Pavilion grounds, Tingley saw three fire engines, a Fire Service Heavy Rescue vehicle, an ambulance and a paramedic car outside the main entrance, as well as two police vehicles.

He drove past the cluster of trailers, pulled up as close as he could to the main entrance, then hurried across, flashing his ID at two security guards. They told him to go inside and turn right.

The last time he had been in this building was years

back, on a school history outing. It had the same smell of all museums and galleries, but he had forgotten just how ornate and splendid it was. As he entered the Banqueting Room, a surreal vision lay in front of him. It was as if a *Pause* button had been pressed, freeze-framing some people in the room, but not everyone. And the smell was quite different. A vile, sickening stench of drains.

Members of the film crew, scruffily dressed and with shocked expressions, stood motionless, seemingly rooted to the spot. One woman, in baggy jeans, had turned away from the horror in the centre of the room, and was sobbing in shock in the arms of a huge, bearded man, who was holding an aluminium foil lamp reflector behind her back.

The fallen chandelier looked like a giant, beached, jewel-encrusted jellyfish, with tentacular chains sprawling all around, a metal shaft, like a broken spear, protruding several feet from the top of it.

Two paramedics were in the middle of the wreckage, while one team of fire officers were manoeuvring cutting gear into place, and another two officers were working on placing a blue and yellow airbag, attached by a line to a compressed air cylinder, under one part of the wreckage. A third officer stood beside them, with a small stack of wooden blocks to place beneath as the wreckage rose.

A young uniformed woman police officer greeted Detective Inspector Tingley's arrival with relief, as if happy she could now delegate responsibility to someone more senior.

The Detective Inspector stared up at the ceiling. He could see the dragon claws and the painted palm leaves, with a small, dark hole in the centre, where he presumed the shaft had been. Then he turned to the PC.

'What do we know so far?' Tingley asked her.

'Well, sir, I just got here a few minutes ago. What I've

been able to ascertain so far is that there is one person, male, known to be under the chandelier.'

'Could there be others?'

'No, sir. I've spoken to several eye witnesses who say there is just one person.'

'What do we know about how this happened?'

'Well, it's very sketchy. It seems that Gaia's son was sitting at the table, playing. This man, who must have seen that the chandelier was about to come down, dashed across the room and literally threw the boy clear.'

'Is the boy all right?'

'Yes, sir, he's with his mother in her trailer.'

'Who is the man? One of the film crew?'

'So far, no one recognizes him.'

'A maintenance worker, perhaps?'

'Could be, sir.'

Tingley looked around. 'Right, get some back-up here fast. I'm treating this as a crime scene. I want the entire building cordoned off, get everyone out, but take the names and addresses of everyone in the building, including the security guards, as they leave.'

She nodded, looking around, taking it all in.

'Start with this room,' he said, helpfully. 'Tape it off. No one leaves until you have their name and address.'

'Yes, sir.' She radioed for assistance, then hurried out.

Tingley strode across the room towards the wreckage. As he did so he caught the eye of the male paramedic, Phil Davidson, whom he had met on several previous occasions.

Davidson nodded grimly. 'It's like that scene in *Only Fools and Horses* when the chandelier came down.'

'What do we know about who's under there?' Tingley asked, ignoring the comment about the TV sitcom.

'One male, according to witnesses.'

Aware of almost everyone in the room looking at him, Tingley went as close as he could to the edge of the chandelier.

'Fifteen,' the female paramedic announced grimly.

'It's looking like it's going to be a fatality,' Davidson said quietly to the detective. Then, using gallows humour jargon he added, 'A scoop and run at best, I'd say.'

An agitated American voice said, 'Excuse me, can I help you?'

Jason Tingley turned and found himself facing a short, lean man, with a tanned bald dome, dressed in a black shirt with silver buttons, open almost to the navel, black jeans and Cuban-heeled boots. The detective flashed his warrant card in his face. 'Detective Inspector Tingley, Sussex CID. Can I help *you*?' he said, pointedly.

'Good to meet you, sir. I'm the producer of this movie. Larry Brooker.'

Tingley shook his hand. It felt like patting the head of a poisonous snake whose venom had been removed.

'I just heard you've ordered the entire building to be cleared,' Brooker said. 'Did I hear right?'

'You did.'

'Well, the thing is, officer, we have a bit of a situation here, as you can see.'

The detective gave him a sideways look. 'I think you could say that, yes.' Out of the corner of his eye, he saw the young woman PC hurrying back into the room with a reel of blue and white police crime scene tape.

'Like, I have Gaia, and Judd Halpern, and Hugh Bonneville, Joseph Fiennes and Emily Watson all waiting in their trailers. We gotta get some footage in the can tonight – because of our schedule.'

The DI looked at Brooker, incredulously. Then he

pointed at the chandelier and the emergency service workers. 'You're aware that there is a man underneath that? A
human being?'

'Sure, of course. Like, I'm as shocked as everyone else.'

'So what actually is your point, sir?'

'My point is that we're already behind schedule. This
is terrible. Tragic. Fucking English maintenance, right – I
mean – where else in the world could this happen?'

He seemed oblivious to the Detective Inspector's stony
glare.

'The thing is, we have to get some footage in the can
tonight. Like, I'm just wondering how fast this mess could
be cleared? So we could carry on? We can shoot around the
chandelier, not a problem.'

Jason Tingley simply could not believe what he was
hearing. 'Mr Brooker, we have a possibly fatally injured
person. This is now a crime scene.'

'Crime scene? It's a goddamn accident! A terrible accident.'

'With respect, sir, at this point in time I have no evidence to support it being an accident. Unless – or until
– I do, this is a crime scene. *My* crime scene. *I* own this
now, do you understand? I'm clearing everyone from it,
and no one is going to be filming here tonight or any time
soon. I apologize for inconveniencing you, but do you
understand that?'

Brooker stared back at him and began stabbing at the
air with his finger. 'Listen to me and listen good, Detective
Inspector Tingles.'

'*Tingley.*'

'Yeah? Well, whatever, you'd better listen good, Detective. You'd better understand me. I have your Director of
Tourism, Adam Bates, totally on board. This is the biggest

goddamn motion picture your city's ever had shot here. I'm not having my multi-million-dollar production set back because of this building's shit maintenance.'

Jason Tingley, standing his ground, said, 'At this point, my priority is to ensure the safety of everyone in this building, Mr Brooker.' He pointed up at the other four, smaller, chandeliers. 'I'm going to have someone from Health and Safety here at any moment, wanting a full check. One chandelier's come down. Do you really want to risk the lives of those stars by not having proper safety checks on the others?'

Brooker looked at his watch, a big, chunky digital thing that looked like it belonged on the instrument panel of a Space Shuttle. 'You know, with respect, officer, this is not your call.'

'Fine. Speak to the Chief Constable. But until he directs me otherwise, this is my crime scene, and I have to warn you that if you attempt to obstruct me I will arrest you.'

Brooker glowered at him. 'You know what you are? You're fucking unreal!'

You are too, Jason Tingley thought.

# 95

Roy Grace, almost home, was hunting for a parking space near Cleo's house when Jason Tingley phoned him to tell him what had happened.

He listened intently, all his instincts telling him this was not coincidence, and he said he was on his way. It was only a few minutes' drive from here to the Pavilion. Moments after the DI hung up his phone rang again. As he answered he heard the nasal James Cagney voice of Gaia's security adviser Andrew Gulli.

'Detective Superintendent Grace?'

'Yes, how are you?'

'Do you want to tell me what's going on, Detective Grace?'

'I'm actually on my way to find out myself.'

'I understand that Gaia's kid was almost killed just now. This is not an acceptable situation.'

'How is he?'

'He's fine. But Gaia's pretty distressed.'

'If you want to meet me at the Pavilion—'

'I'm already there,' Gulli cut him short. 'I need to know what's going on. Is your goddamn building falling down, or is there someone behind this? I have to make decisions regarding my client's security. Am I making myself clear?'

'Meet me at the front entrance in five minutes.'

'I'm there.'

Grace hung up and immediately phoned Cleo, warning her he didn't know what time he would be home now. She told him she understood – not something Sandy had said to him very often.

Then his phone rang yet again. It was the Chief Constable. 'Roy, what information do you have about this incident at the Pavilion?'

'I'm on my way there now, sir.'

'I don't like the sound of it at all.'

'No, sir. I can call you back and give you an update after I get there.'

'Yes, please do.'

A few minutes later he drove into the Pavilion grounds, which were ablaze with blue flashing lights. A large crowd of onlookers was gathered along the far side of the perimeter wall, camera flashes popping intermittently. Two PCSOs were busily cordoning off the entire Royal Pavilion building, and another was already in situ as a scene guard. A dozen bewildered-looking people, film crew he supposed, were milling around on the lawn beneath the darkening sky which was threatening rain, some making phone calls, some smoking. A police van, laden with uniformed officers, siren wailing, turned into the archway as he got out of his car.

Andrew Gulli was standing beside the scene guard. As Grace approached he said, 'This goddamn officious bastard won't let me through.'

'I'm sorry,' Grace said. 'Until we've established what happened, we're treating this whole building as a crime scene; I can't allow you in. My advice would be to get Gaia and Roan back to the safety of their hotel.'

Gulli shook his head. 'The director's asked her to wait – they may shoot some exterior footage tonight.'

'In that case keep a very close eye on her. Put her security guards around her trailer.'

'That's already in place.'

Grace signed the log, ducked under the tape, and hurried through the front of the building. A security guard directed him to the Banqueting Room and Tingley greeted him as he entered. He observed several fire officers working around the edges of the huge, fallen chandelier, and two paramedics on their stomachs in the middle of the debris. He heard the whine of hydraulic cutting gear. Three police officers seemed to be taking down details of the people in the room. 'What's the latest?' he asked.

'The victim's died, sir,' Tingley said, quietly.

'Shit. What information do we have about him?' He looked up, then back at the DI. 'Was he part of the film crew?'

'Not from what I've been able to find out so far. Two of the security guards said he appeared from a part of the building not open to the public, in panic. He punched one of the guards who tried to apprehend him in the corridor, ran into this room and pushed Gaia's son clear seconds before the chandelier came down.'

'What was the boy doing in here?'

'Playing, while his mother was in make-up.'

'He's safe and unhurt?'

'Yes, he's back with his mother.'

'This man – show me where he came from.'

Tingley pointed to the corridor Grace had just walked along.

A voice from behind startled them. 'Oh my God, oh my God, I can't believe this.'

Both detectives turned to see a tall, elegant man in his fifties, in a chalk-striped suit, come into the room. He was looking ashen. 'This was King George's worst nightmare. I can't believe it.' Then he looked at them both. 'I'm David Barry, the Curator of this building.'

Grace and Tingley introduced themselves.

Barry looked up at the ceiling. 'This is isn't possible. I'm sorry, it's just not possible. Oh God. Oh my God! There's someone trapped underneath – what is the poor man's condition?'

'The paramedics say he's died, I'm afraid,' Tingley responded.

'This is terrible. Unbelievable.' He looked at the two men. 'You have to understand, you *must believe me* when I tell you this is simply not possible!'

Jason Tingley pointed at the wreckage and said, pragmatically, 'I'm finding that a little hard to accept at this moment, sir.'

Roy Grace found it a little hard to accept, too. The man had punched a security guard in the corridor and then run into this room. It was impossible to see the chandelier from the corridor. So what did the man know – whoever he was – and how?

'Was this chandelier checked regularly?' Grace asked Barry. 'Does someone carry out safety checks on the fixings?'

The Curator raised his arms, helplessly and bewildered. 'Well, I mean, every five years the entire thing is cleaned. All fifteen thousand lustres – it takes about two months.'

'Could it be metal fatigue?' Jason Tingley said.

'We carry out safety checks regularly on everything,' Barry said. 'Queen Victoria had the original shaft replaced with aluminium. We never had any reason to change it. You have to believe me – this just could not happen. It couldn't!'

Grace was trying to recall who it was who said, *The moment the world ends, the last sound you will hear is the voice of an expert explaining why it could not happen.* 'I'd like to have a good look around the building,' he said. 'Can you take me up to the space above the ceiling?'

'Yes, yes, of course. Can I help in any way here before we do that?'

'There's nothing anyone can do here – we have to stop all work now until the Coroner's Officer arrives,' Tingley said.

Grace told Tingley to stay in the room, then followed the Curator out of the Banqueting Room, along the corridor, past a sign to the toilets, and in through a door in the main hallway. 'We have a bit of a climb up a spiral staircase,' David Barry said. 'Can I ask you not to put your hand on the railings – they are very unstable – this is why we don't let the public in here.' He pulled out a torch.

Grace followed him up a steep, winding spiral staircase that seemed never-ending. Halfway up, Grace stopped and touched the handrail. It felt extremely wobbly, with a long drop beyond it into darkness. He stepped away and moved as close to the wall as he could get, hugging it as he climbed; heights had never been his strong point.

Finally, both men puffing, they reached the top and entered what looked to Grace like a derelict bedroom, mostly covered in dust sheets over angular shapes. Even in the waning light of the June evening, he could see ancient, mottled wallpaper, with graffiti scrawled over much of it, and oval leaded-light windows overlooking the Brighton skyline.

David Barry decided they could see well enough without his torch. He spoke with a pleasant, cultured voice. 'This was where the king's senior household staff had their quarters, back in Prinny's day. I don't know how much you know about the history of this palace, Detective Superintendent, but during the First World War it was used as a hospital for wounded Indian soldiers – hence the graffiti. It's been derelict since that time, largely because the stair rail is in such dangerous condition. Oh, and – er – please be careful where you tread, we have a lot of dry rot up here.'

To his unease, Roy Grace saw that he was standing on a large trapdoor secured by two rusting bolts. It felt decidedly unsafe and he quickly stepped aside and off it.

'That trapdoor opens downwards on to a forty-foot vertical drop to a store room above the kitchen scullery. There used to be a dumb waiter for hauling meals up to the residents here from the kitchen.' He pointed upwards to reveal a primitive block and tackle fixed to the ceiling, with rope wound around it. Grace looked down at the floor again. At the large sign which read: DANGER – STEEP DROP BELOW. DO NOT STAND ON DOOR.

Suddenly he saw something glint on the floor beneath a dust sheet hanging over the bed, and knelt down. It was a chocolate wrapper. A Crunchie bar. 'Did they have these in King George's day?' he asked.

The Curator smiled, looking sinister in the shadows. 'I'm afraid there have been a few unofficial visitors up here in more recent times. We've had a number of break-ins. It's almost impossible to maintain one hundred per cent security in a building of this size.'

'Of course.' Grace stared again at the chocolate bar wrapper, as the Curator walked across the room. Putting on a pair of gloves, Grace picked up the wrapper and sniffed it, expecting it to smell stale. But to his surprise it seemed fresh, as if it had been opened very recently. Then he noticed a tiny smear of lipstick where the front of it was folded back.

He put it down carefully where he had found it in order

that it could be photographed by a SOCO officer, and followed the Curator out on to the roof, ducking through a small door that was barely bigger than a serving hatch. The sky had turned ominously dark, as if it were about to rain. Barry strode ahead, along a narrow steel platform, with a sheer drop to the ground to his left, and Grace followed gripping the handrail, trying not to look down. Ahead of him and all around was a spectacular view across the roofs of the Pavilion, with its onion domes and minarets. Down below he could hear sirens and see more blue flashing lights of vehicles pulling up.

'That's the dome of the Banqueting Room, right ahead,' David Barry pointed. They scaled a short, metal ladder, then went along another narrow walkway. Then they climbed a long, steep ladder, Roy Grace nervously clinging on tightly as the Curator, above him, clambered as confidently as a mountain goat.

Grace hauled himself on his knees on to a narrow platform, with the dome curving majestically skywards above him. And now he really did not dare look down.

Then his phone rang.

He debated for a moment whether to answer it, then very carefully pulled it out of its cradle. 'Roy Grace,' he said.

It was ACC Peter Rigg, and he sounded anxious. 'Roy,' he said. 'I don't know if you've heard, but I gather there's a bit of an incident at the Royal Pavilion.'

'Er – yes, sir, I have.'

'I think you'd better get there PDQ.'

Grace looked out across the city rooftops. 'I am actually here, sir.'

'Good, excellent! Anything to report?'

'Yes, sir, I have a great view.'

'View?'

He saw Barry was crawling through a tiny inspection hatch door.

'Can I call you back in a few minutes, sir?'

'Please. The Chief Constable's fretting.'

'Yes, I know, sir.' He ended the call and followed Barry through the hatch, having to ease himself in backwards, into almost total darkness and the musty smell of old wood, and something acrid and deeply unpleasant.

'This is the second skin of the building,' the Curator said, shining his torch beam around. 'Outside you have the visible bottle-shaped shell of the dome. This is the wooden framework supporting it.' Both men coughed. Grace's eyes were stinging. He could see wooden slats, like a primitive ladder, rising above him and getting increasingly narrow.

The Curator shone the beam upwards, illuminating a wooden cross beam, with a severed metal shaft suspended from it. It looked, to Roy Grace, the same diameter as the shaft sticking out of the top of the fallen chandelier. Wisps of smoke or steam were curling upwards from it. Grace frowned, then coughed again. Then he looked down, and through a small hole, a large section of the Banqueting Room was visible beneath. He could see the two paramedics still on all fours, in the wreckage of the chandelier.

The Curator swung the torch beam down and something glinted in the light. It looked like a metal bottle cap. Then Roy Grace noticed a discarded San Pellegrino bottle. Near it were fragments of broken plastic.

'Bloody litter louts!' the Curator said, reaching for the bottle.

Grace grabbed his hand. 'Don't touch it – it could be a crime exhibit and it might contain acid.'

'Acid?'

Grace guided the beam up the severed shaft again. 'What do you suppose that is?'

Barry stared at him. 'I don't understand.'

Then they both saw the rucksack wedged between two slats, a short distance above them. Grace took the torch and climbed up to it, then shone the beam inside. He saw an opened all-day-breakfast pack of sandwiches, a can of Coke, a bottle of water, a Kindle, a battered leather wallet, and what looked like an iron tyre lever.

Tucking the torch under his chin, he again pulled a pair of protective gloves from his pocket and snapped them on. Then he took out the wallet and opened it. Slotted in one pocket he saw a photograph of a small boy in a baseball cap, and a plastic Grand Hotel room key jammed in another. He put the wallet into a plastic evidence bag and slipped it into his pocket.

Then he coughed again, just grabbing the torch before it fell. He shone the beam back on the shaft. The end of it, with wisps of smoke still rising, had melted into a bulbous shape that reminded him of mercury in a thermometer. 'What do you know about chemistry?' he called down to the Curator.

'Never my strong subject,' David Barry said, staring up at the end of the shaft.

'That makes two of us,' Roy Grace said. 'But I can tell you one thing. Your chandelier didn't fall by accident.'

'I don't know if I'm happy to hear that or not.'

Grace barely heard him. He was thinking about Gaia's son Roan, who had apparently been sitting beneath the chandelier seconds before it fell. Had the boy been the intended target?

No. He did not think so. His immediate hypothesis was

that Gaia was the target. Something had gone wrong in the assailant's plans. Timing? The appearance of Roan?

Who was the man crushed beneath the chandelier? The perpetrator? Or a heroic innocent bystander?

He did not think the latter. Innocence didn't play any part in what had just happened.

# 96

Roy Grace and a subdued David Barry strode quickly back into the Banqueting Room. The film crew had now been cleared from the room, and two police officers stood by the doorways. A large number of Fire Brigade officers were standing by with their equipment, waiting for a decision that would be made by the Coroner's Officer and the Home Office pathologist, who would be called out, whether the body could be recovered to the mortuary, or the first part of the post-mortem was to take place here.

A Crime Scene Photographer had arrived, as well as the Coroner's Officer, who was talking to DI Tingley. Grace hoped there were sufficient people from the mortuary on call so that Cleo would not be dragged out here from her much needed rest this evening.

Jason Tingley turned to Grace. 'Chief, we can't get a Home Office pathologist until first thing in the morning. Nadiuska's going to be doing the post-mortem. I explained the situation and she's given permission for the body to be recovered to the mortuary.'

'Good.' He looked up, briefly. 'I think we're going to have a difficult balancing act with the film people. It looks to me that someone deliberately brought down this chandelier. I want the dome above it treated as a crime scene – get SOCO up there right away, and warn them there are some hazardous substances.'

One of the police officers at the door came over to him.

'Sir, there's a gentleman who says he is the film's producer who's insisting on speaking to you.'

Grace walked across to the door and saw a short, bald man, expensively dressed in casual clothes, who was looking indignant.

'You the officer in charge around here?' Larry Brooker said imperiously.

'I'm Detective Superintendent Grace – I'm in charge of Major Crime for Sussex.'

'Larry Brooker, I'm the producer of this movie.' He stabbed a finger towards Jason Tingley. 'I gotta problem with that colleague of yours. I'm making a multi-million-dollar movie and he won't let me on my own set!'

'I'm afraid that's correct,' Grace said. 'No one is permitted in the building while we carry out our investigations. I'm afraid I'm going to have to ask you to leave, too.'

'I'm sorry, I can't let this happen,' Brooker said.

'With respect, it's actually not your decision to make,' Grace said.

The producer glared at him. 'So just whose decision is it, for fuck's sake?'

'Mine,' Grace said.

'You have to get real, Detective – do you have any idea—'

'Is a dead body under that chandelier real enough for you?' Grace said, cutting him short, barely containing his anger now.

'So, like, what's the score?'

*Did this creep really not care?* Grace stared at the bald runt, highly tempted to say something that would really piss him off. *The score is three–two to Manchester United*, perhaps. *The Test Match score in Bangalore?* But he remembered the importance of this film to his beloved city. 'Mr

Brooker, I'm conscious of your situation, and I'll be as fast as I can. I'm going to bring in a team to work overnight. I'm afraid we do have to seal off the whole building, but subject to what the maintenance and Health and Safety people say, I'll try to give it back to you tomorrow afternoon. Would that be acceptable?'

'What time tomorrow afternoon?' Brooker growled.

'What time do you need it?'

'We were planning to shoot after it closes to the public: 5.45 p.m. onwards.'

'Chief!' Tingley cautioned.

'Fine,' Grace said, ignoring Tingley's protestation. 'You'll have it back for then. Are you able to do any filming outside, or in a different location tonight?'

'That was the plan – we have over one hundred extras here. It's a very important scene – it's a key scene in the movie. But how can we even shoot outside with all these police vehicles here?'

'We'll get them moved – if you tell us which area you want cleared outside, we'll make that happen.'

Then he turned to the DI. 'My car's outside. Meet me there in five minutes.'

He hurried out of the building, looking around for Andrew Gulli, but could see no sign of him. Then he crossed the lawns towards the little village of motorhomes and trailers. Four man-mountain security guards stood by the steps to Gaia's motorhome. Grace showed his warrant card, then asked if any of them had seen Mr Gulli.

'He went over to the hotel to see about stepping up security there,' one of them replied, talking in a voice that sounded like he had a mouth full of ice cubes.

Grace knocked on the door. It was opened a few moments later by a female assistant, who he had seen before in Gaia's suite in The Grand. She had ginger hair, cut in a fashionably skewed style, and wore a black T-shirt and black jeans over deck plimsolls. 'Lori, right?'

She smiled in recognition, but looked uneasy. 'Inspector Grace – what can I do for you?' she said in a clipped American accent.

'I wanted to check that Roan is okay.'

'Uh huh, he's fine, thank you.'

'He's not injured?'

'No, he's good, he's not even upset – I think he was more confused than anything. Thank you for asking. What's actually happened? Andrew Gulli told us there's been some kind of accident with a chandelier, but we don't have any details.'

'Yes, I'd just like to explain the situation – is Gaia here?'

The assistant stepped back for a moment and called out, 'It's Inspector Grace!'

Moments later she beckoned him to come on board.

He climbed the steps and entered the cavernous interior of the vehicle, which smelled of a very appealing perfume, and the fainter smell of a recently smoked cigarette. A television was on, tuned to a cartoon channel, and Roan sat at a table, wearing his baseball cap, a computer game in front of him, staring at the cartoon with a rather bored expression, then turned his attention to his game.

'You okay?' Grace asked him.

He shrugged and pressed a toggle on his game.

Then a woman he did not at first recognize appeared through a partition door, wrapped in a cream silk dressing gown, her blonde hair cropped short in a male cut. She looked tearful, but greeted him with a cheery and very sexy voice. 'Hey, Mr Paul Newman Eyes!'

He smiled at her; she looked different but still strikingly beautiful.

'What's going on? Is the goddamn building falling down or something?'

He shook his head. 'I'm really sorry – we're doing our best to establish what happened.'

She strode up to him, put her arms around him and hugged him hard. 'This is scary,' she said.

'We'll get to the bottom of it quickly, I promise you.'

Suddenly, she gave him a quick – but not *that* quick – peck on the cheek, then stared into his eyes for some moments. Staring back into hers, he felt an electrifying frisson between them.

'I know you will. Thank you for everything you're doing while we're here in your city, Chief Inspector.' Her breath smelled minty.

He shrugged and blushed. 'I'm afraid with this incident in the Banqueting Room, it's clearly not enough.'

'Can I offer you a drink?'

He shook his head. 'Thank you, but I have to get on in a second. I just wanted to make sure Roan was okay. It's too early to say whether there's any foul play, but we've closed down the Pavilion in order to conduct our investigations, so there won't be any filming in there tonight.'

'You think someone might have done something to bring that chandelier down?'

'I wouldn't want to alarm you, but it's a distinct possibility.'

'They were targeting my son?' Her eyes opened wide in fear.

'If what happened is connected to the email that was sent last night, and that's pure speculation at this stage, I'd say it was more likely they were targeting you and got their timings wrong. But I wouldn't want to say anything that might cause you to worry unduly at this stage.'

She stared him in the eyes again. 'So long as you're around, Chief Inspector, I won't be worried!'

He thought for a moment she was going to kiss him again, and he took a step back, half turning away, trying, albeit rather unconvincingly, to retain a professional detachment. 'Thank you,' he said. 'Thank you for being so understanding.'

'*De nada!*' She blew him a kiss.

# 97

Grace hurried back across the Pavilion lawns towards his car with a spring in his step. Despite his worries, he felt he was walking on air. He'd never imagined the day might come when he was kissed by an icon!

'What are you smiling about, chief?' Jason Tingley greeted him, standing by his car. 'You look like you just won the lottery!'

'Gaia's kid's okay, thank God. I'm relieved, that's all.'

'You sure that's all it is?'

'What's that meant to mean?' Grace grinned at him. Tingley was a sharp detective who missed nothing.

The DI looked at his watch. 'That was a long five minutes. Get lucky in there, did you?'

'It was a purely professional visit.'

'Oh yes?'

Ignoring the innuendo, Grace climbed into the car and pulled his seat belt on. Tingley sat in the passenger seat. 'None of my business, of course,' he said.

There was a rap on Grace's window. He lowered it to talk to the tall woman with long fair hair who was holding a reporter's notepad.

'Detective Superintendent Grace?' she queried. 'Sorry to bother you. Iona Spencer, from the *Argus*.'

*Shit*, Grace thought, cursing silently. He should have known that Spinella would be replaced pretty smartly. 'Can I help you?'

'Is there anything you could tell me about what's happening in the Pavilion? I gather there's been a fatality.'

'There'll be a press conference in the morning,' he said, politely. 'It would appear at the moment that a maintenance worker has been fatally injured in an industrial accident.'

'Are any of the cast of the film involved?'

'No, I can assure you of that. I'm sorry, we are in a hurry, but I will have more information for you tomorrow.'

'Thank you,' she said.

As he drove off, Tingley commented, 'Well, at least she's better looking than Spinella.'

'And better mannered,' Grace said, inserting his phone into the hands-free cradle, then calling the Chief Constable's number.

*

Five minutes later Grace pulled the car up on the driveway in front of The Grand Hotel, and they went inside and straight up to the front desk. Grace was aware that, strictly speaking, he shouldn't be doing this kind of legwork they were embarking on, and should have delegated it to a much lower rank – a DC or DS. But, having been given overall responsibility for Gaia's security, at this moment he wanted to be hands on. Equally importantly, he genuinely loved real, old-fashioned detective work – the slog to find clues and unravel tiny parts of the puzzle. If he let it, his work would keep him permanently desk-bound, and he never wanted that to happen.

He showed his warrant card to a young woman on duty on reception, then handed her the plastic room key he had retrieved from the wallet inside the rucksack in the Pavilion's roof space.

'We need to identify someone who has been fatally

injured in an accident, and we found this in what we believe are his belongings. Could you tell us who this room is registered to, please.'

She inserted the key into her computer and moments later said, 'Room 608, Mr Jerry Baxter. I have an address for him in New York.'

Tingley jotted it down.

'Can we see the room, please?' Grace asked.

'I'll phone the duty manager – actually, the General Manager is here, I'll call him.'

Andrew Mosley had, it seemed to Grace, all the qualities required of a consummate hotelier. Smart appearance, a charming manner, an efficient air and impeccable manners. He took them up in the lift, along the corridor then knocked, dutifully, on the door of room 608 and waited some moments. Then he knocked again. When he was satisfied no one was answering, he inserted the key and pushed the door open, calling out a cautious 'Hello?' before switching on the lights.

The two detectives entered the small room, which was furnished with twin beds, an armchair, a round table on which sat a copy of *Sussex Life* magazine and *Absolute Brighton*, a side table, and a desk fixed to the wall, littered with receipts. There was a window overlooking an internal courtyard, and another door, ajar, leading through to the bathroom.

A suitcase lay open on the floor, and on the top of the clothes inside it lay a dark-blue passport bearing a crest and the words UNITED STATES OF AMERICA.

Grace pulled on a pair of gloves; Tingley followed suit. Then Grace picked up the passport and opened it, flicking rapidly through the pages until he came to the identification one.

There was a typically poor quality, photo-booth image

of a hostile-looking man, in his forties when it was taken, he calculated from the date of issue, with greying hair brushed forward in a pageboy fringe. It gave his name as *Drayton Robert Wheeler*, and date of birth, 22 March 1956, which put him at fifty-five years old. His place of birth was New York City, USA.

'I think this could be our man,' Tingley said, staring at a receipt. 'This is from Halfords. Receipt for a car battery and a tyre lever. You said there was a tyre lever in the rucksack, right?'

Grace nodded. 'Odd things for a tourist to buy.'

'Not as odd as six thermometers, paint stripper and chlorine,' the DI said, looking at some of the other receipts. 'Were you any good at chemistry at school?'

'Not much. I thought you did a CRBN course a few years back?' CRBN was training for Chemical, Radiological, Biological and Nuclear incidents.

'I did, but I'd need to go online to check what could be made with this lot. Mercury is used sometimes in bomb-making.'

Grace turned to the hotel manager. 'How's your chemistry knowledge?'

Mosley shook his head. 'Only very rudimentary, I'm afraid. Stink bombs at school were about my limit!'

Tingley was frowning at another receipt. 'A baby monitor from Mothercare?'

Grace stared at the receipt. Then realized what the broken plastic fragments he had seen up above the chandelier were. Had Drayton Wheeler been listening to the Banqueting Room from up above?

Then the DI said urgently, 'Look at this, chief!'

It was a receipt from an internet café, Café Conneckted, dated yesterday, Monday.

Grace looked at it. It was for one hour's connection, coffee, mineral water and carrot cake. Ten pounds. 'Do you know this place?'

'Yes,' Tingley said. 'Top of Trafalgar Street.'

Grace's mind was whirring. Thinking about the threatening email that had been sent last night.

The two detectives looked at each other. 'Shall I send someone over there?' Tingley asked.

Grace shook his head. 'No, you and I are going there. I want to find out for myself.'

Tingley walked through into the bathroom. On the shelf above the sink was a row of plastic medication tubs. Grace followed him. There were six of them, each labelled with a New York pharmacy prescription band. Grace read them all.

'This guy was some sort of junkie,' Tingley commented.

Grace shook his head. 'No, he was ill.'

'How ill?'

Grace stared at one label in particular. 'It looks to me like he had cancer. I recognize this – my father died of bowel cancer and was taking this medication, too.' He thought for a moment. 'That rude guy, the producer. Do you have his phone number?'

The Detective Inspector fished out his notebook and flicked through several pages. 'Yes, I have his mobile number here.'

Grace keyed it in. He got Larry Brooker's voicemail and left a message for him to call back urgently.

# 98

Larry Brooker called back just as they pulled up outside Café Conneckted.

'Does the name Drayton Wheeler mean anything to you, Mr Brooker?' Grace asked him, then immediately put his phone on loudspeaker.

'Drayton Wheeler?' the American said. 'Um, right, well, yes.'

Grace could detect the unease in the American's voice.

'He's just an asshole – trying to make a claim on our story. That kind of thing happens every time you make a high-profile movie. There's always some creep comes crawling out the woodwork claiming it was their idea and you stole it.'

'Might he have had a genuine grievance against you, or your production?' Grace asked, glancing at Tingley.

'Oh sure, he was threatening to sue us. No big deal – I told him to contact our lawyers.' Then, sounding distinctly edgy, suddenly he asked, 'Has he been in contact with you, or something?'

'We think he might be the man lying under the chandelier.'

There was a long silence. 'You're serious?'

'I won't know for certain until we've formally identified him.'

'Is there anything I can do from my end?'

'Not at the moment. If we make positive identification, then we'll need to interview you tomorrow.'

'Of course.'

'Have you been able to do some filming outdoors tonight? The weather seems to be holding, just.'

'We are. Your officers here are being very co-operative. We'll be shooting until around midnight.'

'Good.'

Grace then rang Andrew Gulli, to ask him if to his knowledge a Drayton Wheeler or Jerry Baxter had ever sent any obsessive or threatening messages to Gaia.

Gulli was certain he had never heard either name.

Grace ended the call and they went into the café, which was almost empty. A heavily pierced woman in her twenties, in jeans and a baggy blouse, stood behind the bar counter, working an espresso machine. There was a lounge seating area to the left, and an archway beyond the bar, through to what looked like a larger area at the rear. On the right was a row of ten workstations, each with a computer terminal. Two were occupied, one by a ponytailed man in his twenties, the other by two teenage girls, one standing looking over the other's shoulder, both of them giggling.

Grace looked up at the ceiling and noticed a CCTV camera covering the row of terminals. They walked up to the bar. The woman finished making the coffee, gave them a cursory nod, acknowledging their presence, then took the coffee across to the ponytailed man.

When she returned, Grace showed her his warrant card. 'Detective Superintendent Grace from Sussex CID Major Crime Branch and Detective Inspector Tingley from Brighton CID.'

She looked a tad bewildered. 'Yes – er – how can I help you?'

Grace held out a cellophane evidence bag containing Drayton Wheeler's passport, which was open at the page showing his photograph. 'Do you recognize this man?'

She studied it carefully for some moments, then shook her head. 'I'm sorry, no I don't.'

'He hasn't been in here?'

'Not while I've been here, I'm sure.'

'We believe he was here yesterday evening and paid for one hour's internet access.'

'Ah, right, I wasn't here last night.'

'Who was here?'

'The owner and his wife, but they're off today.'

'Can you contact them?'

She looked at her watch. 'They've gone to a George Michael concert in London. I shouldn't think they'll hear the phone. But they'll be here all day tomorrow. I can try, if you like?'

'We'll come back tomorrow,' Grace said.

Jason Tingley pointed up at the CCTV camera. 'Is that working?'

'Yes, I think so.'

'How long is the footage kept before it gets wiped?'

'I'm not certain – I believe it's a week.'

'Do you know how to replay footage on it?' Grace asked.

'No, and I wouldn't dare touch it!'

'Okay, what time do you open tomorrow?'

'Ten.'

'Right, now this is really important,' Grace said. 'Can you please ask the owners, or leave a message for them, to make absolutely sure all footage from yesterday is retained?'

'Yes, yes of course,' she said.

Grace gave her his card, then they left.

As they climbed back into the car, Jason Tingley said, 'We have a motive. The Café Conneckted receipt puts Drayton Wheeler in a place where he could have sent that email last night. In my view we could start making some assumptions.'

'I hate that word, Jason,' he said with a wry smile. 'As I've often said, in my experience *assumptions* are the mother and father of all cock-ups. I prefer to stick with *hypotheses.'*

The DI grinned. 'Okay, *hypotheses.* Drayton Wheeler believes he has been screwed by Larry Brooker – or his company. So he decides to hit back by sabotaging the production? By killing the leading lady?'

'Why didn't he just sue?' Grace replied. 'Presumably it was money he was after?'

Tingley tapped the side of his head. 'Dealing with a crazy?'

Grace was thinking about the vials of medication in the bathroom. Was this some kind of desperate act by a dying man? But with what aim? 'Did you ever hear that expression, "The more I do this job, the less I know?" ' he asked.

Tingley smiled. 'No, but I understand it.'

Grace nodded. 'Please God it was Drayton Wheeler who sent that email last night, and that he's the guy under the chandelier. That would be a rather tragic but very elegant solution.'

'Beware of assumptions, didn't you say, chief?' the DI remarked with a cheeky grin.

Roy Grace, deep in thought, did not respond. He was thinking hard what he needed to do to step up the security for Gaia and her son, regardless of cost, until they could be sure that the threat to her was over.

And he had a nagging doubt. Some of it stacked up, but not all of it. Not enough.

# 99

It was late when he finally got home to Cleo. She was lying, half-asleep in bed, with an old Miss Marple episode playing on the television. *Murder At The Vicarage*, he recognized after a few moments.

'How are you feeling?' He kissed her forehead.

'I'm okay. But Bump's training for the Olympics!' She guided his hand to her stomach, and he could feel their baby zapping around as if on a trampoline. He smiled, proudly and lovingly. It was such an amazing sensation. Their child. His and hers. Alive inside her.

He lay beside her for some minutes, just holding her tightly and feeling the baby's exertions. Then he kissed her. 'God, I love you so much,' he said.

'I love you too,' she said. 'But it's no good you coming to bed on an empty stomach – I don't want to lie here listening to it rumble all night!' She kissed him. 'There's a Marks and Sparks fish pie on the worktop. Give it a few minutes in the microwave – it says how many on the pack. And there are some peas in a saucepan – just bring them to the boil.'

'You spoil me!'

'You're worth spoiling. So, did you save the world tonight?'

'Probably.'

'That's what I love about you, Detective Superintendent Grace. Your modesty.'

He kissed her again. 'It sort of comes naturally!'

'Oh yes? By the way, Humphrey refused to go out. He needs to do his business – if we don't want a prezzie on the carpet in the morning!'

'I'll take him for a walk. Do you still want the telly on?'

'You can turn it off, please, I'm going to try to sleep, if I can convince Bump! Don't forget about that Gaia documentary I recorded.'

'I had forgotten – thanks for reminding me.'

He went downstairs, clipped the lead on Humphrey's collar with some difficulty, while the overjoyed creature kept jumping up and down licking his face. Then he took a plastic bag from under the kitchen sink, crammed it into his pocket and led the dog out of the front door.

Humphrey squatted the moment they were in the cobbled courtyard.

'Wait!' Grace hissed.

The dog took no notice, defecating firmly and proudly, as a neighbour wheeled his bicycle past. 'Hope you're going to pick that up,' the man mumbled.

Grace scooped it up, dearly tempted to push it through the rude cyclist's letterbox. Then he threaded his way with Humphrey through the narrow streets of the North Laine district of Brighton, heading for his favourite part of the city, the seafront itself, and the promenade beneath the Arches. He deposited the bag in a designated bin, relieved that at least now the dog had performed, he would be able to let it off the lead.

As he walked, he was deep in thought. Thinking about the email. Was the man under the chandelier the sender? He read it again on his BlackBerry.

**I still cannot believe how you cut me dead. I thought your whole point in coming to England was to see**

> me. I know you love me, really. You're going to be
> sorry you did that. Very sorry. You made me look a
> fool. You made people laugh at me. I'm going to give
> you the chance to apologise. You are soon going to
> be telling the whole world how much you love me.
> I will kill you if you don't.

It chimed but it didn't fit. 'I thought your whole point in coming to England was to see me.' That did not make sense in the context: 'You made people laugh at me. I'm going to give you the chance to apologise. You are soon going to be telling the whole world how much you love me. *I will kill you if you don't.*'

Drayton Wheeler's actions were just not consistent with that. These weren't the words of a man who believed his story or his script had been ripped off. Unless he was a totally confused crazy. Also, from what he knew, an American would have spelled *apologise* with a *z* not an *s*.

Was sacrificing his life to save Gaia's child some kind of desperate gesture to make Gaia love him?

It was a dark night but the rain was still holding off. There were dozens of people out and about. He walked in the shadow of the Palace Pier, so preoccupied he barely even clocked it as the place where he and Sandy, some twenty years ago, had had their first kiss.

He called Humphrey, clipped his lead back on, then, still deep in thought, he headed home.

# 100

Twenty minutes later, Roy Grace put the fish pie into the microwave, switched on the hob and placed the saucepan of peas on top. Then he took his Policy Book out of his briefcase and sat down on the sofa to update it. Humphrey entered into a life-or-death tussle with a squeaky stuffed elephant on the floor.

It was 12.30 a.m. and he felt wired. He picked up the Sky remote and clicked through the saved programmes until he saw the one Cleo had recorded for him on Gaia, and clicked on it.

*Squeak-squeak-squeak, grrrrrrrrrrrrrr.* Humphrey's tussle continued.

He scooped his food on to a plate, put it on a tray with a napkin and cutlery, and a glass of Spanish Albarino from the fridge, and sat back down. For the next twenty minutes as he ate, tuning out the dog, Gaia's life unfolded in front of him. From the modest house where she lived as a child on Brighton's Whitehawk housing estate, to her first success at the age of fifteen on a television talent show, to her move to Los Angeles in her late teens, where she started off waiting tables, followed by an affair with a record producer who picked her up in a noodle bar on Sunset, and gave her her big break, cutting her first single with the same session musicians that had been behind both Madonna and Whitney Houston's early recordings.

There were periodic close-ups of Gaia saying how important it was for everyone to treat the planet with respect. '*I love you love me*' was one of her catchphrases for that message.

There followed vignettes of concerts she had performed around the globe. Grace grinned at one, in Munich, where she appeared in German national costume of a dirndl, holding an accordion, and knocking back beer from a gigantic stein. Then another in Freiburg, capital of the Black Forest, where she was kitted out in lederhosen. Then, suddenly, in a costume switch, she stormed on stage, in front of an enraptured audience, in a cloud of swirling dry ice, jumping right, then left, holding a hunting rifle, wearing a man's tweed suit.

A bright yellow ochre suit with a loud check pattern.

Grace's tray crashed to the floor as he grabbed the remote, and froze the image. He ignored the up-ended plate and his spilled wine glass as he stared, transfixed, at the screen. He wound it back some seconds, then let it play and then froze it again.

It was exactly the same fabric that had been found in the chicken farm. The same fabric that had been found at the fishing lake. He was certain.

Beyond certain.

Gaia was wearing it on stage, in front of him, on the Bavarian leg of her German tour last autumn.

He froze the image again, reached for his phone, and dialled Andrew Gulli.

'Inspector Grace?' he answered. 'How can I help you?'

'I apologize for calling so late but this could be important.'

'No problem, Inspector, do you have any news for me?'

'Well, this may sound a strange request,' Grace said. 'I gather Gaia often auctions off the clothes she wears at concerts, and gives the money raised to green causes. Is that correct?'

'She's very committed.'

'I need to know about a yellow tweed suit that she wore at a concert in Bavaria last autumn.'

In a wry tone displaying rare humour, Gulli said, 'You're not going weird on me are you, Inspector?'

'I'm not going weird on you, I can assure you! I need to know about that suit really urgently. It could be relevant to her safety. Would you by any chance recall if she put it up for auction?'

'You wanna describe it to me?'

Grace gave him the details.

'I'll come back to you in the morning.'

'No, I need you to come back to me tonight. If you have to wake her up, then apologize to her for me, but it is really urgent.'

'Okay, leave it with me, Inspector.'

Grace continued to play and replay the scene. Fixated on the suit. Then he cleared up the mess on the floor and was just pouring himself another glass of wine when Gulli called back.

'Inspector Grace, I just spoke with Gaia. This was a while back, you have to appreciate. But so far as she can remember, that suit was auctioned last fall, October or November. She seemed to think it fetched quite a large sum – more than usual.'

'Thank you,' Grace said.

'Anything else I can help you with tonight? Have you made any progress on the chandelier?'

'I have a Crime Scene Team and a Police Search Team working through the night.'

'I appreciate your increasing the police presence around the hotel tonight,' Gulli said. 'But I'm minded to recommend Gaia flies back to Los Angeles tomorrow. I'm looking into flights.'

'Wouldn't you have an issue with the film schedule?'

'Yeah, but her safety and the kid's safety are more important.'

'I'd appreciate if you waited for our findings tomorrow.'

'I'm not happy with the situation,' Gulli said.

To Grace, he did not sound like a man who was ever happy. But he didn't tell him that. Instead he replied, 'Then I guess my job is to make sure you are happy.'

'I remain to be convinced.'

He ended the call, then immediately phoned Glenn Branson to update him about the fabric. Then he replayed the entire scene in the video again.

Thirty minutes later, when the documentary had reached Gaia's first movie role, he fell asleep on the sofa.

# 101

The production did not wrap until almost 1 a.m. Part of the problem causing constant delays to the outdoors filming, Anna Galicia could see, watching among the thinning crowd of onlookers from New Road, was the constant coming and going of Police, Fire Brigade and Scientific Support vehicles.

The scene they were filming was Gaia, or rather Maria Fitzherbert, bewildered and in tears, storming out of the front entrance of the Pavilion, having been dumped by her royal lover.

Although the crowd were kept too far back to hear what was being said, except for that final call announcing it was a wrap, it was clear that Gaia had been keeping everyone waiting and was in an irritable mood tonight. *Big surprise there! Bloody bitch.*

She watched her return to her motorhome.

Finally, at 1.20 a.m. someone emerged, a fit-looking female in jeans and a blouson jacket, and it took Anna a moment to realize this was Gaia with cropped hair. She was accompanied by an assistant, and instantly surrounded by her security guards. Much earlier, Anna had watched the boy leave, accompanied by another assistant and two security guards. Presumably back to the hotel, to bed.

There were rumours going around the crowd that he'd narrowly missed being killed by a falling chandelier. Shame that, she thought. She'd have liked to have seen Gaia grieving. Although it would have messed up her plans.

The convoy of five black Range Rovers swept out of the

grounds, and there was a general hive of activity in their wake. Lamps being shut down, equipment being moved and stowed in the trucks parked in the grounds. The police cordon broke up, and within ten minutes several white Sussex Police vans had arrived and were loading up with officers. Anna, watching keenly, began walking, looking for her opportunity.

It came sooner than she had anticipated. As she reached the entrance to the car park at the rear of the Dome concert hall, she saw that the three police officers who had been manning the cordon were walking away. Two people were closing up the catering truck and four men were occupied in lifting some camera dolly track.

No one took any notice of her as she slipped between the trucks, then over to the motorhomes. She paused in the shadows between Judd Halpern's and Gaia's and looked around. Neither had lights on inside. She saw a security guard standing nearby, smoking a cigarette and talking on his phone or radio, looking away from her.

Now!

She stepped up to the front door of Gaia's trailer, clutching the key she had collected from AD Motorhomes in St Albans earlier in the day, and slipped it into the lock.

Then she turned it.

# 102

Roy Grace woke up at 2 a.m. in front of the television, to see Jack Nicholson on the screen, in a hard hat, standing in flat, open land in front of the nodding-dog arm of an oil derrick. He yawned and hit the off-button. Humphrey was fast asleep beside him, the half-destroyed stuffed elephant lying on the floor below him.

He hauled himself upstairs, brushed his teeth and fell into bed. But for the next three hours he barely slept a wink, a jumble of disturbed thoughts playing, like a video, inside his head. Gaia was in all of them. So was the Chief Constable Tom Martinson, repeatedly berating him for missing a vital clue.

Completely wide awake at 5 a.m., he slipped out of bed, careful not to disturb Cleo, padded through into the bathroom and closed the door. He showered, shaved and brushed his teeth, then dressed and went downstairs. Humphrey was still curled up on the sofa, asleep. He picked up his briefcase and stepped out into the courtyard. It was now almost full daylight and raining lightly.

Fifteen minutes later, using his security card, he let himself in through the front door of Sussex House, climbed the stairs, walked through the deserted offices of the Major Crime Branch and entered his office. He put his briefcase down, went into the kitchenette area and made himself a strong coffee, which he carried back to his office.

Then he logged on to the internet and entered a Google search for *Gaia* and *auctions*.

There were thousands of results, but it didn't take him long, narrowing down the criteria he entered, to find what he was looking for. The auction for the yellow check suit had taken place over two weeks last November. The suit had been sold for £27,200.

Although he didn't know much about these things, that struck him as a lot of money, however good the provenance might have been that it really had belonged to Gaia. To pay that amount it needed someone either very rich, or seriously fanatical.

Or both.

# 103

On a whiteboard in the Conference Room of the Major Crime Suite was a blow-up of Drayton Wheeler's passport photograph.

'The time is 8.30 a.m., Wednesday, June the fifteenth. This is the twenty-first briefing of *Operation Icon*,' Roy Grace said to his team, which this morning included DI Tingley, Haydn Kelly, and Ray Packham from the High Tech Crime Unit. 'We have developments that are leading me to believe *Operation Icon* may have links to the real-life icon who is currently here in Brighton shooting a movie – Gaia.'

He registered the immediate highly focused attention he had from every single member of his team. Then he relayed the events of last night, his viewing of the Gaia video, and his search on the internet this morning. He looked at DC Reeves. 'Emma, I found the winning bid amount that was paid for the suit from the eBay site, but it would not give me any details about the bidders. We need to find that out very urgently. I'm tasking you to contact eBay and find out the names of all the people involved in that auction. As soon as you have them I want them checked against all databases. In particular, we need to find the underbidder who didn't get it.'

'Yes, sir,' she said.

He turned to Ray Packham. No one could look less like a computer geek than the High Tech Crime Unit analyst, but his mastery of technology was better than anyone Grace had ever met. 'You've looked yourself, Ray, and not been able to find it either?'

'No, chief – but eBay should be able to come up with the information pretty quickly.'

'Good. And you have a result for us on the email sent on Monday night?'

'I do,' he said proudly. 'We've looked at the IP address on it, and I've got some good news. It's a fixed IP registered at the internet café – Café Conneckted in Trafalgar Street. It was sent from there at 8.46 p.m. Monday night.'

'You're a genius!'

'I know,' Packham said, with a tongue-in-cheek grin.

Grace pointed at Drayton Wheeler's passport photograph on the whiteboard. 'The man's body has not yet been formally identified, but we are satisfied that this is the man crushed to death by the chandelier last night.' Grace then listed the receipts found in his hotel room. 'The Café Conneckted receipt puts Wheeler in that café on Monday, the day the email was sent – we need to find out what time he was there. Norman, I want you to be there at 10 a.m. when it opens.'

Potting nodded. 'Yes, chief.'

'If we can establish Wheeler was there at 8.46 p.m. on Monday, that could be good news. If he wasn't there at that time, we need to know who was. Hopefully you can get a result from the CCTV.'

'Leave it with me.'

Grace glanced at his notes. 'SOCO, who have been working through the night, reported their findings to me a short while ago. Mercuric chloride is an acid that apparently can be synthesized very easily from mercury, obtained from thermometers, sulphuric acid, from car batteries, and hydrochloric acid found in paint stripper. Receipts for all these items were present in Wheeler's room at The Grand. SOCO tell me that mercuric chloride is particularly efficient at dissolving aluminium – which is what the shaft support-ing the chandelier was made from.'

'Chief,' DS Guy Batchelor said, 'I'm having problems connecting the dots between the suit fabric and the chandelier.'

'Join the club,' Grace said. 'The connection is Gaia, and I can't guarantee we can connect the dots, Guy. But I'm treating it as a line of enquiry, okay?'

The DS nodded.

'The most urgent thing we need to do at this moment is establish whether or not Drayton Wheeler sent that email,' Grace continued. 'I'm hoping he did. Because if he didn't, we have a big problem.'

# 104

This was not Norman Potting's idea of a café. This was just another instance of how the world was changing in ways he didn't like and didn't understand. Fancy leather sofas and computer terminals. Couldn't people even have a cuppa without needing to be online, for God's sake? He liked traditional greasy spoons, with Formica table tops, plastic chairs, the odour of fried food, a menu chalked up on the wall, and a good, honest mug of strong tea.

Why, he wondered, looking up at the menu, printed in some barely decipherable fancy lettering, was there no such thing as an ordinary cup of coffee any more? Why did everyone have to dress the menu up in an incomprehensible bloody arcane language of its own?

Although he did eye the range of cupcakes greedily.

'Can I help you?' said a solidly built Goth woman behind the bar, wearing blue dungarees, tattoos running down both her arms, and so many rings through her nostrils he wondered how she managed to breathe or blow her nose. He noticed a tongue stud, too. And her forehead piercings which made him wince. Apart from the two of them, at a few minutes past 10 a.m. the place was deserted.

Potting produced his warrant card.

'Ah, yes, Zoe said to expect you.'

He showed her a copy of the receipt found in Drayton Wheeler's hotel room. 'We are anxious to establish what time this person was here on Monday.' Then he placed a blow-up of Wheeler's passport photo in front of her. 'Do you remember this man?'

She studied it for a moment. 'Yes, absolutely I do. He was, frankly, very rude, American, really quite unpleasant.'

'Can you remember what time he was in here? Was it Monday evening?'

She studied the photograph again. 'No, I think it was lunchtime. I remember we were very busy, and he got angry because he was having problems getting online – we had a server crash. He started shouting abuse at one of my staff. My husband gave him his money back and told him to leave.'

'You're certain?'

'One hundred per cent.'

'You have CCTV here?'

She pointed up at the ceiling-mounted camera. 'Yes, we installed it after we had a couple of terminals nicked.'

'You get such a nice class of people in this city.'

'You're telling me.'

'Would you be able to show me the footage between 8.30 p.m. and 9 p.m. on Monday?'

'I'll ask my husband – he knows how to operate it.' She turned and shouted through the archway, 'Craig! I need you!'

Moments later a short, thin man appeared, with a shaven head, even more tattooed and pierced than his wife. Late at night, in a dark alley, he'd have scared the shit out of anyone, Potting thought. But here in daylight he looked surprisingly meek and spoke with a friendly, rather weedy, voice.

Potting explained what he needed, and five minutes later was seated, with a trendily large tea cup with a clumsy handle, in a sparse office at the back of the café, staring up at a monitor. The time was displayed digitally in the top right-hand corner of the screen. The image quality wasn't great, but clear enough for his purpose. He could see five of the ten terminals were occupied.

Three were young men who looked like students. The fourth was an attractive girl, in her early twenties. The fifth was a middle-aged woman, wearing a leather baseball cap, a polo-neck sweater and a bomber jacket with the collar turned up.

By 8.35 p.m. four of the occupants had left, leaving the woman in the leather baseball cap on her own. Shortly after 8.46 she rose and walked up towards the counter, out of shot. Then a couple of minutes later she came back into frame, leaving the premises.

'Her!' Potting said. 'Do you remember her?'

'Yes, I do,' Craig said. 'We get a lot of oddballs in here. She was definitely one of them.'

'In what sense?'

'Well, sort of just her manner, and she had a very husky voice, you know, like someone who's a heavy smoker. Before she started her session she asked how much we charged and I told her two pounds for half an hour or three pounds for an hour. She said she needed to draw some cash out and asked if there was a hole-in-the-wall machine anywhere around. I remember telling her the nearest one was just up in Queen's Road – an HSBC.'

'She went to it?'

He shrugged. 'She went out and came back ten minutes later. I remember she paid with a brand new ten pound note, and I thought that must have come straight out of the machine.'

'I need to borrow the disc,' Potting said. 'Do you have any objection?'

The man hesitated.

'I can get a warrant, if you insist.'

Craig shook his head. 'No, that's fine.'

Potting took the disc, then hurried up to the top of Trafalgar Street, walking through the archway beneath Brighton Station, then turned left into Queen's Road. He saw the HSBC bank, with two cash machines, diagonally across to his left.

# 105

Glenn Branson sat at his terminal in MIR-1 with a row of index cards laid out in front of him. On one was written, *Torso at Stonery Farm*. On another was, *Arms and legs found in West Sussex Piscatorial Society lake*. On the third, *Suit fabric at Stonery Farm, West Sussex Piscatorial Society Lake and Gaia German tour*. The fourth was headed, *Myles Royce*. The fifth, *Drayton Wheeler*.

It was a method he employed whenever he found himself stuck. Each card related to photographs pinned to the whiteboards above the workstations where the investigation team were working in mostly silent concentration. Every few moments, he could hear Norman Potting's irritating voice. The DS always seemed to speak louder than anyone else when he was on the phone, as if assuming the person down the other end of the line was hard of hearing.

Then a female voice interrupted Branson. 'Sir?'

He looked up to see the tall figure of DC Reeves, in a bright red dress and flaxen hair, standing over him, looking excited. 'I have something from eBay that might be significant.'

'What?'

'They've been really helpful. I've got the entire history of the auction for Gaia's suit, and all the names of the bidders. It ended up with just two people who between them drove the price up from seven hundred pounds to the final winning bid of twenty-seven thousand, two hundred.'

'That was some bidding war. Incredible!'

444

'I know! And the winning bidder was none other than our jigsaw puzzle man, Myles Royce.'

'Royce?' Branson said. He frowned. 'I thought he already had this suit – he bought one.'

'Yes, sir,' Emma Reeves agreed. 'But he didn't own *this* one. Gaia's personal suit, worn by her at a concert. That's what gives it kudos and value to a collector.'

'Yeah, I get it, but shit, you've got to be sad to pay that kind of money.'

'Gaia gives it all to charity, apparently,' Emma Reeves said. 'And for the collector it could be a good investment.'

Branson shrugged. 'Even so, you'd have to want something real bad.'

'I think these collectors do, sir. Anyhow, I gave the names of all the other bidders to Annalise Vineer, and she's run checks on them. Remember an incident at The Grand Hotel, last week, when an over-zealous Gaia fan got pushed over by one of her security guards? This fan called the police, who attended; subsequently it was found that she had given them a false address.'

'Yep,' Branson said. 'Her name was Anna Garley – Galicia – or something like that, right?'

'Spot on! *Galicia*. Well, she was the underbidder on this auction for the yellow suit.'

Branson absorbed this for some moments. A possibility was shaping in his mind. A motive? Had they been looking down the wrong track? Could anger over the suit be behind this murder? Were the yellow cloth fragments at the deposition sites put there deliberately? Out of some kind of spite?

Norman Potting, who had just ended his call, looked up. 'You're talking about a female Gaia obsessive?'

Branson gave him a surly look. 'Possibly.'

'I just got back a short while ago from that internet place, Café Conneckted.' He held up a CD. 'This is the footage of the person who was online at 8.46 p.m. Monday night, when the threatening email was sent to Gaia.' Like an actor playing to an audience, Potting took a deliberate pause before going on. 'It's a woman.'

This was greeted by frowns, and a brief silence.

'A woman?' Guy Batchelor said.

'Yep.'

'Is there footage of her walking?' Haydn Kelly, sitting just opposite him, asked.

'I think so, a bit,' Potting said.

'May I see it?'

Potting handed him the disc. Kelly loaded it immediately.

'This person, whoever she is, went to an HSBC bank hole-in-the-wall machine in Queen's Road around 8.30 p.m. on Monday to make a cash withdrawal,' Potting said. 'There are two ATMs, side by side. I've just been on to the bank asking them to let us have details of all the people who made cash withdrawals from these machines between 8.15 and 9 p.m. on Monday – to allow for the machine clocks being slightly wrong. I should have it a bit later today.'

Glenn Branson stood over Haydn Kelly's shoulder and studied the distinct, if poor quality, colour image.

'You can fast forward through the first few minutes as the others leave the café, Haydn,' Potting said.

The forensic podiatrist did so, then slowed as the clock counter approached 20.44. Only the woman in the leather cap was there now. From her body language it was clear she had a decisive moment around 20.46. Shortly after that she appeared to log off, then stood up and walked towards the counter, and out of shot.

'You see her again shortly,' Potting said.

Two minutes later, she walked back into frame, briefly, then left the premises.

'Shit!' Haydn Kelly exclaimed.

'What?' Branson asked him.

'I can't be sure, I need to see more footage,' the podiatrist said.

'Sure of what?'

'The gait.'

'What is it telling you?'

'I need to see more of this person walking before I can be certain.'

'The CCTV room at John Street Police Station would be bound to have caught her on camera,' Guy Batchelor said. 'The whole of Queen's Road's covered.'

Branson turned to Nick Nicholl. 'Nick, take Haydn down there right away.'

As Nicholl stood up, Glenn Branson asked, 'Does anyone know how to get still photographs off video like this?'

'Ask Martin Bloomfield down in Imaging – he'll be able to do it.'

*

Thirty minutes later Branson left the building, with two printed and enhanced blow-ups of the woman in the leather cap. One was full-length, the other of just her face. He climbed into his allocated unmarked car and drove out through the green gates of the building, heading towards the seafront, and The Grand Hotel.

# 106

The pavement outside The Grand was crowded with fans with their mobile phone cameras, and paparazzi with their long lenses, all hopeful of catching a glimpse of the icon.

The doorman stood well back against the front entrance, as if defending it, as he studied the photograph Glenn Branson held up.

'Yes,' he said. 'Oh yes, very definitely.'

'No doubt at all?' Glenn asked.

'Part of my job is to remember faces, sir,' Colin Bourner said. 'I've been doing this a long time. Regulars get upset if you don't recognize them. I never forget a face. If you need verification, we are bound to have her on CCTV.'

'I would like to see that,' he replied. 'Not because I don't trust your judgement, but I'd like to take a look for myself.'

'I'll speak to Security, sir, won't keep you a moment.' He hurried into the building.

Glenn looked at his watch. 11.23 a.m. Gaia was staying here. One of the greatest stars in the world, and Ari had refused to let their kids play with her son. How shit was that? He stared up, wondering which her room was. One of these on the front façade, with a sea view, for sure. He had to make sure he got her autograph for Sammy and Remi while she was staying here, at least. He stared at the slow-moving traffic, and at people ambling along the promenade on the far side, occasionally being pinged out of the way by an irked rider as they trespassed unwittingly on the cycle path. Early June, and already it looked as if many of them were holidaymakers.

Holiday, he thought wistfully. The last holiday he'd had was in Cornwall with Ari nearly two years ago. It had rained for a solid fortnight. That hadn't done their failing relationship much good.

'Right, sir, they're just setting it up for you now!'

Branson turned. 'Great, thank you.'

'No, sir, it's my pleasure, absolutely my pleasure.'

*

Roy Grace had just arrived back from two awkward meetings. The first with ACC Peter Rigg who wanted to know how, despite the tight security that Grace had been requested to plan, someone had managed to hide directly above where the filming was taking place – and had been a fraction of a second away from killing Gaia's son. The second had been with the Chief Constable, who had been a little more understanding, but unhappy, nonetheless.

But Rigg had not tried to hide his fury. Sitting in front of him, Roy Grace felt as if he were back in the presence of his former boss, the acerbic Alison Vosper, who delighted in putting him on the spot at any opportunity. When he attempted to explain the difficulties of securing a site to which the general public had daily access, the ACC snorted in derision. 'My dear fellow,' he said, pompously, 'You were tasked with overall responsibility for Gaia's safety while she is a guest in our city – and so far you've given a less than impressive performance. You knew there was a threat to her life; did it not occur to you to check the roof spaces, as something utterly elementary?'

'It did, sir, and they were checked. The police checked thoroughly, initially, and it has been down to the Pavilion's own security since then. I'm a homicide investigator, not a security analyst or expert.'

'Thank God you're not. I'd hate to be in a situation where my life or the safety of my family was dependent on any plan you produced to protect them. What's up, man, were you sleepwalking, or something? It's all over the bloody news – you've seen the front page of the *Argus*?'

## Gaia son escapes death by inches

The ACC's criticism wasn't fair, Grace knew. If they'd had an unlimited budget, no one would have got into that damned roof space, but the truth was, with the battle he'd had to get even very limited resources for Gaia's security, there were inevitably going to be gaps. It wasn't unreasonable to expect that the Pavilion would have been capable of protecting itself.

And Rigg was very definitely being unreasonable at this moment. But he wasn't about to tell him that. The police force was a hierarchical system. In many ways it was like the military; you respected ranks senior to yourself and obeyed them without question, whatever you really thought.

'There were gaps in the security that should not have been there,' Roy Grace conceded. 'It looks like we were lucky.'

'I don't like that word *lucky*,' the Assistant Chief Constable said.

Being lucky was better than the alternative, Grace thought, but did not say.

# 107

Shortly after 4 p.m., the steady concentration of the seventeen people currently packed around the three large workstations in MIR-1 was broken by a loud curse from Norman Potting. Several people looked up. Then the steady putter of keyboards resumed. A mobile phone rang, playing 'Greensleeves', and Nick Nicholl answered it quickly.

Bella crunched on a Malteser. She had been tasked with contacting all the bidders on this and previous eBay auctions of Gaia memorabilia, in the hope one of them might know the elusive Anna Galicia personally. Meanwhile, down in the High Tech Crime Unit, Ray Packham was trying to navigate a path through a complex trail of encrypted email accounts. If they'd hoped to find her quickly by following the trail back from PayPal, they were going to have to be very patient. It was going to take days, and possibly weeks – if ever.

Potting cursed again. Then he said, 'Bloody banks! Can you bloody believe it?'

'Believe what, Norman?' Glenn Branson asked, secretly pleased that Potting was struggling. Badly though he wanted this case solved, he really hoped it wouldn't be Potting who made the breakthrough.

Potting turned to face him. 'We're reasonably certain that Anna Galicia went to one of the two HSBC hole-in-the-wall machines in Queen's Road, at around 8.30 p.m. on Monday. The CCTV room has images of her approaching the machine and then leaving at around that time. The bank are telling me there were seven withdrawals from those two machines between 8.15 and 9 p.m. that night – and all of them were male accounts.'

'Maybe her card didn't work in those machines?' Branson said. 'We've all had that happen. Don't they have CCTV running – a lot of them have a camera that looks outward – so you can see the faces of everyone using the machines.'

'I've asked for that,' Potting said. 'It's going to take them an hour or so – they're going to email me the image sequence they have, along with all the names and addresses of the people who used the machine. So we'll see then if she appears.'

'Have you got a list of all the other cash machines in easy walking distance from those two?' Bella asked him.

Glenn watched her face. She looked more attractive every time he looked at her, and it really stung him to see this interaction between her and Potting. It was almost like she was feeding him a pre-rehearsed prompt, to big him up.

'I have,' Potting said, grinning smugly as ever. There's a Santander Bank, a Barclays and a Halifax. I'm waiting for information back from all of them.'

Roy Grace entered the room, turning his head to see who was here. Then he turned to Glenn. 'How are we doing?'

'Apart from the doorman of The Grand confirming the Anna Galicia we are looking for is the same person involved in the incident with Gaia's bodyguards last week, nothing else so far, boss. What's happening at the Pavilion?'

'The chandelier's been removed into police storage,' Grace reported, 'much to the outrage of the Curator. The Search Team have found a baby monitor transmitter underneath a table in the Banqueting Room – it's a Mothercare make, consistent with the receipt in Wheeler's hotel room – and consistent with the broken receiver up in the roof space above the chandelier. I've given permission to the producers to re-enter the building and film in the Banqueting Room tonight – they're planning to shoot indoors, without the chandelier. The producer just told me that they will be able to add it in afterwards through some computer generated technique.'

Grace looked at his watch, worried. 'So, we can't be certain that email was not sent by Wheeler, but it's looking unlikely. Is that about the right assessment?'

'The timings don't work for Wheeler,' Branson said.

Timings were very much on Grace's mind at the moment. Within the next hour Gaia would be leaving the security of her hotel suite and going to the Pavilion. On his advice she had remained in her suite all day, and her son was staying in the suite this evening. Grace had arranged for his god-daughter Jaye Somers to come over for a couple of hours to play.

He knew Gaia was safe all the time she was in the hotel, but he was worried about the Pavilion. Had Rigg been too harsh on him, or did the ACC have a valid point? Had it been a visit from a member of the Royal Family or a senior politician, they would have searched the building with a fine-toothed comb, and sealed off all areas such as cellars and roof spaces where a potential perpetrator could hide either themselves or a bomb. But as the film company required unrestricted daily access, and it remained open to the public, security was always going to be an issue.

Had he been too complacent?

Well that wasn't going to happen again tonight. During

the past two hours the building had been searched with the same rigour as if a political conference were being staged there.

But even so, it was impossible to protect someone totally against a lone fanatic. He was still mindful of the chilling words of the IRA after they blew up The Grand Hotel back in 1984 in a failed attempt to murder the then Prime Minister Margaret Thatcher. They sent a message saying, 'Today we were unlucky, but remember we only have to be lucky once. You will have to be lucky always.'

He was not going to let Gaia be lucky. Luck was damned well not going to come into this equation. Quality police work, that was all. And everyone was briefed.

# 108

Much of the central area of the city was under constant CCTV surveillance, with cameras capable of zooming in to a tight close-up from a distance of several hundred yards.

The nerve centre of the operation was the CCTV room on the fifth floor of Brighton's John Street Police Station. It was a large space, with blue carpet and dark blue chairs. There were three separate workstations, each comprising a bank of monitors, keyboards, computer terminals and telephones.

Civilian controllers sat behind two of the workstations. One of them, wearing a headset, was busily engaged in a police operation, tracking a drug dealer's movements, but the other, Jon Pumfrey, a fresh-faced man in his late thirties, with neat brown hair, wearing a lightweight black jacket, was occupied with helping Haydn Kelly navigate through the system in his search for sightings of Anna Galicia.

The forensic podiatrist, cradling a tepid Starbucks coffee, had cramp in his right thigh. He had been seated at this console since shortly before midday, with the exception of one quick break to grab a sandwich and this coffee. It was now coming up to 5 p.m. A kaleidoscope of images of parts of the city of Brighton and Hove, and other Sussex locations, changed constantly on the multiple screens. People walking. Buses moving. A sudden zoom shot on to a man standing by a wheelie bin.

Kelly had spotted Anna Galicia on six different cameras so far, during Monday evening. In the first she was seen

455

walking in the direction of Café Conneckted. In the second she was heading towards the location of the HSBC cash machines in Queen's Road. In the third, fourth and fifth images she was walking around the outside of the Pavilion grounds, threading her way through the crowds of onlookers. In the sixth, she was walking towards the Old Steine, at 11.24 p.m. Although there was extensive camera coverage around that area, she did not reappear. Jon Pumfrey told Kelly that her disappearance from vision indicated she had probably taken a bus or jumped into a taxi and gone home for the night.

They were now scrolling through the images in the area around the Pavilion grounds from yesterday, fast-forwarding through the whole day on each of the different cameras in turn, in the hope of seeing her again. Kelly glanced at his watch, mindful that he needed to be back at Sussex House for the 6.30 p.m. briefing. It was almost 5 p.m. He already had more than enough for his purposes, and he was excited about what he had to report.

Then something caught his eye. He frowned.

'Jon, go back a few seconds!'

The controller moved his joystick, and the image began reversing.

'Stop!' Kelly commanded. The time on the screen displayed as 1 p.m., yesterday, Tuesday.

The image froze.

'What street is this?' Kelly asked.

'New Road.'

'Okay, zoom in on that guy, please.'

The image of a balding man in a business suit filled the screen. He stepped out of the front door of an office building, hesitated, held a hand out as if to check if it was still raining.

'Now, go slow forward, please.'

Kelly watched, with growing excitement, as the man walked out of frame. Then he said, 'Keep it running – you can fast forward. I think he'll be back.'

The forensic podiatrist was right. Ten minutes later the man returned, holding a small paper bag. He shot a glance at a bicycle chained to a lamp post, then went back into the office building.

'I need a copy of that, please,' he said to the controller.

A few minutes later, when Pumfrey handed it to him, he loaded it straight into his laptop, then ran the software he had developed for gait analysis on it. After he had taken off the measurements and calculations, he made a comparison with the figures computed from the footage of Anna Galicia walking.

And now he could barely contain his excitement.

# 109

Norman Potting sat at his workstation in MIR-1, puzzled. He now had images emailed to him from all the hole-in-the-wall machines within a short walking distance of Café Conneckted. HSBC, Barclays, Halifax and Santander banks had responded quickly and efficiently.

He scrolled through them, looking, in turn, at four female and sixteen male faces, and something was not making sense. All twenty people had made cash withdrawals from these machines, within his parameter of 8.15 and 9 p.m. Monday evening. Despite the poor image quality, one woman bore a reasonable resemblance to Anna Galicia. She had apparently attempted a transaction from an HSBC machine on Queen's Road at 8.31 p.m. But there was no withdrawal showing under her name. One explanation, the bank had told him, was that her card had been declined. But they were still a bit mystified why no record showed up at all. Another suggestion was that she was using a card that had been stolen but not yet reported missing: a withdrawal was made one minute later, at 8.32 p.m. in a man's name.

The Detective Sergeant was on the verge of deciding he had drawn a blank with this particular line of enquiry, when for the second time this afternoon, the normal studious quiet of the Major Incident Room was broken. This time there was an exuberant whoop from Haydn Kelly, who entered with such speed and force that the door swung back and struck the wall behind it with a bang loud enough to make everyone look up with a start.

'I've cracked it!' he shouted across the room at Roy Grace, beaming like an exuberant kid and brandishing two CD cases in the air.

'What? What have you cracked? Anna Galicia?' Grace asked.

The forensic podiatrist moved Grace's keyboard aside and set his laptop down on the worktop. He flipped open the lid and tapped in his code. Moments later Grace was staring at a screen that was split vertically. On the left-hand side he saw what looked like CCTV footage of the woman he recognized from earlier, Anna Galicia, walking along a street in Brighton. On the right-hand side of the screen was a balding man in a business suit. Along the top were several columns of spinning numbers and algebraic symbols that seemed to be calibrating and re-calibrating as each person walked.

Haydn Kelly pointed at the left screen. 'See our mysterious Anna Galicia?'

Grace nodded.

'There's a good reason why no one's been able to find her.'

'Which is?'

Kelly pointed at the right-hand screen. At the balding man in the business suit. 'Because that's *her*.'

Grace looked at the forensic podiatrist's face for an instant, in case he was joking. But he appeared deadly serious. 'How the hell do you know?'

'Gait analysis. See all those computations on the screen? I can do the analysis visually, to a pretty high degree of accuracy because I've done it for so long, but those calculations done by the algorithm I developed add certainty.

There is a very minor variation because the woman is on high heels and the man is wearing conventional male shoes. But they're the same person. No question.'

'Beyond doubt?'

'I'd bet my life on it.'

# 110

Roy Grace stared at the screen, his eyes switching from the woman to the man to the woman again, feeling a sudden chill deep in the pit of his stomach. 'Glenn,' he said. 'Come and see this.'

Branson stepped over, looked at the screen and exclaimed, 'That looks like our friend Eric Whiteley!'

'Whiteley?' Grace said, the name ringing a strong bell, and trying to place it.

'Yeah – the weirdo accountant me and Bella interviewed. That's the outside front door of his office – who's taken it?'

Norman Potting looked up. 'I've got something interesting here about Eric Whiteley, assuming it's the same one, Glenn.'

'In what context?'

'Could just be a strange coincidence. I've got the name *Eric Whiteley* just come in on an email from HSBC,' Potting said. 'I've got a list of all people who made cash withdrawals at hole-in-the-wall machines close to Café Conneckted on Monday night. According to the bank, he drew fifty pounds out of one of their machines in Queen's Road, at 8.32 p.m.'

'Do they have his photograph?'

'Well, this is the strange thing, they haven't.' Potting pointed at his own screen. 'This is the person who appears to have withdrawn the money – Anna Galicia. The bank think it's possible she's stolen his card.'

Glenn Branson was shaking his head. 'No, she hasn't stolen Eric Whiteley's card. She *is* Eric Whiteley!'

Grace looked at his watch. 5.20 p.m. He radioed the Control Room and asked for the on-duty Ops 1 Controller. Moments later he was through to Inspector Andy Kille, a highly competent man he liked working with. He explained the situation as quickly as he could, and asked for uniformed and plain clothes officers to go to Whiteley's office, with luck catching him before he left for the day, and arrest him. He told Kille to warn them the man could be violent.

When he ended the call he instructed Guy Batchelor and Emma Reeves to take an unmarked car to Whiteley's home address, and sit close by in case Whiteley showed up. Next he told Nick Nicholl to get a search warrant for both Whiteley's home and his office signed by a magistrate, and then to head directly to Whiteley's house.

Next, he spoke to the Ops 1 Controller again, and asked for a unit from the Local Support Team – the public order unit which specialized in executing warrants and wore full protective clothing, including visors, for the purpose – a POLSA and Search Officers to stand by near to Whiteley's house, but out of sight, until Nicholl arrived with the search warrant, then to go straight in, accompanied by DS Batchelor and DC Reeves. Again he cautioned the man might be violent.

Less than five minutes later, Andy Kille radioed Roy Grace back with news from two Response officers who were now on site at the offices of accountants Feline Bradley-Hamilton. Eric Whiteley had not turned up for work today. His office hadn't heard from him and he had not responded to their calls.

*Shit*, Roy Grace thought, *shit, shit, shit*. The deep chill inside him was rapidly turning into the white heat of panic.

The innocuous ones. So often it was the meek, mild-looking guys who turned out to be monsters. The UK's worst ever serial killer Harold Shipman, a bearded, bespectacled, kindly looking family doctor who just happened to have a penchant for killing his patients, and despatched 218 of them, and possibly many more.

He stared at Whiteley's image on the screen. One thing he knew for sure: someone who was capable of killing once was well capable of killing again. And again. His mind was spinning. *Whiteley had not showed up for work all day.* He turned to Glenn Branson.

'Glenn, you spoke to Eric Whiteley's boss a few days ago, didn't you?'

'Yes, chief.'

'Do I remember right that he said the man was a bit of an oddball but a very reliable employee?'

'Yes. Said he was a loner, but yes, totally reliable.'

'So him not showing up for work all day without contacting the office, or having an outside appointment in his diary, is out of character?'

'It would seem so, but we do know that he occasionally works away from the office at the premises of clients.'

Grace was liking this less and less. Hopefully the man was sick, in bed. But in his bones he didn't think so. He called Guy Batchelor. 'How are you doing?'

A blast of expletives came back down the phone, followed by, 'That sodding bus lane! Sorry Roy, but we're sitting in gridlock from Roedean all the way through to Peacehaven.'

'Okay, let me know when you are on site.' Grace immediately radioed the Ops 1 Controller again. 'Andy, do you have a unit in the Peacehaven area?'

'I'll check.'

'Send the nearest one straight to Eric Whiteley's house. I need to establish if he's at home – top priority.'

'Leave it with me.'

Grace was suddenly craving a cigarette. But he didn't carry any on him these days, and he didn't have time to find someone to bum one from – and even less time to go outside and smoke it. *Please God, let Whiteley be at home.*

And if he wasn't?

He was thinking of Gaia, she seemed to be a sweet and fragile person behind her tough public persona. He liked her, he was utterly determined to do all he possibly could to protect her and her son. After the incident with the chandelier, the consequences of any similar occurrences were not worth thinking about. Neither morally, nor career-wise.

He glanced at the serials – the log of all incidents in Sussex that was updated constantly. So far it was a quiet afternoon, which was good because that meant most of the officers on duty would be available if needed. He was thinking ahead. Clearly Andrew Gulli had not managed to convince Gaia to leave town, as the production's call sheet, which he had requested and was lying in front of him, required her in make-up at 4 p.m. and on set at 6 p.m.

Andy Kille called him back. 'Roy, I've got a Neighbour-hood Policing Team car at Whiteley's house now. They're not getting any response from the doorbell or knocking and they can't see or hear any signs of movement inside the house.'

Grace was tempted to instruct them to break in. If Whiteley was unconscious or dead, it would change the whole dynamics. But the fact the man had not turned up for work wasn't sufficient grounds. They needed the warrant.

Twenty anxious minutes later, Nick Nicholl called him to say he had the warrant signed by a magistrate who lived close to Whiteley's house in Peacehaven, and he was standing by, two streets away, with DS Guy Batchelor, DC Emma Reeves and six members of the Local Support Team. The POLSA and four Specialist Search Unit officers were minutes away.

'Send the LST in,' Grace instructed, urgently. 'Now!'

# 111

Eric Whiteley's house, 117 Tate Avenue, was near the top of a hill, in a network of streets filled with post-war houses and bungalows, all fairly tightly packed together. It was a quiet area, with the cliff-top walk above the sea a quarter of a mile to the south, and the vast expanse of farmland and open grassland of the South Downs just two streets away to the north.

Number 117 had a rather sad look about it, Guy Batchelor thought. It was a modest, drab 1950s two-storey brick and wood structure, with an integral garage, and fronted by a tidy but unloved garden. A sign on the garage doors, in large red letters on a white background, proclaimed, DON'T EVEN THINK ABOUT PARKING HERE.

He waited on the pavement with DCs Nicholl and Reeves as the six officers from the Local Support Team went down the drive, two peeling off and hurrying down the side alley, past the dustbins, to cover the rear of the property. All six were in blue jump suits, with body armour, and military-style helmets with the visors down. One carried the cylindrical battering ram. Another two carried the hydraulic jamb spreader, and its power supply, which was used for forcing apart the steel reinforced door frames that drug dealers were increasingly fitting to slow down entry of any police raid. A fourth officer, the Sergeant in charge of this section, carried the search warrant.

Shouting, 'POLICE! OPEN UP, POLICE!' the first officer banged on the door, rang the doorbell and banged hard on the door again. He waited some moments, then turned, looking for a signal from his Sergeant, who nodded. Immediately, he swung the battering ram at the door. It burst open on the second strike, and three LST officers rushed in, bellowing, 'POLICE! POLICE!' while the Sergeant held back, in case their intended target tried to do a runner out of the garage door.

Guy Batchelor, Emma Reeves and Nick Nicholl stayed outside, until they got the all clear, confirming that the rooms had all been checked and there was no threat. Then they entered.

And stopped in their tracks in astonishment.

Nothing about the exterior of the house had given them any hint of the quite astonishing room they had stepped into.

There was a marble floor that would have looked more at home in an Italian palazzo than an urban annexe of Brighton and Hove. The walls were ceiling-to-floor mirrors, decorated with Aztec art and posters of Gaia. Batchelor stared at a signed monochrome of the icon in a black negligee – one of her most famous images. But it was ripped through several times with what must have been a knife blade, so that parts had peeled away and were hanging down. In angry red letters across it was daubed, *BITCH*.

He looked uneasily at Emma Reeves. She pointed to the left, above a white leather armchair. At another huge framed poster, in which Gaia was wearing a tank-top and leather jeans, captioned GAIA REVELATIONS TOUR. Across it was daubed in the same red paint, *LOVE ME OR DIE, BITCH*.

Above the fireplace, clearly in pride of place was a blow-up of the icon's lips, nose and eyes in green monochrome, captioned, GAIA UP CLOSE AND PERSONAL. It was also personally signed. It too was slashed to ribbons in parts, and painted across, again in red, was the word *COW*.

One of the Specialist Search Unit officers, gloved and wearing black, was opening drawers in a chest on the far side of the room. Batchelor stared at each of the posters, at the violent rips, at the red paint, feeling deep, growing unease. He glanced out of the window; it was a grey, blustery afternoon and he could see a neighbour's washing flapping in the wind, in front of a breeze-block garage. Something flapped in his belly. He had been in a lot of bad situations in his career, but he was experiencing something new to him at this moment. It was an almost palpable sense of evil. And it was spooking him.

A shadow moved, making him jump. It was a small Burmese cat, back arched, eyeing him suspiciously.

'Take a look up here!' another Search Unit officer called down to them from upstairs.

Batchelor, followed by Emma Reeves and Nick Nicholl, charged up the stairs, and, following the direction he was signalling, entered a room that felt like a cross between a museum and a shrine. And in which there had been a recent explosion of anger.

Shop window dummies lay on their sides on the floor, wearing dresses covered in clear plastic, and daubed in red paint. More autographed posters on the walls were ripped and daubed. CDs, tickets to Gaia concerts, bottles of Gaia's mineral water, a smashed Martini glass and a fly-fishing rod snapped in two were among the other detritus that lay on the floor streaked, like blood, in red paint.

Some items remained in their glass display cabinets, but many of these were barely visible behind the furious red words all over the glass. *BITCH. COW. DIE. LOVE ME. I'LL TEACH YOU. FUCK YOU.*

DC Reeves was looking around, wide-eyed. 'What an incredible collection.'

'You a Gaia fan?' Nick Nicholl asked.

She nodded vigorously.

'Sir!'

They all turned. It was one of the Search Unit officers, Brett Wallace, and his face was ashen. These officers, he knew, saw everything and it took quite a bit to shock any of them. But this officer was definitely shocked at this moment.

'This house has just become a crime scene. We're going to have to lock it down and not disturb anything else.'

'What have you found?' Batchelor asked.

'I'll show you,' Wallace said.

They went back downstairs, and followed him into the kitchen, a spotless room with dated furniture and appliances. Two other Search Unit officers were standing in there, both looking uncharacteristically uncomfortable. Wallace pointed at an open door, and Batchelor, followed by the other two, walked across to it. Beyond was a tiny pantry, mostly filled with a chest freezer, the lid of which was raised. A few supermarket ready meals lay on the floor, along with several packets of frozen sausages, and three picnic freezer blocks.

'Take a look inside,' Wallace said, indicating for him to go in.

Warily, Guy Batchelor took a couple of steps forward and peered down. Instantly he stepped back a pace, in shock.

'Oh shit,' he said.

# 112

'Where – the – fuck – is – she . . . ?' Larry Brooker glared at Barnaby Katz, the Line Producer, his voice tight with fury. They were standing by the doorway, inside the Banqueting Room of the Pavilion. Thirty actors, including all the rest of their stars – Judd Halpern, Hugh Bonneville, Joseph Fiennes and Emily Watson – were seated around the table, waiting and looking increasingly impatient as they grew hotter and sweatier in their costumes and wigs. All the film lights were on, bathing everyone at the table in a surreal glow – and roasting them at the same time.

The table had been temporarily botched back together. Above it was a small but gaping hole in the dome, where the chandelier had been hanging just twenty-four hours ago.

Katz raised his arms in a shrug of helplessness. His hairline appeared to have receded a couple of inches in the past few days of constant stress.

'I knocked on her trailer door twenty minutes ago and someone shouted she'd be out in a few moments.' He adjusted his headset then spoke urgently into it. 'Joe, any sign of Gaia?'

Brooker checked his watch. 'Not *twenty* minutes ago, Barnaby. That was *thirty* minutes ago. Prima donnas! God I hate them. Goddamn actresses! Thirty fucking minutes she's kept us.' He turned to the director, Jack Jordan. 'You know what thirty minutes costs us, don't you, Jack?'

Jordan gave a benign shrug, long used to being messed

around by out-of-control egos on both side of the lens. With his mane of white hair flowing from beneath his baseball cap, the veteran film-maker looked as ever like an ancient soothsayer and, true to that persona, was keeping his calm. He needed to. This was the most important scene in the movie and with every single one of the stars featuring, the most expensive. The *money shot*.

Brooker banged his fists together. 'This is ridiculous. Has someone pissed her off today or what?' He glared at Jordan. 'Have you had another argument with her over her lines?'

'Darling, I haven't had a peep out of her since yesterday. She was as good as gold last time we spoke. Just give her a few more minutes. She has to be patient for her heavy make-up and her wig is damned uncomfortable, it tickles her face, poor love.'

Poor love, Brooker thought, cynically. Gaia was getting paid fifteen million bucks for just seven weeks' work. He could put up with his face being tickled for seven weeks for that kind of dough, he thought.

'Goddamn ridiculous wig,' Brooker said. 'Can hardly see her face. Makes her look like a sheep in a corset. I'm paying all this goddamn money to have Gaia, and we could have had anyone inside that dress and hair.' He looked at his watch again. 'Five minutes. If she's not on set in five minutes I'm gonna – I'm gonna . . .' He hesitated, wary of making a fool of himself and of upsetting the icon. The truth was, when you worked on a small independent production with an actress as big as Gaia, you had to tread carefully. Irritate her and she might start to slow down even more and run you days – if not weeks – over schedule, with all its crippling consequences. There had already been a couple of occasions during this past week when Gaia, turning suddenly imperious, made Brooker realize that, without ever saying as much, she knew very well that there was only one reason he had managed to get this movie into production. That all of them were only here making this movie for that same one reason.

Which was, that she, Gaia, had said *yes*.

# 113

It took Guy Batchelor a moment to pluck up the courage to step forward again and look back into the chest freezer. The cold air swirling around him felt part of the same ice that was coursing his veins.

A human head lay on the bottom, face up, between several packs of frozen peas, beans and broccoli, like some hideous ornament. A man's face. The flesh was grey, flecked with frost, and the hair was coated with frost, as if he were wearing a white beanie. The eyes were shrunken, like tiny marbles.

Despite the discoloration and the patches obscured by frost, he recognized the face instantly from the photographs he had seen: Myles Royce, winner of the auction for Gaia's yellow tweed suit.

As he turned away and stepped back into the kitchen, Brett Wallace said, 'Is that the bit you're missing from "Unknown Berwick Male"?'

'Yes, I'd say it is,' Batchelor replied.

One of the other Search Unit officers, who was busily peering beneath a dishwasher with a torch, looked up. 'Brett's mum said he was always good at jigsaw puzzles as a kid.'

The DS smiled, then pulled out his phone and called the SIO.

\*

Grace listened intently to the news from Guy Batchelor, trying to think clearly through the panic engulfing him, trying to make some fast decisions. The Chief Constable and the Assistant Chief Constable needed to be informed before they found themselves in the embarrassing situation of hearing about the discovery of Royce's head on the news. But before he did that, Grace had one absolute priority.

He rang the US cellphone number of Gaia's head of security.

'Andrew Gulli,' he answered, almost instantly, as if expecting a call.

'It's Roy Grace.'

'Inspector Grace – I—' The James Cagney whine sounded uneasy.

'We have an emergency situation, Mr Gulli. I have a copy of the production call sheet, and see your client's shooting at the Pavilion this evening. I'm extremely concerned for her safety – I've reason to believe there's a person out there intent on harming her. He's already killed at least once. We know what he looks like and we know his disguise, and I think we have a good chance of catching him very quickly. But I don't want to take any risks with your client so what I'd like to do, with your support, is remove her from the set and keep her and her son indoors in her suite, under guard, for the next twenty-four hours. Is that possible?'

'Hey, Inspector, you and I are on the same page. But I can't help you. I got fired this morning.'

'Fired?'

'I'm flying back to LA tomorrow.'

'Gaia? Gaia fired you? In the middle of this situation?'

'Yeah, well, the thing is, I told my client I was insisting on her leaving England right away, today, and flying back to

474

the States – and to hell with the consequences. She wouldn't have it. So we had a kind of a Mexican stand-off. She told me if I didn't change my attitude, I'd be fired. I told her, "Ms Lafayette, I'm not risking your life, nor your son's life. You crazy or something? To hell with the consequences."' There was a brief silence then Gulli went on. 'I tell you, Inspector, she was getting paid peanuts for this film compared to what she earns performing, so what the hell, let them sue, I told her. Better to be sued than dead. But she wouldn't have it. I told her, I was not letting her go on set. So she fired me.'

'Want me to try speaking to her?'

'Gaia Lafayette does what Gaia Lafayette wants, Inspector. She doesn't listen to anybody.'

'I'm going to go talk to her right now,' Grace said.

'Good luck. You're gonna need it.'

He ended the call with Gulli and immediately phoned the Ops 1 Controller Andy Kille, glad that he was still on duty. 'We've found Myles Royce's head,' he informed him. 'And the suspect's at large with, I believe, real intent to harm Gaia. I'm circulating images of Eric Whiteley and his Anna Galicia persona – I'm printing copies for all officers on duty, and PCSOs. And I want every available officer and PCSO we have, deployed to the Pavilion right away. I want to make it an island site.'

'I could draft in some Specials as well,' Kille said helpfully.

'Anyone you can get,' Grace replied. 'Until we've got this maniac locked up.'

'I'm upgrading this to a Critical Incident,' Kille said. 'Graham Barrington's Duty Gold and Nick Sloan's Silver.'

Grace thanked him and looked at his watch: 6.15 p.m. According to her schedule on the call sheet, Gaia had been required in her trailer for make-up and wardrobe at 4 p.m., two hours before she was due on set. He turned to the forensic podiatrist. 'Haydn, I want you to go back to the CCTV room – I'll get anyone who's available to help you there. I need you to watch the cameras on the streets around the Pavilion for any sign of Eric Whiteley – or Anna Galicia.'

'Sure – now?'

'Yes, right away, we have to find him, and fast.' He looked around. 'Bella, I want you to blue-light him down there, then meet me at the front of the Pavilion. Okay? Go!'

Bella Moy and Haydn Kelly both stood up hurriedly and headed towards the door. Grace addressed the rest of the team. 'We all know what Whiteley looks like in both guises – I want as many as possible of us down there looking out for him. I can't be sure he's going to turn up, but I'll be surprised if he doesn't, and we can't take the risk of missing him.'

He checked the calls log on his phone, found the numbers corresponding to the time he rang Larry Brooker last night and the time the producer returned the call and rang it again.

'Brooker.' He did not sound in a sunny mood.

'It's Detective Superintendent Grace, Mr Brooker.'

'This is not a good moment,' Brooker said. 'We're about to start shooting a major scene. Can I call you back later?'

'No!' Grace said emphatically. 'Is Gaia on set?'

'She goddamn well isn't – we're waiting for her.'

'Mr Brooker, I need a big favour from you. We believe her life may be in real and present danger. I want to take her under police guard back to her hotel room and keep her there until the threat is over. Is there any filming you could do tonight without involving her?'

'Detective Grace, she's already delayed us enough. You have to get real. Stars get threats from crazies regularly. She's got her own goddamn security, we've got the Pavilion's security, the film unit's security and we've got the whole of your police force. This location is more secure than Fort Knox. A mouse isn't getting in here without ID. This is the safest place in Brighton right now.'

'So in which case, how come the chandelier came crashing down yesterday?'

'Everyone's tightened up since then. We've battened down the hatches. The whole place has been searched. She'll be totally safe on set – if we can ever get her out of her goddamn trailer.'

Grace hung up, exasperated.

'What's happened, chief?' Glenn Branson asked.

'Sorry, thought you'd been told. They've found Myles Royce's head.'

Branson looked at him. 'They have? Where?'

'In Eric Whiteley's freezer.'

'Ohhhhh shit.'

'Yes, and I have a bad feeling his next intended trophy is Gaia's. Judging by the state of his house, he's lost it. He ripped all his Gaia memorabilia to shreds, daubed his walls in anti-Gaia hate slogans and disappeared.'

'Where do you think he might be?' Branson asked.

'I talked to a psychologist this afternoon, who's written extensively on stalkers and celebrity obsessives, a Dr Tara Lester. She said these obsessive fans frequently build themselves an imaginary relationship with the celeb. They *know* the celeb is just waiting for that right moment to show reciprocation. That the celeb is, secretly, as much in love with them as they are with the celeb. When they get rejected by the celeb, sometimes they can flip. I think we're dealing with such a situation now. I think he's going to position himself near her, either at her hotel or the Pavilion.'

Branson nodded.

'Forget this evening's briefing, you and I are going down there ourselves right now.'

# 114

'Gaia's left her trailer, she's on her way,' Barnaby Katz announced at last to Larry Brooker and Jack Jordan. Then he listened on his earpiece for a moment to the voice of the Third Assistant Director who was accompanying her, before speaking to the producer and director again. 'Joe's with her and there's two police officers escorting her to the door.'

'Tell 'em to switch their sirens on and shift it,' Brooker said impatiently.

The black Range Rover, followed by a marked police car, drove the 300 yards across the lawns to the front of the Pavilion. The police officers hurried out of their car and stood a few feet away, as one of her minders held the rear door open, and the icon slowly emerged, carefully ducking her head so as not to knock her mass of hair against the door frame, or snag any of the multiple layers of her dress and high collar on anything.

There was a ragged cheer from the crowd of general public assembled beyond the wall in New Road, and a whole battery of flashes strobed in the grey, early evening light, as Gaia stepped down on to the drive. She walked slowly, seemingly a little uncertainly, following the AD into the building, then right, along the corridor towards the Banqueting Room.

Into a sea of faces.

A distinct sense of relief spread through the room. Several of the actors at the banqueting table turned to look at her. A make-up artist was working her way around their chairs, dabbing shiny noses and foreheads, and one of the hairdressers was making a minor adjustment to Hugh Bonneville's wig. Suddenly the entire assembly of actors burst into spontaneous applause.

*Oh shit*, Brooker thought. *Oh shit, she is not going to be happy with this.*

It wasn't the applause of a warm greeting, nor the applause for a fine performance. It was a sarcastic demonstration by her thirty fellow actors that they had not been amused to be kept waiting.

Then, to his amazement, Gaia smiled and curtsied. First to the cast at the table. Then to the Director of Photography and his camera crew. Then to the sound crew. To the continuity girl. To the director and to the producer, and to each grip and spark present. She curtsied as if her career depended on it.

She curtsied smiling and proud, totally misreading the situation, as if relishing being the centre of attention, the centre of adulation that was not there.

Brooker frowned. Her behaviour was totally out of character. There was also something else very strange about her.

# 115

Roy Grace wondered why, whenever Glenn Branson got behind the wheel of a car, he drove it as if he had just hot-wired it although he now had a legitimate reason. Glenn was weaving through the thinning rush hour, on blues and twos, and Grace spent much of the journey fearing for his life, or the life of anyone who stepped into their path. To distract himself, he phoned and updated first the Chief Constable, via his Staff Officer, and then ACC Rigg.

At 6.30 p.m., just seven minutes after leaving Sussex House, they tore into the Pavilion grounds and pulled up behind a black Range Rover. Grace was a little relieved to see that already the police presence here was markedly increased from yesterday.

As they walked up to the front entrance, two uniformed security guards, each wearing earpieces, blocked their path. 'Sorry, gentlemen,' said one of them. 'No one's allowed in, they're about to start shooting.'

Grace fished out his warrant card and held it up.

The same guard shook his head. 'Sir, you don't under-stand, they're about to do a take. There has to be absolute silence. I can't let you in until they've finished this scene.'

'We'll be quiet,' Grace said. 'This is an emergency.'

'I'm afraid they've already lost almost an hour tonight. Madam's been in a particularly tricky mood, if you get my drift,' one guard said. He had a nicotine-stained moustache, a stocky but bolt-upright posture, and exuded the officious, no-nonsense air of a former army Sergeant-Major.

*She's damned lucky to still be alive, if you get mine,*
Grace nearly retorted. 'I'm sorry, we need to go in the
building.'

'Phones off?'

'No, we're not turning our phones or radios off.'

'Then I'm afraid you can't go in until the end of this
scene, gentlemen.'

'How long will that be?'

'Depends how many takes Madam requires to get her
lines right.' Both officers noted the sarcasm in his voice.

Grace decided not to push the point, turned and walked
a few steps away, followed by the DS.

'Sodding jobsworth!' Glenn Branson said. 'I'd love to see
some of the filming.'

'I'd like to see the finished result, knowing that we kept
Gaia alive,' Grace replied grimly.

There were a good 200 members of the public lined up
along the wall, watching. He saw Glenn warily scanning
their faces. Was Eric Whiteley among them? A man who was
prepared to pay more than £27,000 for a suit worn once by
his idol. A loner, with nothing in his life but his doomed-to-
be-unrequited – and unreciprocated – passion for an icon.
A loner who had been spurned by her, probably humiliat-
ingly for him, in the front entrance of The Grand Hotel.

Was he so desperate for anything belonging to his idol,
that he had killed and butchered his rival bidder for that
suit?

What was next on Whiteley's agenda, after destroying
his entire collection of Gaia memorabilia?

Destroying the icon herself?

Which would, of course, instantly make him almost as
famous.

# 116

Along with Larry Brooker, several of the cast and crew were staring uneasily at Gaia. Jack Jordan frowned, wondering whether his star was on drugs. She was definitely looking very odd this evening, he thought. Her hair was obscuring much of her face, her make-up was far too heavy and her voice sounded strange, as if she had aged overnight; nor did she appear to have remembered anything from their rehearsals over the weekend. Had it been the shock of her son nearly being killed yesterday? Would it have been more sensible to have given her a couple of days off to recover? Too late for that now.

Patiently he repeated the line for her, putting the emphasis where he wanted her to put it. 'This is *not* how a *queen* expects to be treated, my dear Prinny. I have *never* in my life been *so* humiliated.' He paused. 'Okay? Much more emphatic! In these last few takes you're almost mumbling. You are saying this loudly to everyone, playing to your audience – all the king's friends and associates. You must really *project*! What you are doing is trying to humiliate him publicly.'

Gaia nodded.

He turned to the banqueting table, to King George. 'Judd, immediately you respond with, "You never *were* a damned queen. You were just a *posh tramp*."' He turned back to Gaia. 'That's your cue to burst into tears and run, wailing, from the room. Are we all clear?'

Judd Halpern and Gaia both nodded in turn.

The First Assistant Director, headset on, strode across the floor and called out, 'Right, first positions everybody!'

The Camera Operator announced, 'Rolling!'

The Clapper Boy jumped in front of the camera lens with the digital clapperboard. 'Scene One-Three-Four, take three.' There was a sharp crack, and he moved clear.

Jack Jordan called out, 'Action!'

'Gaia,' she said, addressing first the king, then everyone at the table, before turning dramatically around and addressing Jack Jordan. 'You never were a queen! You were always just a posh tramp! Just a poser! You made people believe you loved them just for your ego, didn't you? Well, you're not special, see, anyone can do what you do. Look at each one of you in this room!'

Faces froze. There were looks of astonishment, bewilderment. Jack Jordan took a step towards her. 'Gaia, love, do you want to take a few minutes' break?'

'You see?' she was screeching now. 'You can't tell! You really can't tell! So you don't need *her* any more, anyone would do!'

She turned and ran, stumbling, from the room.

Jordan turned in bewilderment to Larry Brooker, then to the Line Producer. 'That – that's not her,' Barnaby Katz said. 'That's not Gaia!'

Brooker was shaking his head. 'Has she goddamn flipped?'

'That's not her – that wasn't her!' Katz said again. 'Shit, I'm telling you, *that was not Gaia*!' He sprinted for the corridor and ran down it, into the hallway where there was the door to the public toilets. Brooker and Jack Jordan followed closely behind him.

'Not Gaia?' Brooker called out.

'No!'

'Then who the hell was it?' Brooker said. 'Is this her idea of a goddamn practical joke or something?'

'Where's she gone?' Katz pushed open the door to the ladies and peered in, then the men's room. Then he hurried across to the front entrance, and out to the two guards. 'Did you guys see anyone come out? About a minute ago?'

Both men shook their heads. 'No one's been in or out in the past fifteen minutes, on your instructions, sir.'

'You didn't see Gaia – or someone resembling her?'

'No one.' They looked adamant.

He squeezed past them, followed by Brooker and Jordan. A few yards away, he saw Roy Grace standing beside a tall black man in a sharp suit. 'Neither of you saw Gaia just now?' he asked.

'Gaia?' Grace said. He did not like any of their strange, baffled expressions.

'Or someone dressed as her?' Katz asked.

'She ran out of the Banqueting Room and goddamn vanished,' Brooker said.

'No one's come out of this entrance since we've been here,' Glenn Branson said. 'Not for at least the last seven or eight minutes.'

Roy Grace stared at Brooker. 'Would you mind telling me what's going on? What do you mean, you can't find Gaia?'

'I would if I goddamn knew.'

'Gaia came on set looking very strange, and acting completely out of character,' Jack Jordan said. 'Then she went totally off-script, spouting a whole load of nonsense, and ran out of the room.'

'It wasn't her,' the Line Producer said. 'I'm certain.'

'Everything's secure, the whole building,' one of the security guards said. 'All the keys have been removed from the locks – one of the measures we were advised to take by your colleagues. We did that as soon as the public had left. If she was in the building five minutes ago, she is still there, I can assure you.'

'If you're saying it wasn't Gaia,' Grace said to the Line Producer, 'then where is Gaia?'

He shrugged. 'I dunno. Maybe still in her trailer?'

Grace felt his earlier panic returning, gripping and twisting his insides. *Still in her trailer?*

Jordan and Katz went back into the building.

'Want me to go and check?' Katz said to Grace.

'No, I'm going.' He turned to Branson. 'Glenn, get the building surrounded, put someone on every exit, no one leaves, okay? Not even the damned Curator until I say so. No one leaves the grounds, either – I want a total lockdown, and right now.'

'Right, chief.'

Grace ran along the drive then across the lawns, then stopped by the two police officers standing guard near the front of Gaia's motorhome. Two of Gaia's own security guards were chatting a little further back, one smoking a cigarillo.

'Has anyone gone in or come out of this since you've been here?' he asked the two officers.

Both shook their heads. 'Not since Gaia left to go on set, sir,' said one.

Grace went up to the door and rapped hard on it. He waited a moment, then rapped again. Then he pulled it open, calling out a cautious 'Hello? Hello?'

Silence greeted him.

He climbed up the steps and entered. And felt as if a fish hook had suddenly and viciously snagged him in the gullet.

For an instant the entire interior of the motorhome seemed to swivel on its axis, its walls shrinking in, then expanding again. His ears popped in terror at what he saw. 'Oh, Jesus,' he said. 'Oh, sweet Jesus.'

# 117

Grace shouted at the two officers on guard outside the mobile home. 'In here, quick!'

Then he dashed over to the three bodies on the floor, each bound head-to-foot, and gagged, with a mixture of twine and grey duct tape. The eyes of all three were moving, thank God, he thought. One he recognized as one of Gaia's assistants. But neither of the other two was Gaia.

'I'm a police officer, are you all right?' he asked each of them, in turn, and got frightened but positive nods back. Carefully removing the tape from their mouths, he established these other two were the hairdresser and the make-up artist.

He turned to the two officers behind him. 'Call for three ambulances, then try to free them, but be careful, that tape's bloody painful.' Then he went through to the rear, pushing through a curtained-off section, checking that a shower on one side and a toilet on the other were both empty, and then opened a door into what appeared to be the master bedroom, which smelled of Gaia's perfume but was empty. A few clothes were strewn on the unused bed. He looked around carefully, pulling open cupboard doors, then went down on his knees and peered under the bed, just in case, but to no avail.

Gaia wasn't in this motorhome.

He radioed Ops 1, and moments later was through once more to Inspector Andy Kille. He gave him a quick summary.

'So we can't be sure of the time she was abducted, can we, Roy?' Kille asked.

'Any time between 4 p.m. and two minutes ago.'

'Over three hours. She could be anywhere. I don't think there's much value in road blocks – they could be too far away by now.'

'I think the perp's in the Pavilion with her,' Grace said. 'I agree, no point in road blocks. Is Hotel 900 or Oscar Sierra 99 available?' Hotel 900 and Oscar Sierra 99 were the call signs of the two helicopters of the South East Air Support Unit.

'Yes.'

'Get one up and over the Pavilion, in case he's up on the roof somewhere. There are lots of spaces up there. They can also see if he tries to leave.'

'I'll have it overhead within ten minutes, tops.'

*Please God let her be alive*, Grace prayed, silently. His mind was spinning, trying to get traction. He'd worked on child abductions and on kidnap cases, and was a qualified hostage negotiator. From his experience, he knew how badly the odds were stacked against them. In child abductions, forty-four per cent of the victims died within the first hour. Seventy-three per cent were dead within three hours. Just one per cent survived more than one day. And forty per cent were dead before they were even reported missing.

Those figures applied to children, but if the psychologist Dr Lester was right, inside Eric Whiteley's warped mind, now that Gaia was no longer his lover, he might well be viewing her as a child who needed to be taught a lesson.

Every single second mattered right now.

'We need a PNC broadcast, as well, Andy, just in case.'

'Do we know Whiteley's vehicle?'

'He's got a Nissan Micra, but it's still in the garage. It's possible he rented something bigger – he wouldn't be able to conceal a person in a Micra very easily.'

He was staring at a small sign just by the rear window of the bedroom. EMERGENCY EXIT.

He had to walk around the far side of the bed to reach it, and then he saw the handle in a raised, unlocked position, as if the door had recently been opened – and not properly closed from the outside.

He ended the call with Kille, pushed the door open and looked out and around the rear of the vehicle. Two other smaller motorhomes were parked directly behind, blocking the view of this exit from anyone more than a few yards away. No windows overlooked them. This seemed the likely route that Whiteley would have taken her, but they would have had to come into open view within ten yards or so, surely?

Then, looking down, he noticed the jagged, uneven dark rectangle in the grass, as if it had been made with a very thin trail of weed killer.

He knelt down, and the rectangle wobbled beneath him, just a fraction. He clambered back into the vehicle, checked that the two officers were making progress on freeing the victims, then rummaged in the kitchen drawers, and took out a heavy-duty knife and a metal spatula.

Then he got down on his hands and knees behind the motorhome, and using the two implements as a lever, prised open an ancient, heavy metal cover, the top of it turfed, which he lifted aside. He could see steep stone steps leading down into darkness. He'd often heard rumours of secret passages under the Pavilion, and wondered if this was one of them.

He went back into the motorhome and asked if either of the officers had a torch on them. One produced a small, sturdy-looking one and handed it to him. He switched it on, went out again, then began to descend the steps, breathing in dank air. After about twenty feet he found himself in a tunnel just high enough to stand in. It had faded white-washed walls and a whitewashed brick floor, and stretched away into the distance toward the main building of the Pavilion. Lagged pipes, copper tubes and bare power cables, clipped to the top of the walls on both sides, appeared to run its full length, and every few yards there were unlit lights mounted on the walls.

He began walking along the tunnel, as quickly as he could, being careful not to trip on the uneven floor, shadows jigging ahead of him from the throw of the beam, his nerves jigging inside him. He passed an old wooden door lying on its side, then a large dusty pane of glass, and a short distance further along, a busted wicker chair. Two tiny pinpricks of red momentarily froze in the darkness, then vanished. A rat. He passed an orange and white traffic cone, incongruously placed on the floor, then reached an old, grimy white door, with a shiny new chrome handle on it. He hesitated for a moment and glanced down at his phone. There was no signal. Which meant no chance of calling back-up if he needed it. If Whiteley came at him, he would have to cope on his own.

He gripped the handle, switched the torch off, not wanting to make himself a target just in case. Then he jerked the door open and snapped on the beam again.

It shone on a fire hose attached to a brick wall. He stepped forward and swung the beam down another corri-dor, much wider and higher, angled off to the right, with some dim lights on further along it. All the cables and piping were bunched together in this section, running along the ceiling. The brick floor was uneven and unpainted, repaired in places with ugly concrete patches. He passed a row of plastic chemical drums, then saw a decrepit green door, sagging on its hinges, with a yellow and black DANGER – HIGH VOLTAGE sign on it, to his left. A broken cobweb across the top left corner of the door showed it had been opened recently. Bracing himself, and stepping aside as he did so, he pulled it open. The hinges shrieked, the bottom scraping noisily on the bricks. Then he stabbed the beam inside. It lit up a wall of fuses and electrical switchgear, and pipework lagged in asbestos, but otherwise it was bare.

He walked on and saw a pool of light ahead of him now. Then he heard voices, and froze.

They sounded directly above him. Then footsteps. Clumping down steps. Now his nerves were really jangling. He took several deep breaths, firmly gripped the torch – the only weapon he had – and eased himself forward, keeping as flat against the wall as he could. He saw a shadow, growing larger. Then suddenly the ex-Sergeant-Major security guard loomed into view. The old soldier jumped with shock when he saw him, shouted something, and dropped his torch, which hit the ground with a loud crack and went out.

'Blimey, you gave me a fright, sir!'

'That makes two of us,' Grace said. 'What's happening? Has anyone found anything here?'

The guard knelt down, bending his stiff frame with some difficulty, and picked up his torch. 'Nothing, sir, not so far. But it's a bloody big place to search and you have to know your way around to do it. So many corridors – it was designed as a sort of a double skin, so that staff could move all around the ground floors without going into any of the main rooms unless needed. I've been here seven years and even I keep finding new spaces all the time. Be easy for someone who knows it well to avoid being seen.'

'What's up there?' Grace pointed to the steps he had just come down.

'Takes you up to the main hallway, just inside the front entrance, and the toilets.'

'I'm certain Gaia's abductor must have brought her along here, sometime in the past couple of hours. Where could he have taken her from here?'

'Well, he couldn't go any further along this passage. If you shine your beam along there you'll see.' He pointed along the continuation of the tunnel and it was bricked off a short distance along. 'He'd either have to have taken her back the way he came or up these stairs.'

Grace suddenly recalled the smell of fresh chocolate. The abandoned Crunchie wrapper with a trace of lipstick on it.

Anna Galicia's lipstick?

'Follow me, will you?' Grace said, and sprinted up the stairs, through the open half-gate, then across the hall to the half-concealed door on the far side, where he had been taken by the Curator yesterday. He pulled it open, then began to lope up the spiral stairs.

Some way behind him, he heard the panting voice of the elderly security guard. 'Don't touch the handrail, sir, it's dangerously rickety!'

He reached the top and entered the old, abandoned apartment beneath the dome, with its unpleasant musty smell and dust sheets over the uneven, angular shapes. But he didn't even notice the smell. Or the dust sheets. Or the Crunchie wrapper still lying on the ground.

He was staring, transfixed at the bizarre and horrific tableau facing him. It could have been two actors rehearsing a scene in a play. Except neither of them was acting. They were both standing on a dangerously rotten trapdoor, and one had a noose around her neck.

# 118

Gaia, in jeans and a sweat-darkened white T-shirt, her face glistening with the perspiration of fear, stood on tiptoe, a noose of razor wire around her neck pulled tight and looped around the pulley system high above the trapdoor. Blood trickled down parts of her neck where the wire had dug into her skin. A small strip of duct tape lay, curled, on the floor. The skin around her mouth looked red and raw, probably from that bit of tape that had been ripped away, Grace thought, feeling fury at what he saw, tinged with relief that she was still, at this moment, alive.

Her hands were tied behind her back. Inches from her sparkly trainers was the sign on the trapdoor that read in bold letters, DANGER – STEEP DROP BELOW. DO NOT STAND ON DOOR.

Her eyes, filled with stark terror, locked on to his. He tried to flash back reassurance. His heart went out to her, she looked so vulnerable and helpless.

Crouched beside her was an apparition, caked in make-up, dressed in female Regency clothing and wearing a huge, lopsided wig, staring at him with a strangely triumphant smile. One hand was on each of the two rusty bolts that secured the trapdoor from opening downwards – and taking them both with it, plunging through the hatch, down the forty-foot drop straight to the store room above the kitchens. On the floor beside this creature was a vicious-looking open-bladed hunting knife and a mobile phone.

There was a sudden, sharp crack, like a gunshot.

Gaia yammered in terror. The apparition's eyes darted momentarily down.

Grace realized what it was. The trapdoor was starting to give way. His mind was racing, spinning, trying to get traction and figure what to do. The two of them were about ten feet in front of him. Three fast paces, he assessed. The bolts could be slid long before he even got close. He couldn't take the risk, not at this moment.

There was another crack. This time the trapdoor visibly sagged a fraction, tightening the razor wire even more. The door was going to cave in at any moment.

'Detective Superintendent Roy Grace,' the apparition smiled, speaking through gleaming white teeth in a seductive, gravelly voice that mimicked Gaia's. 'I recognize you from the *Argus*. How nice of you to join our little private party!'

Gaia was pleading with her eyes for him to do something.

His heart was hammering so hard he could feel pulsing in his ears. 'Eric Whiteley?' he said. 'Or should I call you Anna Galicia?'

He heard footsteps behind him, then heavy panting.

'Get rid of your fat friend with the tash, hon, he's so ugly,' the apparition continued in her Gaia voice. 'I'll talk to you, but I'm not talking to any bullying thug.'

Grace hesitated.

The creature slid the bolts back a good half inch. The panic in Gaia's eyes deepened into wild terror. There was another, smaller crack, and the apparition jolted, but seemed not to care. 'Get rid of your fat friend or the bitch and I go. You have five seconds, Detective Superintendent.' He tightened his grip on the bolts.

Grace turned and said urgently to the security guard, 'Do what she said!'

The guard gave him a look, as if questioning his sanity.

'GET OUT OF HERE! GO!' Grace yelled at him.

It had the desired effect. The security guard turned in shock and lumbered out of the room. Grace turned back to the transvestite, thinking fast. He was trying to remember all he had been told by the indexer Annalise Vineer, who'd had researchers delving back as far as they could into Whiteley's past. As well as all the insights he'd had from the psychologist Dr Tara Lester. But the first stage was to get a rapport going, to try to bond with Whiteley. And at the same time to make his Plan B.

'Tell me what you would like me to call you,' he said. 'Anna Galicia or Eric Whiteley?' He looked up at the wire above Gaia for an instant.

'Very funny,' Whiteley snapped back. It came out as a male snarl. 'I'm not afraid to kill her.'

'You've killed before haven't you, Anna? Shall we stick with Anna?'

'Anna will be very happy with that.' Now she sounded like Gaia again.

A chill wave swept through Grace. It felt as if he were dealing with two totally different people in one. 'And how about Eric? Will he be happy?'

'Eric will do what Anna tells him,' Whiteley said in his Anna voice.

'You killed Myles Royce, didn't you. Why did you kill him?'

'Because he was richer than me. He kept outbidding me on things I really wanted. I couldn't let that go on. I invited him round to see my collection and then I killed him. I collected him! He was a nice trophy to have. Eric approved!'

Grace was conscious of Gaia desperately staring at him, but at this moment he didn't want to break eye contact with Whiteley. He needed to try to find some common ground, some way to start to bond with him. And he knew he didn't have much time. Maybe only seconds.

There was another splintering crack.

'You'd better be quick, Detective Superintendent, we're going down!' Whiteley said, again in Anna's seductive Gaia voice.

Whiteley had been clever. The wire had been wound several times around the winch in large loops, then he had bent it several times just above Gaia's head, to take up the slack and force her on to her toes. There was about six feet of slack in those loops. If the hatch collapsed, Gaia would fall that distance, and even if her neck wasn't broken instantly, or her head severed completely by the wire, it would be impossible to reach her. It would be equally impossible to haul her weight up by that single strand of sharp wire.

Suddenly he heard the wakka-wakka-wakka-wakka thrashing of a helicopter, roaring overhead. He saw Whiteley's eyes dart apprehensively towards one of the dusty oval windows, and realized to his dismay he had missed a split-second chance of jumping him while he was distracted.

The sound faded away.

'I don't think a helicopter's going to do you much good in here, Detective Superintendent Grace, do you?' Anna said, then looked up at Gaia. 'Don't get your hopes up, know what I'm saying? About someone coming to save you? It's not going to happen.' Then he raised his right hand, pressed his thumb, middle finger and ring finger together and raised the other two fingers in the air. 'Secret fox!' He winked at her.

She stared back at him, icily and terrified.

Grace's phone rang. He ignored it.

'Eric says you can answer it,' Anna said sweetly.

It carried on ringing.

'Eric says you can answer it,' Anna repeated.

Grace continued to ignore it. He wanted to keep both his hands free. It stopped ringing.

'It might have been an important call!' Anna Galicia said. 'You are a very important man, aren't you?'

'Aren't you important too, Anna?' he replied.

'Eric thinks so!'

Grace shot another quick glance at Gaia. Her eyes were still locked on him. He wondered what the security guard was going to do. But short of putting a sniper on the roof to take a shot through the window at Whiteley, and he did not have the time, there wasn't anything he could think of. Down below he heard the wail of sirens, followed by a series of deep honks, then more sirens. It sounded like fire engines on their way. But that wasn't going to help. There wasn't time to get any back-up. The shadow of a seagull flitted past one of the windows behind Whiteley, and was gone.

Whiteley looked up at the icon. 'How's it feeling, Gaia? Is it nice to be with your number one fan? Is it nice to be adored? Hey?'

She tried to respond but only a gurgling croak came out.

'Did you ever think what you would be if it wasn't for me, and all the others? Hey?'

'Why don't you give her some slack, or take the noose off, so she can answer you?' Grace said calmly.

'Haha! Very funny, Detective Superintendent!' Anna retorted.

'What is it you want from Gaia, Anna?'

Grace was poised, ready, like a coiled spring. Listening. Waiting for the next crack. He didn't know if his plan would save her but at this moment he was totally out of alternatives, except to try negotiation with the man. With only minutes, maybe only seconds, left to do it.

After some moments' silence, Whiteley responded, staring directly back at him. 'I want her to say *sorry*.'

Grace felt a tiny ping of hope. 'Sorry for what, Anna?'

Whiteley looked up at her. 'You know, don't you, Gaia?' Then he looked back at Grace.

'Take the noose off,' Grace said firmly but pleasantly. 'Let her speak to you.'

Suddenly, in a very masculine voice, Whiteley snapped at him, baring his teeth in an animal snarl. 'Anna won't take the noose off. Stop bullying her!'

Grace stared back at him. 'Bullying, did you say?'

Whiteley looked up at Gaia again. Anna spoke. 'All you had to do in the lobby of The Grand Hotel was smile and say *hello*. Instead you humiliated me. You snubbed me in front of everyone. You made me look a fool. You made me a Ubu, didn't you. *Useless, Boring, Ugly.* You pretend to love everyone, but you're just a greedy bully, really, aren't you, Gaia? So how does this feel now? I bet you wish you'd been nicer to me in The Grand, don't you?'

'Give her a chance to talk to you, Anna.'

Whiteley snapped his head round and glared at Grace. 'Anna's not talking to you,' he said in his Eric Whiteley voice.

Then he turned back to Gaia and it was Anna speaking again. 'You see, Gaia, you're not as special as you think. Anyone can be *you* if they have enough make-up on. They all thought I was you! I could have done the rest of the film and they'd never have known! You're not very special at all really. You're just lucky and very cruel and very ungrateful.'

Grace was looking at the wire again. And trying very subtly to signal to Gaia. He looked pointedly down at the trapdoor, at the warning sign, then jerked his eyes over to the right. She clocked him, in a fleeting, puzzled glance before his eyes went back to Whiteley.

'You know what they say, don't you?' Anna Galicia's voice asked her. 'Be careful how you treat people on the way up, because you never know who you're going to need when you're on the way down.' Whiteley lifted a hand from a bolt, and pointed at the trapdoor. '*On the way down!* Gettit?' Anna's voice suddenly cackled with laughter. '*Gettit?*' he repeated to Gaia. 'How will that feel for you in your last few seconds? Dying with your number one fan! But we won't tell anyone, will we?' Again he raised his hand and formed his fingers into the symbol. 'Secret fox!'

'Anna,' Grace said, 'I have an idea. If you gave Gaia your phone, she could call anyone you wanted and tell them whatever you would like her to say. She could apologize to the newspapers, the radio, television, her Twitter followers, her Facebook fans – she could tell the whole world that you really are her number one fan. That all she had been doing was testing you. Because she has so many imposters claiming to be her number one fan, she had to make sure you were the real one. And she is sure now. No one else would be willing to die with her. That is real love, Anna, and she knows that now. You can film her telling you that with the camera – put it on YouTube!'

He saw the sudden change of expression in Whiteley's eyes. Like a cloud moving away from the sun. They shone briefly and he smiled, like a child who had just been given a new toy.

For an instant.

Grace caught Gaia's eye again, moved his eyes to the right. She frowned. She didn't get his plan.

Then Whiteley's face turned to hostility again. 'You're

lying, Detective Superintendent. This is all bullshit. You're lying!'

'Ask her,' Grace said. 'Go on!'

'Stop bullying me.'

There was another crack. He saw the alarm on Whiteley's face.

This was the moment.

Grace raised his voice, deliberately, in anger. 'I am not bullying you! You are not ugly, boring or useless – that's what they called you at school, isn't it? Ubu?'

Whiteley froze for an instant. He looked panic-stricken. In Anna's voice he said, 'That's – that's what they called Eric. How do you know? How do you know that?'

'I found out, okay? Someone told me. Give Gaia the phone. Let her start telling the world that you are none of these things. She'll tell her fan club that you truly are her number one fan. You'll be a hero! Wouldn't it be nicer to be a living number one fan than a dead one?'

'Anna doesn't think so, I've just asked her,' Whiteley said in his male snarl.

'The phone!' Grace jabbed a finger at it. 'Give her the phone!'

Whiteley's snarl turned to a whine. 'You're bullying me.'

'GIVE HER THE SODDING PHONE!' Grace bellowed at the top of his voice.

It threw Whiteley for an instant. He turned, almost like an automaton, reached out for the phone and picked it up. Then he froze, confused, his arm momentarily suspended in mid-air, as Grace launched himself forward.

Grace took one step, then sprang off his right foot in a long-jump stance and landed with both feet exactly where he had aimed, in the centre of the trapdoor, inches from

Gaia. He heard a loud crack, and felt the wood splintering instantly beneath him, his legs plunging through. But he barely noticed, barely heard Whiteley's yelp of surprise, he was totally focused on positioning his hands on the floor either side of the trapdoor, directly beneath Gaia so his shoulders would take her weight.

For an instant he was aware of hands grabbing his right leg, sliding down it, and a deadweight that was pulling him down, with Gaia's feet pushing down on his shoulders. He scrabbled desperately with his fingers to keep a grip on the floor, oblivious to the splinters ripping into his skin and under his nails, just concentrating in these few split seconds on stopping himself – and equally importantly, Gaia – plunging through the open hatch. His arms were being pulled out of their sockets.

He could feel the weight of her feet on his shoulders even more heavily now. She was pushing him down. He was going. His hands were stinging like hell and he was struggling to keep a grip. He was being pulled down by his right leg, his hands dragging across the wooden floorboards. He heard Whiteley screaming. The weight was pulling him further down, down, too much for him to hold back. Then he felt hands sliding down his ankle. Heard Whiteley screaming pitifully for help again. Then, suddenly, like a hooked fish that has freed itself from a line, he felt his right shoe come off, and the weight was instantly gone.

He kicked out, but was just kicking air. His feet dangling over the forty-foot drop, he was acutely aware that only his hands, which were still sliding agonizingly across the wood towards the rim of the hatch, were holding him. And Gaia's weight on his shoulders was pushing him down. He kicked out, desperately trying to find something for his feet to grip on, in case by some miracle there was a ladder beneath him. Gaia's feet kicked, wildly, stamping on him as she scrabbled for grip on his shoulders. Pushing him down further, his hands slipping, slipping, his feet flailing in the air.

His arms and shoulders were in agony. He tried desperately to pull himself up, but the more he pulled, the more Gaia pushed down with her full weight. His arms were starting to give way and he didn't know how much longer he was going to be able to hold on.

*Can't fall. Can't fall. Can't fall.* The words played in his brain like a mantra. *Can't fall. Can't fall. Can't fall.*

He thought suddenly of Cleo. Of their unborn baby. Of all the new life that lay in front of him. He was not going to die. Not going to.

'Gaia,' he yelled. 'You're going to kill us both! Get off me, get on to the floor, there's enough slack in the wire, trust me!'

His hands slipped further, agonizingly, across the boards.

Further.

She pushed even harder on his shoulders. She was clearly in total hysterical panic, beyond any ability to hear him.

He was going. He could not hold on any more. His fingertips were sliding over the raised edge of the rim.

Then, suddenly her weight lifted off him. It was gone completely. But he still could not hold his own body up; his fingers were slipping. Slipping. He did not have the physical strength in them, nor the grip, to hold on any more. Somehow, he had to haul himself back up through the hatch, but he couldn't. His arms were spent. He didn't have the energy. For an instant he thought, it would be easier to fall. Simpler. Just let go.

Then he saw Cleo's face again. Saw the bump. Their baby. Their life.

But his fingers slipped further. His body hung from them like a lead deadweight. He felt his fingertips right on the edge. They were losing their grasp. His legs bicycling in the air below him in the hope, again, of finding something, miraculously, to save him.

Slipping.

*Oh shit, no, no, no.* This was crazy. This was not how it was going to end. He fought back, with every ounce of strength he had. But he slipped further.

Then, suddenly, an iron clamp closed around both his wrists.

The next instant he was hanging, swinging from his arms. Moments later he was being pulled, very slowly and very firmly, upwards. He smelled the sour breath of a heavy smoker, looked up, saw a nicotine-stained moustache and heard the voice of the security guard.

'Don't worry, sir,' he wheezed, 'I've got you!'

Moments later he felt a second pair of hands gripping him, securely, under the arms. Near by, he heard a woman sobbing hysterically.

# 119

Seconds later, Roy Grace's feet touched the floor, safely away from the hatch. He barely noticed he was missing a shoe. His hands were raw and bleeding and he had splinters up inside his nails that hurt like hell, but he barely noticed that either at this moment. His sole concern was for Gaia.

She was kneeling, supported by a male and a female police officer who were gently working free the noose around her bleeding neck. She was sobbing and shaking.

'Do you want to sit down, sir?' the guard with the moustache asked.

The other held on to him with a steadying hand. 'I'm fine, I'm fine – is Gaia all right?' he called out. 'Is she all right?'

The woman officer said, 'Yes, she's okay, she's in shock. I've radioed for an ambulance.'

'Shall we get an ambulance for you, too, sir?' one of the guards asked.

Grace shook his head, still getting his breath back. Then he saw the state of his hands. 'I think I need tweezers,' he said distantly, staring at Gaia again, trying to make sense of these last few moments. He stared at the four-foot-wide rectangular hole where the trapdoor had dropped down.

'You've a nasty gash on your face.'

He put a hand up and it came away covered in blood. 'You came in good time, guys. Thank you – for – getting me out of there.'

'I used to be a bit of a weightlifter in my army days, sir. You were nothing compared to the weights I used to do.'

'Thanks a lot!'

'Take it as a compliment, sir.'

Grace gave a wry smile, then crossed over to Gaia. Their eyes connected and for an instant, her sobbing ceased.

'You okay?' he asked.

Through her tear-stained face she managed a weak smile. 'Yes, guess I'm just a little wired.'

Grace grinned. Moments later he heard footsteps, and Glenn Branson charged into the room, then stopped and stared, open mouthed at Grace, then Gaia, then Grace again. 'What's happened? You all right? Everyone all right? Chief?'

The helicopter clattered past overhead, making conversation momentarily impossible as the din of its engine and blades echoed around the bare walls and bare floor. 'We're okay,' Grace said.

Branson looked around wildly. 'Where's Whiteley? They said he was up here.'

Grace dropped down on his knees and crawled towards the edge of the hatch.

'Careful, sir!' one of the guards said.

Grace carried on to the edge, and looked down. Then he backed away and turned to the DS. 'He's in the kitchen.'

'Kitchen?'

'What – what's – like – who's with him? What's he doing there?'

'I'll tell you what he's not doing – he's not cooking dinner.'

Ignoring his bleeding face and increasingly painful hands, Grace hurried down the spiral stairs with Branson close behind. When they reached the bottom, they ran along the corridor, into the Banqueting Room, where there was a bizarre mix of men and women in elegant Regency clothing mingled with the film crew who were mostly in jeans, trainers and T-shirts.

Larry Brooker called out, 'Detective Grace, can you tell us what's—?'

Grace ignored him, pushing the door open and running into the first of the kitchen rooms. It was a small, bare space, with beige walls and brown linoleum on which stood a stainless steel trolley that reminded him of a mortuary gurney. He looked up, but there was no hatch above, just a low ceiling.

Followed by Branson he pushed open a sludge-coloured door and went into the next room, which was similar, but smaller. There was a faint smell of human excrement. He crossed over and opened another door, which was slightly ajar. Both men recoiled at the sight.

'Jesus,' Branson said.

There was a strong stench of fresh human excrement.

Grace stared levelly ahead. At the man who had nearly killed Gaia, and had come close to killing him, too. He shot a quick glance up at the smashed ceiling, fifteen feet above, which Whiteley had crashed through, and saw the guard with the moustache, forty feet above that, peering curiously down. Then, holding his breath for some moments against the smell, he looked ahead again, at the bizarre sight in the centre of the room.

The wig had gone, and was lying a short distance away. A balding, middle-aged head, with grey hair, protruded from the neck of the elegant Regency dress. Whiteley appeared to have hit the floor feet first, then collapsed back against a stainless steel sink, which was supporting him, giving the illusion he was sitting upright of his own accord. The scarlet dress lay pooled all around him, as if carefully arranged so as not to get creased.

Two pale-coloured sticks, each about eighteen inches long, rose up through rips in the dress below his midriff, like a pair of ski poles. Except they had blood and small strips of sinew and skin on them. Grace realized with horror what they were. The lower sections of the man's legs, driven up through his knees by the impact.

The stench of excrement was even worse now. He walked over, and looked at Whiteley's make-up-caked face. The man was blinking, non-stop, three or four blinks a second, as if some wiring loop inside his head had short-circuited. Tiny moans were coming from his mouth, which was opening and closing slowly, gormlessly, like a goldfish. Grace took hold of Whiteley's wrist and found a pulse. He did not bother to time it, but could tell it was dangerously low. 'He's still alive, just. Call for an ambulance.'

Branson, staring bug-eyed at the stricken man, pulled out his phone.

# 120

'Would she have done the same for you?' Cleo asked.

'That's not the issue.'

'Isn't it?'

'It was my job to protect her.'

'You're a trained hostage – and suicide – negotiator. You told me once, Roy, that part of what you were instructed was never to put your own life in danger. Well, you just did, didn't you? Again.'

It was a warm Friday evening, a glorious summer night, and to celebrate Cleo's last day at work before maternity leave, they'd booked a table at a country restaurant they liked called the Ginger Fox, a short drive out of Brighton. Cleo liked to remind him that with the birth of the baby increasingly imminent, each quiet dinner out together might be their last for a very long time. Roy never took much persuading. There were few things he enjoyed more in life than sitting in a restaurant with Cleo, with some good food and a decent glass of wine.

He ran the shower, removed his tie with difficulty, as his hands were so painful, and had several deep splinters still embedded in them. He took off his suit jacket and trousers, then sat on the edge of the bed to pull off his socks. He was hot and sweaty, and felt drained after what seemed like a very long week. And an even longer past two days.

Two press conferences in the past twenty-four hours; a referral to the Independent Police Complaints Authority, because he had been directly involved in the serious injury of a suspect; an enquiry by Professional Standards as to why he hadn't brought up the issue of the information Kevin Spinella kept obtaining, much sooner than he had. Plus he had all the paperwork dealing with *Operation Icon* to go through. And as a bit of icing on the cake, there were major issues with the playing fields that the police rugby team, which he managed, would be using when the season started.

On top of everything else, he'd had to travel up to London today, as he'd been called as a witness earlier than he'd expected in the Carl Venner trial. Except, having got all the way to the Old Bailey, he was told he now would not be needed until next Tuesday.

A shower, followed by a blast out into the countryside in Cleo's Audi TT with the roof down, a cold beer and a few glasses of wine and he would feel a lot better. He might even treat himself to a cigarette. One big advantage of Cleo's pregnancy was there were no drink-driving issues, no arguments about who would drive home.

'It's not a question of training, my darling,' he replied. 'There was a scandalous hoo-hah a few years back when two PCSOs in another county didn't jump into a lake to try to save a drowning boy, because their training forbade them. That's pretty rare – I don't think I've met a single police officer in Sussex who would have held back from jumping in. It's not about training, it's something any human being would do. You can't just stand by and watch someone die.'

She kissed him. 'You know, I've never been a worrier.' She gave a small laugh. 'Not until I met you.'

'Are you sure it's not part of the package? All the stuff we've read, we both know that pregnancy messes with the mother's hormones. Worry is one aspect of the protective mothering instinct. You don't have to worry about me.'

'It's not the baby, Roy. It's you. Every time you walk out

the front door, I wonder if you'll be coming back. Or whether it will be two of your colleagues knocking on the door instead.'

'Cleo, darling!'

'Did Sandy have to put up with all this? The same fears?'

The reminder of Sandy stung. The mention of her name invariably set off a small pang of sadness and loss, despite the good mental place that he was in, and all he now had. He shrugged. 'She never said anything – not about danger. Her gripe was always my unpredictable hours.'

'I'm sorry that I worry, I can't help it, I love you. But just look at all the crazy stuff you've done in the past year. You've been in a burning building. Over a cliff in a car.'

'Not exactly.'

'The car went over a cliff, Roy.'

'Yes, okay, but I wasn't in it.'

'You were in it ten seconds before it went over.'

He smiled. 'True.' He stood up and pulled his boxer shorts down.

'You dived into Shoreham Harbour in front of a ship.'

It was strange, he thought. He felt perfectly comfortable standing naked in front of Cleo. But Sandy had an almost Victorian prudery about nudity. Except in bed where she could be wild, she always had something wrapped around her, and would insist that he put something on, even if it was just to walk from the bedroom to the bathroom. And she had a thing about the toilet, as well, an obsessive privacy. He once, way back, had joked to a friend that in all the years he and Sandy had lived together as man and wife, so far as he knew, she had not yet been to the toilet.

'I didn't have any choice with Gaia,' he said. 'If I hadn't done what I did, she would be dead or maimed. My career would have been over. But that was not the reason I did it.'

'The police force isn't the only job in the world, Roy. If you ever got demoted or got the sack, I wouldn't love you any the less. Okay?'

'And if someone died because I had been a coward?'

The question hung in the air.

'History is full of dead heroes, Roy. I'm not ready for you to be history.'

He blew her a kiss and stepped into the bathroom, then checked his face in the mirror. The gash on his left cheek had required three stitches, but it looked to be healing all right. As he turned on the taps, his mobile phone, lying on the bed, pinged twice with text messages.

'Could you see if there's anything urgent!' he called out.

She picked up the phone. The first message was from Jason Tingley.

**Do you need me 2morrow or can I play golf?**

The second was from a number that meant nothing to her. She opened it.

**Hey Mr Paul Newman Eyes! I want to thank you properly sometime for saving my life. XXXXXXXXXXXXXXXXXX**

Roy Grace adjusted the shower temperature then, before stepping into it, called, 'Anything important?'

'Jason Tingley wants to play golf tomorrow. And Gaia wants to have sex with you.'

He grinned and closed the shower door behind him.

*

Five minutes later as he came back into the bedroom, with a towel wrapped around him, Cleo paraded the loose, turquoise dress she had chosen. She looked stunning.

'What do you think? This or my black one? Or the beige one you like?'

He could not remember either the black or the beige ones. 'This looks great.'

'Which shoes?'

'Which ones were you thinking of?'

'Well, I can't wear anything with heels. So I'm not going to be able to compete with Gaia, am I?' Her tone was unusually sarcastic.

'Hey, come on!' He picked up the phone and looked at the text, then smiled, proudly. Not every cop got a text from one of the world's greatest stars. And a row of kisses.

'So would you?' she said.

'Would I what?'

'Go to bed with her, if you had the chance?' She was staring at him strangely.

'Don't be ridiculous, absolutely not! Hey, come on, let's not go there.'

He picked up the Alfa Romeo brochure that was lying on his bedside table, and flicked through it for distraction, to avoid having to look back at her. He stopped on the Giulietta page, and stared at the car with longing.

Cleo looked over his shoulder. 'Go with your heart!' she said. 'You love that car, right?'

He shrugged. 'Yes.'

'So, you've nearly died I don't know how many times in your career, and you've still got a third of it to go. You're probably not going to make old bones, so go on, treat yourself while you can. Enjoy!'

'I'm tempted,' he said.

'It'll suit you. And, hey, *Mr Paul Newman Eyes*, Gaia will think you are so cool.'

# 121

Over the course of the following week, to Roy Grace's relief, press coverage about his rescue of Gaia began to move from the front page and dwindled, although the jibes from his friends and colleagues continued. He gradually reduced the *Operation Icon* team numbers, until by the following Friday's morning meeting there was just himself, Glenn Branson, Norman Potting, Bella Moy, Nick Nicholl and a handful of others.

They had a lot of work to do still, collecting statements, preparing for the inquests into the deaths of Drayton Wheeler and Myles Royce. Meanwhile they awaited the daily medical bulletins on Eric Whiteley, who remained on life support in the ICU at the Royal Sussex County Hospital, under police guard.

He hadn't been able to resist showing the text from Gaia around to his colleagues and he was now the butt of a number of saucy but good-humoured jokes about her.

'So how's your new lovebird today, chief?' Norman Potting asked.

'She's been back on set all week, I gather, thank you, Norman. She's tough.'

'I'll bet she is,' he said with a dirty chuckle.

'Leave it alone, will you, Norman?' Glenn Branson snapped at him.

Grace had been noticing a certain tension between Branson and Potting recently. But his mate had refused to be drawn on it, on the couple of occasions he'd tried to bring the subject up while they were having a drink after work. Another thing he had noticed a few times was a sly exchange of glances between Potting and Bella.

There couldn't be anything going on between them, could there? To him, Potting was just about the most physically unappealing man he'd ever encountered. Surely Bella could do better than him?

On the other hand, nor could he see the appeal a Brighton copper might have to one of the world's greatest and sexiest rock and movie stars. But he was getting a constant stream of increasingly flirty texts from Gaia. It did not seem to matter how neutral and guarded his replies were, the innuendo from her was increasing daily.

Of course he was flattered. And they were too much of an ego boost to delete. But they changed nothing in his love for Cleo. He had thought several times about that question she'd asked him last week in their bedroom. Would he go to bed with Gaia if he had the chance?

And his answer was no. An emphatic no.

\*

On the following morning he drove to his house to check on its condition. Sometimes his now long-stay lodger, Glenn Branson, kept it neat and tidy, other times it looked like he'd had a herd of hyenas rampaging through it. Also he could never quite trust his friend to remember to feed his venerable goldfish Marlon.

He pulled up outside shortly after ten, nodded at his neighbour across the street, Noreen Grinstead, the local gossip, a hawk-eyed, jumpy woman in her seventies, who was forever outside the front of her house, washing something. Right now she was hosing down her spotless silver Nissan car.

He did not want to have to talk to her about the recent events, and was equally happy not to get drawn into a tedious conversation with her about the lives of everyone in the street, which sometimes happened. He had moved on from this place, which Sandy, years back, had fallen so in love with. He was now house-hunting with Cleo, and they were taking advantage of this free weekend to look at a number of houses in the city and in the surrounding countryside.

He walked up the path, and let himself in through the front door. 'Hi, matey!' he called out, as a warning that he was here, not wanting to disturb Glenn if he had some bird back here – which he was always secretly hoping Glenn would have, to get him over his marriage-from-hell.

But there was no reply. He knew that on his weekends off, Glenn liked to sleep in and then go to the gym, or cycling, which he had recently taken up, in the afternoon.

He stooped and picked a bunch of mail off the mat, sifting through it as he walked through into the kitchen, which Sandy had once made so modern and high tech, but which now looked sadly dated.

'Hi, Marlon, how are you doing?' he said, peering into the bowl, pleased to see there was still plenty of food in the hopper.

The fish, as surly as his namesake, ignored him as usual, slowly gliding to the surface and gulping down yet another tiny globule of his food.

'Not in a chatty mood today? That makes a change, right?'

Marlon did a single circuit of his bowl, and for a moment their eyes met. Then the fish rose to the surface and gulped another globule.

'It's okay, old chap, you're not hurting my feelings. I've

got a much sexier admirer than you. Would you be jealous
if I told you who?'

The fish did not look remotely jealous.

Grace turned away and dumped the small pile of letters,
takeaway pizza and Chinese menus, and a blue and white
flyer from the local Conservative MP, Mike Weatherley.
Then he sifted quickly through the letters. One was a brown
envelope that contained a council tax demand. And one
was from the estate agents Mishon Mackay, whose board
was outside the house.

He opened it, and there was a written report on the
recent viewings. Just as he started reading it, his phone
rang.

'Roy Grace,' he answered.

'Oh, Mr Grace? It's Darran Willmore from Mishon
Mackay.'

'Hi,' he said. 'I'm just reading your letter this minute!'

'Right – well – I've got a bit of a development I thought
you might like to hear about.'

'Fire away.'

'We had a viewing recently, a mother and her son. We
did think she seemed quite interested at the time. They're
living overseas at the moment, but want to move to Brighton – I believe she has some past connection here.'

'Okay, sounds interesting.'

'Well, it's looking encouraging. She wants to have a
second viewing.'

That's brilliant news, Grace thought, wondering how he
was going to break it to Glenn.

'I thought you'd be pleased!'

'I am,' Roy Grace said. 'The timing could not be better.'

# 122

Roy Grace was pretty happy with how the Carl Venner trial was going. The ghastly fat snuff movie king and paedophile, with a penchant for Breitling watches, had done himself no favours.

And for the first time in a very long while, to his great relief, Grace had spent an entire week as the Duty Senior Investigating Officer without a single major crime incident happening in the city of Brighton and Hove. Which meant he was available day and night to take Cleo to hospital the moment labour began.

*The King's Lover* was in its final week of location shooting in and around Brighton, before moving up to Pinewood studios, and miraculously was only four days behind schedule. The texts from Gaia, to Grace's relief, but at the same time, slight disappointment, had stopped. Although he had paid a couple of visits to the set and been greeted by Gaia on each occasion as somewhat more than her new best friend.

Eric Whiteley was still on life support in the ICU, tying up valuable resources in what Grace considered a pointless, but requisite, around-the-clock police guard.

It was a Monday afternoon in late June, as he was about to leave for home, when his phone rang. He heard an American accent.

'Detective Grace? This is Detective Myman, from the Los Angeles Police Threat Management Unit. We have kind of a number of loose ends to tie up relating to Gaia Lafayette and, in particular, the deceased Drayton Wheeler.'

'You're telling me. I'm working on it right now.'

'It would speed up the process if it were possible for one of your team to come over here. Wouldn't need them for more than a couple of days.'

'The issue we have right now is our budgets,' Grace said.

'That's not a problem. The LAPD would be happy to pick up the tab for the air fare – and we'd take care of whoever came over. Can you suggest who might be the best person on your team? Yourself perhaps?'

Grace thought hard. Because of the consultant obstetrician's concerns, Cleo was booked into the maternity ward of the Royal Sussex County Hospital the following Monday, to have the baby by caesarean section. With the risk that she might need to go in earlier, there was no way he could go. But a break might do Glenn some good, what with him seeming particularly miserable at the moment.

He told Myman he would get back to him later in the day.

As he hung up, his phone pinged with a text.

> **Hey Mr Paul Newman Eyes! I have some free time on Thursday evening. Leaving town at the weekend. Can I invite you to my suite for a good-bye drink? XXXX**

Thursday was his boys' poker night, a tradition that had been going on for years, and except when work intervened, he tried never to miss a game. Perhaps he could fit in a very quick drink with her before joining the boys. He would do that and then go on to the game.

# 123

On the Friday night, despite being exhausted from all that had happened in recent weeks, combined with the Carl Venner trial, Roy Grace barely slept at all. Whenever he was not wide awake, tossing around, shaking lumps out of his pillows, Cleo was, with Bump going totally berserk inside her.

Somehow, miraculously, around 7 a.m. he fell into a deep sleep, and did not wake until 10 a.m. on Saturday morning.

Despite still feeling groggy, he pulled on his shorts, T-shirt and trainers, and went for his favourite run, down on to the seafront, by the Palace Pier, then along to the Deep Sea Anglers club by Shoreham Harbour and back. A circuit just short of five miles.

When he got back he slipped out of his clothes and went gratefully into the bathroom. One of the many things he loved about Cleo was her taste in showers. A rain shower-head, a face-on jet and sideways jets, if you wanted them on as well. He was luxuriating in them when suddenly the bathroom door opened so violently, he thought it was coming off its hinges.

Cleo stood there, in a baggy shirt-waister, clutching a copy of the *Argus*, with a face like thunder.

He switched the taps off and stepped out, water running down his body.

'So *poker* on Thursday was good, was it?'

She was brandishing the paper like a weapon.

'I sort of broke even, I told you.'

'Sounds like you edited one bit out, Roy.'

'Oh?'

'Oh? Oh yes, actually. Take a look at this! Perhaps it will help jog your memory.'

His heart sank as he saw the front page splash.

## Top cop and Gaia: is it love?

Beneath was a photograph of Roy Grace and Gaia, clearly taken with a long lens, standing side by side, looking out of the window of her Grand Hotel suite.

'Hey, I can explain.'

'Can you?' she said.

Never, in all their time together, had he seen her so angry.

She stormed out. He grabbed a towel, and was just starting to dry himself when she marched back in with an open copy of the Saturday *Mirror*. The headline ran across the top of the page.

## Gaia and Brighton cop's secret love tryst!

Beneath was a similar long-lens photograph to the one in the *Argus*, but in this one, Gaia was giving Roy Grace a kiss on the cheek.

He read the first paragraph of the story:

> Rock legend, Gaia, in Brighton to shoot her latest movie, *The King's Lover*, has been repaying the City's top homicide cop, Detective Superintendent Roy Grace, for successfully foiling an attempt on her life, by secret love trysts with him in her hotel suite. The couple are pictured above about to enjoy a romantic candlelit dinner.

'This is unbelievable!'

'You're right,' she said. 'It is. I just can't believe you'd do this, Roy.'

'Darling, listen! This is bullshit, complete and utter bullshit! I can explain!'

'Great. I am all ears. Explain!'

Then, suddenly she gripped her abdomen and screamed out in pain, all the colour draining from her face. 'Roy, oh my God, oh my God!'

# 124

The obituary in the *Argus* read:

GRACE. Noah Jack
On July 2nd. Died tragically shortly after birth.
Much loved son of Roy and Cleo. Private funeral
for family only.

# 125

Roy Grace had tears in his eyes as he watched Cleo cradling their son, in her bed in the maternity ward of the Royal Sussex County Hospital. The baby's pink face was all scrunched up, his eyes were closed, his lips formed a tiny rosebud. Thin tufts of wavy fair hair lay across his head. He was dressed in a pale blue V-neck cotton top, embroidered with a mouse wearing striped shorts.

It was incredible, he thought, unable to take his eyes off him. His son. Their child. He breathed in the sweet smells of freshly washed skin and baby powder. Looked at Cleo, tresses of her hair lying across the shoulders of her night-dress, her face filled with so much love and care.

Then his phone rang. As he answered it, he stepped away from the bed and went out into the corridor. It was Glenn Branson.

'I'm so sorry, mate, we're all gutted.'

'Gutted? What's happened?'

'Well, you know – I thought the baby was doing fine – then we saw it in the *Argus* this morning. I don't know what to say. How's Cleo?'

'Hang on a sec, saw *what* in the *Argus*?'

There was a moment of awkward silence. 'Well – the obit, right?'

'Obituary?'

'Yes.'

'Who's died?'

There was another silence. 'Your baby, right? Noah Jack Grace?'

'What? Are you serious?'

'Got it on my desk right in front of me. Everyone's in tears here.'

'Glenn, there's been a mistake. We had a horrendous couple of days. Noah was born with breathing difficulties – wet lung syndrome, they called it. They weren't sure if he was going to make it.'

'Yeah, you told me. But, you know, you said he was getting stronger.'

'He was all intubated and wired up in an incubator at first – neither of us was allowed to touch him. But he's fine now, Cleo's holding him; hopefully we can take him home soon.'

'So who the hell screwed up with the obituary?' Glenn asked.

'I can't believe this. You're sure?'

'I've got it in front of me in black and white.'

'Shit. I'm going straight down to the shop to get one. I don't think anyone's screwed up. Obituaries don't get put in by mistake,' Grace said grimly. Inside, he was shaking.

# 126

Freedom for Amis Smallbone, among other things, meant being able to enjoy some of life's simple pleasures. One of them had always been sitting at a table under the Arches on the seafront, right by the beach, staring out at the sea and the Palace Pier and the passing totty.

By night, this area was rich pickings for the network of drug dealers he once controlled, but on a fine summer morning it was mostly tourists promenading along, enjoying the views, the beach, the bars, cafés, shops and other seaside attractions.

And there were few things he enjoyed more than his first coffee of the day with the *Argus* newspaper. Especially when an endless procession of skimpily dressed girls were strutting past at eye level.

With his cigarette in his mouth, smoke curling up between his eyes, he flicked through the pages, aware he still had years to catch up on in this town. He saw an interview with the Chief Constable talking about cuts he was having to make and read the piece with little sympathy. There was talk of a new hospital. A bunch of drug dealers in Crawley, a couple of whom he knew, had been arrested in a raid the police had been working on for ten months.

His eyes widened a little and he read this story carefully. Could be a business opportunity had opened up there. Then he reached one of the pages that always interested him the most. YOUR ANNOUNCEMENTS.

He went straight to the DEATHS, and scanned down the

column. He never ever missed this column, because he liked to know who he had outlived, and who he didn't have to worry about any more.

But today there was a very special entry.

\*

She liked Gatwick Airport; it was much more convenient for Brighton than Heathrow and easyJet had direct flights to Munich.

Holding hands with her ten-year-old son, after security she walked into the duty-free shopping area. Immediately the boy dragged her into Dixons, where she bought him an upgrade for his latest computer gaming machine, which made him happy.

The one good thing that had happened in the past decade was her careful investing of her windfall inheritance from her aunt, enabling her to escape from her relationship with the increasingly insane control freak Hans-Jürgen. She was now a wealthy woman. Well, wealth was all relative, but she had enough to buy the house, if she decided, and to buy things for her son without having to consider the cost.

Emerging from Dixons, she made straight for the WH Smith news and bookstore.

'Just want to get some papers, in case they don't have them on the plane.' Then in German she asked her son if he would like something to read on the flight to Munich. '*Möchtest du etwas zu lesen?*'

He shrugged indifferently, engrossed in the instructions on the game upgrade.

Straight away, she grabbed a copy of the *Argus* from the rack, and flicked it open, scanning the pages eagerly.

# 127

On the Wednesday morning, Roy Grace drove Cleo and Noah home. Cleo sat in the back of his unmarked Ford Focus, with Noah strapped in the baby seat he had fitted temporarily into the vehicle.

There were few moments when he could remember feeling the sense of the richness of human life that he was experiencing at this moment. He had a lump in his throat, tears welling in his eyes as he drove around past the Pavilion; with all the film trucks gone, it seemed strangely quiet. Cleo's tantrum over Gaia seemed long ago now, and she had totally accepted that nothing had happened beyond his having had a drink with the icon.

He looked in the rear-view mirror and saw her smiling at him. She blew him a kiss. He mouthed one back.

The obituary in the *Argus* remained a mystery for the moment. Apparently it had been delivered by a taxi driver who had not yet been traced, the instructions inside an envelope, printed on a local funeral director's headed paper, which turned out to have been forged.

Of course he had his prime suspect. Although it beggared belief that, if it was him, Smallbone could be so stupid – or perhaps so brazen.

Noah made a gurgling sound, as if he, too, was excited at going home, for the first time in his life. The sound made Grace think of the enormity of the task that lay ahead of them. Bringing up their child and protecting him in a world that was as dark and dangerous as it always had been, and probably always would be.

He remembered something he had been told, long ago, by the then Chief Constable who had invited him in for a talk during those first terrible weeks after Sandy had gone missing. The Chief had been a surprisingly spiritual man. He said something Roy had never forgotten, and the words he often returned to strengthened him at tough moments.

*The light can only shine in darkness.*

# ACKNOWLEDGEMENTS

As ever I owe thanks to very many people who so kindly and patiently put up with my endless questions, and generously gave me so much of their time. Most of all is the debt I owe to Sussex Police. My first thank you is to the Chief Constable, Martin Richards, QPM, for his continued help and in particular his very considerable input and wisdom on this book.

Retired Detective Chief Superintendent David Gaylor of Sussex CID, the inspiration behind Roy Grace, gives me continuous insight into the mind of a Senior Investigating Officer, helping to ensure Roy Grace thinks the way a sharp detective would, and to shape my books in so many other ways, too.

Chief Superintendent Graham Bartlett, Commander of Brighton and Hove Police, has also been immensely helpful on this book. Chief Inspector Jason Tingley has been a total star, helping me both creatively and procedurally on many aspects of this story. As also have DCI Nick Sloan, DCI Trevor Bowles and Inspector Andy Kille.

A huge debt also to Detective Superintendent Andy Griffith; Senior Support Officer Tony Case; PC Martin Light of the Metropolitan Police Territorial Support Group; DI William Warner; Sgt Phil Taylor and Ray Packham of the High Tech Crime Unit; Inspector James Biggs; PC Tony Omotoso; DS Simon Bates; Sgt Lorna Dennison-Wilkins and the entire Specialist Search Unit; DI Emma Brice, Professional Standards Department, Sussex Police; Sgt Malcolm Buckingham and John Sheridan, TFU Training; Chris Heaver; Martin Bloomfield; Sue Heard, Press and PR Officer; Neil (Nobby) Hall; John Vickerstaff.

Thanks also to Fire Inspection Officer Tim Eady, Kathy Burke, of West Sussex Fire and Rescue, and to Dave Phillips and Vicky Seal of the South East Coast Ambulance Service.

Very special thanks to the New York Police Department; to Detective Investigator Patrick Lanigan, Special Investigations Unit, Office of the District Attorney; Assistant Chief Michel Moore of the Los Angeles Police Department, and Detective Jeff Dunn of the Threat Management Unit of the LAPD. Thanks also to Robert Darwell and Philip Philibosian of Sheppard Mullin.

And as always I owe massive thanks to Sean Didcott at Brighton and Hove Mortuary. Also to Brighton and Hove Pathologist Dr Mark Howard; Dr Nigel Kirkham, consultant pathologist, Newcastle; Dave Charlton, Senior Fingerprint Officer, and Scenes of Crime Officer James Gartrell; Tracey Stocker; Forensic Podiatrist Haydn Kelly; Forensic Archaeologist Lucy Sibun and Forensic Pathologist Dr Benjamin Swift; Coroner's Officer Tony Beldam; Alan Setterington, Deputy Governor of HMP Lewes.

Thanks also to Michael Beard, Editor, the *Argus*, Brighton; my terrific psychology researchers Tara Lester and Nicky Mitchell; Consultant Obstetrician Des Holden; Rob Kempson; Peter Wingate-Saul; Rosalind Bridges, Anna Mumby and Ceri Glen for their insights into the world of celebrity obsession; Claire Horne of Travel Counsellors; Hilary Wiltshire; pyrotechnics expert Mike Sansom; Valerie Pearce, Head of City Services, Brighton and Hove City Council; Andrew Mosley of The Grand Hotel; Keith Winter of Stonery Farm; Andrew Kay.

I'm very grateful to Dr Lorraine Bell for allowing me to quote from her profoundly informative book *Managing Intense Emotions and Overcoming Self-destructive Habits*, published in 2003 by Brunner-Routledge, Hove, East Sussex.

The team at the Royal Pavilion could not have been more

helpful or supportive. I'm extremely grateful to David Beevers, Keeper of the Royal Pavilion, Louise Brown, Facilities Manager, Alexandra Loske, Royal Pavilion Guide, and Robert Yates, Head of Fundraising, for the terrific help and access they gave me to this magical building.

I would like to point out that during the writing of this novel, I have taken some artistic licence with regards to a few of the exterior and interior descriptions, fittings, security and the general condition of the building, as well as certain historical elements. Also I have taken a degree of artistic licence with Stonery Farm.

If, like me, you are passionate about the Royal Pavilion and could help support it, please visit: www.pavilionfoundation.org

My gratitude as ever to Chris Webb of MacService, who has never let me down in keeping my trusted Mac running, even when at times it has turned flaky on me in some far-flung corner of the globe . . .

Very big and special thanks to Anna-Lisa Lindeblad, who has again been my tireless and wonderful 'unofficial' editor and commentator throughout the Roy Grace series; Sue Ansell, who has read and helped me with every single book I have written; Martin and Jane Diplock; Joey Dela Cruz.

In Carole Blake I'm blessed with a truly wonderful agent and great friend; and I have a dream publicity team in Tony Mulliken, Sophie Ransom and Claire Richman of Midas PR. There is simply not enough space to say a proper thank you to everyone on Team James at Macmillan, but I must thank my wonderful publishing director, Wayne Brookes, the incredibly patient Susan Opie, and my copy-editor, John English, as well as my great US editor, Marc Resnick.

Massive, massive thanks also to my totally brilliant PA, Linda Buckley.

Helen has, as ever, been hugely supportive and patient,

wise with her criticism and constantly encouraging. My three hounds, Phoebe, Oscar and Coco, lie permanently in wait, always ready to hijack me for a walk the moment I step away from my desk . . .

I have to reserve the biggest thank you of all to you, my readers. You've given me an amazing amount of support and it is a joy to write for you. Do keep those emails, tweets, Facebook and blog posts coming!

**Peter James**
*Sussex, England*
scary@pavilion.co.uk
www.peterjames.com
www.facebook.com/peterjames.roygrace
www.twitter.com/peterjamesuk

extracts reading groups
competitions books new events
discounts extracts extracts reading groups
competitions extracts discounts
books new events
reading groups books
events books reading groups
new extracts titles reading groups
interviews events new
books events extracts events books
discounts events
new books events interviews new books
events new events extracts

discounts extracts discounts books

www.panmacmillan.com

extracts events reading groups
competitions books extracts new